ASTRONAUT ACADEMY
ZERO GRAVITY

WRITTEN AND ILLUSTRATED BY

DAVE ROMAN

WITH COLOR BY EMMY HERNÁNDEZ

:01

First Second
NEW YORK

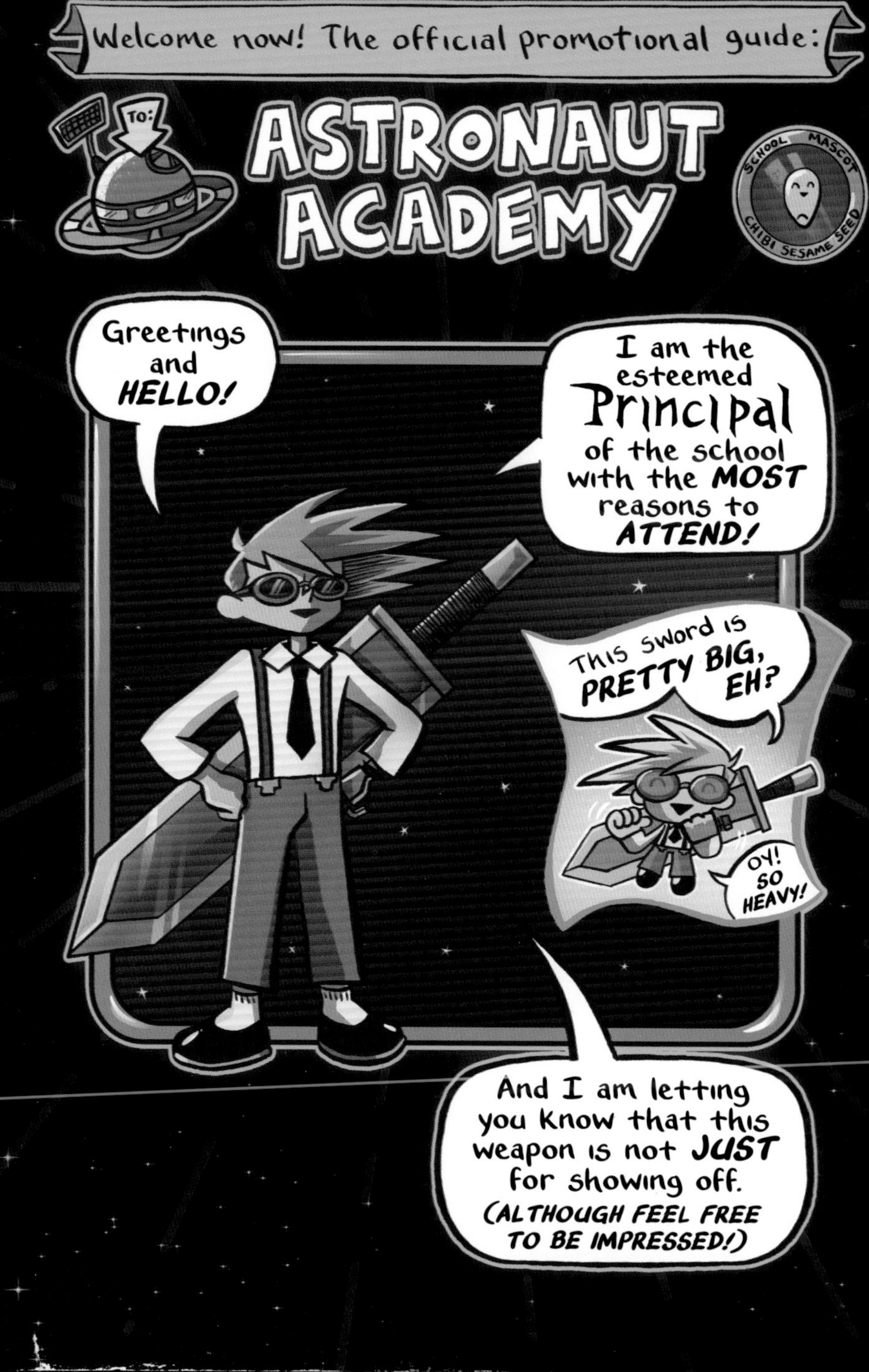
Welcome now! The official promotional guide:
To:
ASTRONAUT ACADEMY
SCHOOL MASCOT
CHIBI SESAME SEED
Greetings and HELLO!
I am the esteemed Principal of the school with the MOST reasons to ATTEND!
This Sword is PRETTY BIG, EH?
OY! SO HEAVY!
And I am letting you know that this weapon is not JUST for showing off.
(ALTHOUGH FEEL FREE TO BE IMPRESSED!)

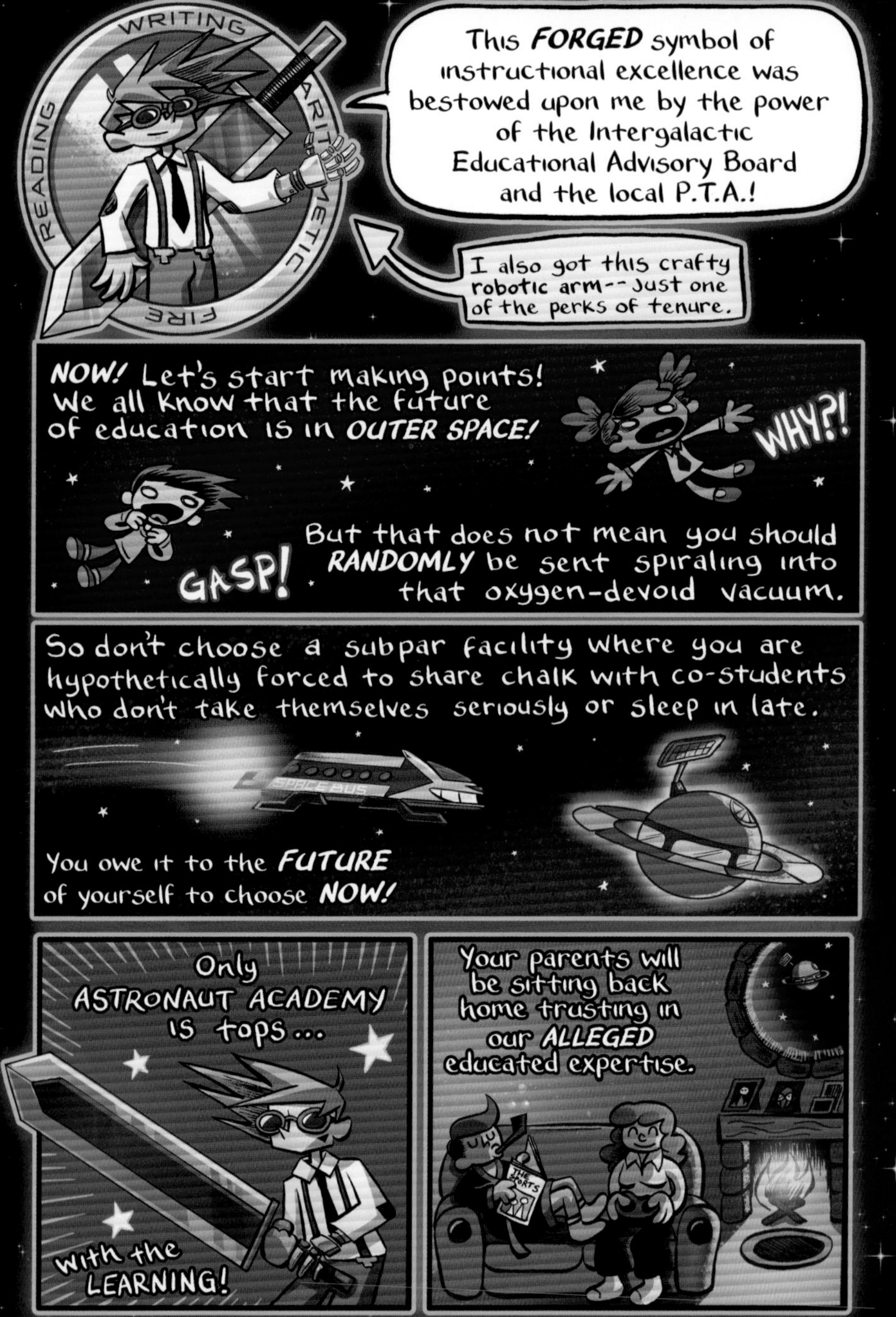
WRITING
ARITHMETIC
FIRE
READING
This FORGED symbol of instructional excellence was bestowed upon me by the power of the Intergalactic Educational Advisory Board and the local P.T.A.!
I also got this crafty robotic arm-- just one of the perks of tenure.
NOW! Let's start making points! We all know that the future of education is in OUTER SPACE!
WHY?!
GASP!
But that does not mean you should RANDOMLY be sent spiraling into that oxygen-devoid vacuum.
So don't choose a subpar facility where you are hypothetically forced to share chalk with co-students who don't take themselves seriously or sleep in late.
SPACE BUS
You owe it to the FUTURE of yourself to choose NOW!
Only ASTRONAUT ACADEMY is tops...
With the LEARNING!
Your parents will be sitting back home trusting in our ALLEGED educated expertise.
THE SPORTS

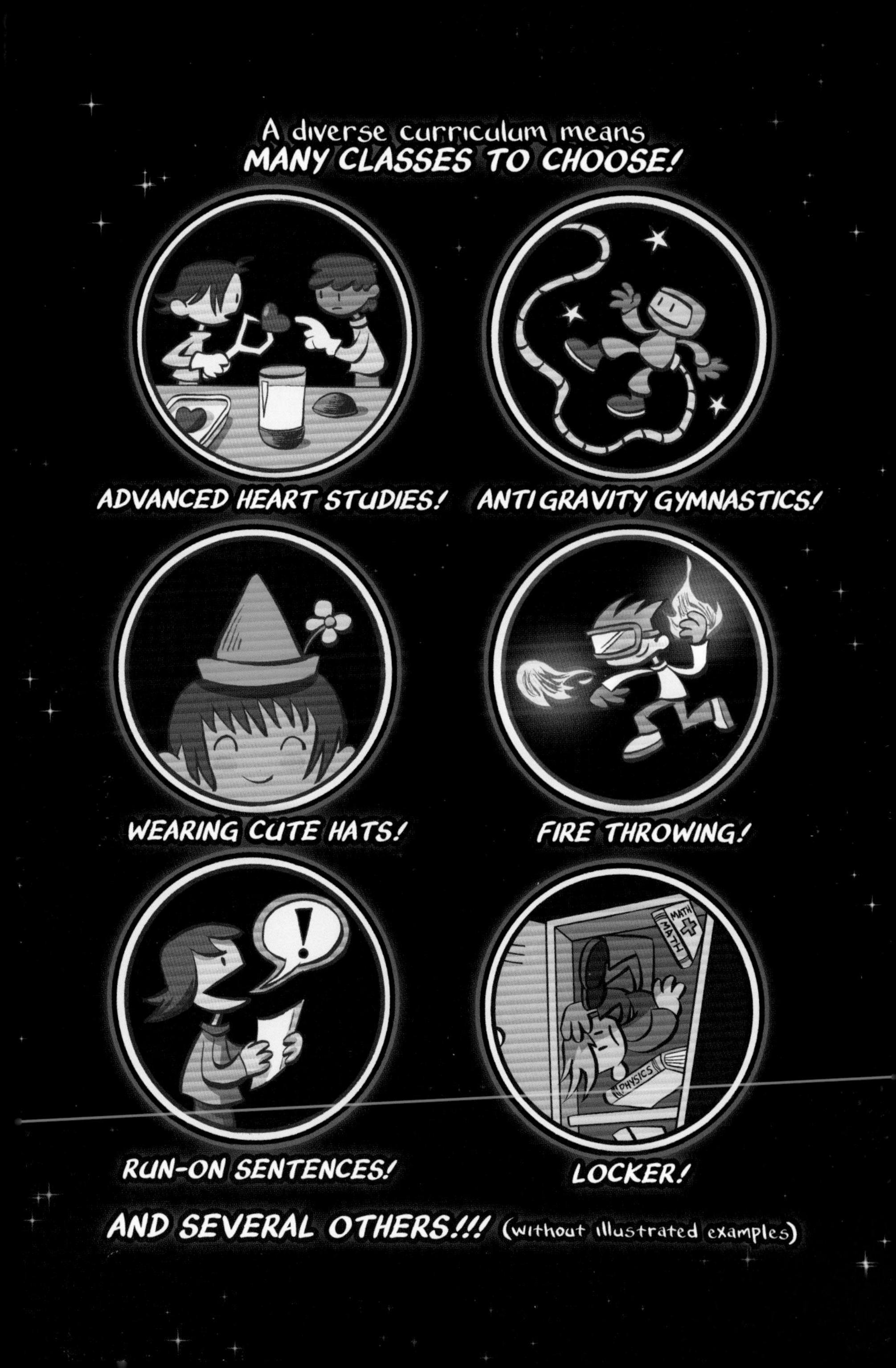
A diverse curriculum means
MANY CLASSES TO CHOOSE!
ADVANCED HEART STUDIES!
ANTI GRAVITY GYMNASTICS!
WEARING CUTE HATS!
FIRE THROWING!
!
RUN-ON SENTENCES!
MATH
MATH
PHYSICS
PHYSICS
LOCKER!
AND SEVERAL OTHERS!!! (without illustrated examples)

If dominating test scores is as important to ***YOU*** as it is to ***MY SWORD***, then you'll love that our teachers are on ***PAYROLL!***

LIKE: Mrs. Bunn

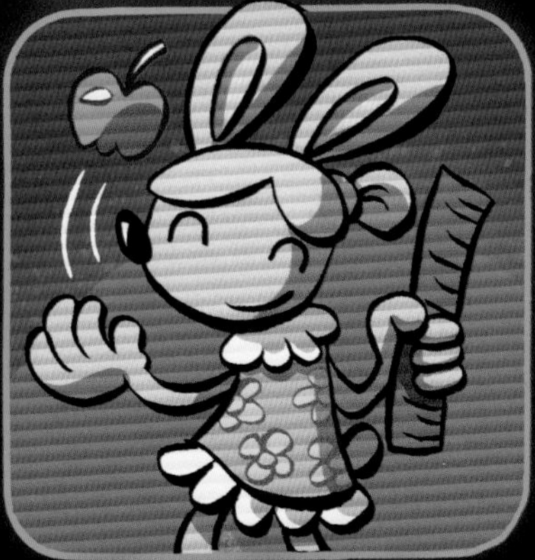

Who is old enough to know so many answers to ***QUESTIONS!***
(YOU MIGHT BE IMPRESSED!)

AND: Mr. Namagucci

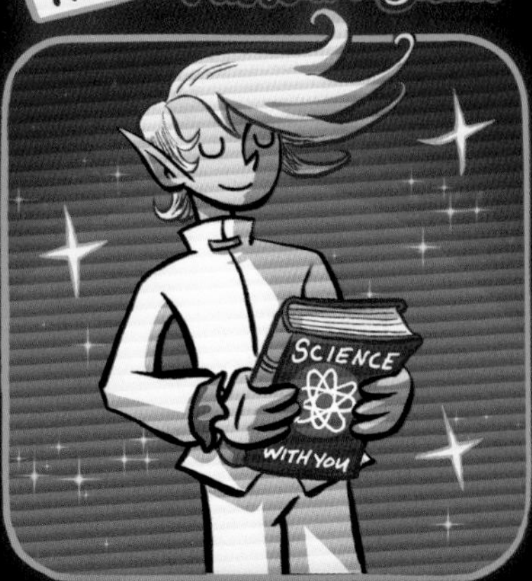
SCIENCE
WITH YOU

Who may or may not have magical powers but is still ***HANDSOME!***
(ASK AROUND!)

AS WELL AS: Senõr Panda

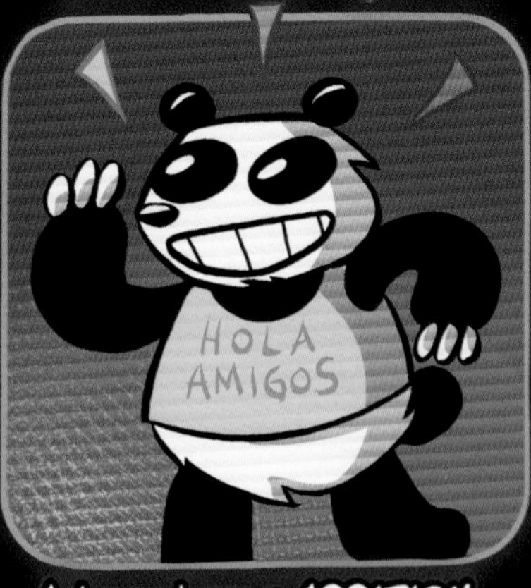
HOLA
AMIGOS

A brand-new ***ADDITION*** to our faculty!
(STILL NOT EXTINCT!)

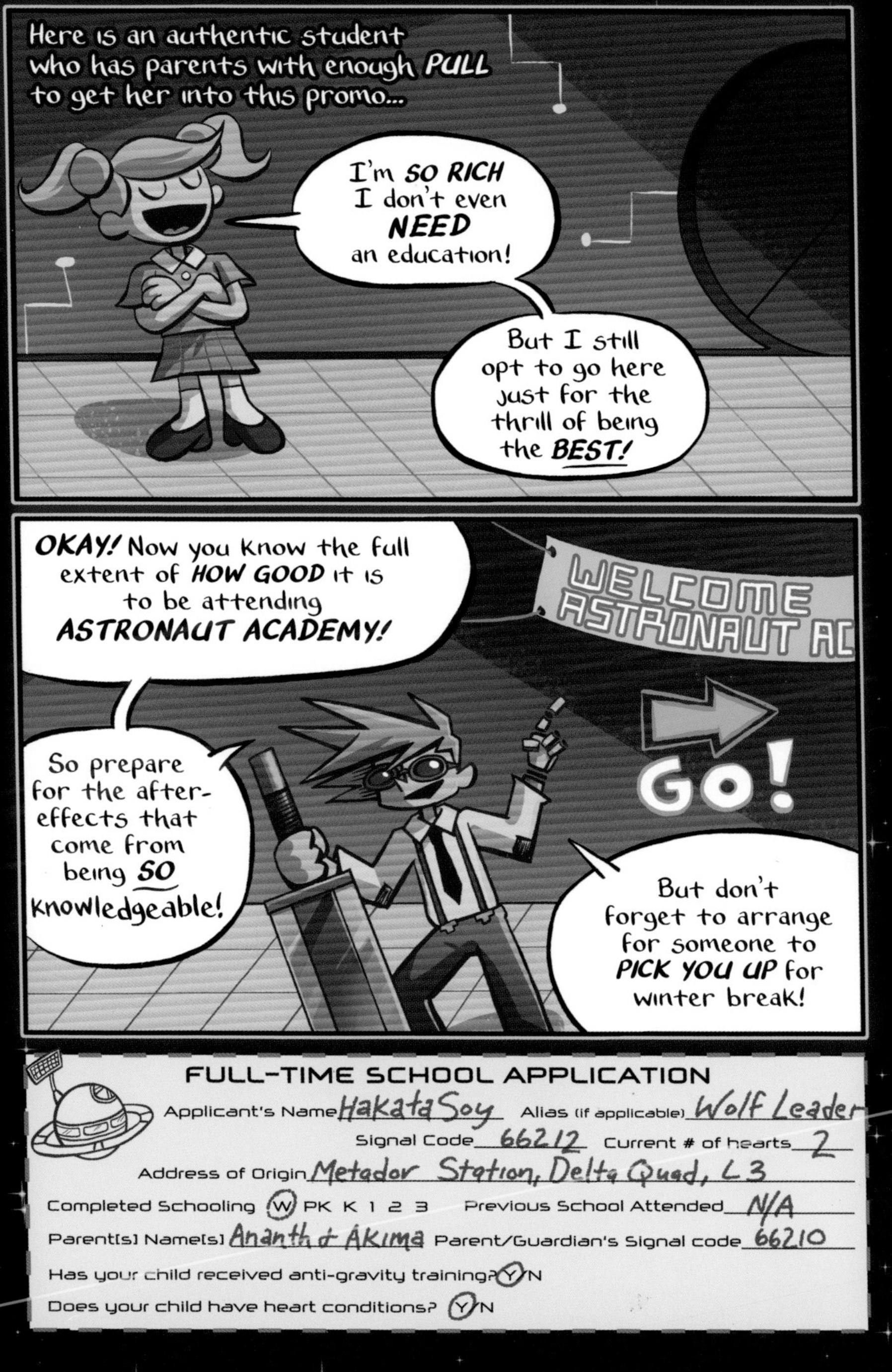
Here is an authentic student who has parents with enough PULL to get her into this promo...
I'm SO RICH I don't even NEED an education!
But I still opt to go here just for the thrill of being the BEST!
OKAY! Now you know the full extent of HOW GOOD it is to be attending ASTRONAUT ACADEMY!
WELCOME ASTRONAUT AC
GO!
So prepare for the after-effects that come from being SO knowledgeable!
But don't forget to arrange for someone to PICK YOU UP for winter break!
FULL-TIME SCHOOL APPLICATION
Applicant's Name Hakata Soy Alias (if applicable) Wolf Leader
Signal Code 66212 Current # of hearts 2
Address of Origin Metador Station, Delta Quad, L3
Completed Schooling W PK K 1 2 3 Previous School Attended N/A
Parent[s] Name[s] Ananth & Akima Parent/Guardian's Signal code 66210
Has your child received anti-gravity training? Y/N
Does your child have heart conditions? Y/N

ASTRONAUT ACADEMY

first semester

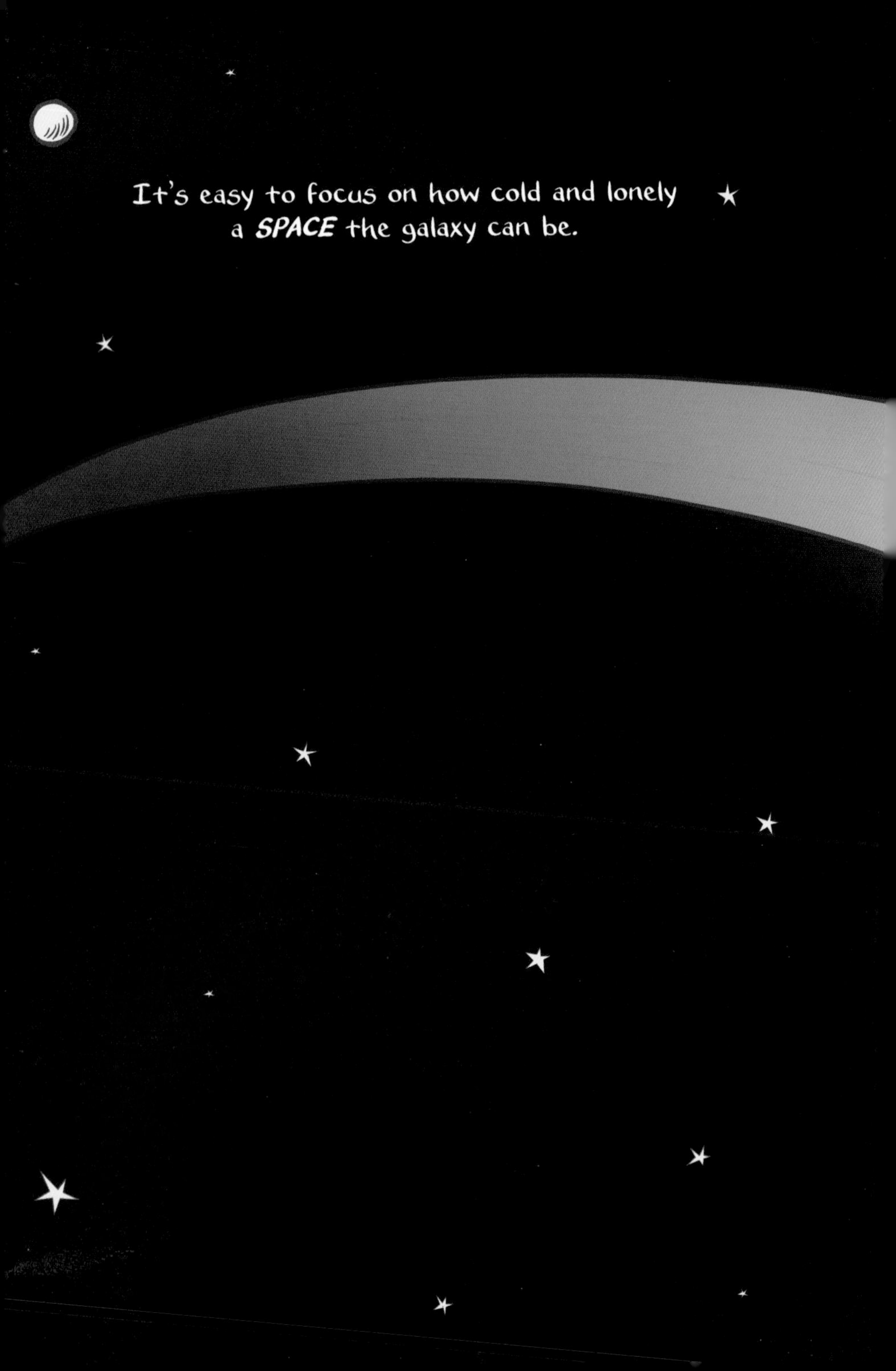
It's easy to focus on how cold and lonely a *SPACE* the galaxy can be.

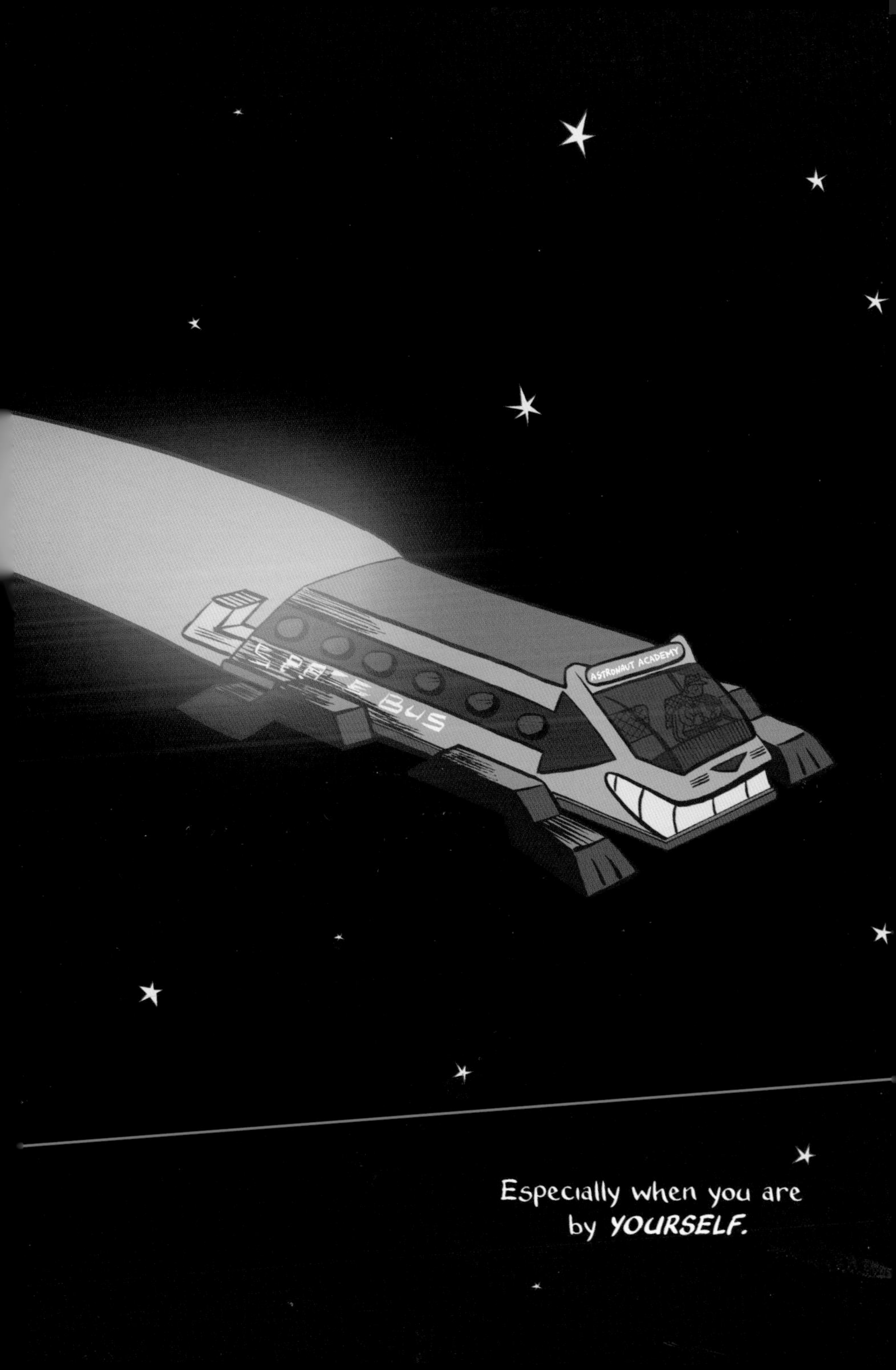
ASTRONAUT ACADEMY
SPACE BUS
Especially when you are by *YOURSELF.*

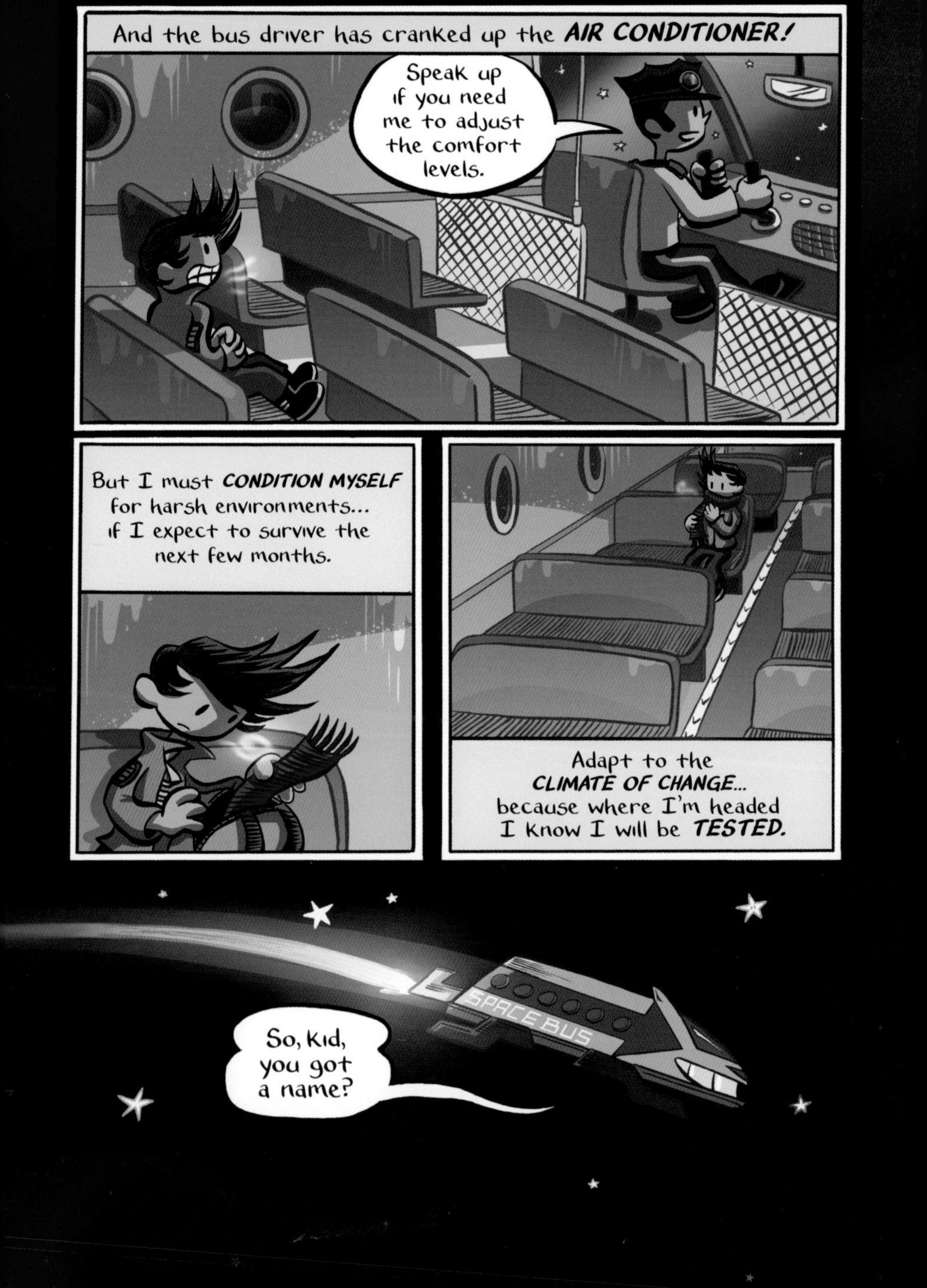
And the bus driver has cranked up the AIR CONDITIONER!
Speak up if you need me to adjust the comfort levels.
But I must CONDITION MYSELF for harsh environments... if I expect to survive the next few months.
Adapt to the CLIMATE OF CHANGE... because where I'm headed I know I will be TESTED.
SPACE BUS
So, kid, you got a name?

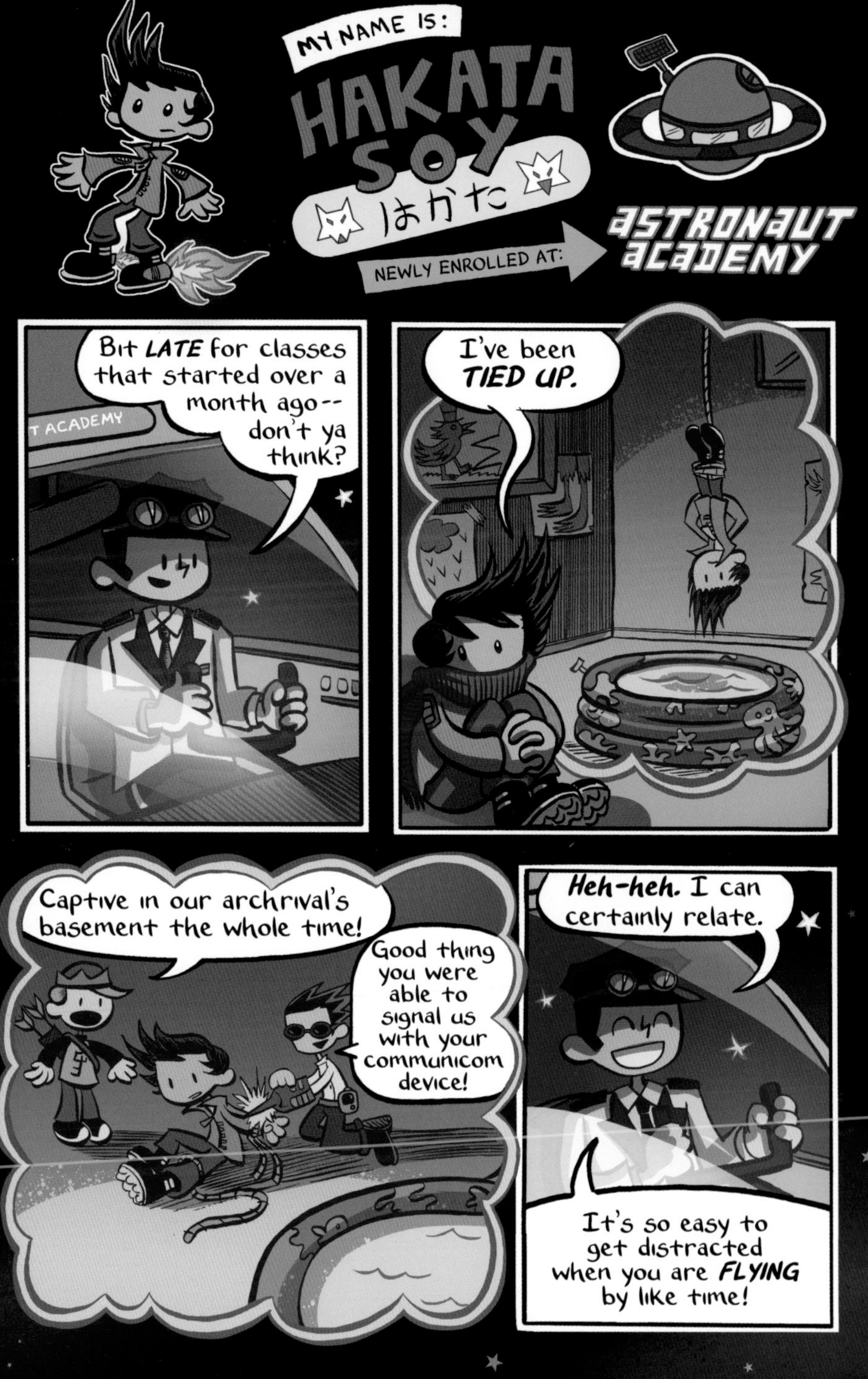
MY NAME IS:
HAKATA SOY
はかた
NEWLY ENROLLED AT:
ASTRONAUT ACADEMY
Bit LATE for classes that started over a month ago--don't ya think?
T ACADEMY
I've been TIED UP.
Captive in our archrival's basement the whole time!
Good thing you were able to signal us with your communicom device!
Heh-heh. I can certainly relate.
It's so easy to get distracted when you are FLYING by like time!

"Before you realize it...you're already gravitating toward a ***MAGNETIC FIELD!***"

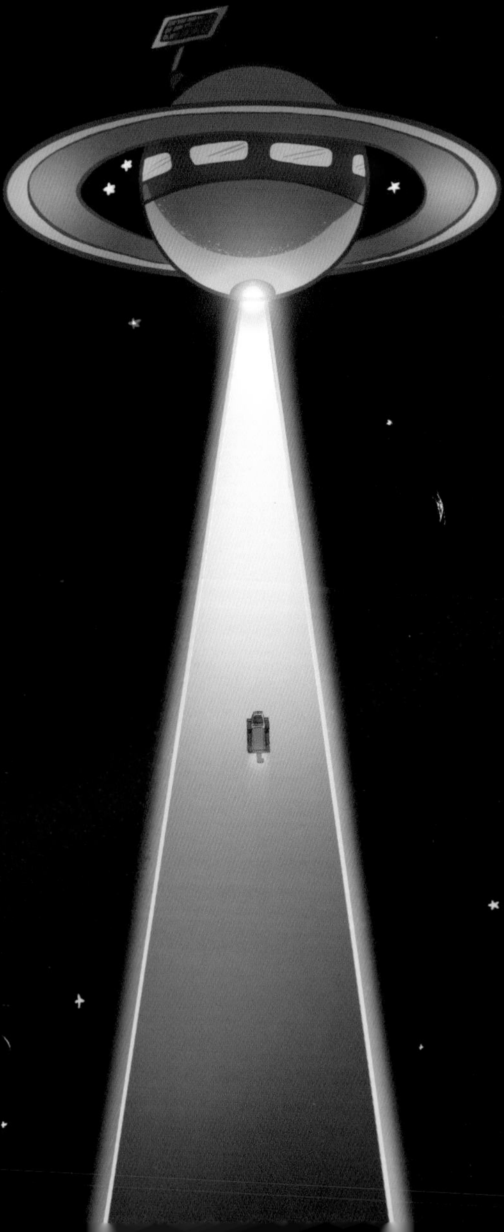

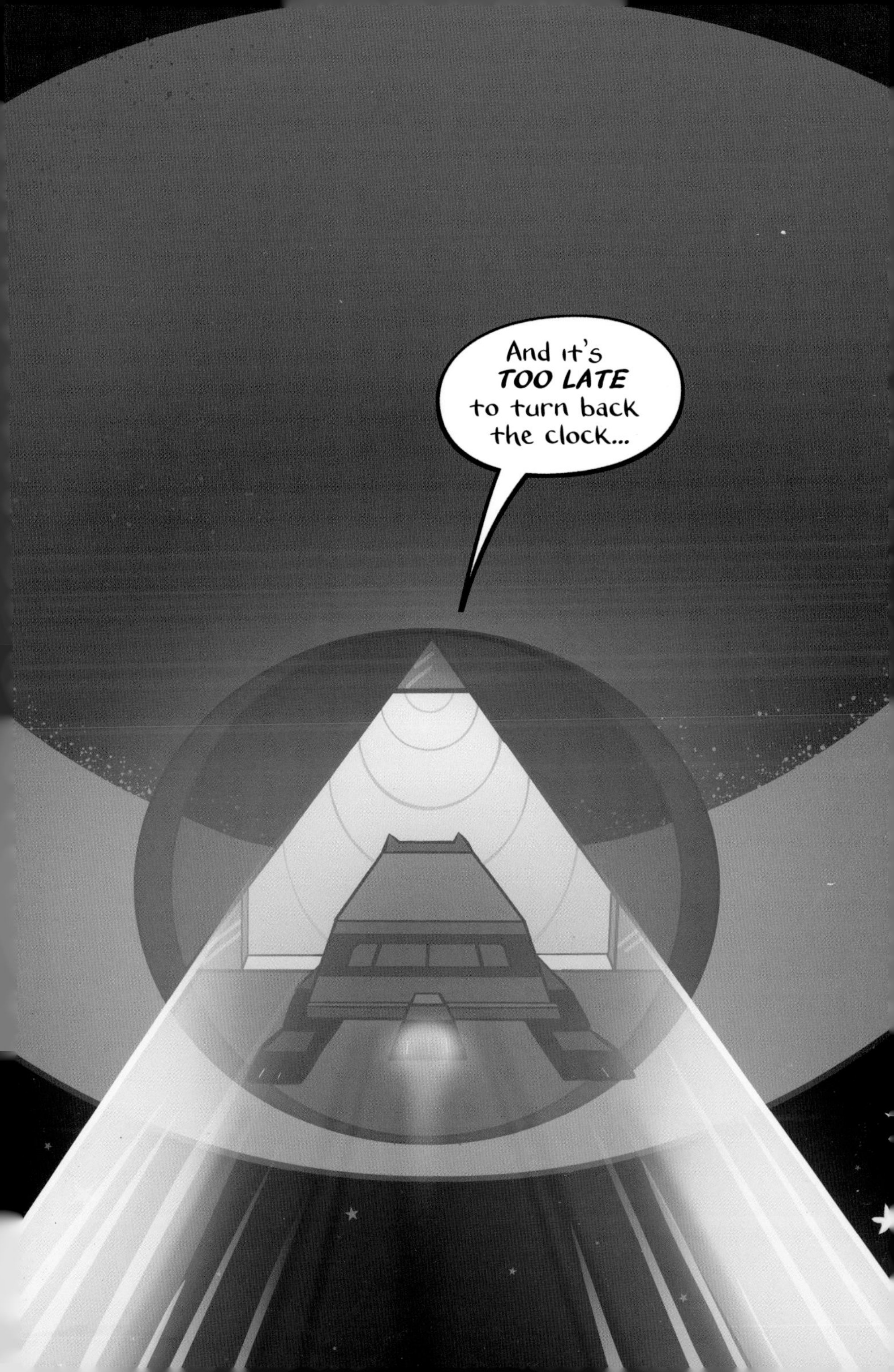
And it's **TOO LATE** to turn back the clock...

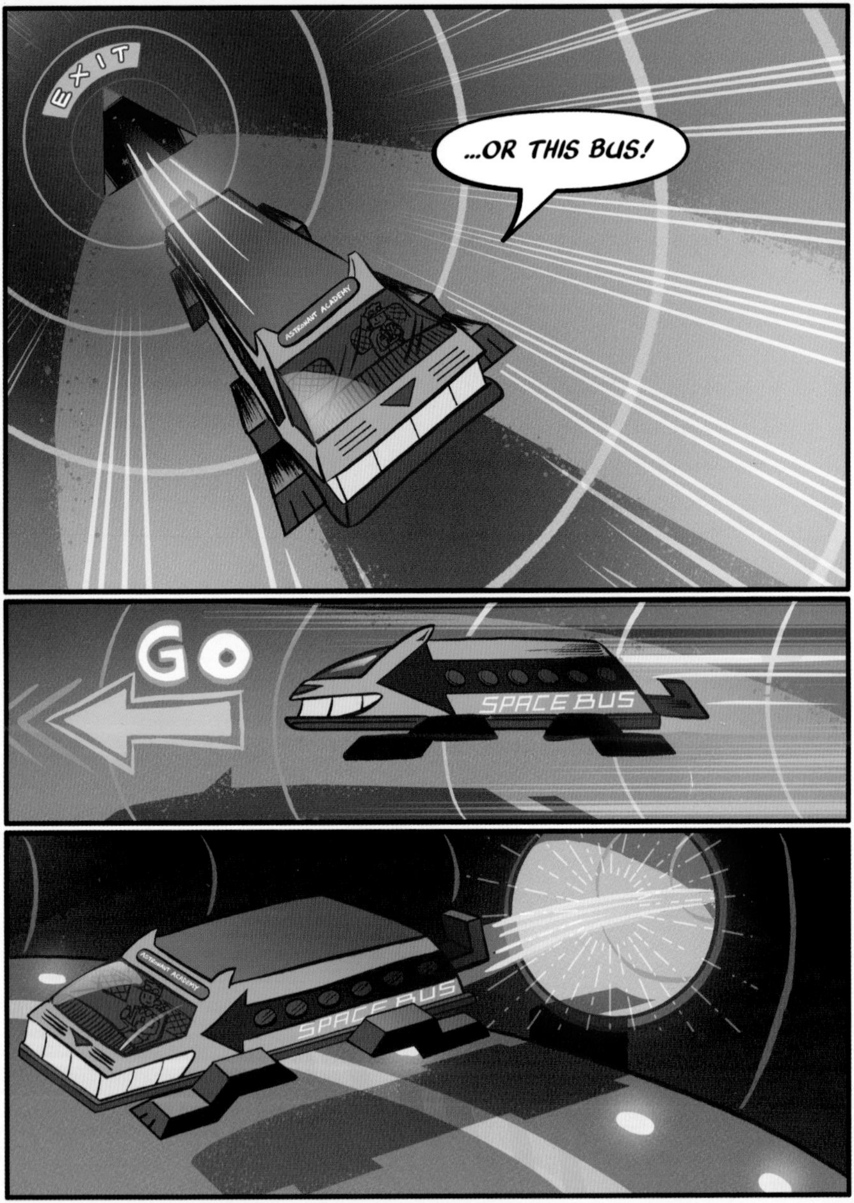
EXIT
...OR THIS BUS!
ASTRONAUT ACADEMY
GO
SPACE BUS
ASTRONAUT ACADEMY
SPACE BUS

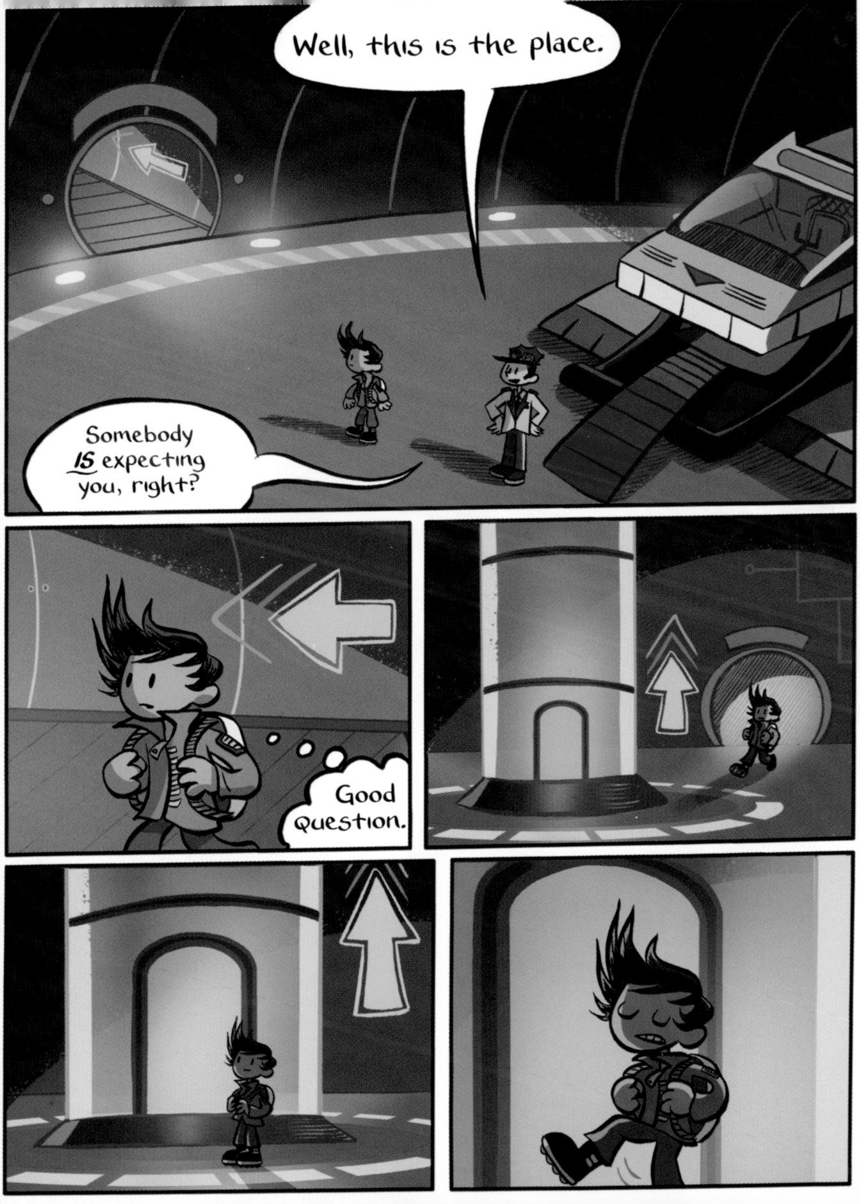
Well, this is the place.
Somebody IS expecting you, right?
Good Question.

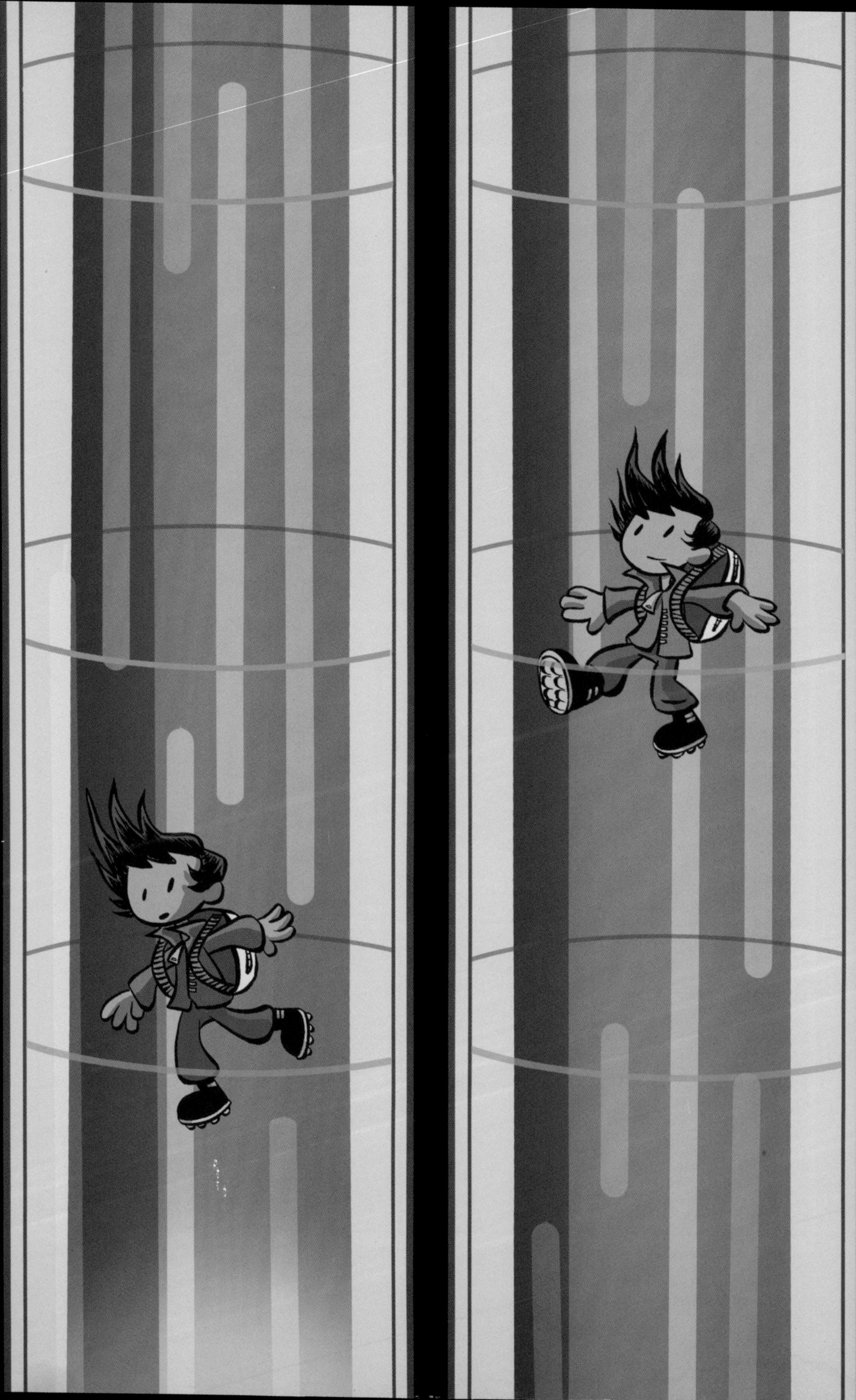

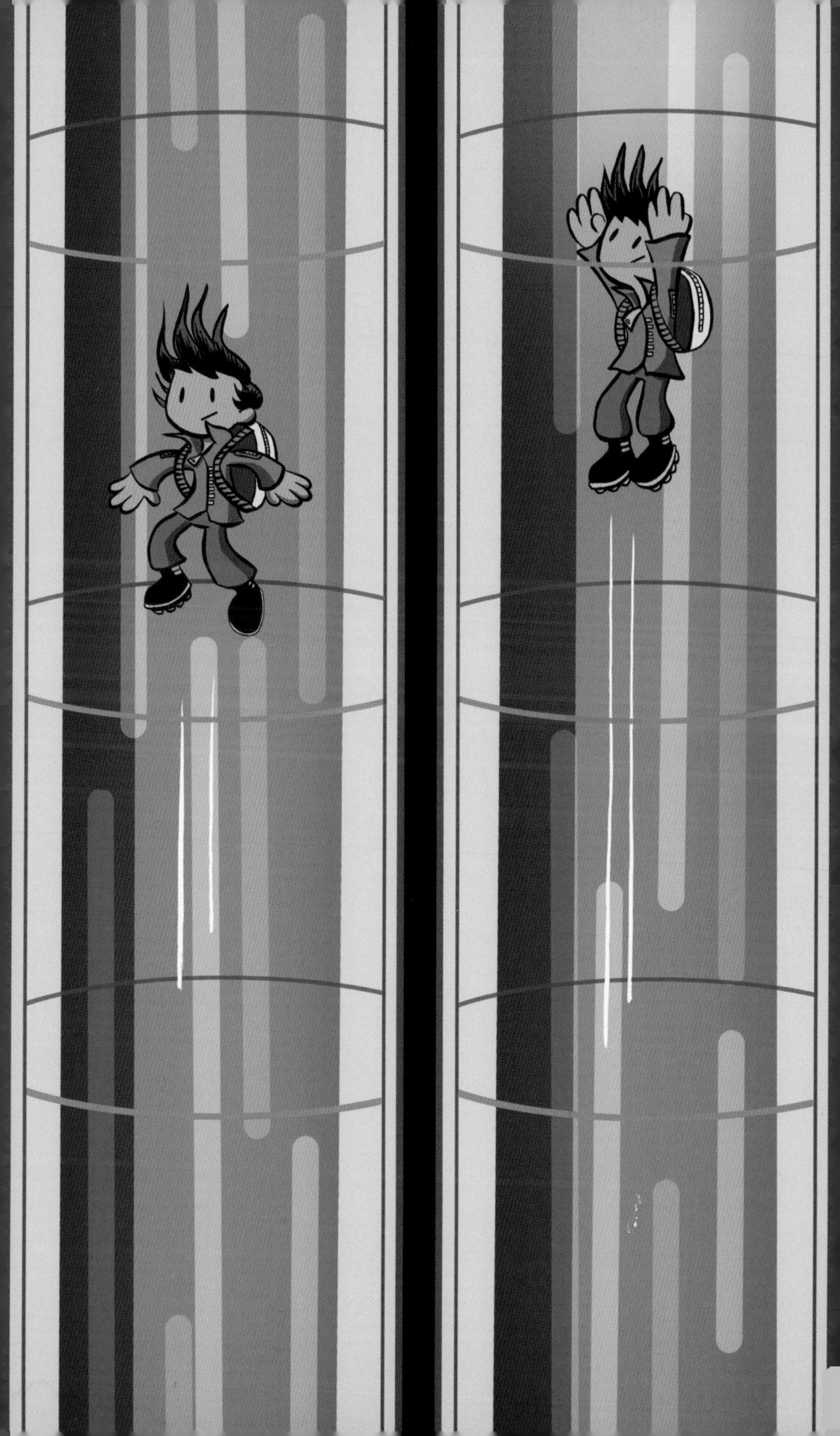

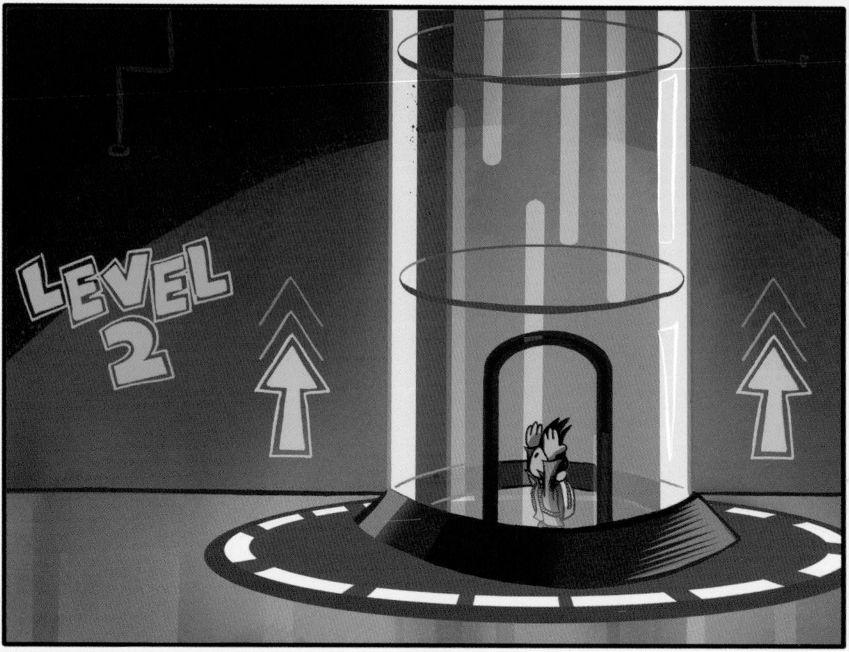
LEVEL 2
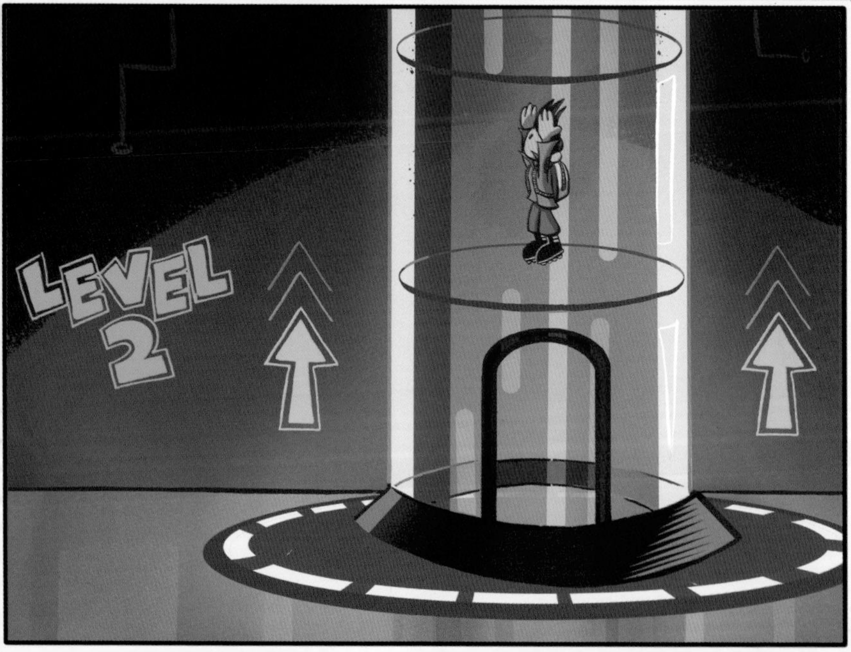
LEVEL 2

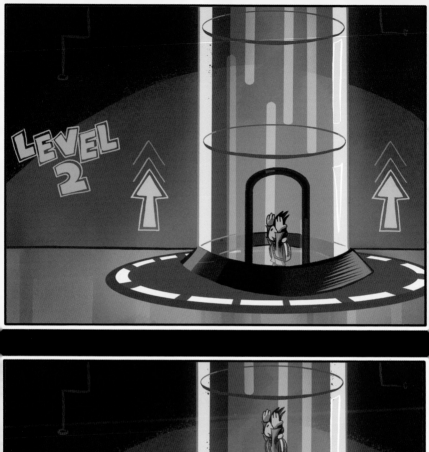

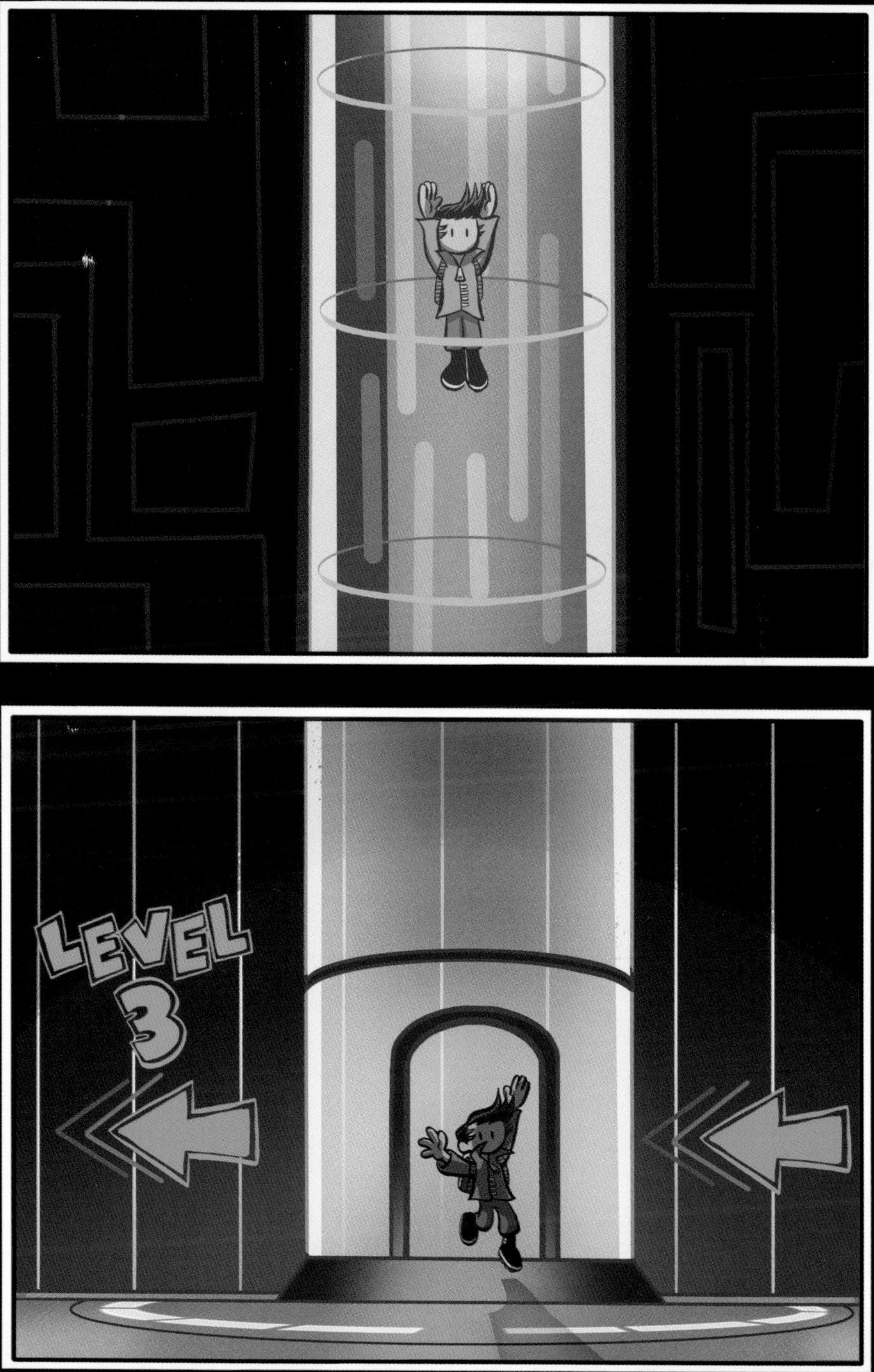
LEVEL
3

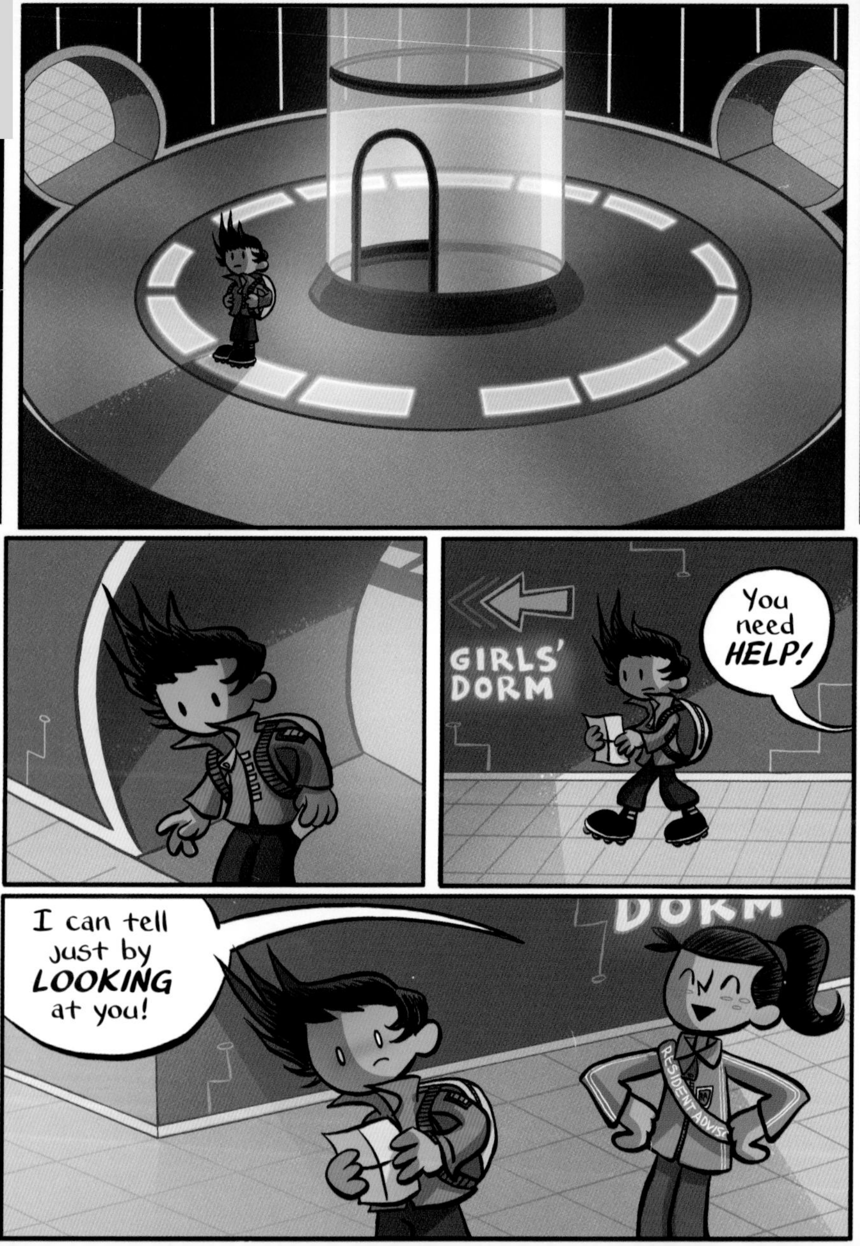
GIRLS' DORM
You need HELP!
DORM
I can tell just by LOOKING at you!
RESIDENT ADVIS

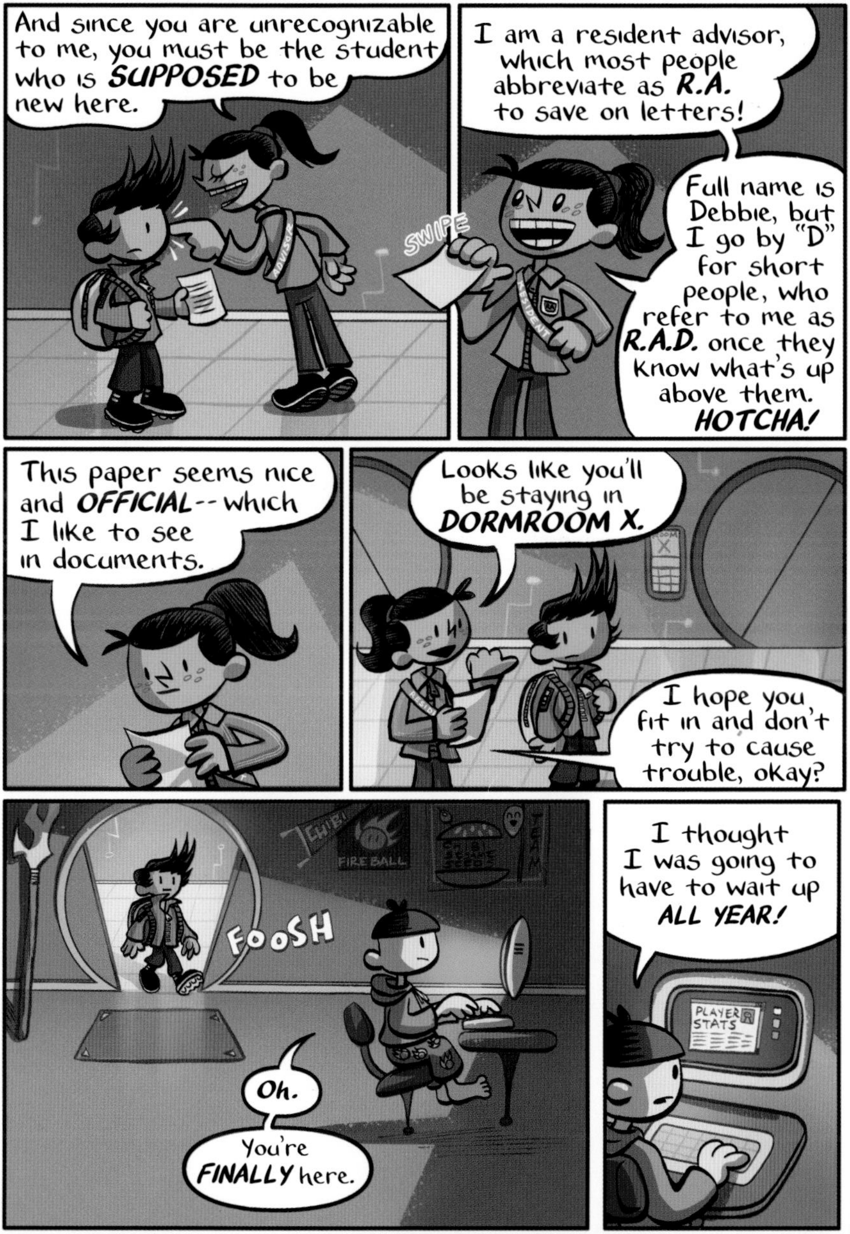

And since you are unrecognizable to me, you must be the student who is SUPPOSED to be new here.
ADVISOR
I am a resident advisor, which most people abbreviate as R.A. to save on letters!
SWIPE
Full name is Debbie, but I go by "D" for short people, who refer to me as R.A.D. once they know what's up above them. HOTCHA!
RESIDENT
This paper seems nice and OFFICIAL-- which I like to see in documents.
Looks like you'll be staying in DORMROOM X.
X
I hope you fit in and don't try to cause trouble, okay?
FIREBALL
TEAM
FOOSH
Oh.
You're FINALLY here.
I thought I was going to have to wait up ALL YEAR!
PLAYER STATS

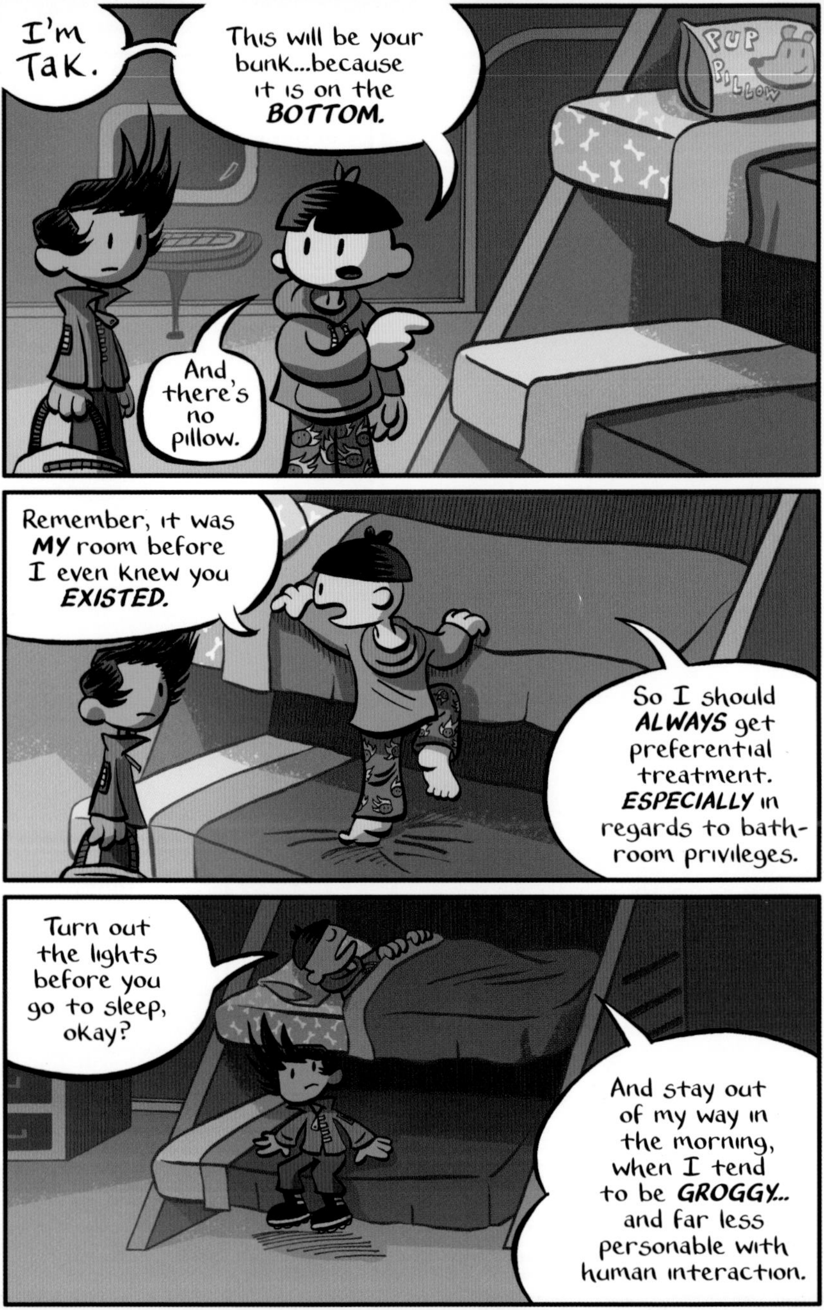

I'm TaK.
This will be your bunk...because it is on the BOTTOM.
And there's no pillow.
PUP PILLOW
Remember, it was MY room before I even knew you EXISTED.
So I should ALWAYS get preferential treatment. ESPECIALLY in regards to bathroom privileges.
Turn out the lights before you go to sleep, okay?
And stay out of my way in the morning, when I tend to be GROGGY... and far less personable with human interaction.

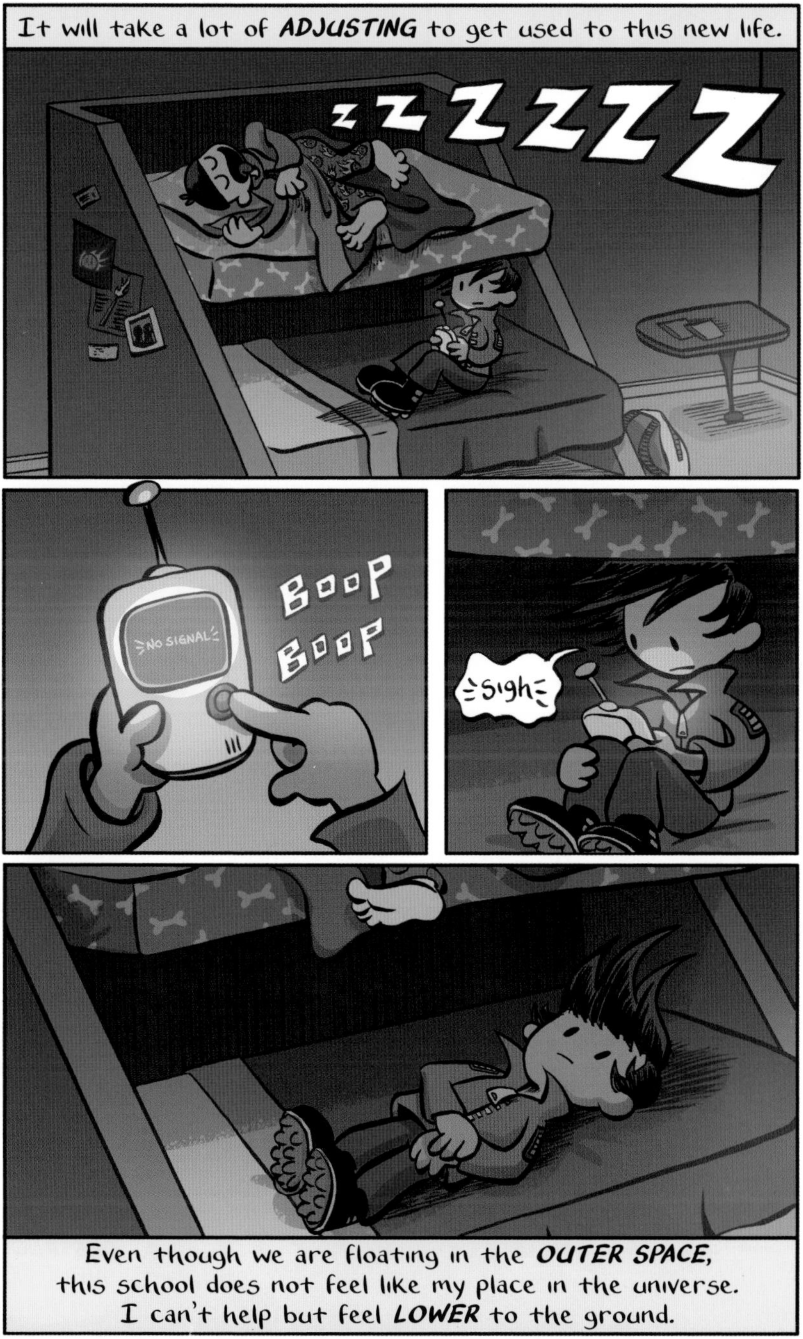
It will take a lot of ADJUSTING to get used to this new life.
ZZZZZZZ
NO SIGNAL
BOOP BOOP
Sigh
Even though we are floating in the OUTER SPACE, this school does not feel like my place in the universe. I can't help but feel LOWER to the ground.

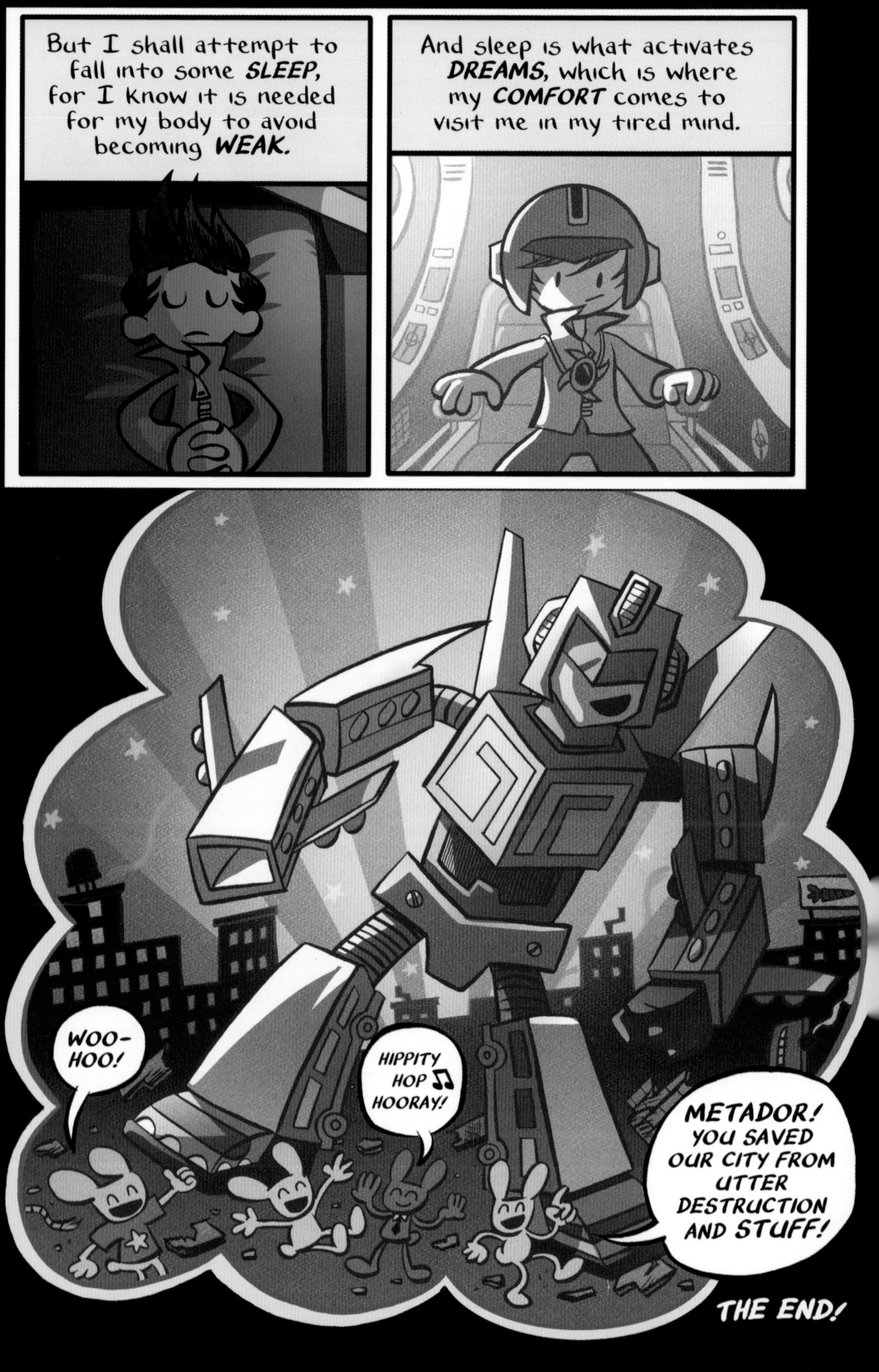

But I shall attempt to fall into some SLEEP, for I know it is needed for my body to avoid becoming WEAK.
And sleep is what activates DREAMS, which is where my COMFORT comes to visit me in my tired mind.
WOO-HOO!
HIPPITY HOP ♫ HOORAY!
METADOR! YOU SAVED OUR CITY FROM UTTER DESTRUCTION AND STUFF!
THE END!

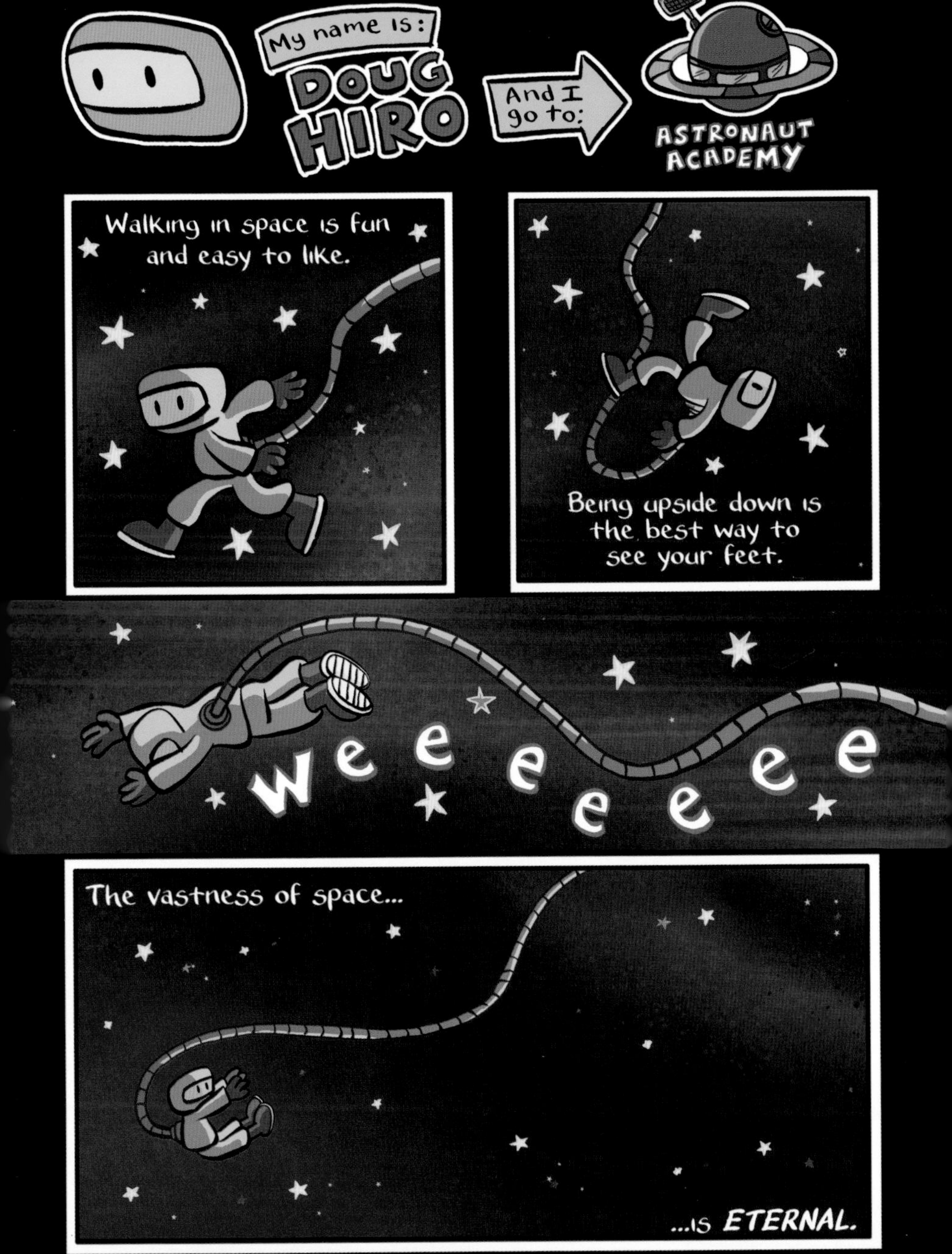
My name is:
DOUG HIRO
And I go to:
ASTRONAUT ACADEMY
Walking in space is fun and easy to like.
Being upside down is the best way to see your feet.
weeeeeee
The vastness of space...
...is ETERNAL.

All right, Doug, class ended **TWENTY MINUTES** ago!
It's time to come back inside.
I don't wanna.
THE END!

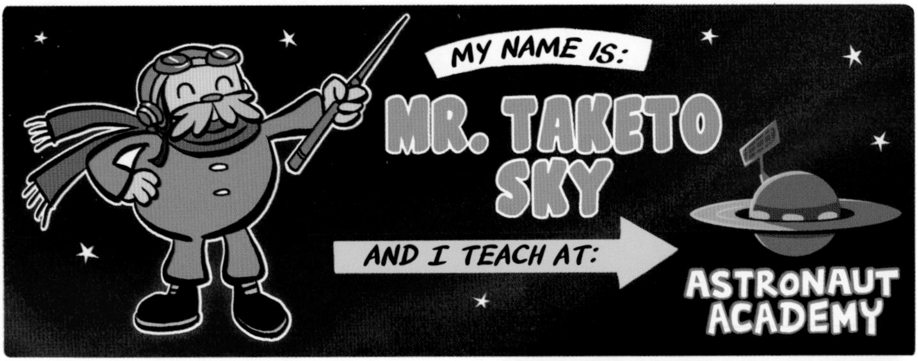
MY NAME IS:
MR. TAKETO SKY
AND I TEACH AT:
ASTRONAUT ACADEMY

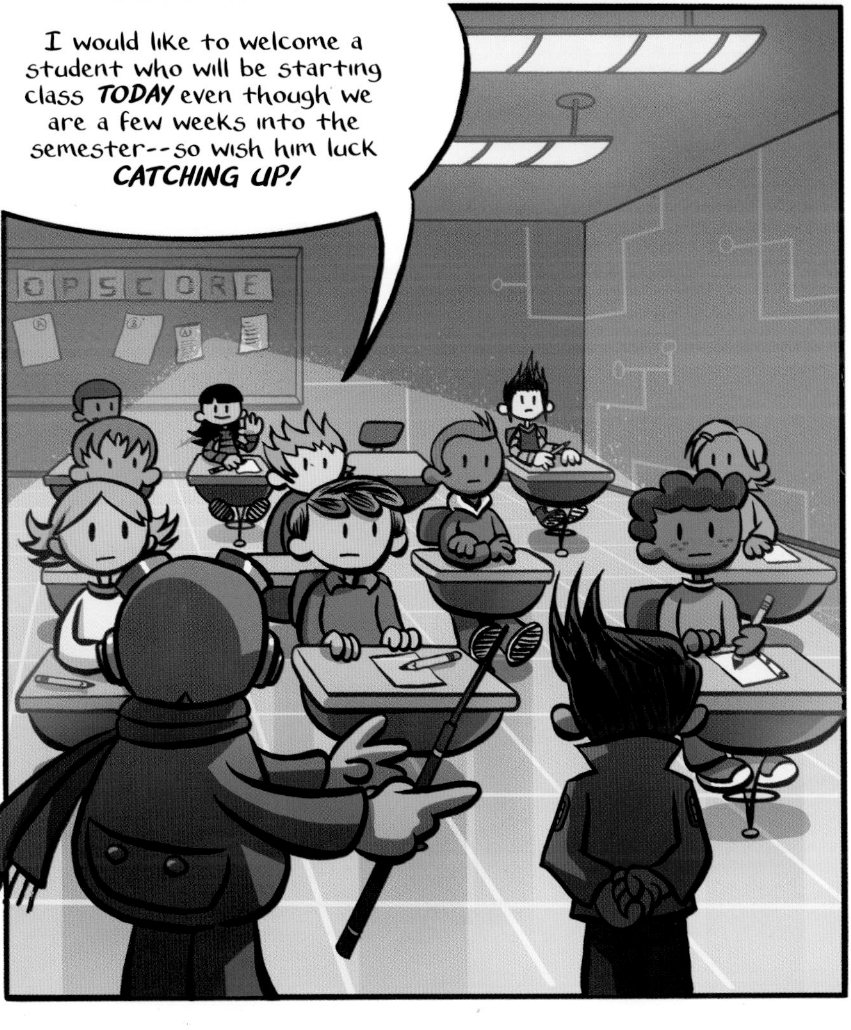
I would like to welcome a student who will be starting class TODAY even though we are a few weeks into the semester--so wish him luck CATCHING UP!
OPSCORE

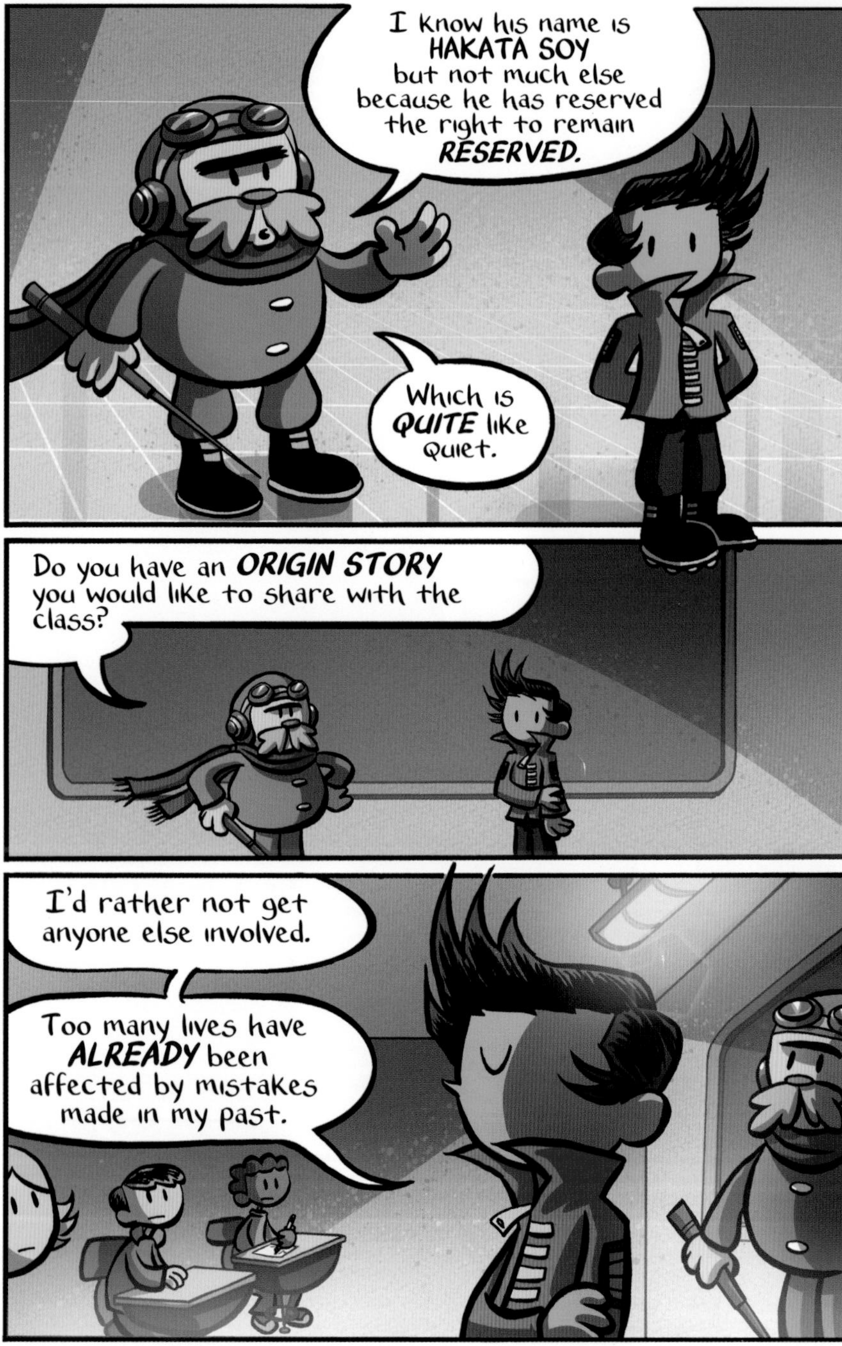
I know his name is HAKATA SOY but not much else because he has reserved the right to remain RESERVED.
Which is QUITE like quiet.
Do you have an ORIGIN STORY you would like to share with the class?
I'd rather not get anyone else involved.
Too many lives have ALREADY been affected by mistakes made in my past.

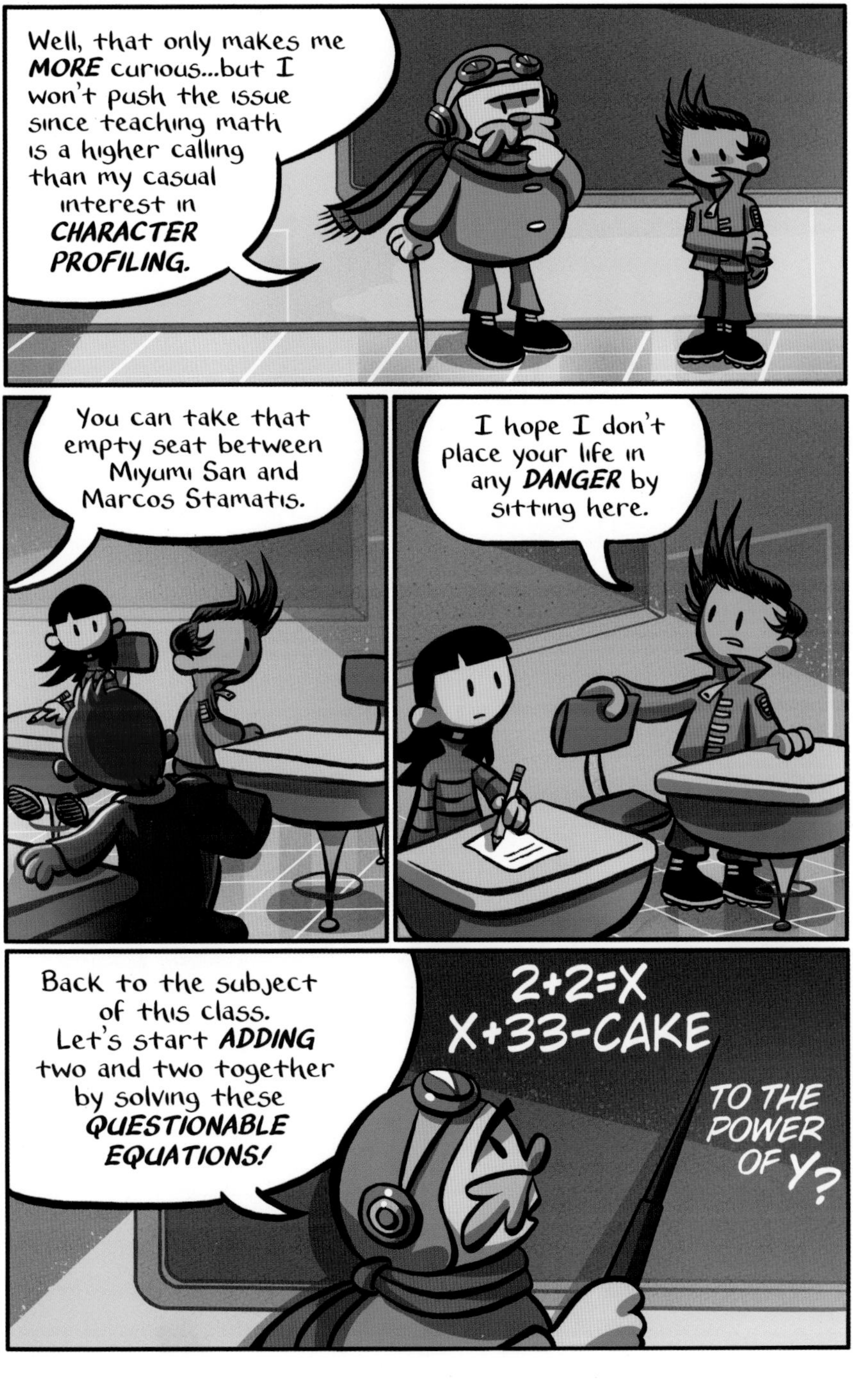
Well, that only makes me MORE curious...but I won't push the issue since teaching math is a higher calling than my casual interest in CHARACTER PROFILING.
You can take that empty seat between Miyumi San and Marcos Stamatis.
I hope I don't place your life in any DANGER by sitting here.
Back to the subject of this class. Let's start ADDING two and two together by solving these QUESTIONABLE EQUATIONS!
2+2=X
X+33-CAKE
TO THE POWER OF Y?

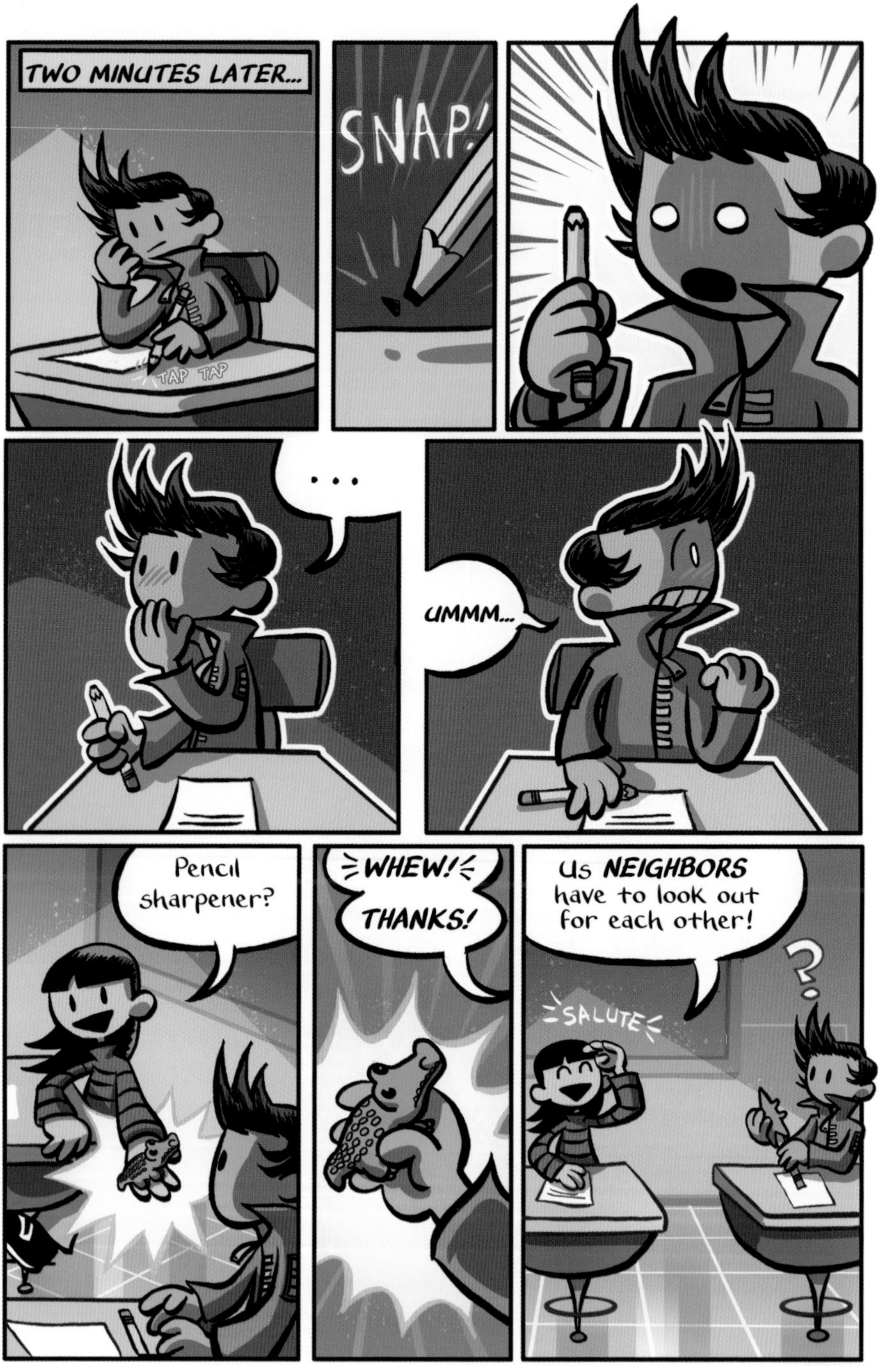
TWO MINUTES LATER...
TAP TAP
SNAP!
. . .
UMMM...
Pencil sharpener?
WHEW!
THANKS!
Us NEIGHBORS have to look out for each other!
SALUTE
?
END!

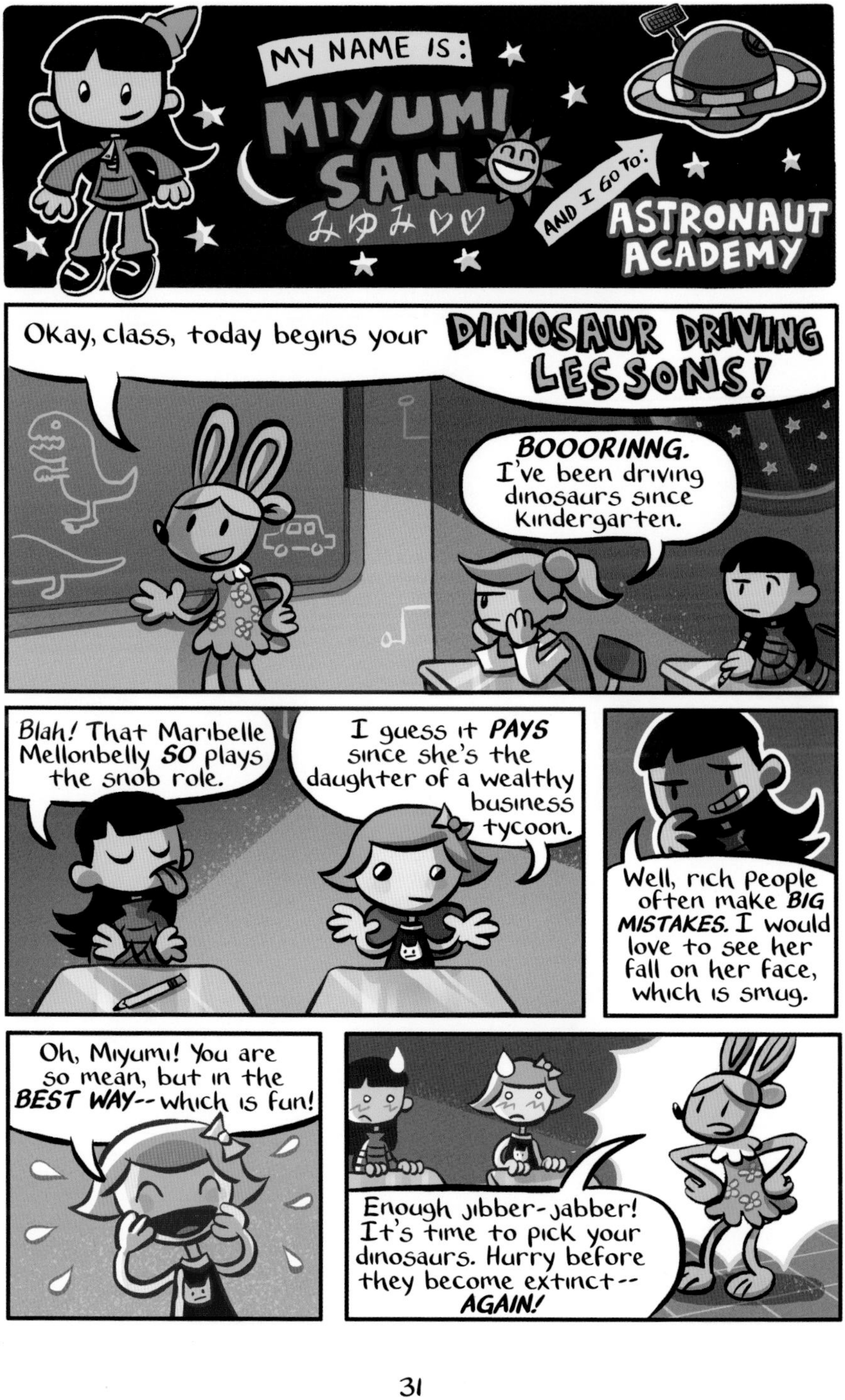
MY NAME IS:
MIYUMI SAN
みゆみ♡♡
AND I GO TO:
ASTRONAUT ACADEMY
Okay, class, today begins your DINOSAUR DRIVING LESSONS!
BOOORINNG. I've been driving dinosaurs since Kindergarten.
Blah! That Maribelle Mellonbelly SO plays the snob role.
I guess it PAYS since she's the daughter of a wealthy business tycoon.
Well, rich people often make BIG MISTAKES. I would love to see her fall on her face, which is smug.
Oh, Miyumi! You are so mean, but in the BEST WAY--which is fun!
Enough jibber-jabber! It's time to pick your dinosaurs. Hurry before they become extinct--AGAIN!

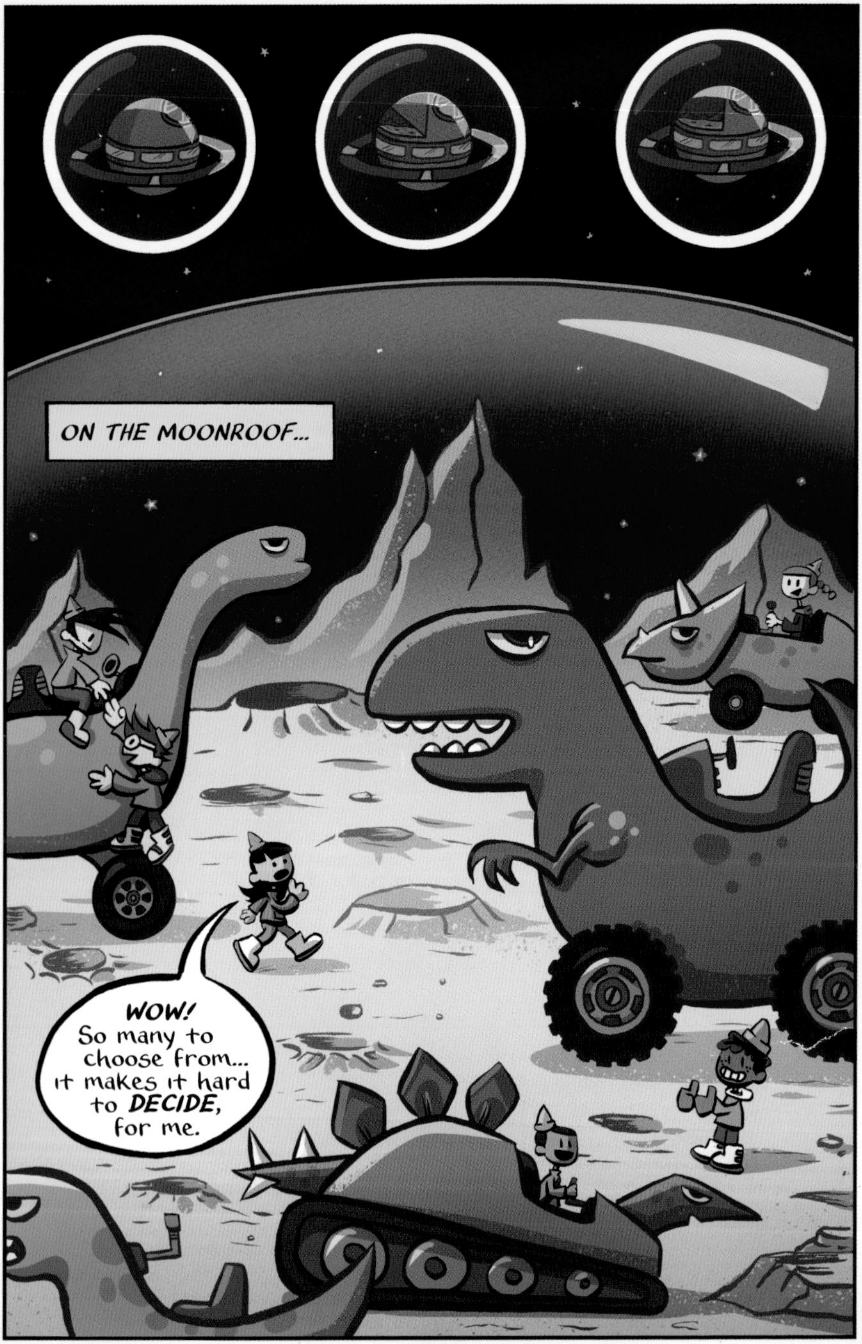
ON THE MOONROOF...
WOW! So many to choose from... it makes it hard to DECIDE, for me.

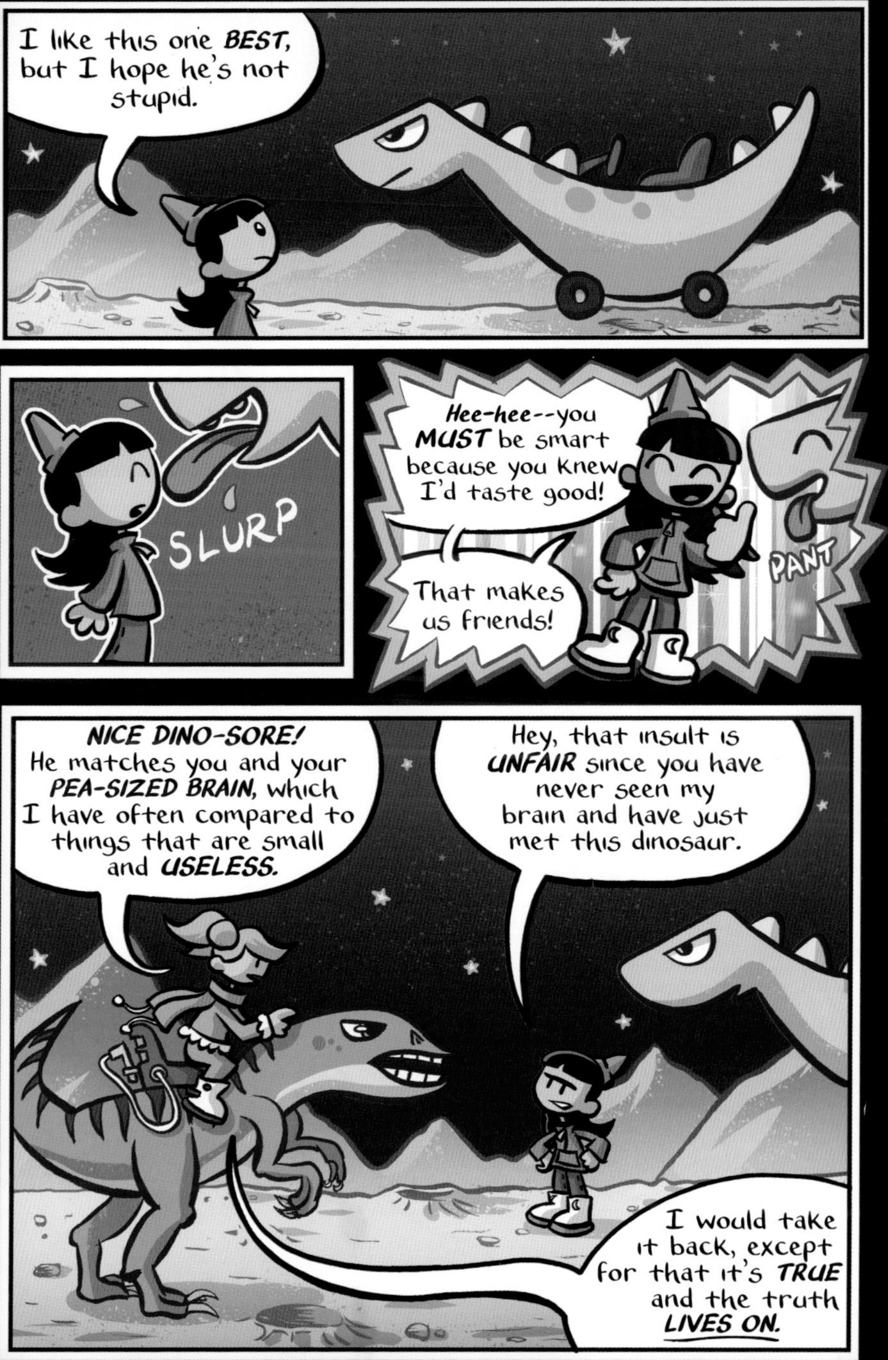
I like this one BEST, but I hope he's not stupid.
SLURP
Hee-hee--you MUST be smart because you knew I'd taste good!
That makes us friends!
PANT
NICE DINO-SORE! He matches you and your PEA-SIZED BRAIN, which I have often compared to things that are small and USELESS.
Hey, that insult is UNFAIR since you have never seen my brain and have just met this dinosaur.
I would take it back, except for that it's TRUE and the truth LIVES ON.

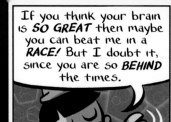

If you think your brain is **SO GREAT** then maybe you can beat me in a **RACE!** But I doubt it, since you are so **BEHIND** the times.

You can't say things like that to **ME!** **I'M RICH!** And I'll race you to **PROVE** how smart I am!

DEAL!

Let the race begin!

Giddyup, dino!

WAIT! You cannot race...it is only your first lesson!

And besides... it's **MY** job to say "let the race begin" since I am the one with the teacher's degree!

Then say it-- because this contest has to be **OFFICIAL** so the world can know that legally I am the best.

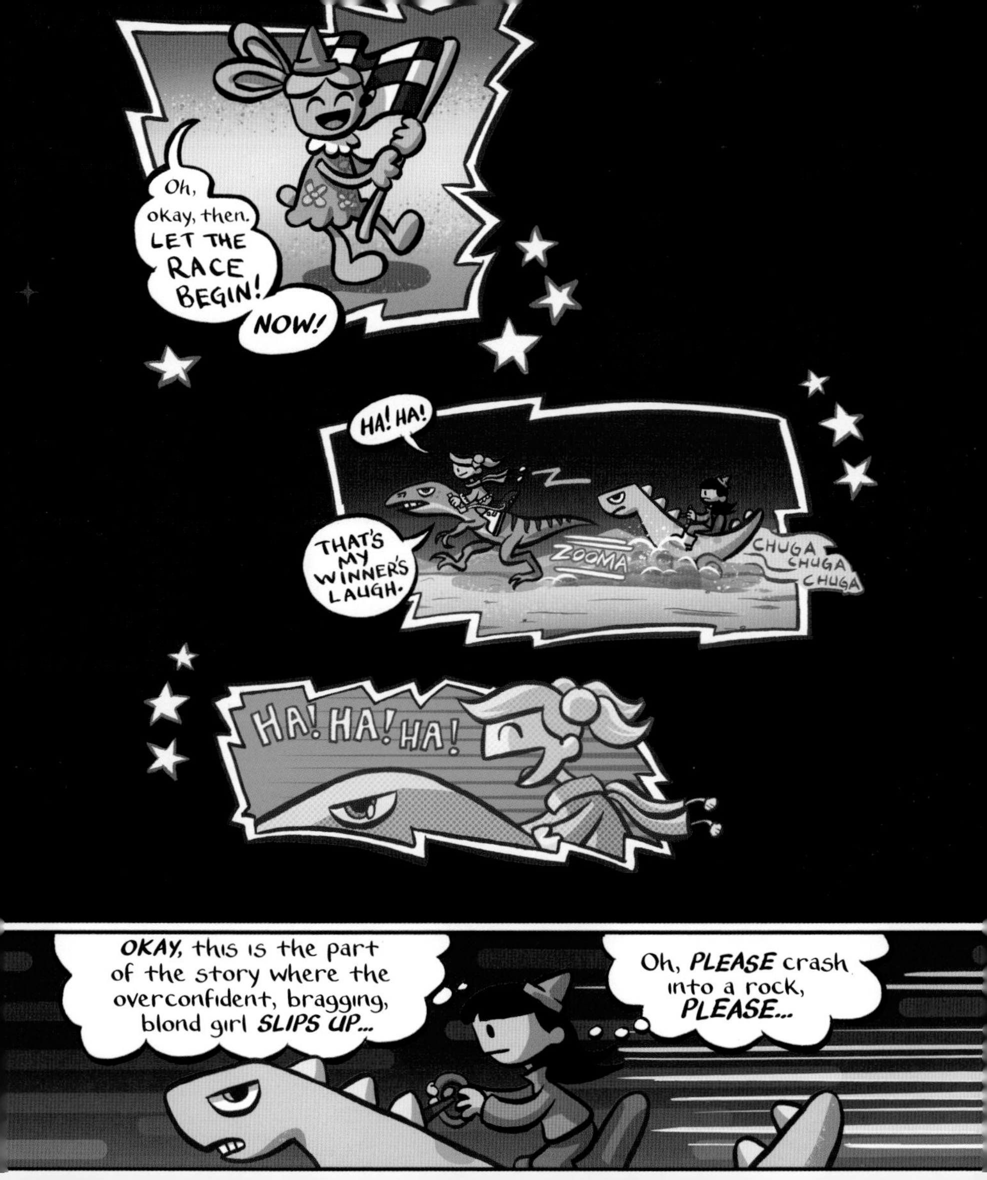
Oh, okay, then. LET THE RACE BEGIN!
NOW!
HA! HA!
THAT'S MY WINNER'S LAUGH.
ZOOMA
CHUGA CHUGA CHUGA
HA! HA! HA!
OKAY, this is the part of the story where the overconfident, bragging, blond girl SLIPS UP...
Oh, PLEASE crash into a rock, PLEASE...

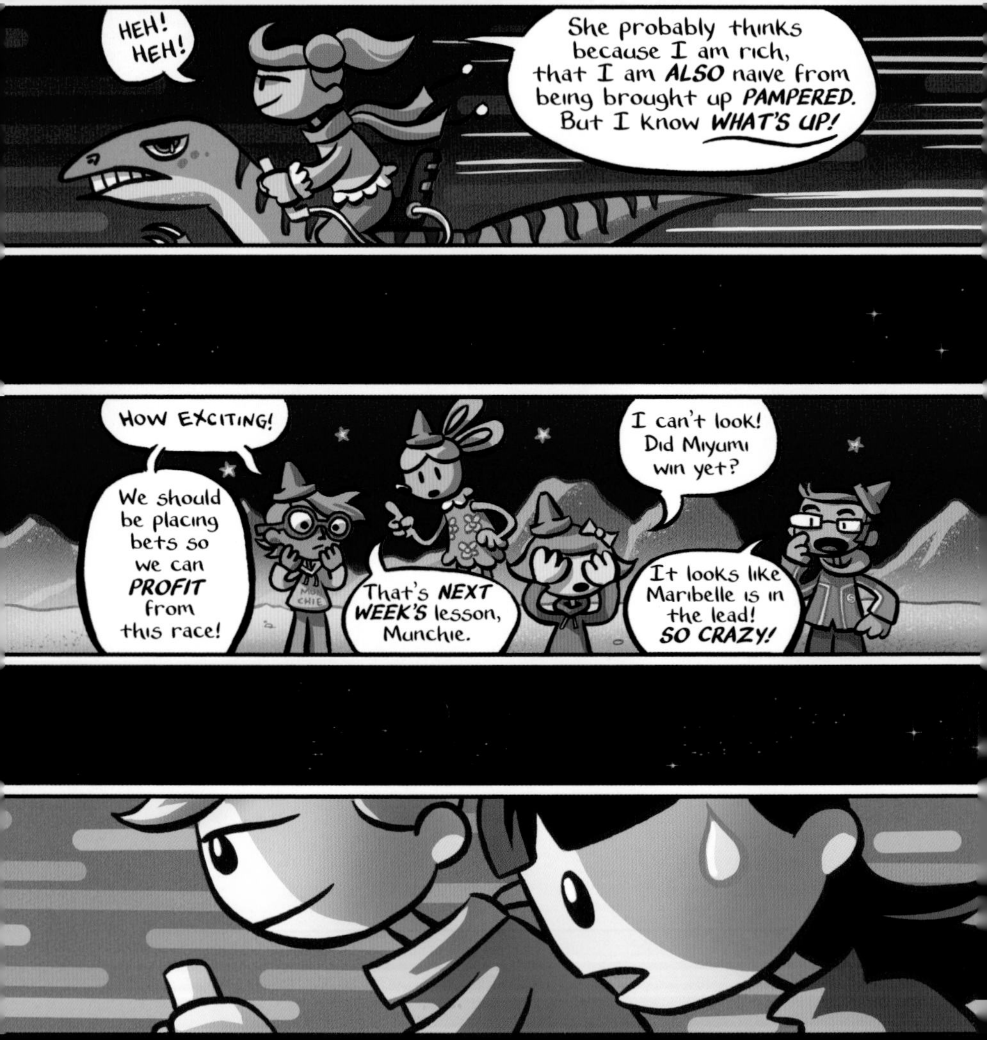
HEH! HEH!
She probably thinks because I am rich, that I am ALSO naive from being brought up PAMPERED. But I know WHAT'S UP!
HOW EXCITING!
We should be placing bets so we can PROFIT from this race!
That's NEXT WEEK'S lesson, Munchie.
I can't look! Did Miyumi win yet?
It looks like Maribelle is in the lead! SO CRAZY!

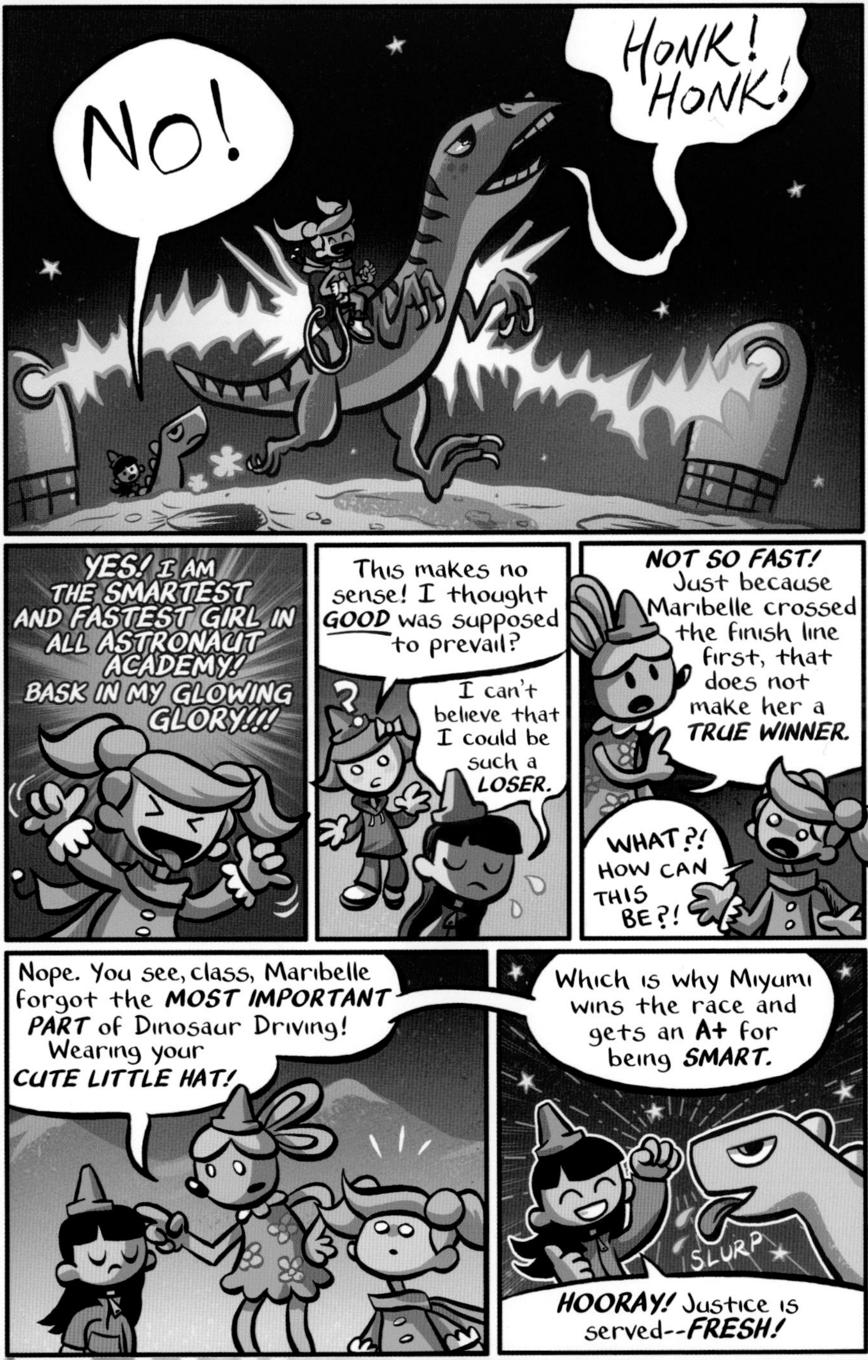
No!
HONK! HONK!
YES! I AM THE SMARTEST AND FASTEST GIRL IN ALL ASTRONAUT ACADEMY! BASK IN MY GLOWING GLORY!!!
This makes no sense! I thought GOOD was supposed to prevail?
I can't believe that I could be such a LOSER.
NOT SO FAST! Just because Maribelle crossed the finish line first, that does not make her a TRUE WINNER.
WHAT?! HOW CAN THIS BE?!
Nope. You see, class, Maribelle forgot the MOST IMPORTANT PART of Dinosaur Driving! Wearing your CUTE LITTLE HAT!
Which is why Miyumi wins the race and gets an A+ for being SMART.
SLURP
HOORAY! Justice is served--FRESH!

PHOTO FINISH!

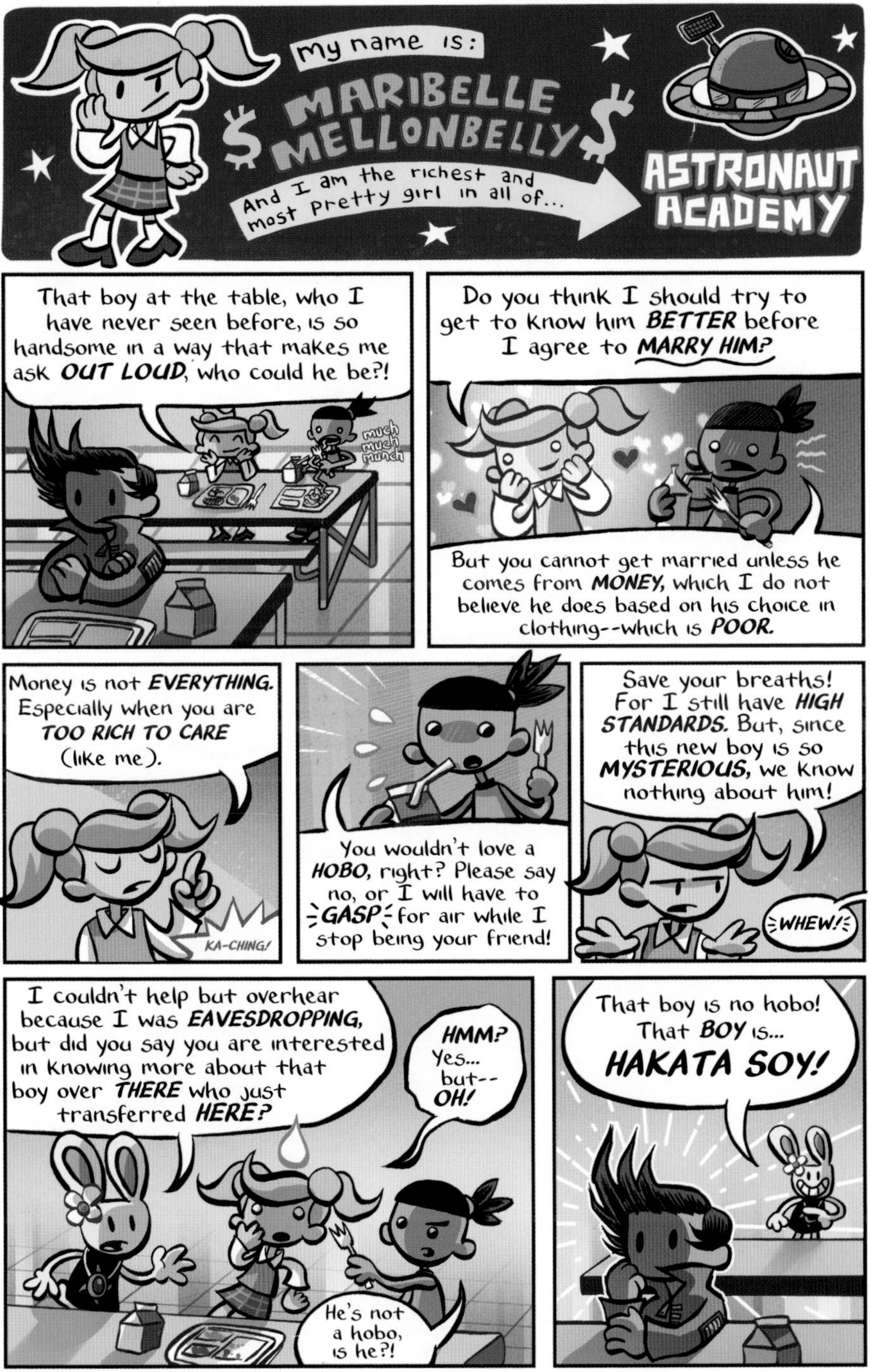
my name is:
$ MARIBELLE MELLONBELLY $
And I am the richest and most pretty girl in all of...
ASTRONAUT ACADEMY
That boy at the table, who I have never seen before, is so handsome in a way that makes me ask OUT LOUD, who could he be?!
much much munch
Do you think I should try to get to know him BETTER before I agree to MARRY HIM?
But you cannot get married unless he comes from MONEY, which I do not believe he does based on his choice in clothing--which is POOR.
Money is not EVERYTHING. Especially when you are TOO RICH TO CARE (like me).
KA-CHING!
You wouldn't love a HOBO, right? Please say no, or I will have to GASP for air while I stop being your friend!
Save your breaths! For I still have HIGH STANDARDS. But, since this new boy is so MYSTERIOUS, we know nothing about him!
WHEW!
I couldn't help but overhear because I was EAVESDROPPING, but did you say you are interested in knowing more about that boy over THERE who just transferred HERE?
HMM? Yes... but-- OH!
He's not a hobo, is he?!
That boy is no hobo! That BOY is... HAKATA SOY!

And *HOW* do you know him *EXACTLY?* You're not an ex-girlfriend, *ARE YOU?!* I hope *NOT,* cuz that would mean you are now *MY ENEMY.*

BACK OFF, SISTER!

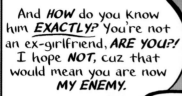

NO! It is *NOTHING* like that conclusion you have jumped to in *COMPLETE INACCURACY!*

My story is less *ROMANCE-BASED* and instead, rather *HEROIC!*

WINK

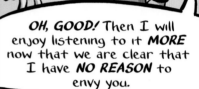

OH, GOOD! Then I will enjoy listening to it *MORE* now that we are clear that I have *NO REASON* to envy you.

A few years ago on the far-off planet of Hoppiton,

I lived hoppily with my family in a peaceful city.

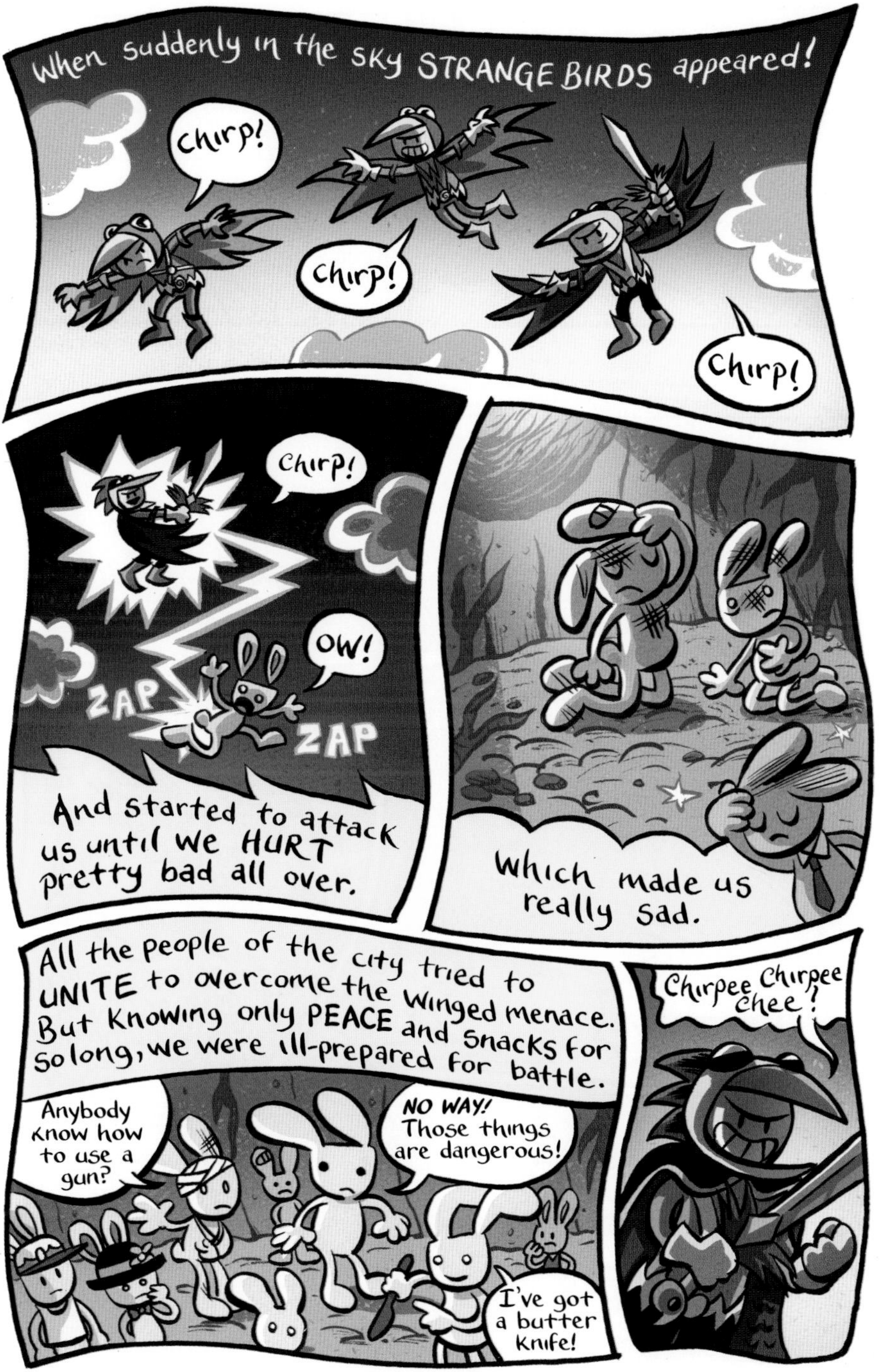
When suddenly in the sky STRANGE BIRDS appeared!
Chirp!
Chirp!
Chirp!
Chirp!
OW!
ZAP
ZAP
And started to attack us until we HURT pretty bad all over.
Which made us really sad.
All the people of the city tried to UNITE to overcome the winged menace. But knowing only PEACE and snacks for so long, we were ill-prepared for battle.
Anybody know how to use a gun?
NO WAY! Those things are dangerous!
I've got a butter knife!
Chirpee Chirpee Chee?

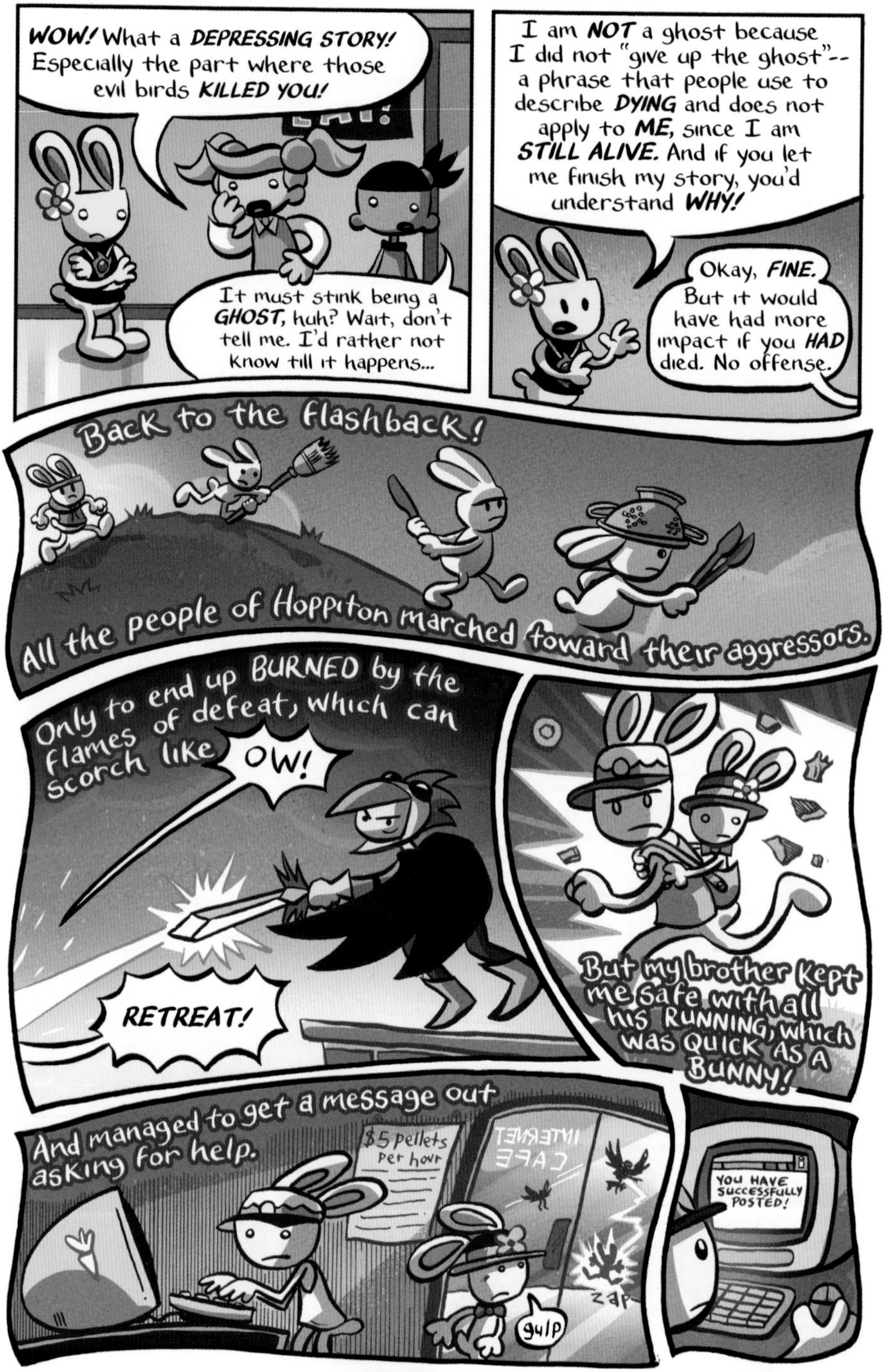
WOW! What a DEPRESSING STORY! Especially the part where those evil birds KILLED YOU!
It must stink being a GHOST, huh? Wait, don't tell me. I'd rather not know till it happens...
I am NOT a ghost because I did not "give up the ghost"-- a phrase that people use to describe DYING and does not apply to ME, since I am STILL ALIVE. And if you let me finish my story, you'd understand WHY!
Okay, FINE. But it would have had more impact if you HAD died. No offense.
Back to the flashback!
All the people of Hoppiton marched toward their aggressors.
Only to end up BURNED by the flames of defeat, which can scorch like
OW!
RETREAT!
But my brother kept me safe with all his RUNNING, which was QUICK AS A BUNNY!
And managed to get a message out asking for help.
$5 pellets per hour
INTERNET CAFE
gulp
zap
YOU HAVE SUCCESSFULLY POSTED!

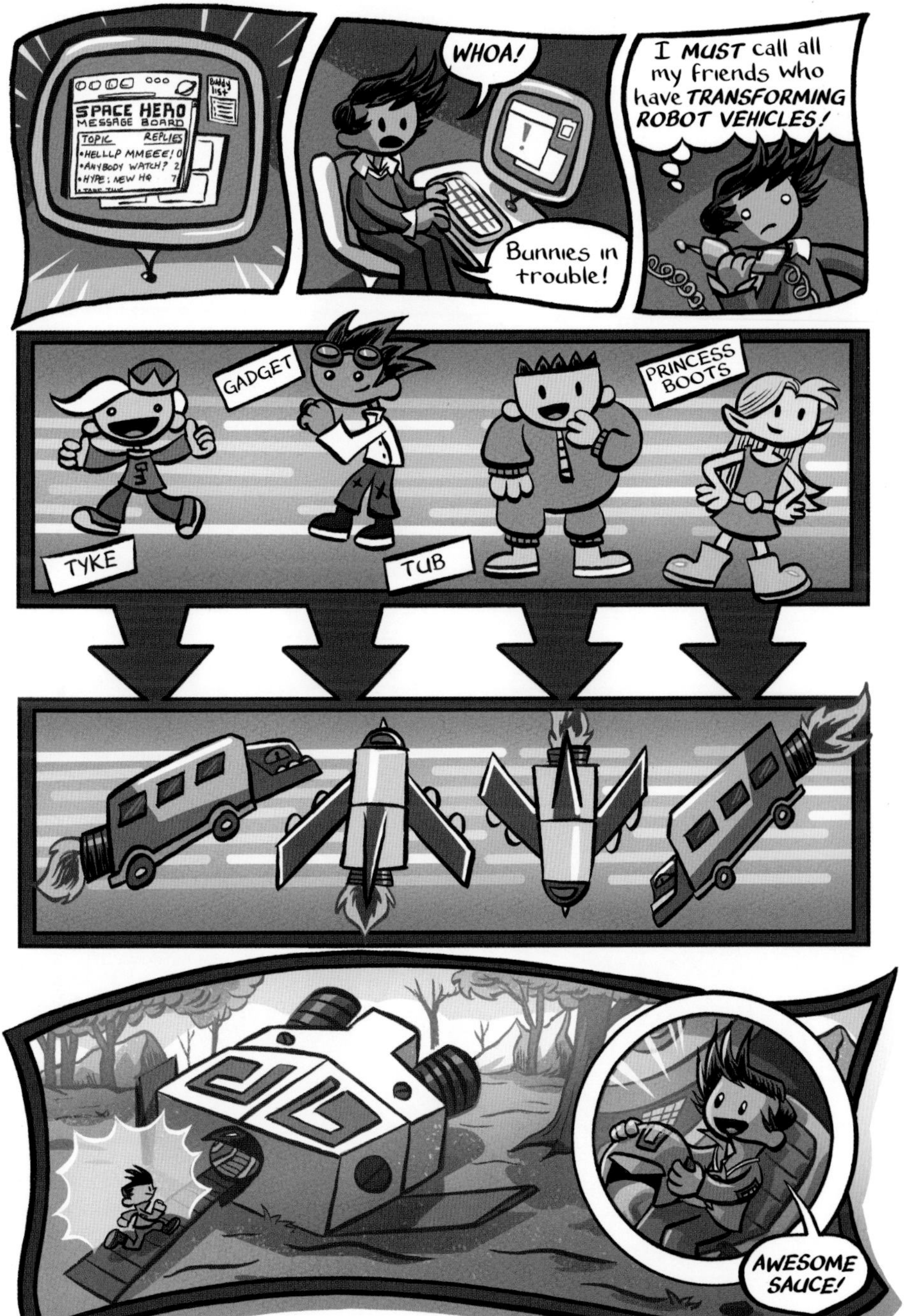
SPACE HERO MESSAGE BOARD
TOPIC REPLIES
•HELLLP MMEEE! 0
•ANYBODY WATCH? 2
•HYPE: NEW HQ 7
buddy list
WHOA!
Bunnies in trouble!
I MUST call all my friends who have TRANSFORMING ROBOT VEHICLES!
GADGET
PRINCESS BOOTS
TYKE
TUB
AWESOME SAUCE!

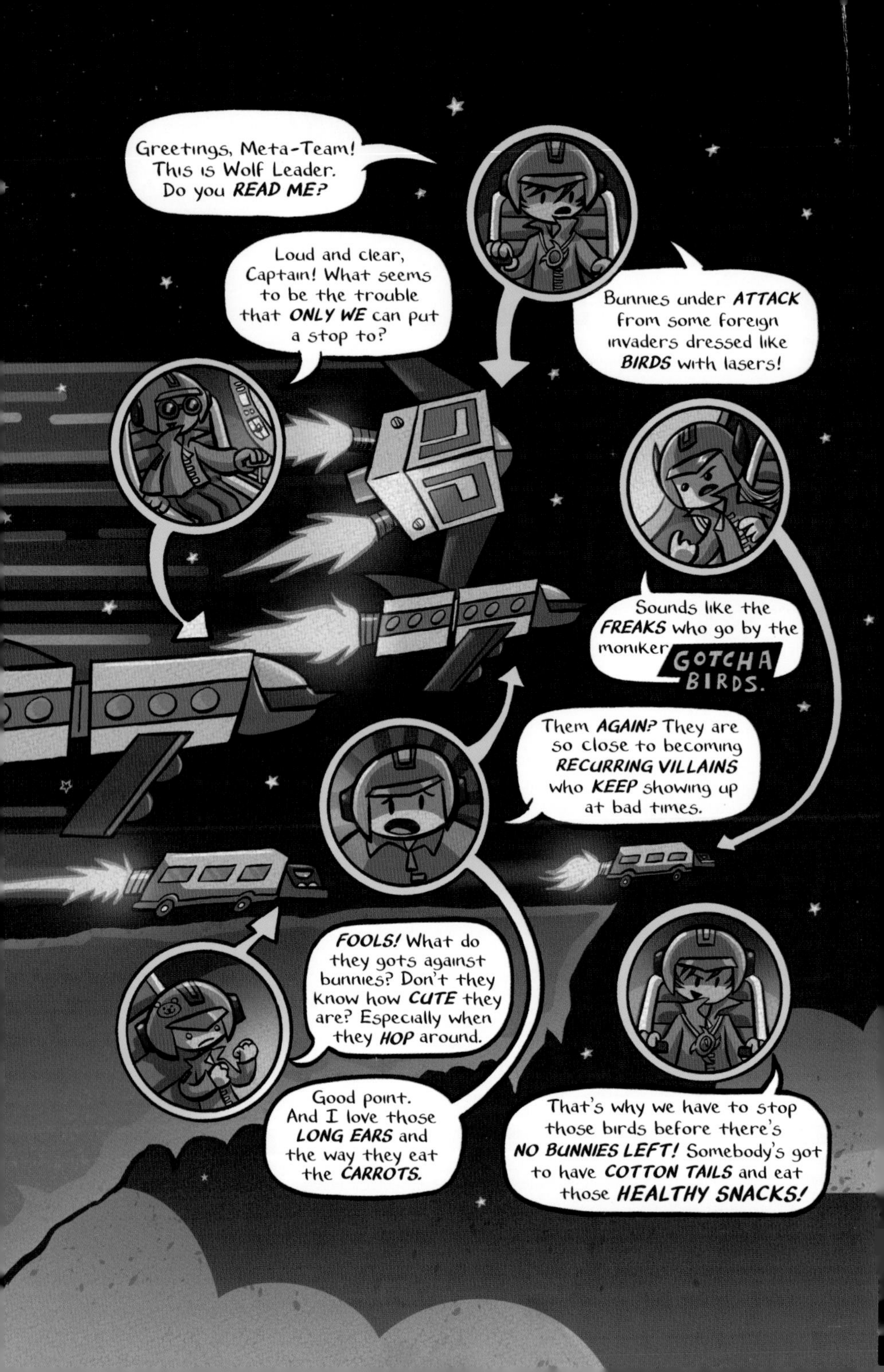
Greetings, Meta-Team! This is Wolf Leader. Do you READ ME?
Loud and clear, Captain! What seems to be the trouble that ONLY WE can put a stop to?
Bunnies under ATTACK from some foreign invaders dressed like BIRDS with lasers!
Sounds like the FREAKS who go by the moniker GOTCHA BIRDS.
Them AGAIN? They are so close to becoming RECURRING VILLAINS who KEEP showing up at bad times.
FOOLS! What do they gots against bunnies? Don't they know how CUTE they are? Especially when they HOP around.
Good point. And I love those LONG EARS and the way they eat the CARROTS.
That's why we have to stop those birds before there's NO BUNNIES LEFT! Somebody's got to have COTTON TAILS and eat those HEALTHY SNACKS!

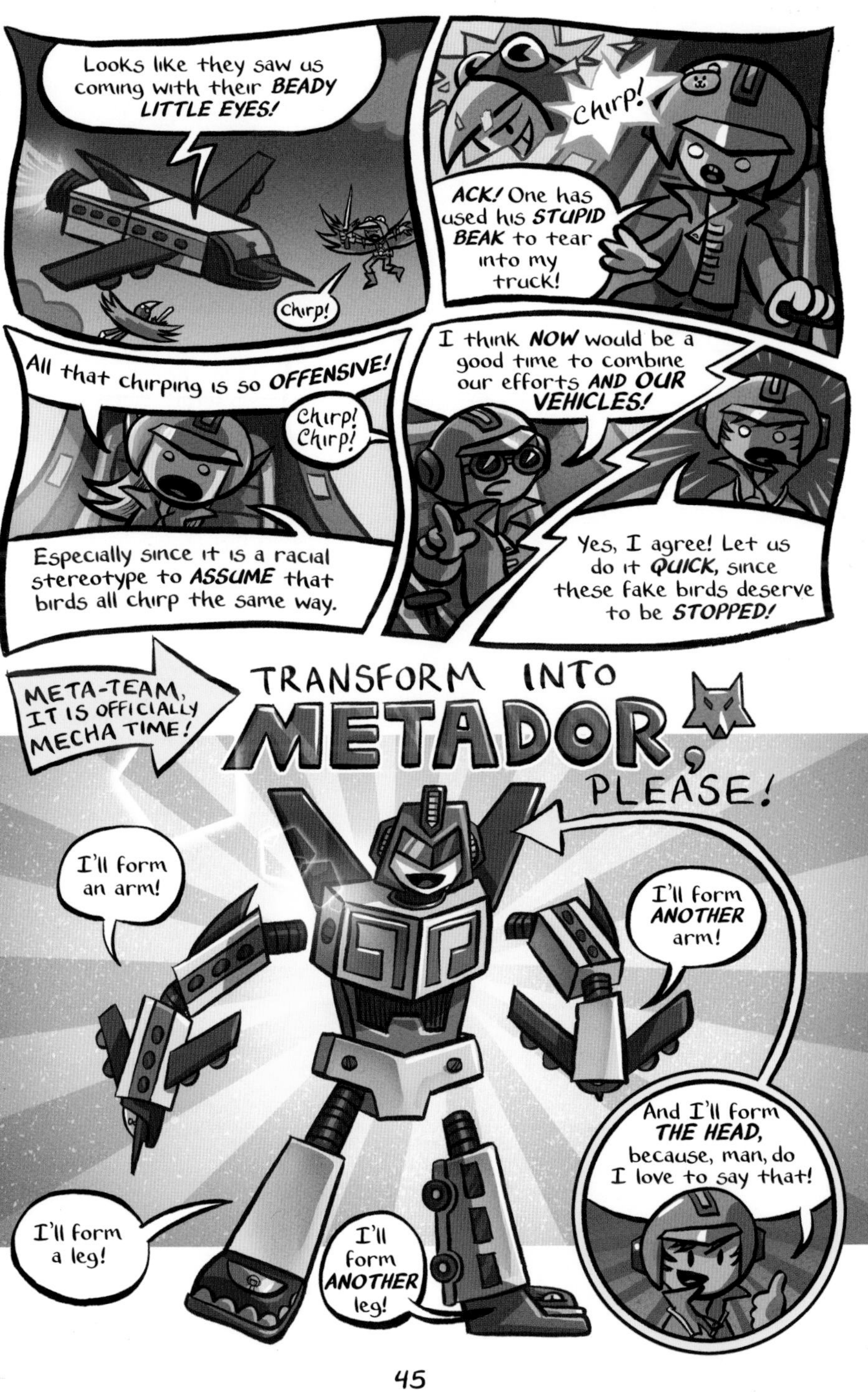
Looks like they saw us coming with their BEADY LITTLE EYES!
Chirp!
Chirp!
ACK! One has used his STUPID BEAK to tear into my truck!
All that chirping is so OFFENSIVE!
Chirp! Chirp!
Especially since it is a racial stereotype to ASSUME that birds all chirp the same way.
I think NOW would be a good time to combine our efforts AND OUR VEHICLES!
Yes, I agree! Let us do it QUICK, since these fake birds deserve to be STOPPED!
META-TEAM, IT IS OFFICIALLY MECHA TIME!
TRANSFORM INTO METADOR, PLEASE!
I'll form an arm!
I'll form ANOTHER arm!
And I'll form THE HEAD, because, man, do I love to say that!
I'll form a leg!
I'll form ANOTHER leg!

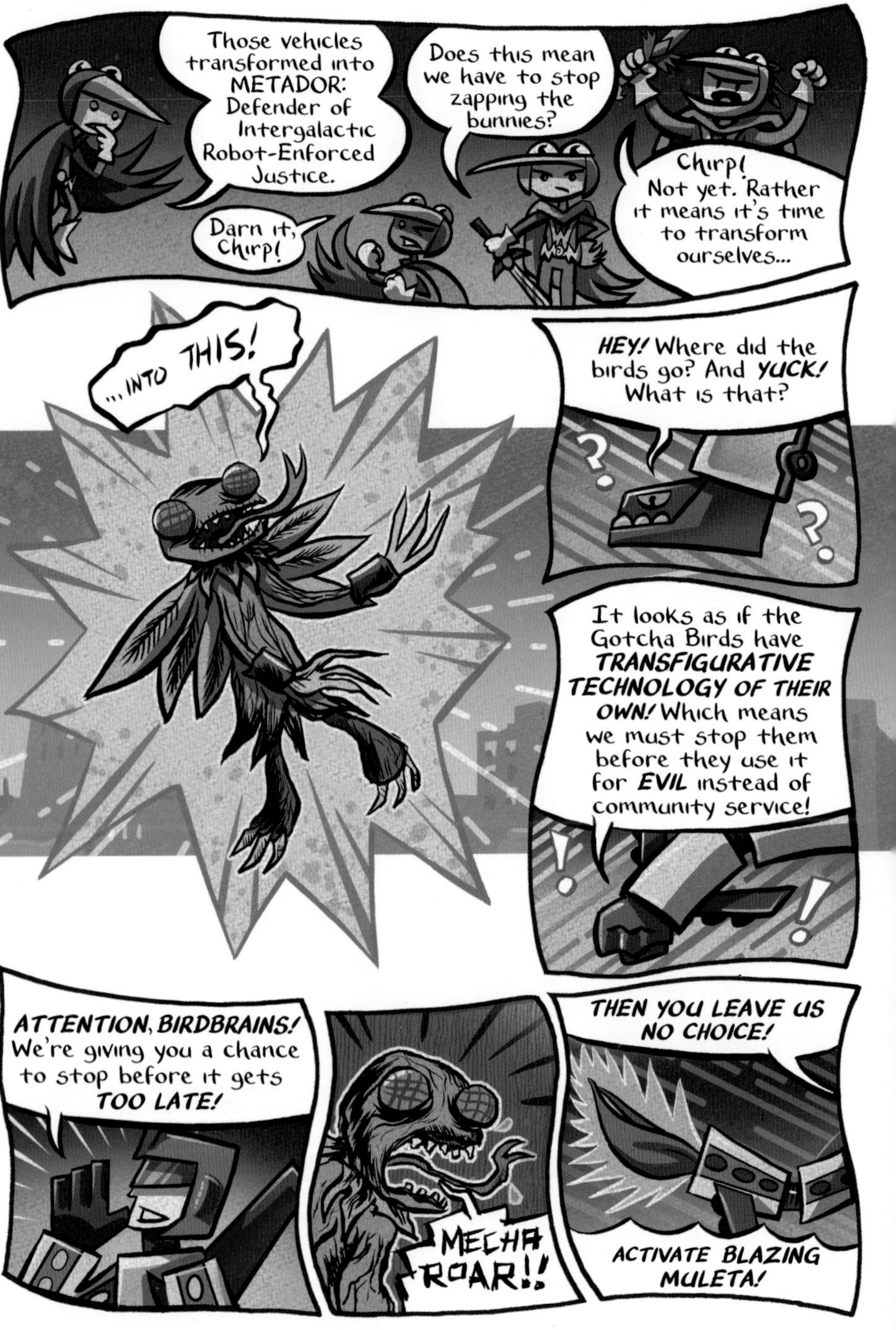

Those vehicles transformed into METADOR: Defender of Intergalactic Robot-Enforced Justice.
Does this mean we have to stop zapping the bunnies?
Darn it, Chirp!
Chirp! Not yet. Rather it means it's time to transform ourselves...
...INTO THIS!
HEY! Where did the birds go? And YUCK! What is that?
It looks as if the Gotcha Birds have TRANSFIGURATIVE TECHNOLOGY OF THEIR OWN! Which means we must stop them before they use it for EVIL instead of community service!
ATTENTION, BIRDBRAINS! We're giving you a chance to stop before it gets TOO LATE!
MECHA ROAR!!
THEN YOU LEAVE US NO CHOICE!
ACTIVATE BLAZING MULETA!

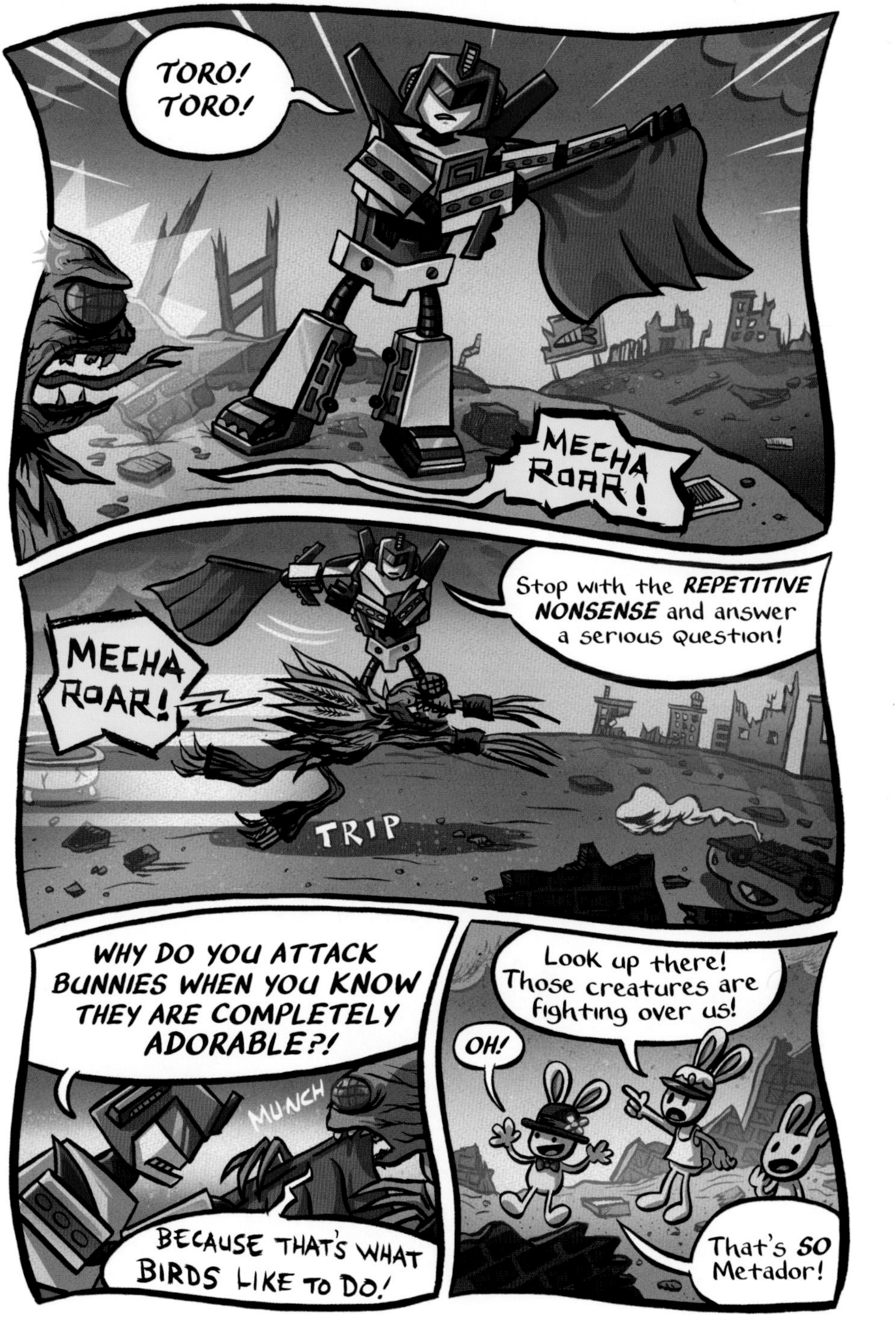
TORO! TORO!
MECHA ROAR!
Stop with the REPETITIVE NONSENSE and answer a serious Question!
MECHA ROAR!
TRIP
WHY DO YOU ATTACK BUNNIES WHEN YOU KNOW THEY ARE COMPLETELY ADORABLE?!
MUNCH
BECAUSE THAT'S WHAT BIRDS LIKE TO DO!
Look up there! Those creatures are fighting over us!
OH!
That's SO Metador!

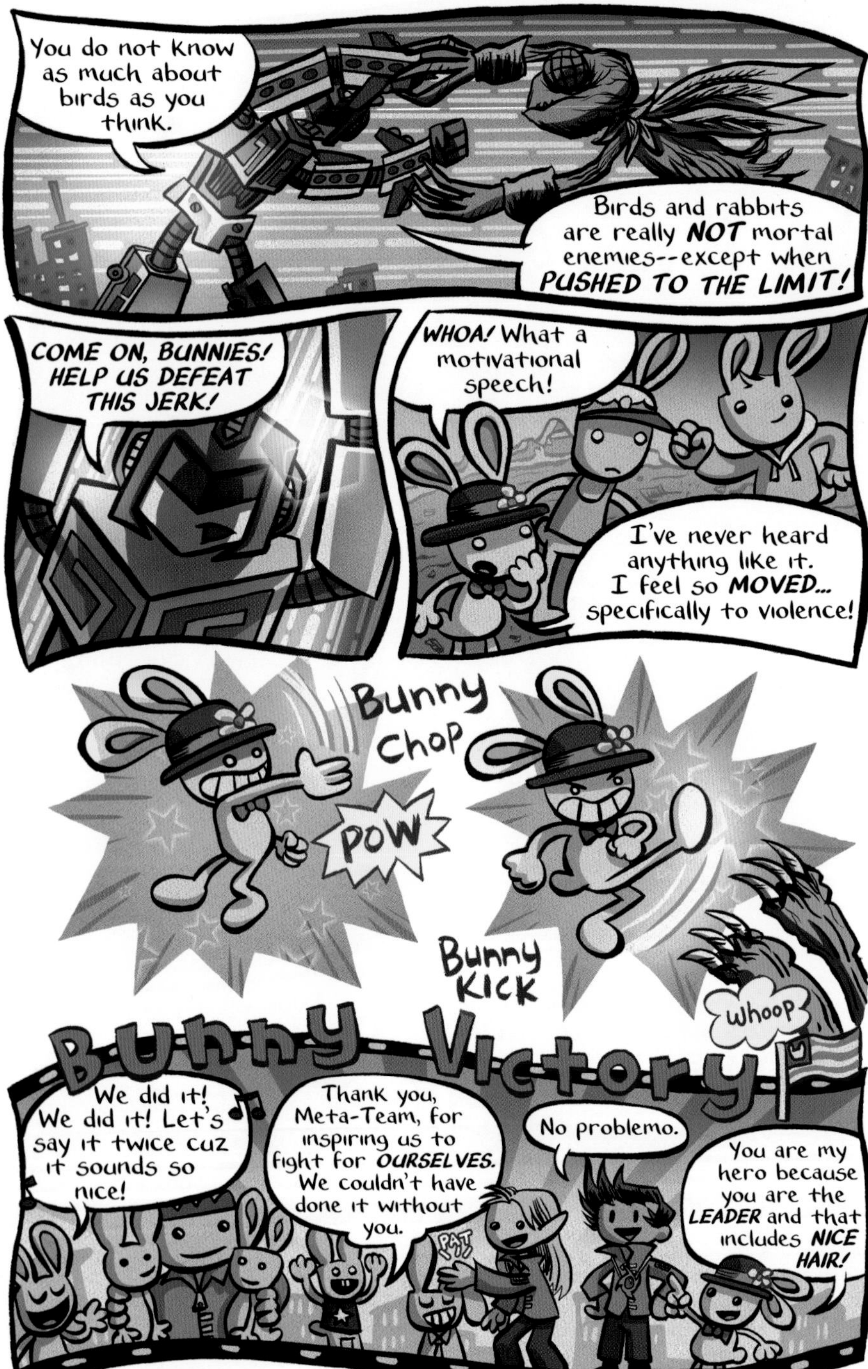
You do not know as much about birds as you think.
Birds and rabbits are really **NOT** mortal enemies--except when **PUSHED TO THE LIMIT!**
COME ON, BUNNIES! HELP US DEFEAT THIS JERK!
WHOA! What a motivational speech!
I've never heard anything like it. I feel so **MOVED...** specifically to violence!
Bunny Chop
POW
Bunny Kick
Whoop
Bunny Victory!
We did it! We did it! Let's say it twice cuz it sounds so nice!
Thank you, Meta-Team, for inspiring us to fight for **OURSELVES.** We couldn't have done it without you.
PAT
No problemo.
You are my hero because you are the **LEADER** and that includes **NICE HAIR!**

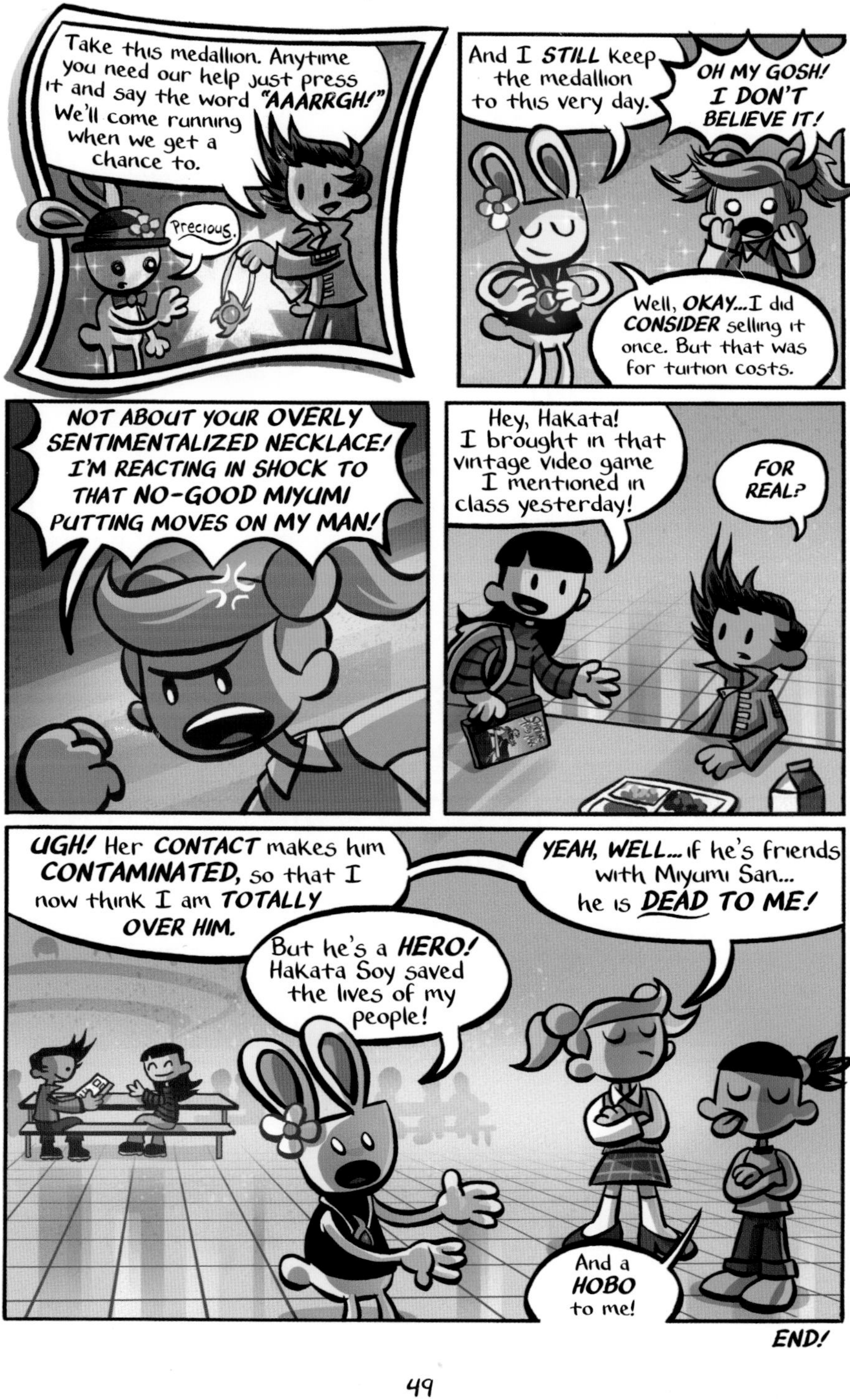
Take this medallion. Anytime you need our help just press it and say the word "AAARRGH!" We'll come running when we get a chance to.
Precious.
And I STILL keep the medallion to this very day.
OH MY GOSH! I DON'T BELIEVE IT!
Well, OKAY...I did CONSIDER selling it once. But that was for tuition costs.
NOT ABOUT YOUR OVERLY SENTIMENTALIZED NECKLACE! I'M REACTING IN SHOCK TO THAT NO-GOOD MIYUMI PUTTING MOVES ON MY MAN!
Hey, Hakata! I brought in that vintage video game I mentioned in class yesterday!
FOR REAL?
UGH! Her CONTACT makes him CONTAMINATED, so that I now think I am TOTALLY OVER HIM.
YEAH, WELL... if he's friends with Miyumi San... he is DEAD TO ME!
But he's a HERO! Hakata Soy saved the lives of my people!
And a HOBO to me!
END!

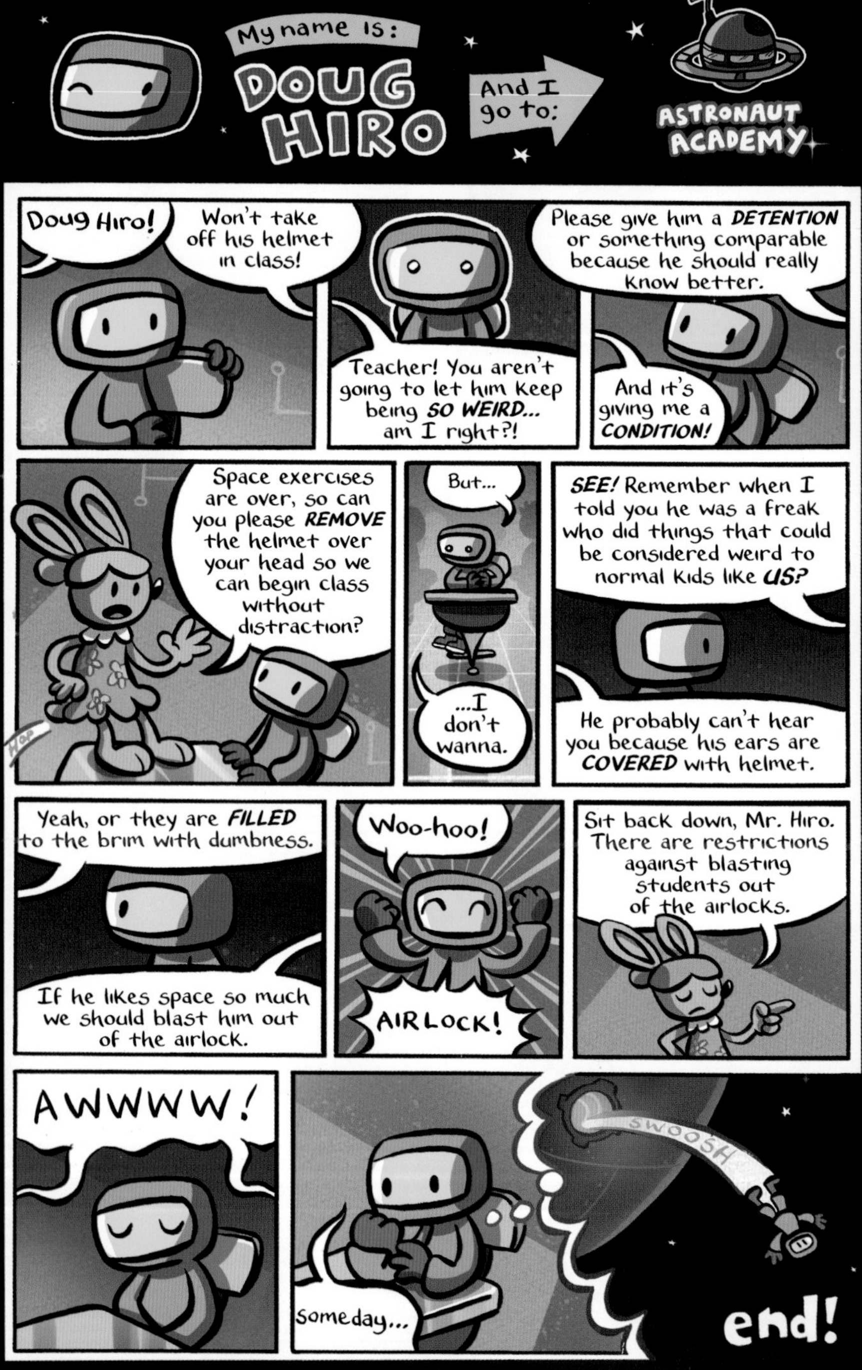
My name is:
DOUG HIRO
And I go to:
ASTRONAUT ACADEMY
Doug Hiro!
Won't take off his helmet in class!
Teacher! You aren't going to let him keep being SO WEIRD... am I right?!
Please give him a DETENTION or something comparable because he should really know better.
And it's giving me a CONDITION!
Space exercises are over, so can you please REMOVE the helmet over your head so we can begin class without distraction?
But...
...I don't wanna.
SEE! Remember when I told you he was a freak who did things that could be considered weird to normal kids like US?
He probably can't hear you because his ears are COVERED with helmet.
Yeah, or they are FILLED to the brim with dumbness.
If he likes space so much we should blast him out of the airlock.
Woo-hoo!
AIRLOCK!
Sit back down, Mr. Hiro. There are restrictions against blasting students out of the airlocks.
AWWWW!
Someday...
SWOOSH
end!

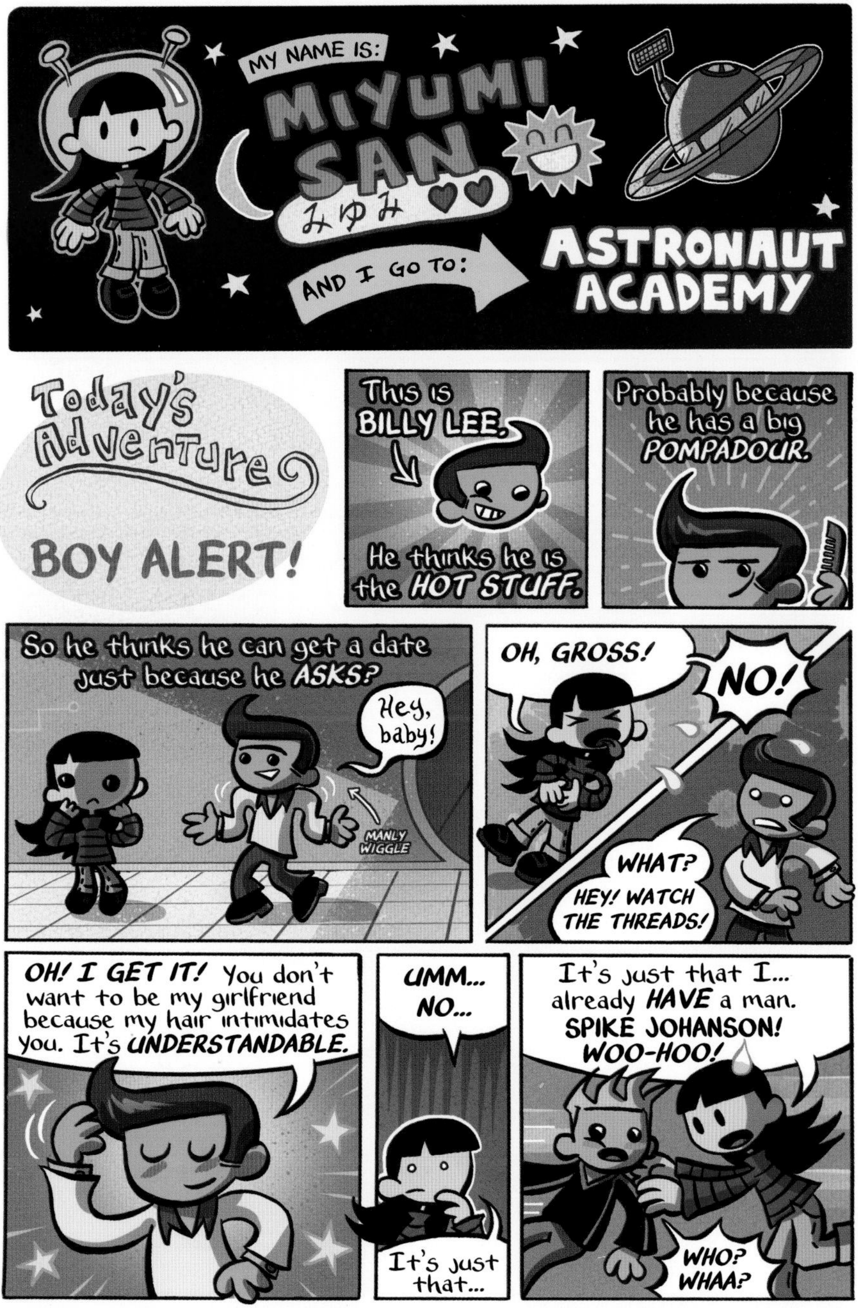
MY NAME IS:
MIYUMI SAN
みゆみ
AND I GO TO:
ASTRONAUT ACADEMY
Today's Adventure
BOY ALERT!
This is BILLY LEE.
He thinks he is the HOT STUFF.
Probably because he has a big POMPADOUR.
So he thinks he can get a date just because he ASKS?
Hey, baby!
MANLY WIGGLE
OH, GROSS!
NO!
WHAT?
HEY! WATCH THE THREADS!
OH! I GET IT! You don't want to be my girlfriend because my hair intimidates you. It's UNDERSTANDABLE.
UMM... NO...
It's just that...
It's just that I... already HAVE a man. SPIKE JOHANSON! WOO-HOO!
WHO? WHAA?

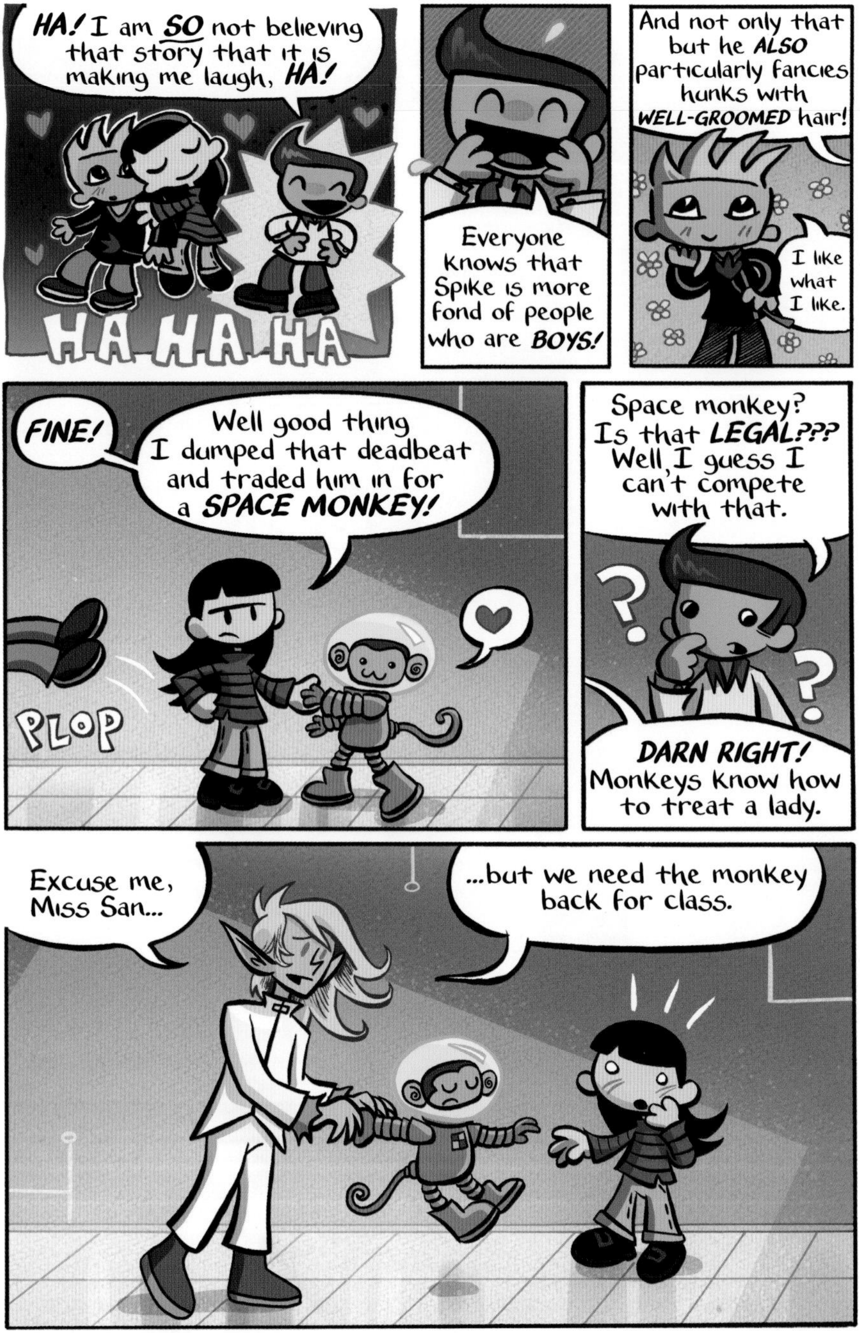
HA! I am SO not believing that story that it is making me laugh, HA!
HA HA HA HA
Everyone knows that Spike is more fond of people who are BOYS!
And not only that but he ALSO particularly fancies hunks with WELL-GROOMED hair!
I like what I like.
FINE!
Well good thing I dumped that deadbeat and traded him in for a SPACE MONKEY!
PLOP
Space monkey? Is that LEGAL??? Well, I guess I can't compete with that.
DARN RIGHT! Monkeys know how to treat a lady.
Excuse me, Miss San...
...but we need the monkey back for class.

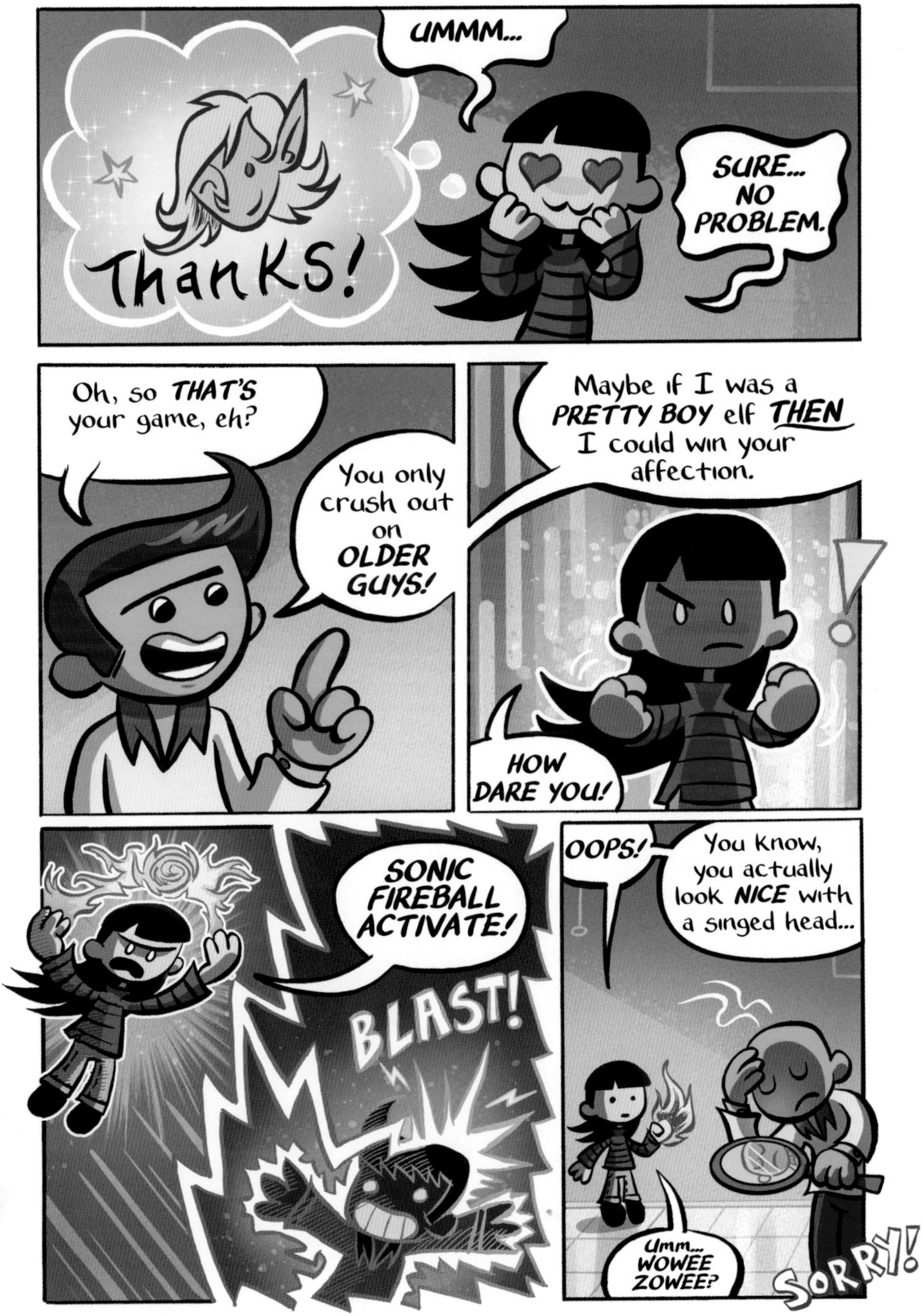

Thanks!
UMMM...
SURE... NO PROBLEM.
Oh, so THAT'S your game, eh?
You only crush out on OLDER GUYS!
Maybe if I was a PRETTY BOY elf THEN I could win your affection.
HOW DARE YOU!
SONIC FIREBALL ACTIVATE!
BLAST!
OOPS!
You know, you actually look NICE with a singed head...
Umm... WOWEE ZOWEE?
SORRY!

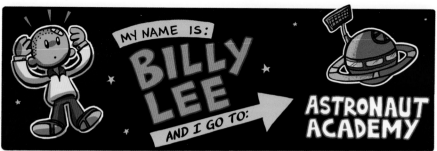

MY NAME IS: **BILLY LEE** AND I GO TO: **ASTRONAUT ACADEMY**

Last week, if an interviewer asked me:

What do you think is your **STRONGEST QUALITY?**

DREAM NEWS

I'd have to say the hair.

Which would have been redundant since my hair always spoke for **ITSELF.**

But due to the sensitive nature of **CURRENT EVENTS...** I'd probably now opt to focus on:

My ability to love.

IMAGINARY PRESS CONFERENCE

And if in a **SPECULATIVE EXPOSÉ** there was a question about what **USED** to be my favorite subject of school, I would have **ORIGINALLY** said:

HUMANITIES
WITH PROFESSOR L

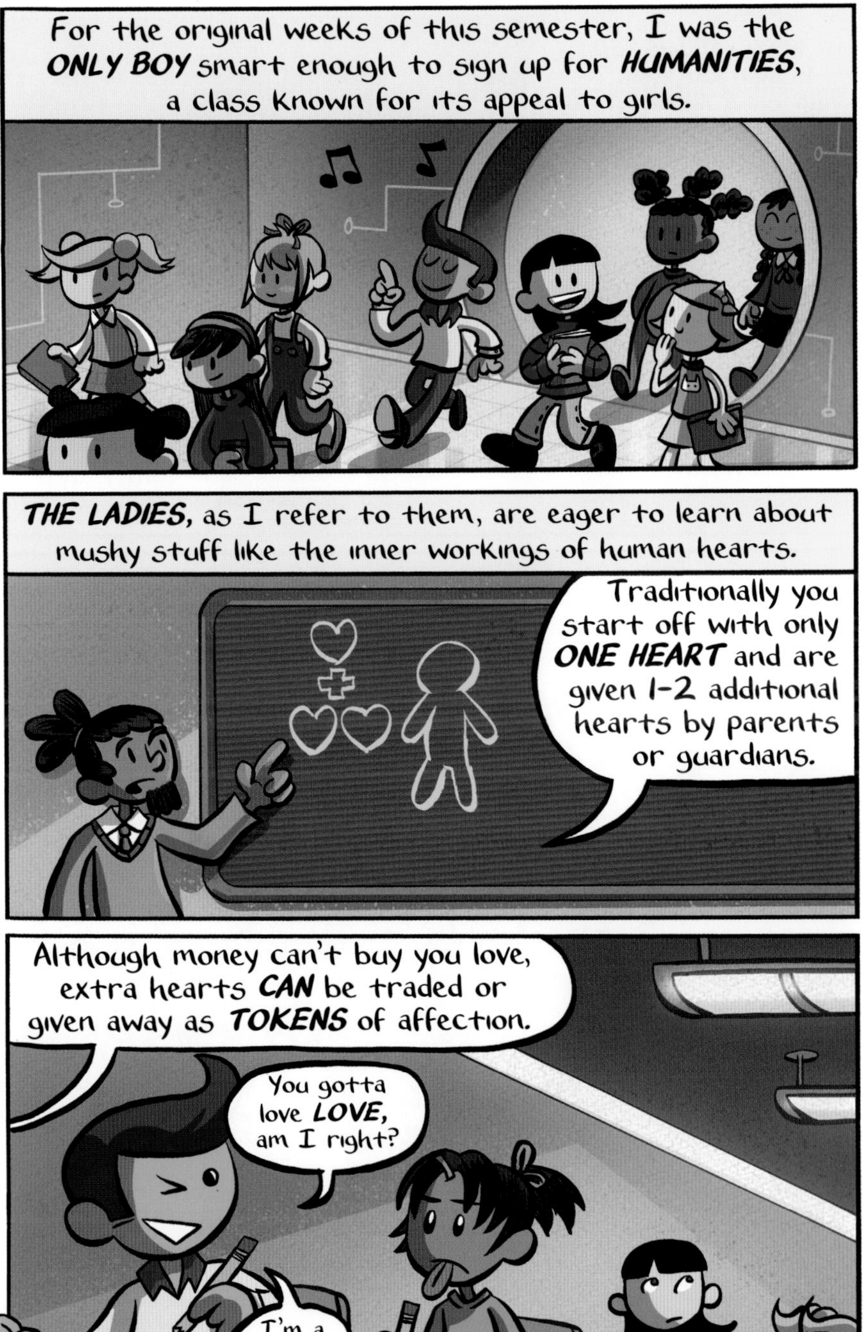
For the original weeks of this semester, I was the ONLY BOY smart enough to sign up for HUMANITIES, a class known for its appeal to girls.
THE LADIES, as I refer to them, are eager to learn about mushy stuff like the inner workings of human hearts.
Traditionally you start off with only ONE HEART and are given 1-2 additional hearts by parents or guardians.
Although money can't buy you love, extra hearts CAN be traded or given away as TOKENS of affection.
You gotta love LOVE, am I right?
I'm a FAN.

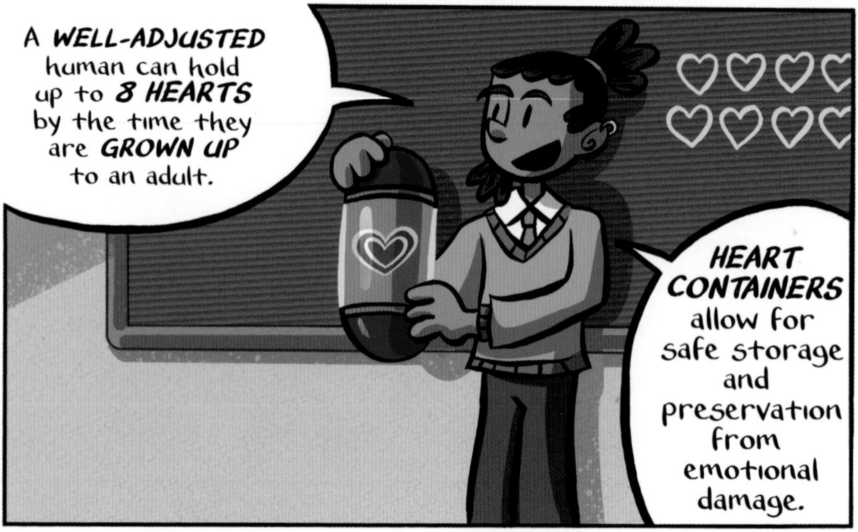
A WELL-ADJUSTED human can hold up to 8 HEARTS by the time they are GROWN UP to an adult.
HEART CONTAINERS allow for safe storage and preservation from emotional damage.

The GOLDEN AGE of this class was becoming lab partners with the two most ANTAGONISTIC girls in school: MIYUMI SAN and MARIBELLE MELLONBELLY!

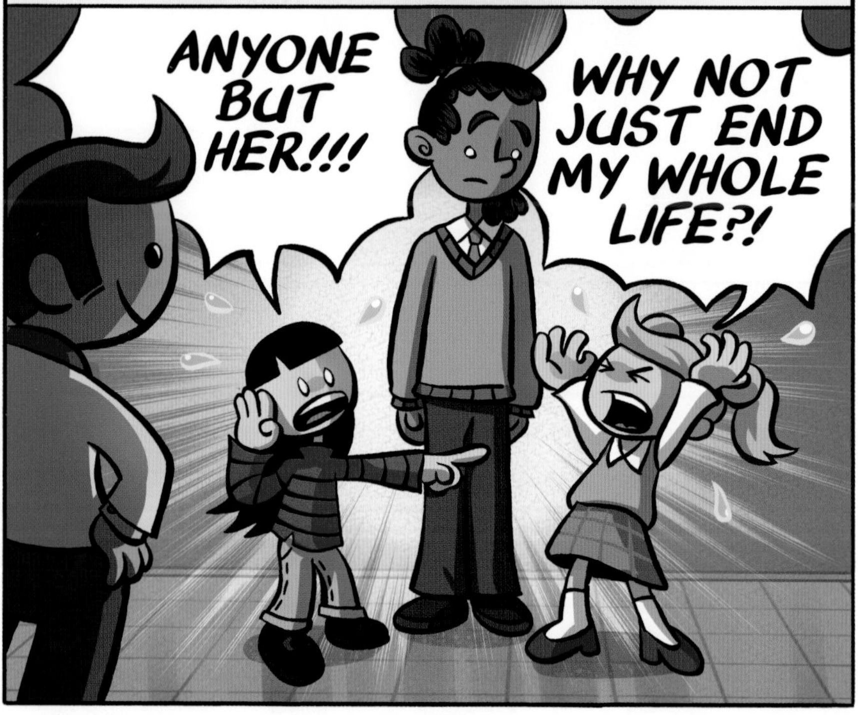
ANYONE BUT HER!!!
WHY NOT JUST END MY WHOLE LIFE?!

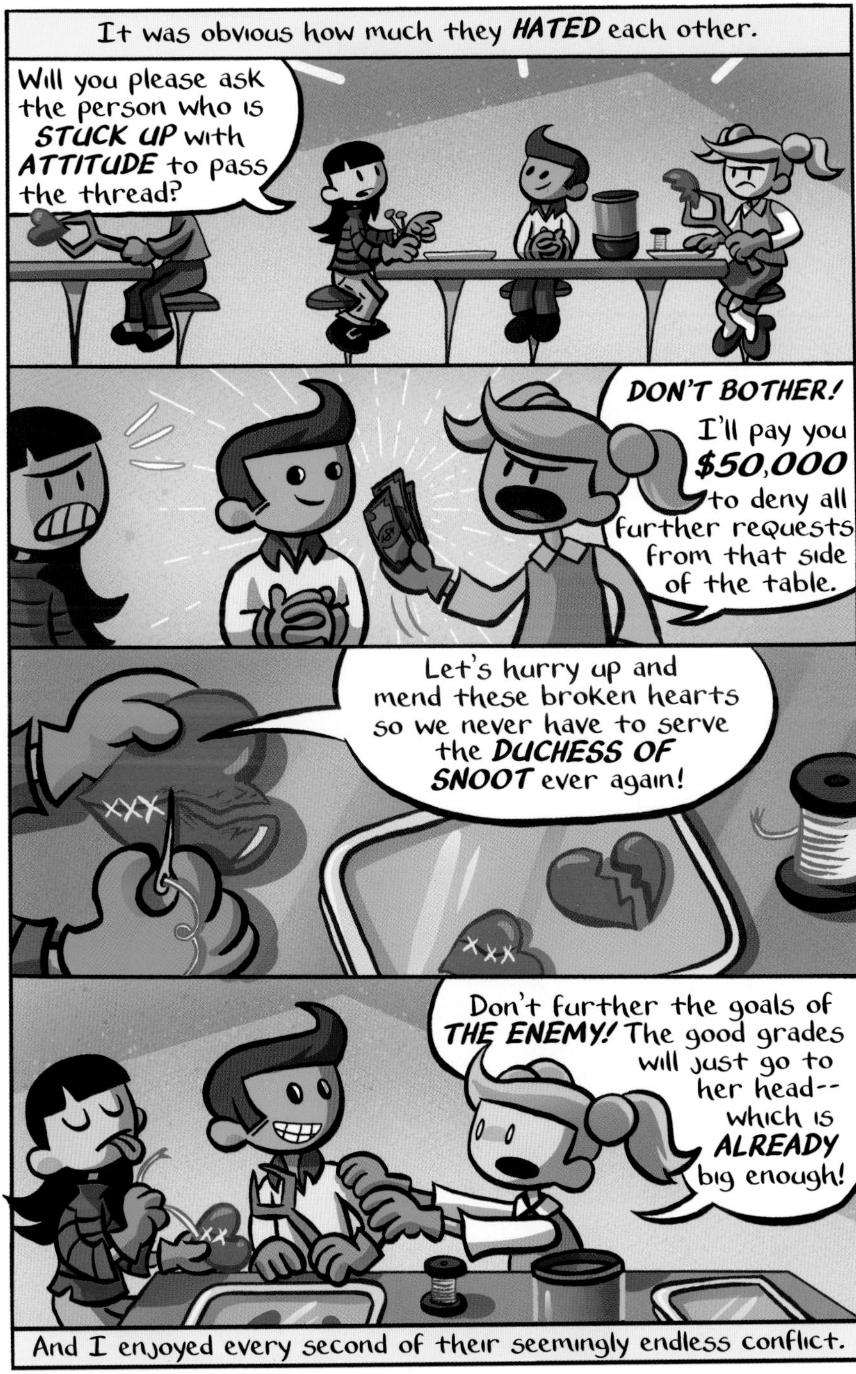

It was obvious how much they HATED each other.
Will you please ask the person who is STUCK UP with ATTITUDE to pass the thread?
DON'T BOTHER! I'll pay you $50,000 to deny all further requests from that side of the table.
Let's hurry up and mend these broken hearts so we never have to serve the DUCHESS OF SNOOT ever again!
Don't further the goals of THE ENEMY! The good grades will just go to her head-- which is ALREADY big enough!
And I enjoyed every second of their seemingly endless conflict.

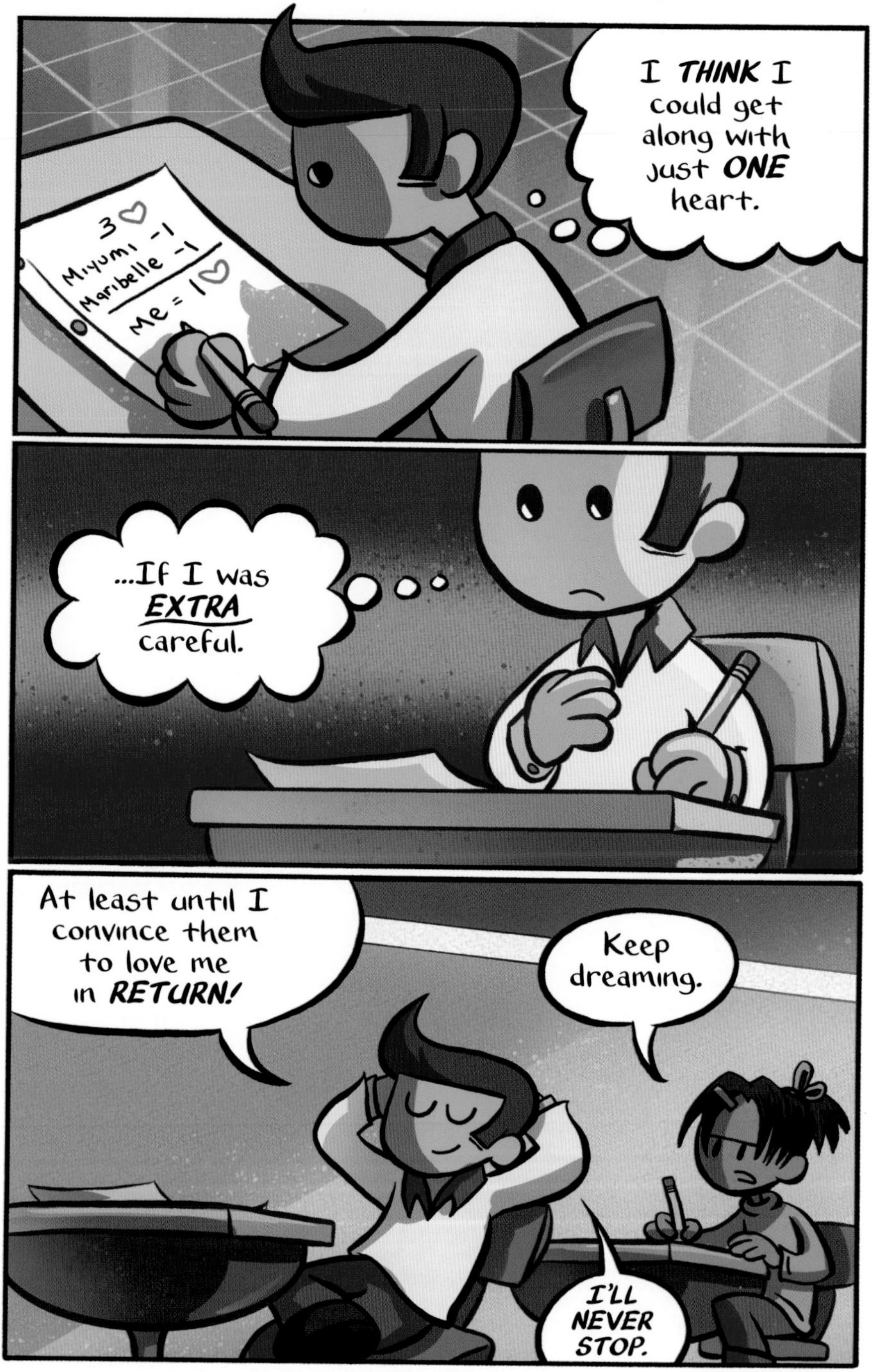
I THINK I could get along with just ONE heart.
3 ♡
Miyumi -1
Maribelle -1
Me = 1 ♡
...If I was EXTRA careful.
At least until I convince them to love me in RETURN!
Keep dreaming.
I'LL NEVER STOP.

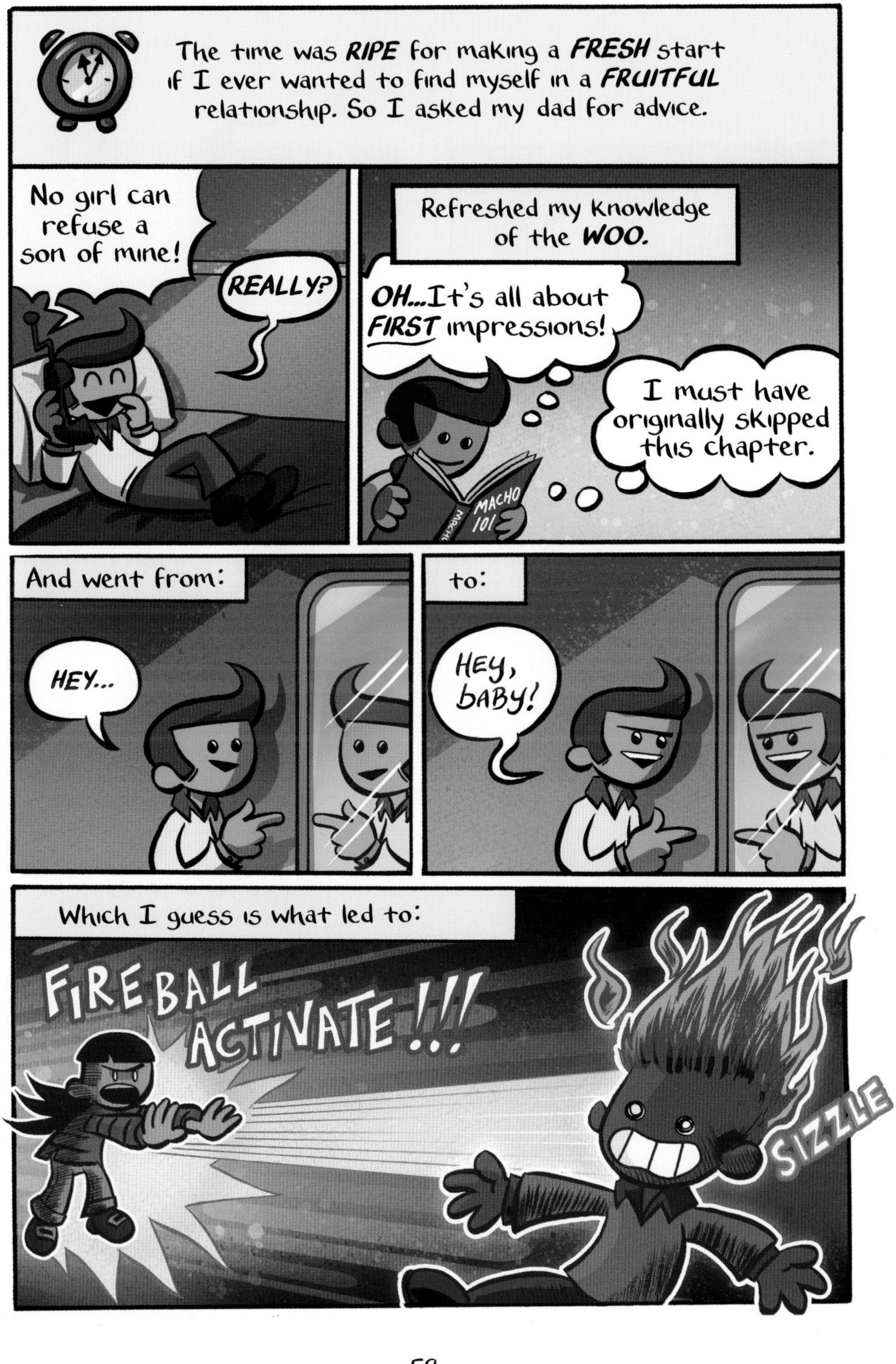
The time was *RIPE* for making a *FRESH* start if I ever wanted to find myself in a *FRUITFUL* relationship. So I asked my dad for advice.
No girl can refuse a son of mine!
REALLY?
Refreshed my knowledge of the *WOO.*
OH...It's all about FIRST impressions!
I must have originally skipped this chapter.
MACHO 101
And went from:
HEY...
to:
HEY, BABY!
Which I guess is what led to:
FIREBALL ACTIVATE!!!
SIZZLE

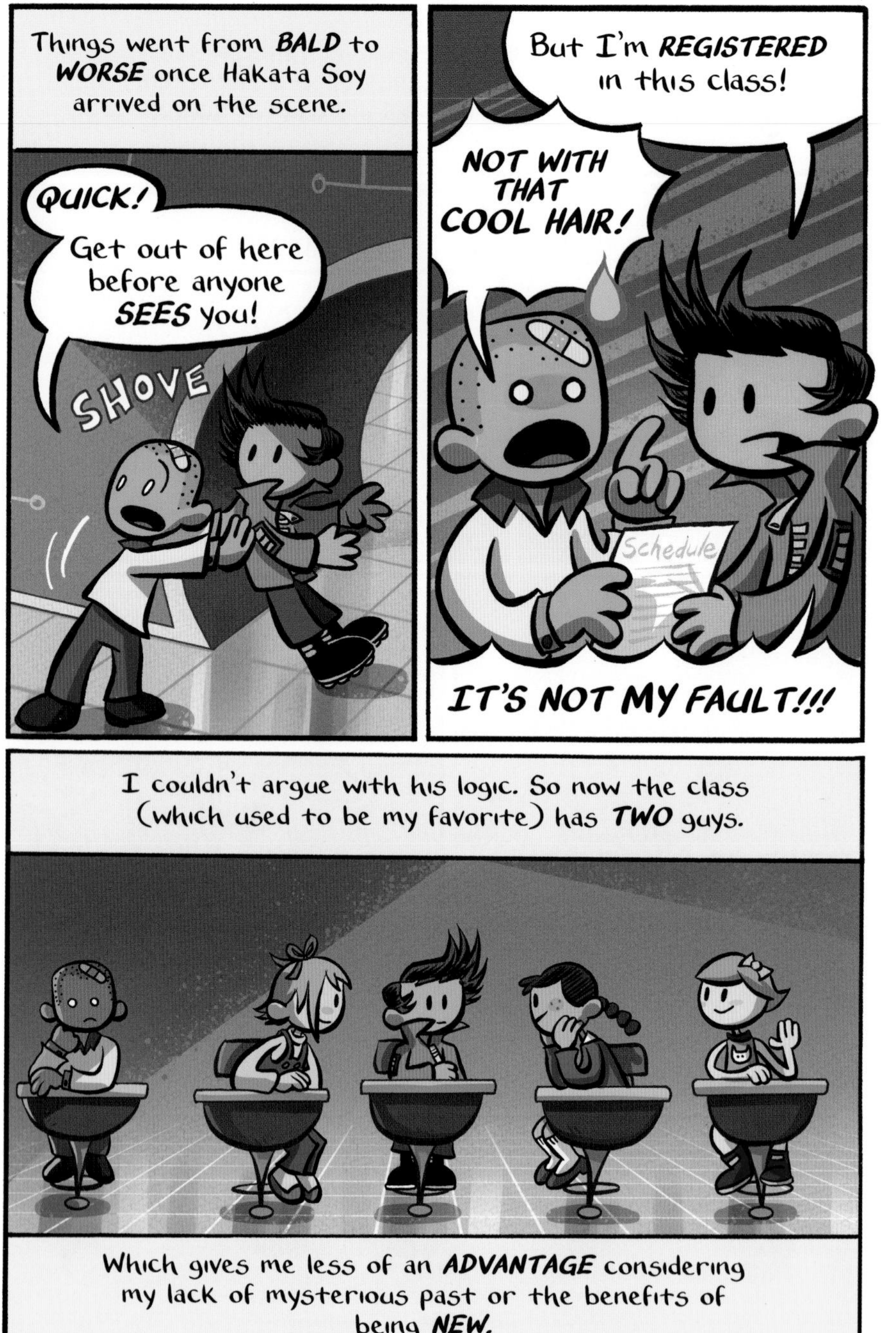
Things went from BALD to WORSE once Hakata Soy arrived on the scene.
QUICK! Get out of here before anyone SEES you!
SHOVE
But I'm REGISTERED in this class!
NOT WITH THAT COOL HAIR!
Schedule
IT'S NOT MY FAULT!!!
I couldn't argue with his logic. So now the class (which used to be my favorite) has TWO guys.
Which gives me less of an ADVANTAGE considering my lack of mysterious past or the benefits of being NEW.

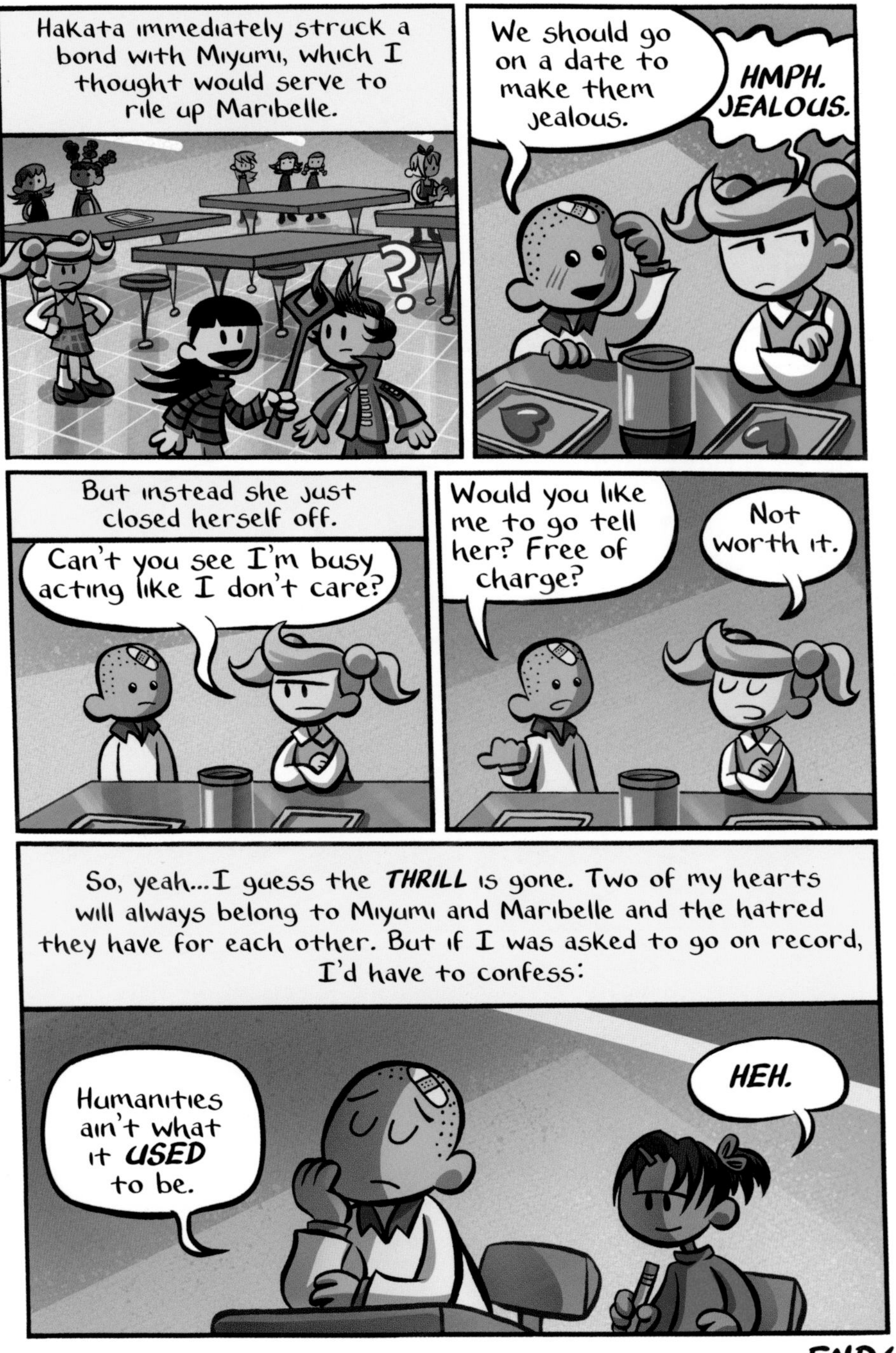
Hakata immediately struck a bond with Miyumi, which I thought would serve to rile up Maribelle.
?
We should go on a date to make them jealous.
HMPH. JEALOUS.
But instead she just closed herself off.
Can't you see I'm busy acting like I don't care?
Would you like me to go tell her? Free of charge?
Not worth it.
So, yeah...I guess the THRILL is gone. Two of my hearts will always belong to Miyumi and Maribelle and the hatred they have for each other. But if I was asked to go on record, I'd have to confess:
Humanities ain't what it USED to be.
HEH.
END!

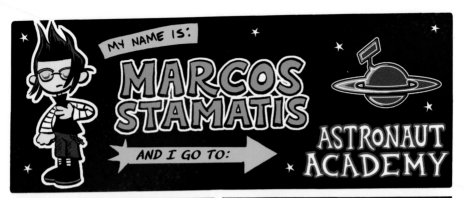

MY NAME IS:

MARCOS STAMATIS

AND I GO TO: ➡

ASTRONAUT ACADEMY

For the past few weeks I've been sitting next to this guy Hakata Soy in math class.

He's also in the same *TACTICAL RANDOMNESS WORKSHOP* as me on weekends.

You, sir? Would you like to buy a banana for eating?

If only I were not a sign post.

STOP

I may not know the guy's *BACKSTORY*, but I can tell you one thing for certain: someone special must have broken at least one of his hearts.

Oh.

I guess I'll stop bothering you, then.

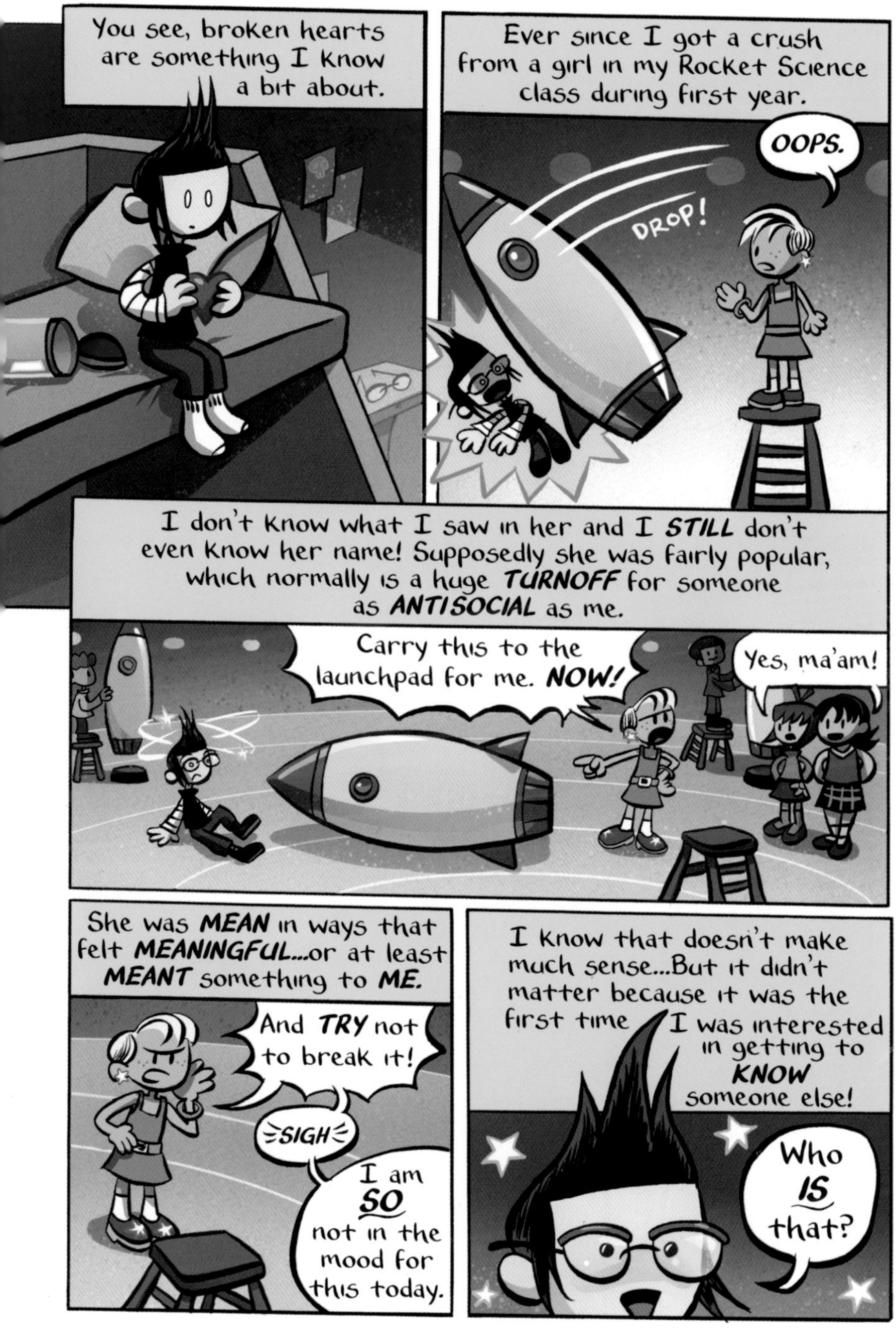
You see, broken hearts are something I know a bit about.
Ever since I got a crush from a girl in my Rocket Science class during first year.
OOPS.
DROP!
I don't know what I saw in her and I STILL don't even know her name! Supposedly she was fairly popular, which normally is a huge TURNOFF for someone as ANTISOCIAL as me.
Carry this to the launchpad for me. NOW!
Yes, ma'am!
She was MEAN in ways that felt MEANINGFUL...or at least MEANT something to ME.
And TRY not to break it!
SIGH
I am SO not in the mood for this today.
I know that doesn't make much sense...But it didn't matter because it was the first time I was interested in getting to KNOW someone else!
Who IS that?

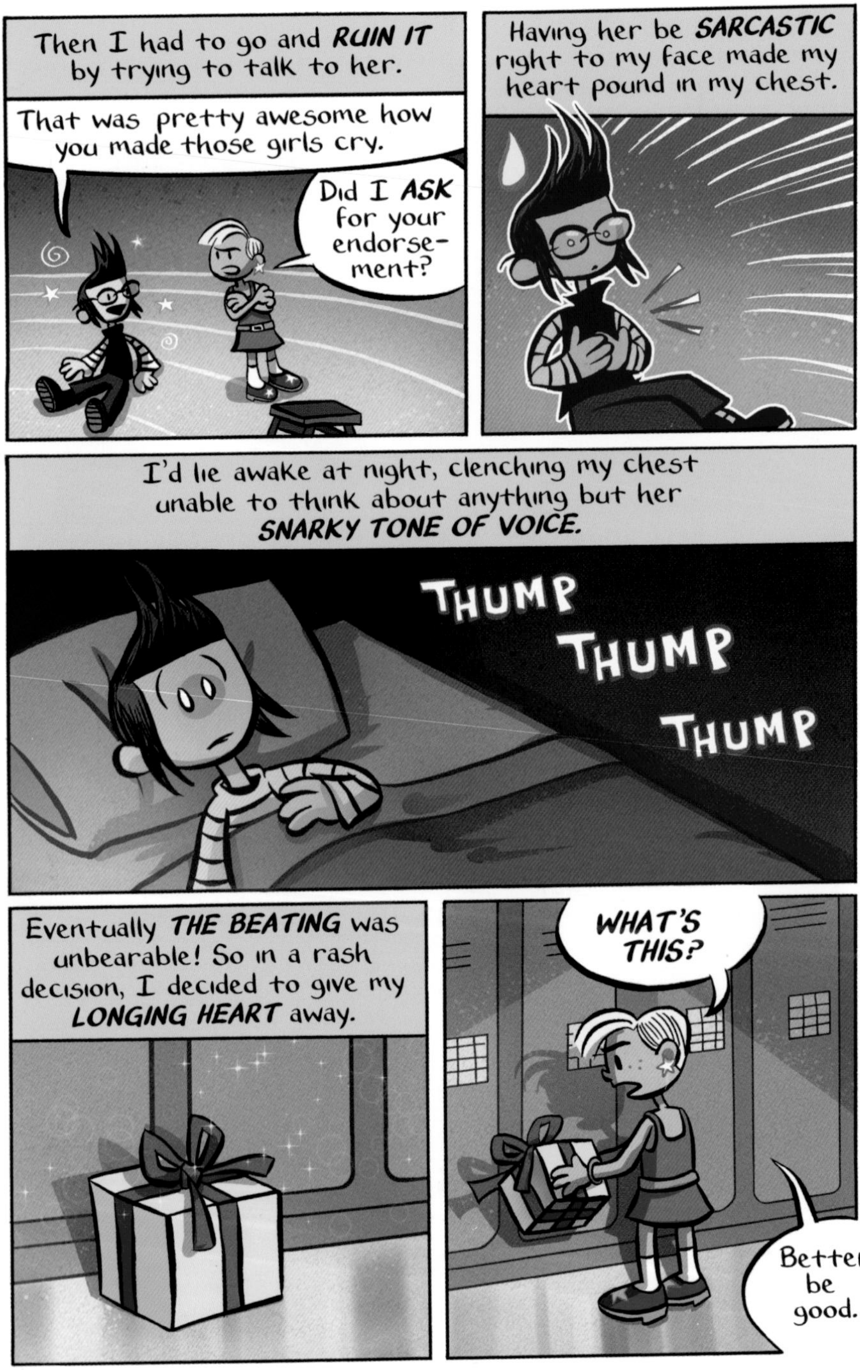
Then I had to go and RUIN IT by trying to talk to her.
That was pretty awesome how you made those girls cry.
Did I ASK for your endorsement?
Having her be SARCASTIC right to my face made my heart pound in my chest.
I'd lie awake at night, clenching my chest unable to think about anything but her SNARKY TONE OF VOICE.
THUMP
THUMP
THUMP
Eventually THE BEATING was unbearable! So in a rash decision, I decided to give my LONGING HEART away.
WHAT'S THIS?
Better be good.

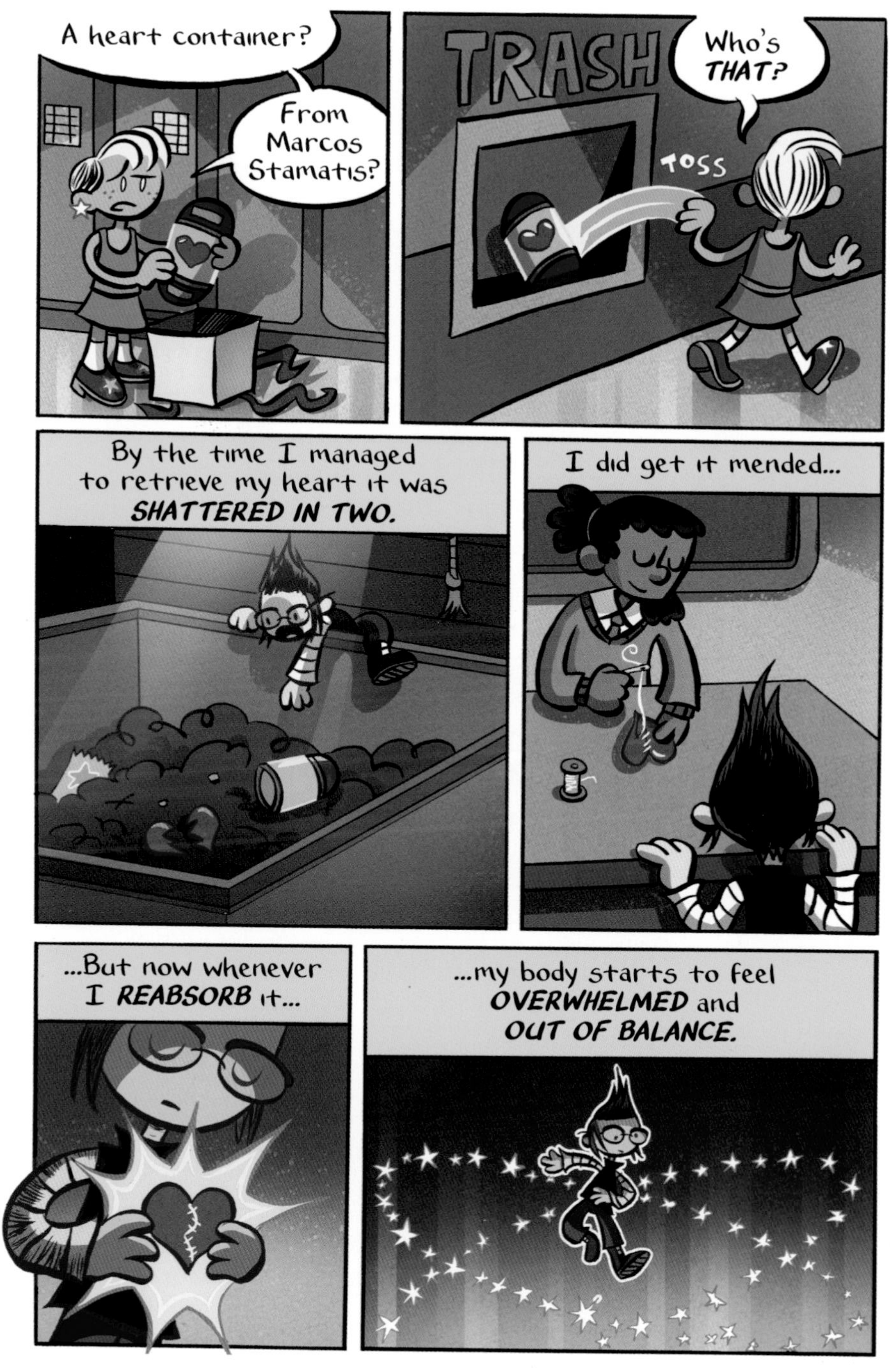
A heart container?
From Marcos Stamatis?
TRASH
Who's *THAT?*
TOSS
By the time I managed to retrieve my heart it was ***SHATTERED IN TWO.***
I did get it mended...
...But now whenever I ***REABSORB*** it...
...my body starts to feel ***OVERWHELMED*** and ***OUT OF BALANCE.***

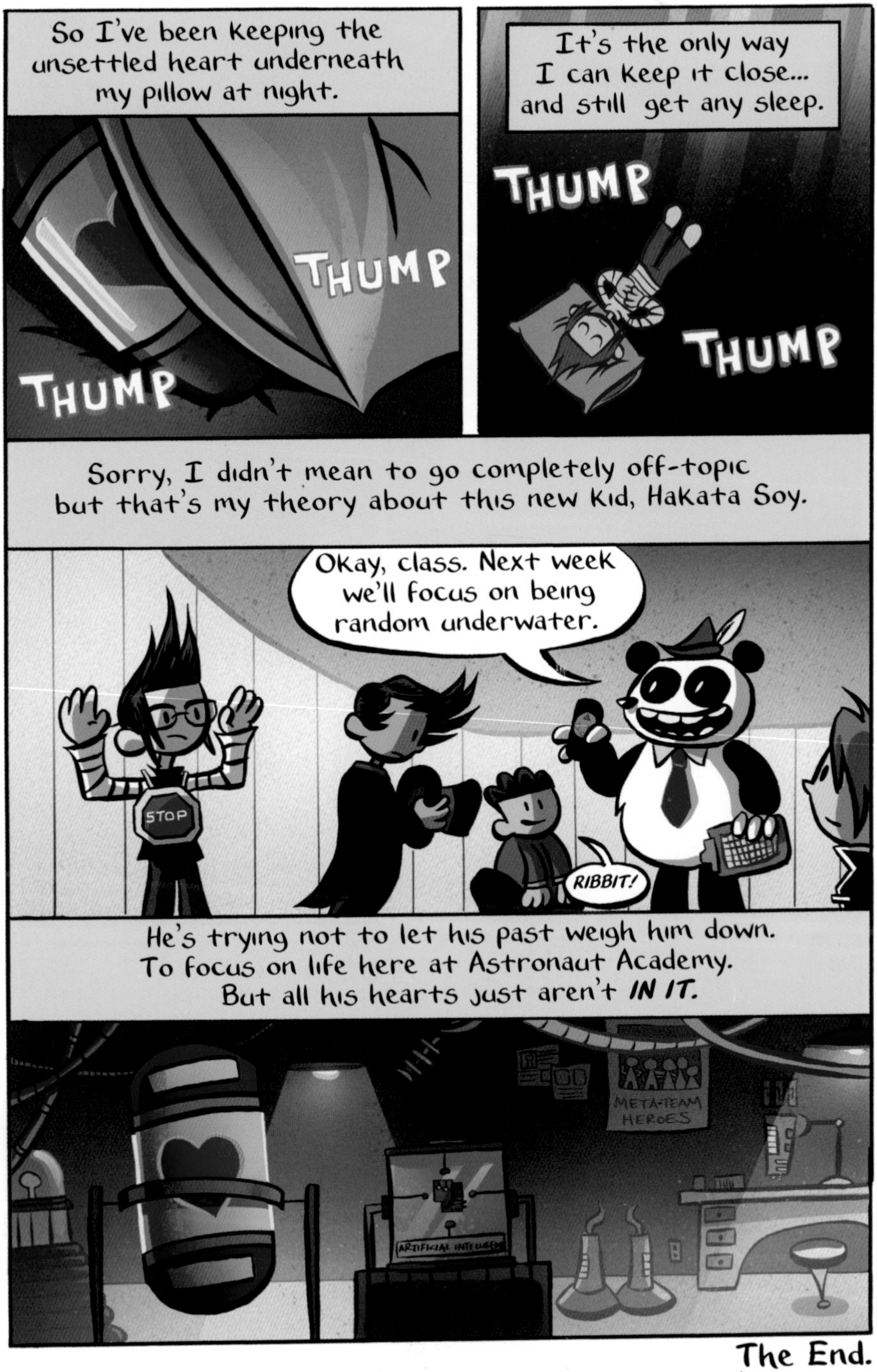
So I've been keeping the unsettled heart underneath my pillow at night.
THUMP
THUMP
It's the only way I can keep it close... and still get any sleep.
THUMP
THUMP
Sorry, I didn't mean to go completely off-topic but that's my theory about this new kid, Hakata Soy.
Okay, class. Next week we'll focus on being random underwater.
STOP
RIBBIT!
He's trying not to let his past weigh him down. To focus on life here at Astronaut Academy. But all his hearts just aren't ***IN IT.***
META-TEAM HEROES
ARTIFICIAL INTELLIGENCE

The End.

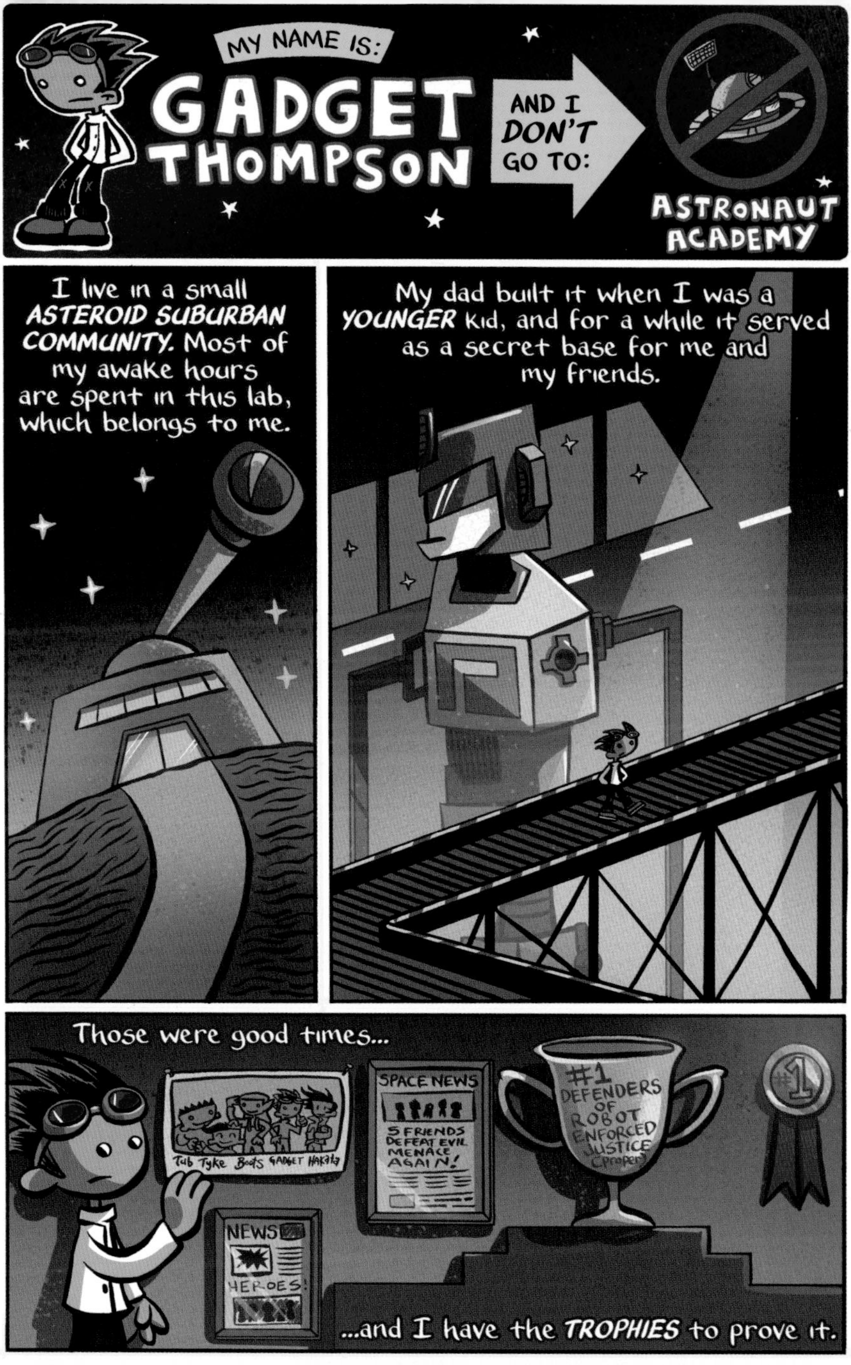
MY NAME IS:
GADGET THOMPSON
AND I DON'T GO TO:
ASTRONAUT ACADEMY
I live in a small ASTEROID SUBURBAN COMMUNITY. Most of my awake hours are spent in this lab, which belongs to me.
My dad built it when I was a YOUNGER kid, and for a while it served as a secret base for me and my friends.
Those were good times...
Tub Tyke Boots GADGET HAKata
SPACE NEWS
5 FRIENDS DEFEAT EVIL MENACE AGAIN!
#1 DEFENDERS OF ROBOT ENFORCED JUSTICE (proper)
#1
NEWS
HEROES!
...and I have the TROPHIES to prove it.

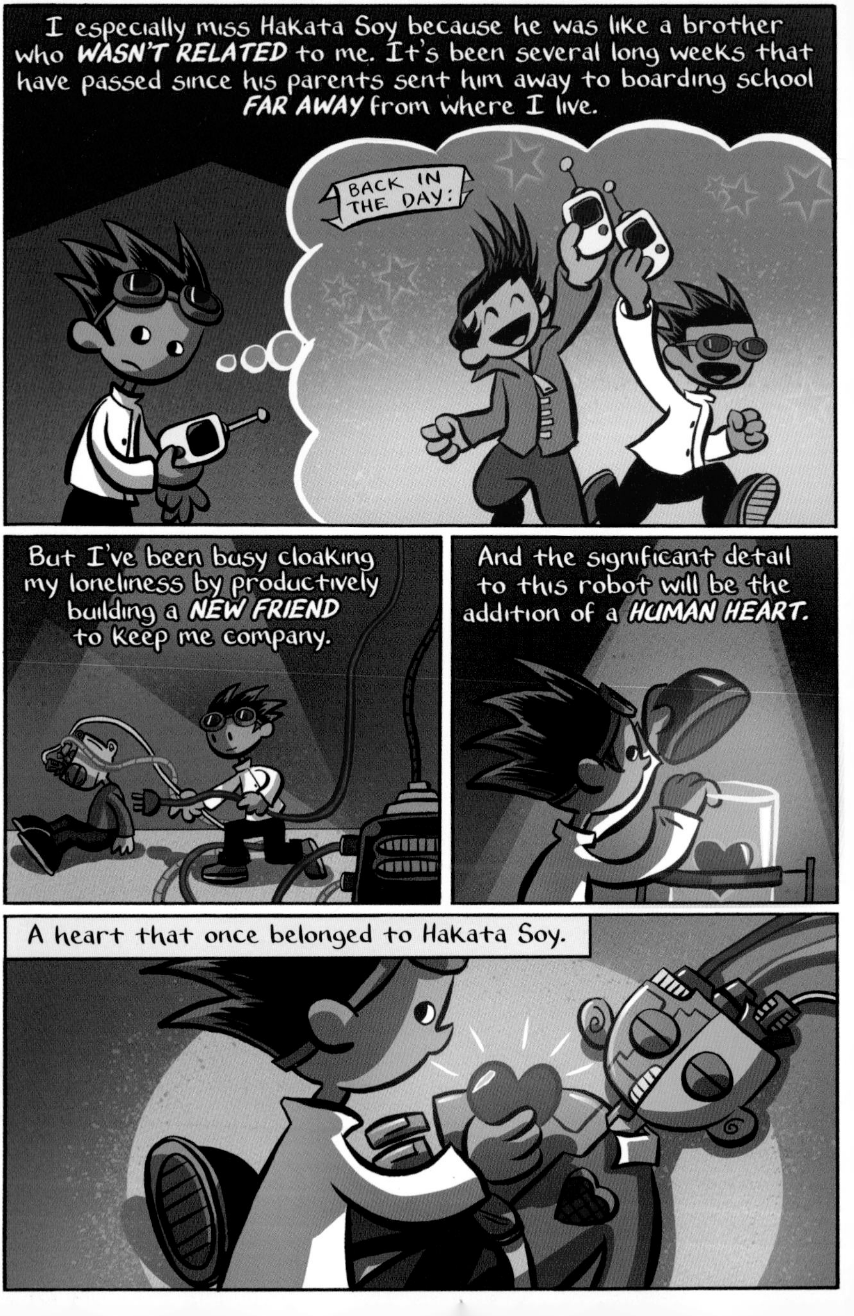
I especially miss Hakata Soy because he was like a brother who WASN'T RELATED to me. It's been several long weeks that have passed since his parents sent him away to boarding school FAR AWAY from where I live.
BACK IN THE DAY:
But I've been busy cloaking my loneliness by productively building a NEW FRIEND to keep me company.
And the significant detail to this robot will be the addition of a HUMAN HEART.
A heart that once belonged to Hakata Soy.

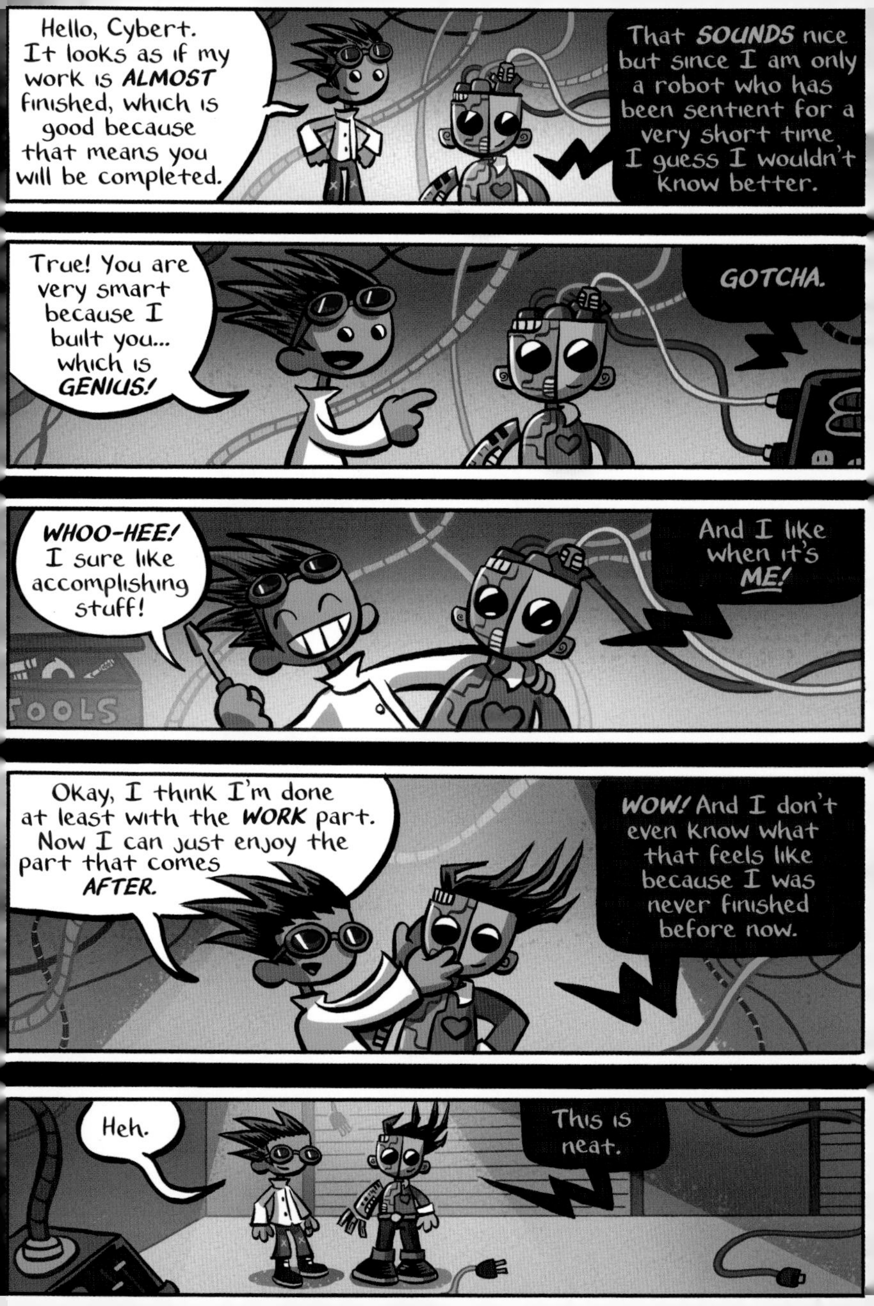
Hello, Cybert. It looks as if my work is ALMOST finished, which is good because that means you will be completed.
That SOUNDS nice but since I am only a robot who has been sentient for a very short time I guess I wouldn't know better.
True! You are very smart because I built you... which is GENIUS!
GOTCHA.
WHOO-HEE! I sure like accomplishing stuff!
And I like when it's ME!
TOOLS
Okay, I think I'm done at least with the WORK part. Now I can just enjoy the part that comes AFTER.
WOW! And I don't even know what that feels like because I was never finished before now.
Heh.
This is neat.

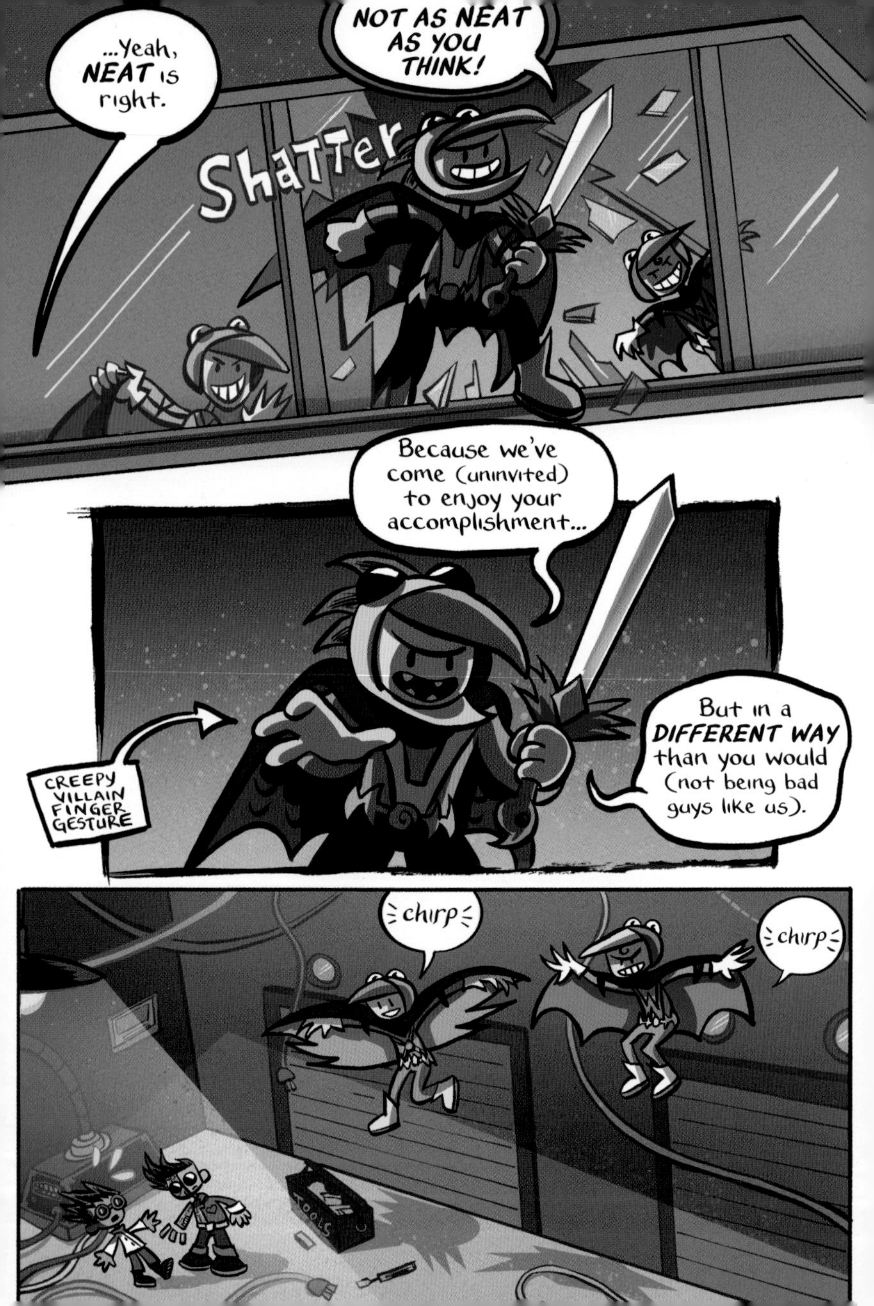
...Yeah, NEAT is right.
NOT AS NEAT AS YOU THINK!
SHATTER
Because we've come (uninvited) to enjoy your accomplishment...
CREEPY VILLAIN FINGER GESTURE
But in a DIFFERENT WAY than you would (not being bad guys like us).
chirp
chirp
TOOLS

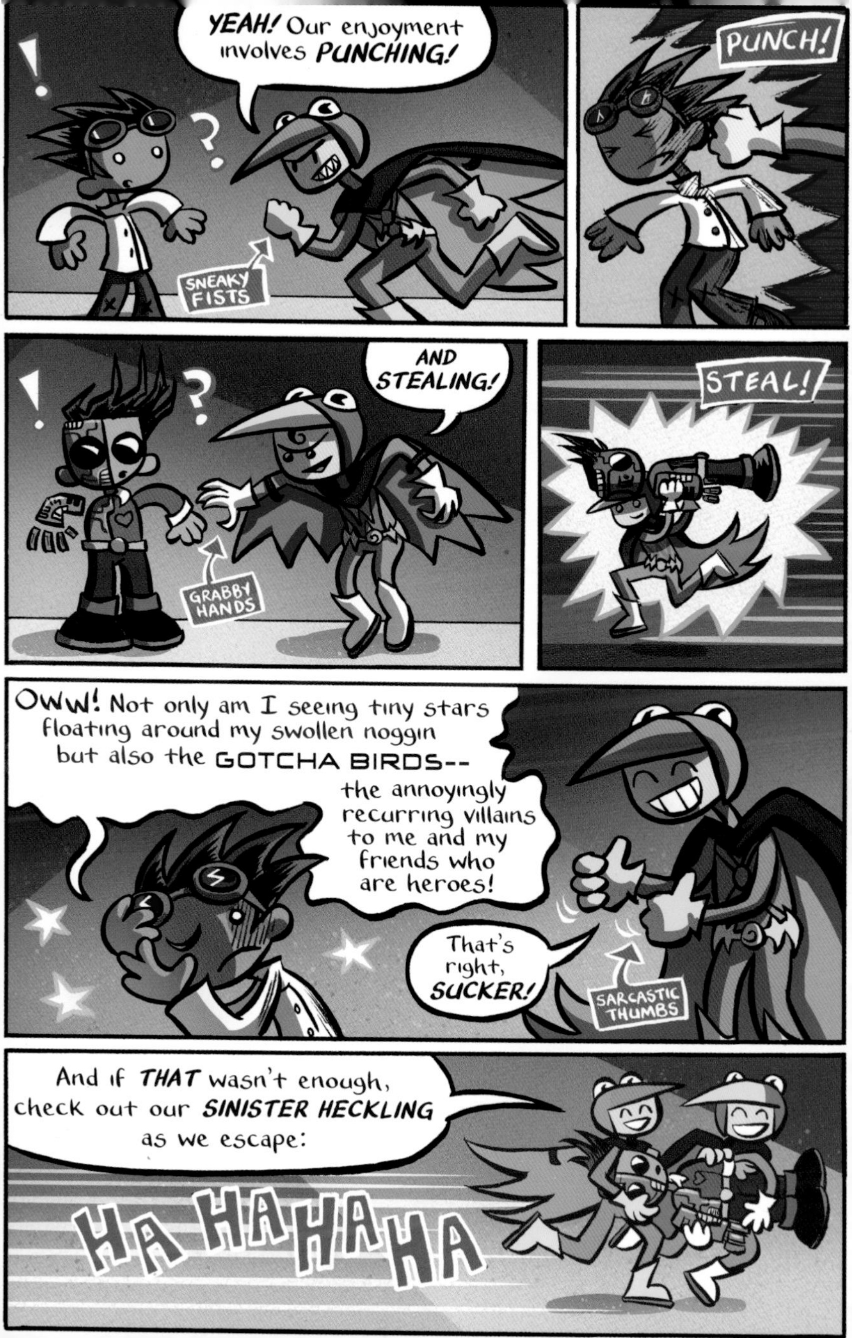
YEAH! Our enjoyment involves PUNCHING!
SNEAKY FISTS
PUNCH!
AND STEALING!
GRABBY HANDS
STEAL!
OWW! Not only am I seeing tiny stars floating around my swollen noggin but also the GOTCHA BIRDS--
the annoyingly recurring villains to me and my friends who are heroes!
That's right, SUCKER!
SARCASTIC THUMBS
And if THAT wasn't enough, check out our SINISTER HECKLING as we escape:
HA HA HA HA HA HA

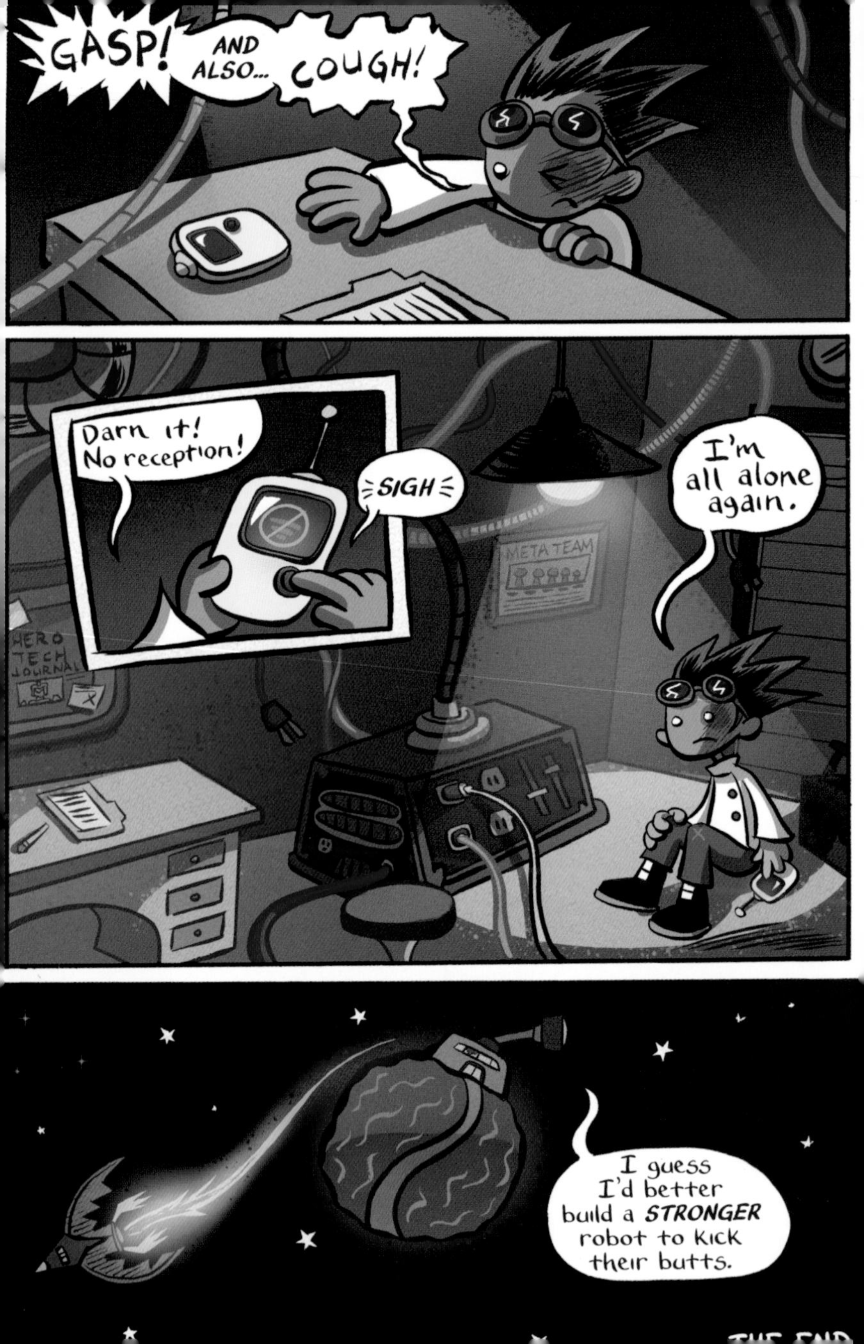
GASP!
AND ALSO...
COUGH!
Darn it! No reception!
SIGH
META TEAM
HERO TECH JOURNAL
I'm all alone again.
I guess I'd better build a **STRONGER** robot to kick their butts.

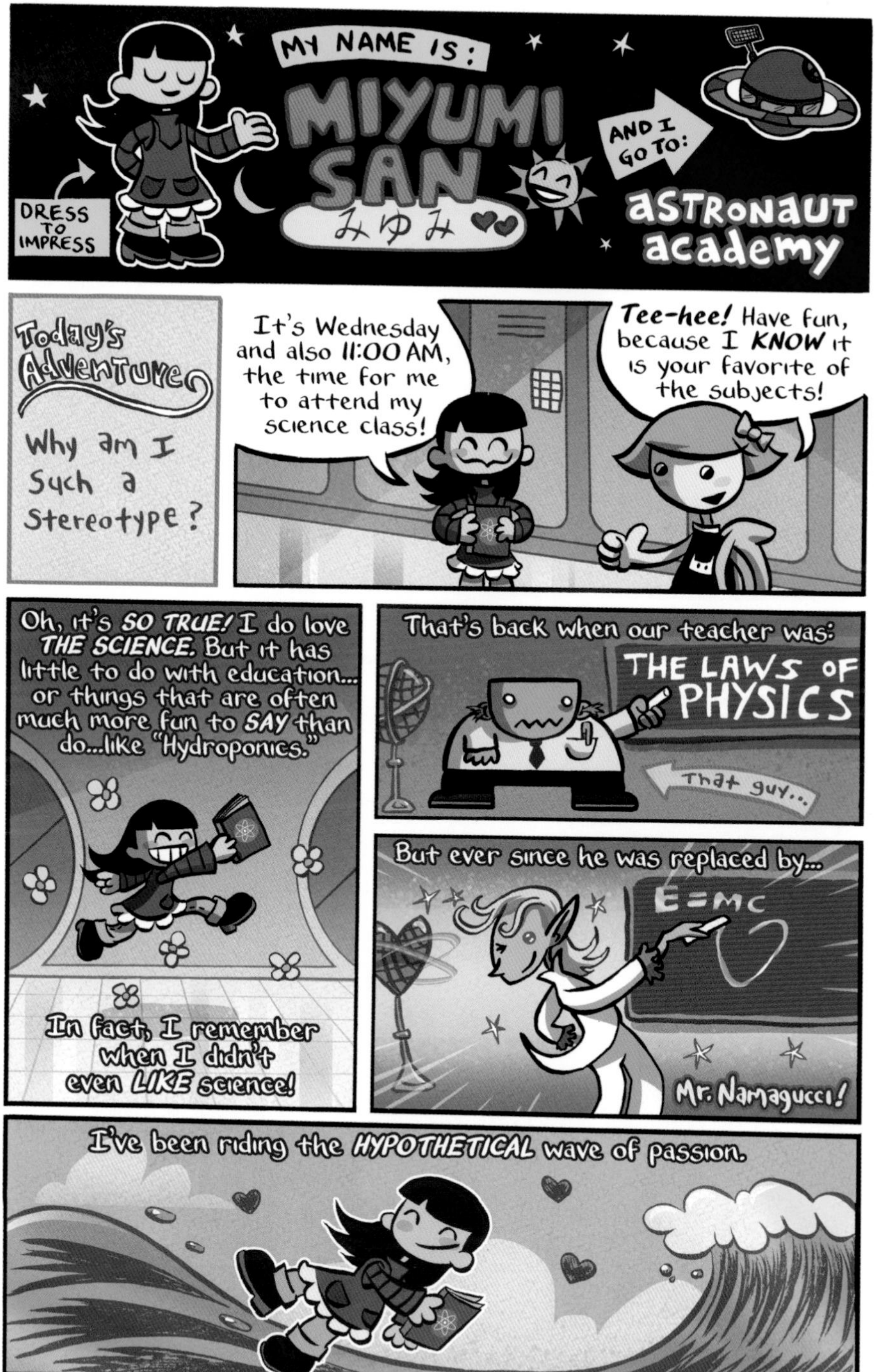
MY NAME IS:
MIYUMI SAN
みゆみ
DRESS TO IMPRESS
AND I GO TO:
astronaut academy
Today's Adventure
Why am I such a stereotype?
It's Wednesday and also 11:00 AM, the time for me to attend my science class!
Tee-hee! Have fun, because I KNOW it is your favorite of the subjects!
Oh, it's SO TRUE! I do love THE SCIENCE. But it has little to do with education... or things that are often much more fun to SAY than do...like "Hydroponics."
In fact, I remember when I didn't even LIKE science!
That's back when our teacher was:
THE LAWS OF PHYSICS
That guy...
But ever since he was replaced by...
E=MC
Mr. Namagucci!
I've been riding the HYPOTHETICAL wave of passion.

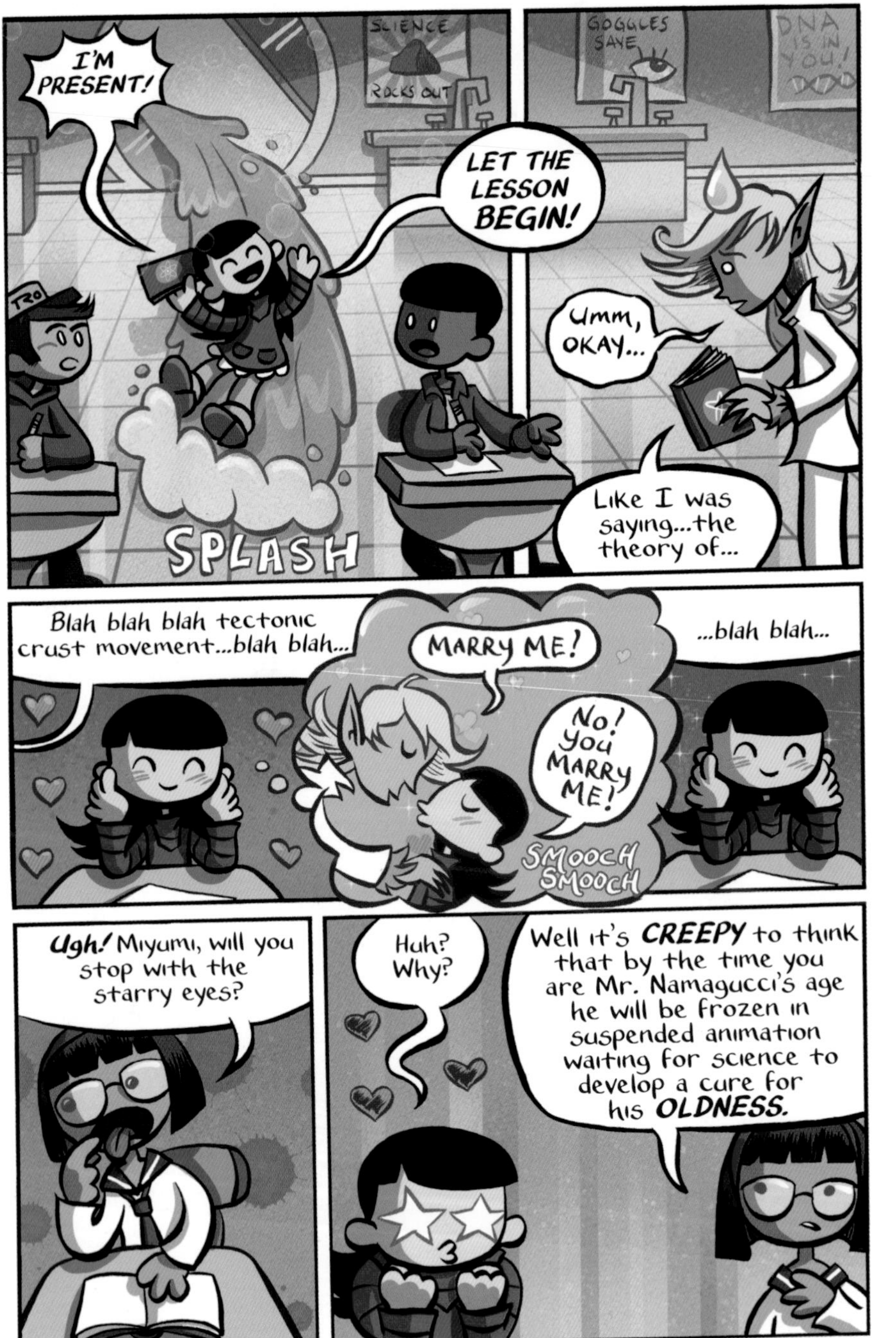
SCIENCE ROCKS OUT
GOGGLES SAVE
DNA IS IN YOU!
I'M PRESENT!
LET THE LESSON BEGIN!
SPLASH
Umm, OKAY...
Like I was saying...the theory of...
Blah blah blah tectonic crust movement...blah blah...
MARRY ME!
No! You MARRY ME!
SMOOCH SMOOCH
...blah blah...
Ugh! Miyumi, will you stop with the starry eyes?
Huh? Why?
Well it's CREEPY to think that by the time you are Mr. Namagucci's age he will be frozen in suspended animation waiting for science to develop a cure for his OLDNESS.

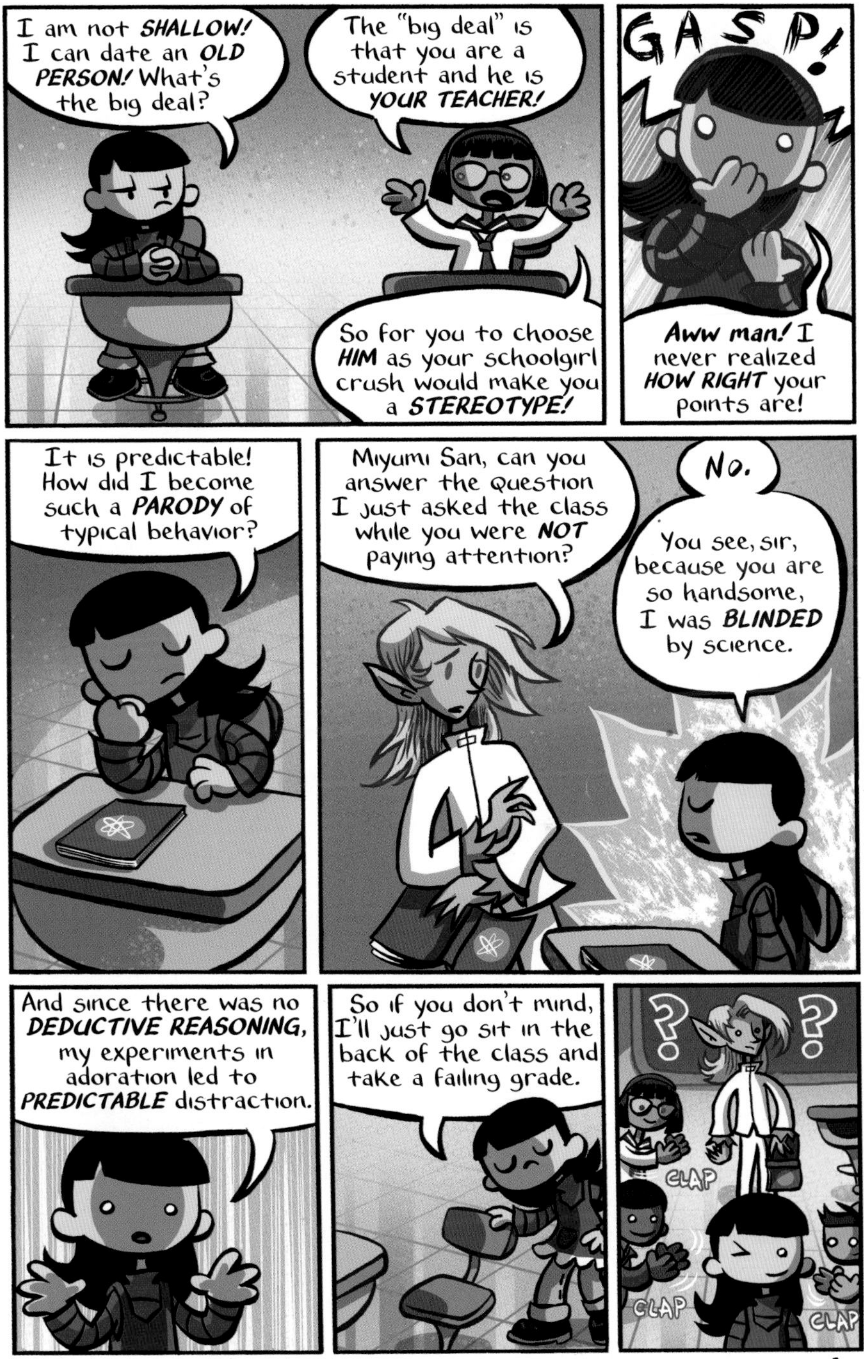

I am not SHALLOW! I can date an OLD PERSON! What's the big deal?
The "big deal" is that you are a student and he is YOUR TEACHER!
So for you to choose HIM as your schoolgirl crush would make you a STEREOTYPE!
GASP!
Aww man! I never realized HOW RIGHT your points are!
It is predictable! How did I become such a PARODY of typical behavior?
Miyumi San, can you answer the question I just asked the class while you were NOT paying attention?
No.
You see, sir, because you are so handsome, I was BLINDED by science.
And since there was no DEDUCTIVE REASONING, my experiments in adoration led to PREDICTABLE distraction.
So if you don't mind, I'll just go sit in the back of the class and take a failing grade.
? ?
CLAP
CLAP
CLAP

♥end♥

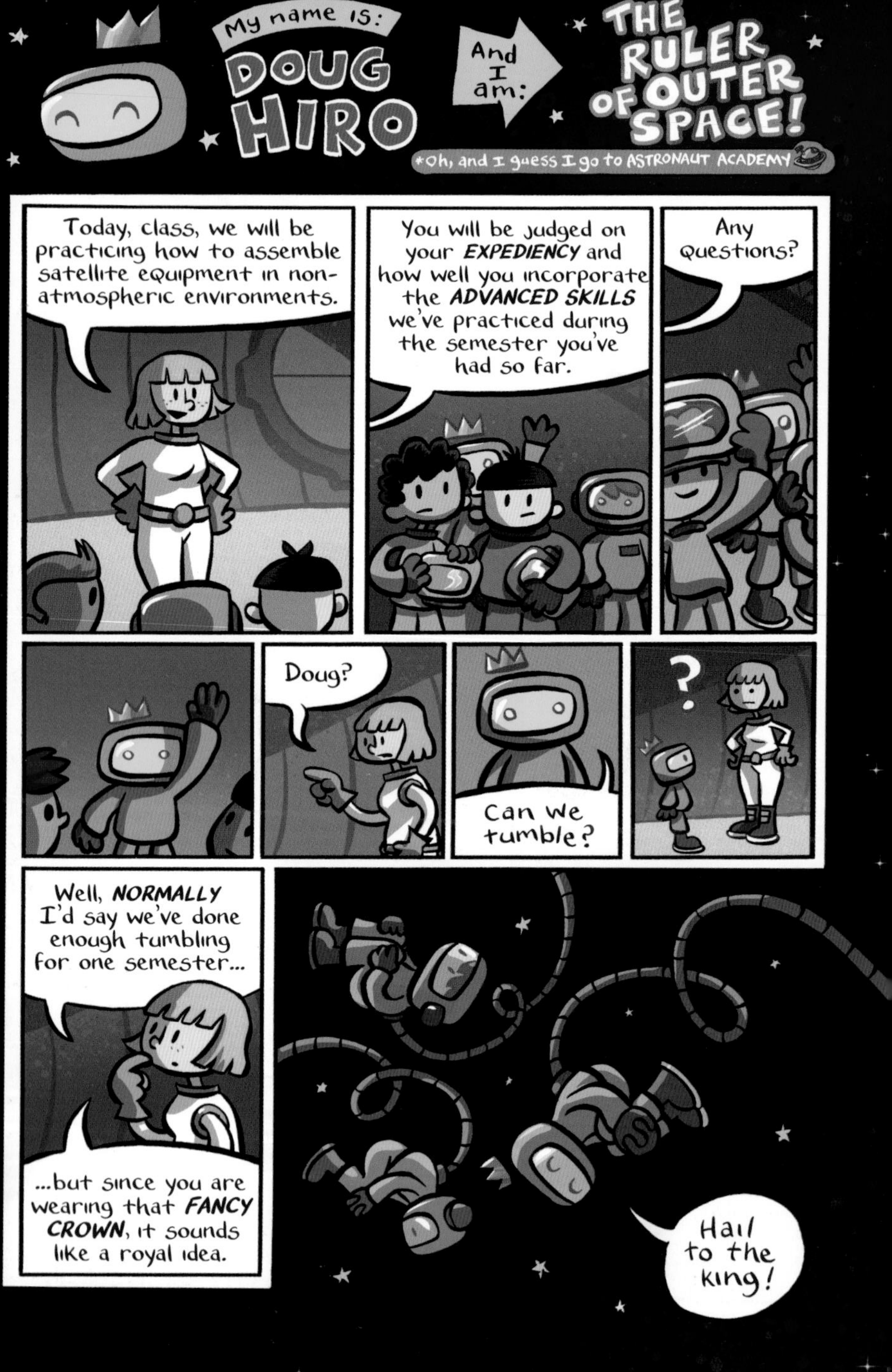
My name is:
DOUG HIRO
And I am:
THE RULER OF OUTER SPACE!
*Oh, and I guess I go to ASTRONAUT ACADEMY
Today, class, we will be practicing how to assemble satellite equipment in non-atmospheric environments.
You will be judged on your EXPEDIENCY and how well you incorporate the ADVANCED SKILLS we've practiced during the semester you've had so far.
Any Questions?
Doug?
Can we tumble?
?
Well, NORMALLY I'd say we've done enough tumbling for one semester...
...but since you are wearing that FANCY CROWN, it sounds like a royal idea.
Hail to the king!

My name is: **TAK OFFSKY** (MVP) at: **ASTRONAUT ACADEMY**

LOOKIT, I'm not an idiot, okay?

I know you're making fun of me.

What makes you think *YOU* are so awesome?

NOTHING, right? So *SAVE IT.*

Besides, I didn't *ASK* to be named "Tak."

MUNCH   MUNCH

It was all my parents' idea, so take it up with *THEM.* And if you're going to all the trouble, tell them I said "hi."

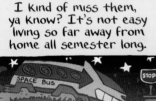

I kind of miss them, ya know? It's not easy living so far away from home all semester long.

SPACE BUS   STOP

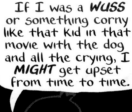

If I was a *WUSS* or something corny like that kid in that movie with the dog and all the crying, I *MIGHT* get upset from time to time.

But Momma says I gotta be *TOUGH* for her.

And being tough comes *EASY* to me.

So stop *JUDGING* me or else I'll *SLUG* you.

Okay, maybe I won't. But that's only because I don't want to ruin my status of being *MOST VALUABLE.* I'd hate to get kicked off the team...

...seeing as how, now, we're considered so *UNBEATABLE.*

CHAMPIONS

FIRE BALL

STAR BURGER

ASTRONAUT ACAD

CURRENT HEROE

MITCH

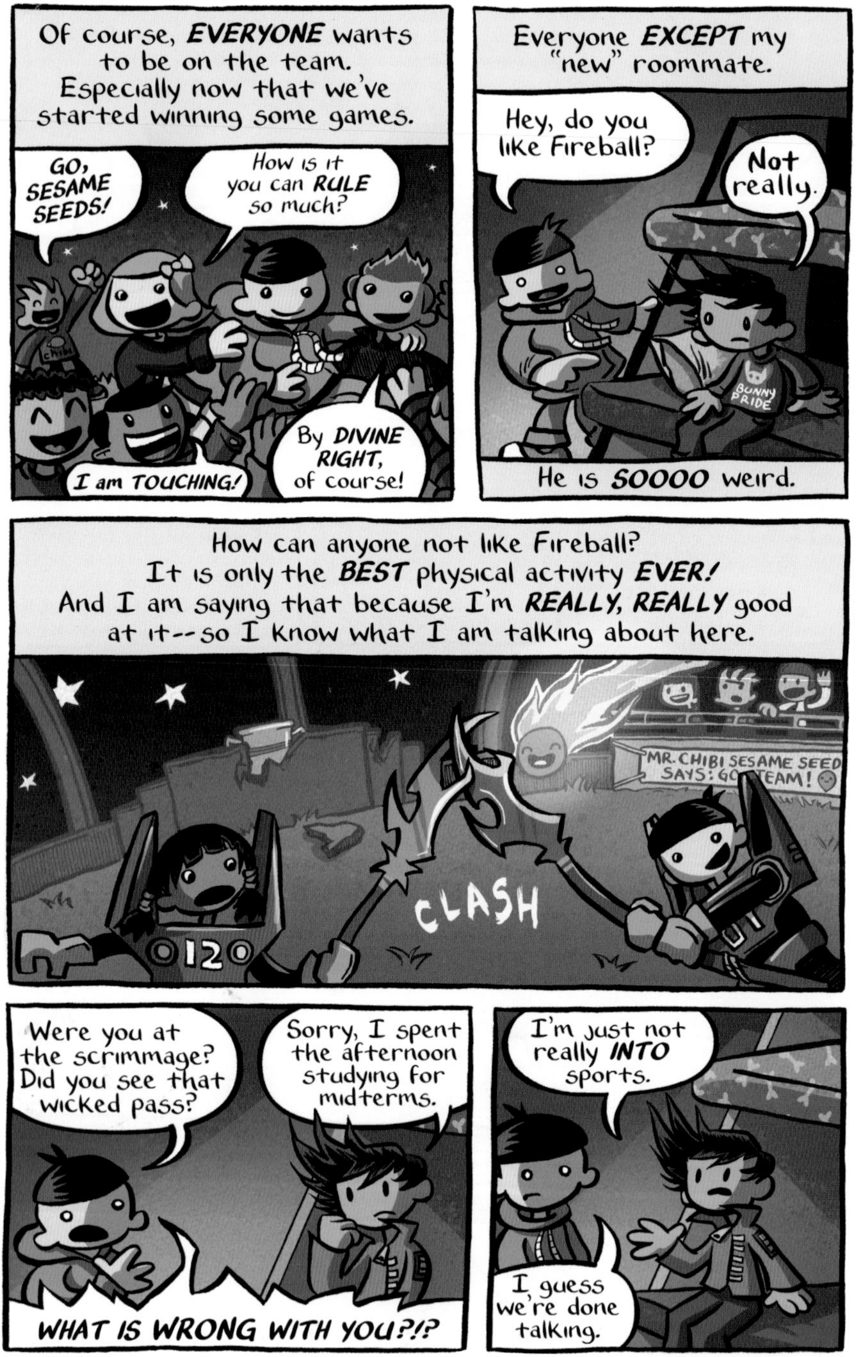
Of course, EVERYONE wants to be on the team. Especially now that we've started winning some games.
GO, SESAME SEEDS!
How is it you can RULE so much?
By DIVINE RIGHT, of course!
I am TOUCHING!
Everyone EXCEPT my "new" roommate.
Hey, do you like Fireball?
Not really.
BUNNY PRIDE
He is SOOOO weird.
How can anyone not like Fireball? It is only the BEST physical activity EVER! And I am saying that because I'm REALLY, REALLY good at it--so I know what I am talking about here.
MR. CHIBI SESAME SEED SAYS: GO TEAM!
CLASH
0120
Were you at the scrimmage? Did you see that wicked pass?
Sorry, I spent the afternoon studying for midterms.
WHAT IS WRONG WITH YOU?!?
I'm just not really INTO sports.
I guess we're done talking.

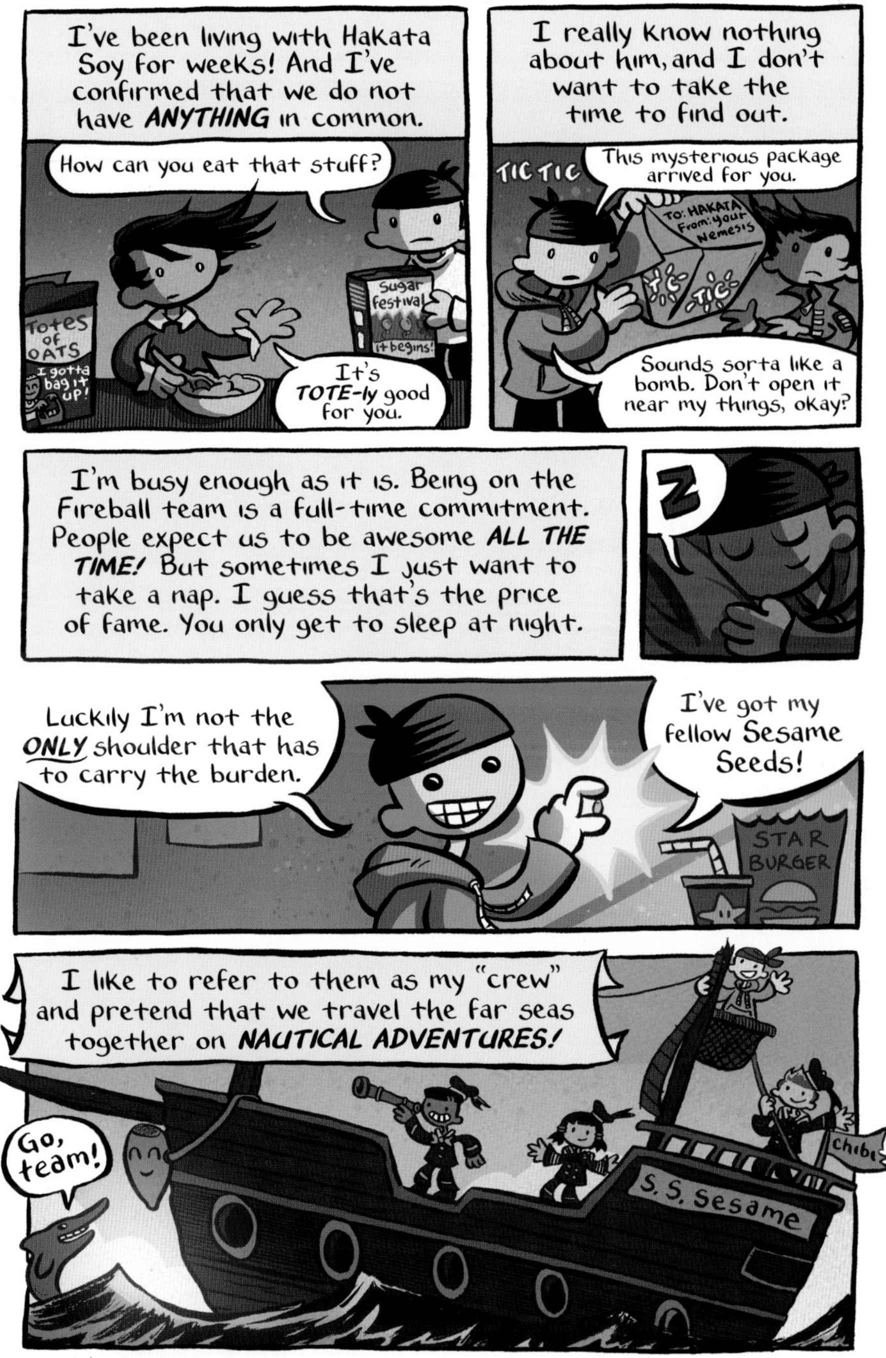

I've been living with Hakata Soy for weeks! And I've confirmed that we do not have ANYTHING in common.
How can you eat that stuff?
Totes of Oats
I gotta bag it up!
Sugar Festival
it begins!
It's TOTE-ly good for you.
I really know nothing about him, and I don't want to take the time to find out.
TIC TIC
This mysterious package arrived for you.
To: HAKATA From: your Nemesis
TIC TIC
Sounds sorta like a bomb. Don't open it near my things, okay?
I'm busy enough as it is. Being on the Fireball team is a full-time commitment. People expect us to be awesome ALL THE TIME! But sometimes I just want to take a nap. I guess that's the price of fame. You only get to sleep at night.
Z
Luckily I'm not the ONLY shoulder that has to carry the burden.
I've got my fellow Sesame Seeds!
STAR BURGER
I like to refer to them as my "crew" and pretend that we travel the far seas together on NAUTICAL ADVENTURES!
Go, team!
Chibi
S.S. Sesame

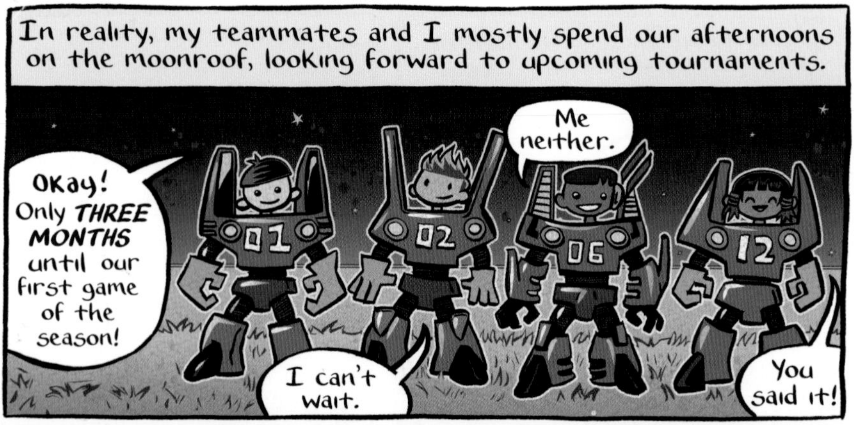
In reality, my teammates and I mostly spend our afternoons on the moonroof, looking forward to upcoming tournaments.
Okay! Only THREE MONTHS until our first game of the season!
I can't wait.
Me neither.
You said it!
01
02
06
12

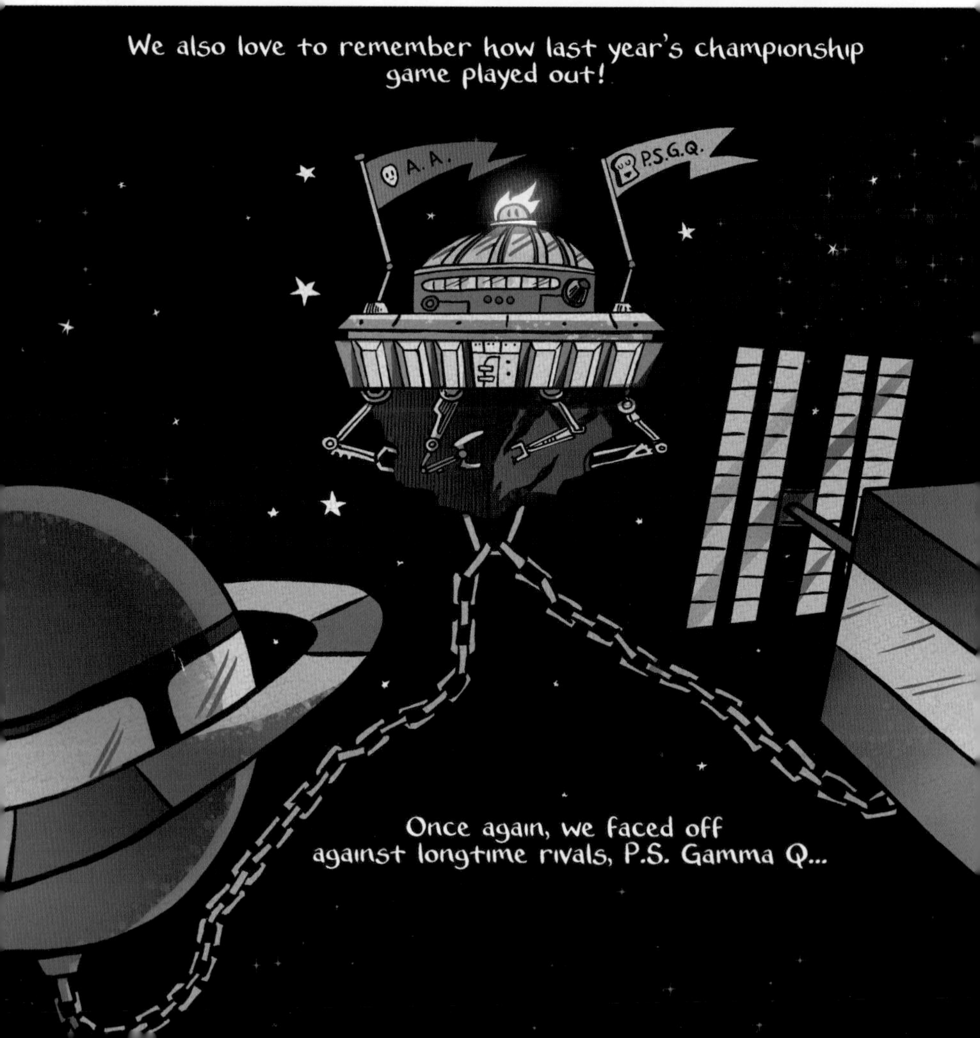
We also love to remember how last year's championship game played out!
A. A.
P.S.G.Q.
Once again, we faced off against longtime rivals, P.S. Gamma Q...

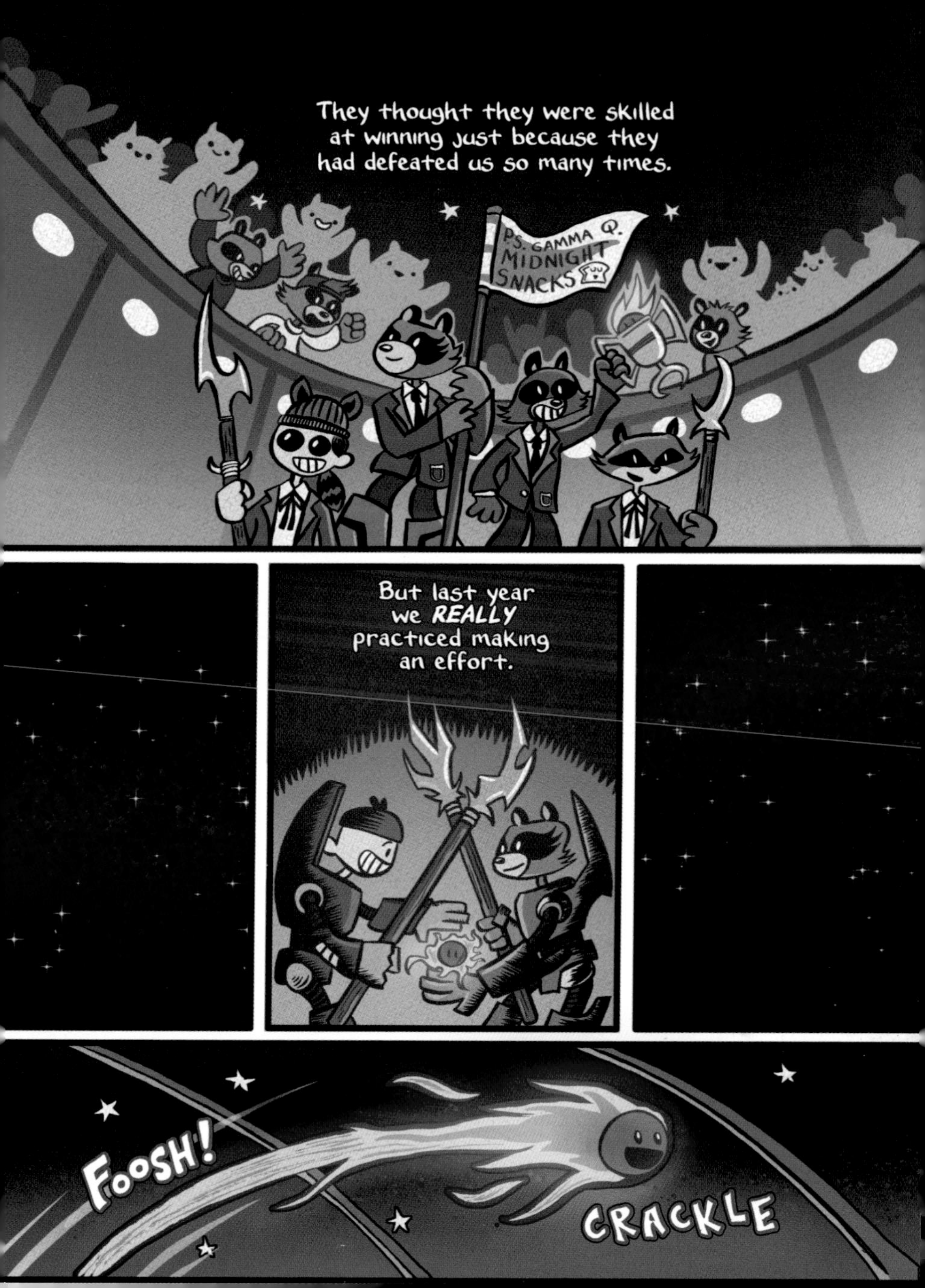
They thought they were skilled at winning just because they had defeated us so many times.
P.S. GAMMA Q. MIDNIGHT SNACKS
But last year we *REALLY* practiced making an effort.
FOOSH!
CRACKLE

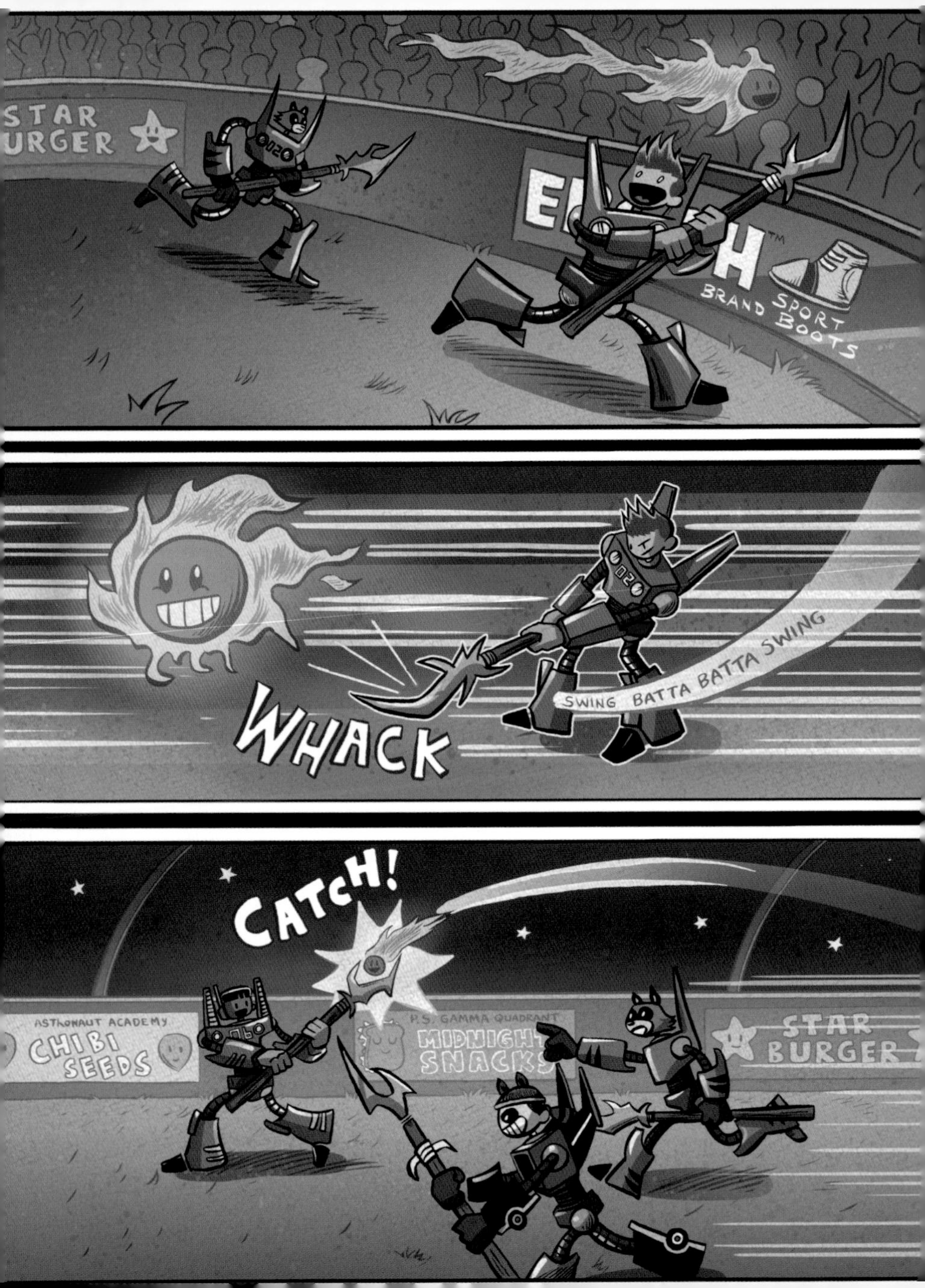
STAR
BRAND SPORT BOOTS
WHACK
SWING BATTA BATTA SWING
CATCH!
ASTRONAUT ACADEMY
CHIBI SEEDS
P.S. GAMMA QUADRANT
SNACKS
STAR BURGER

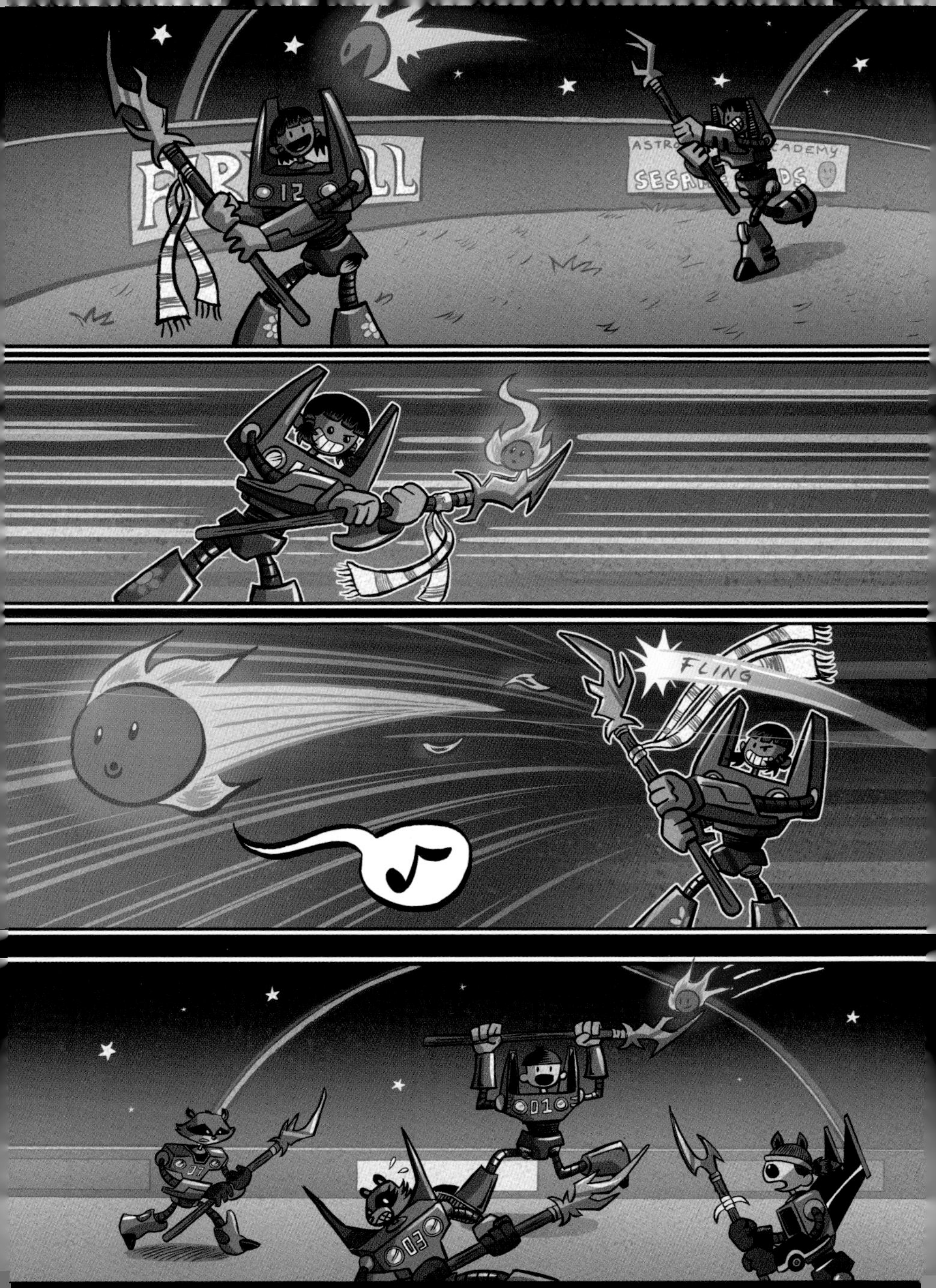
FLING

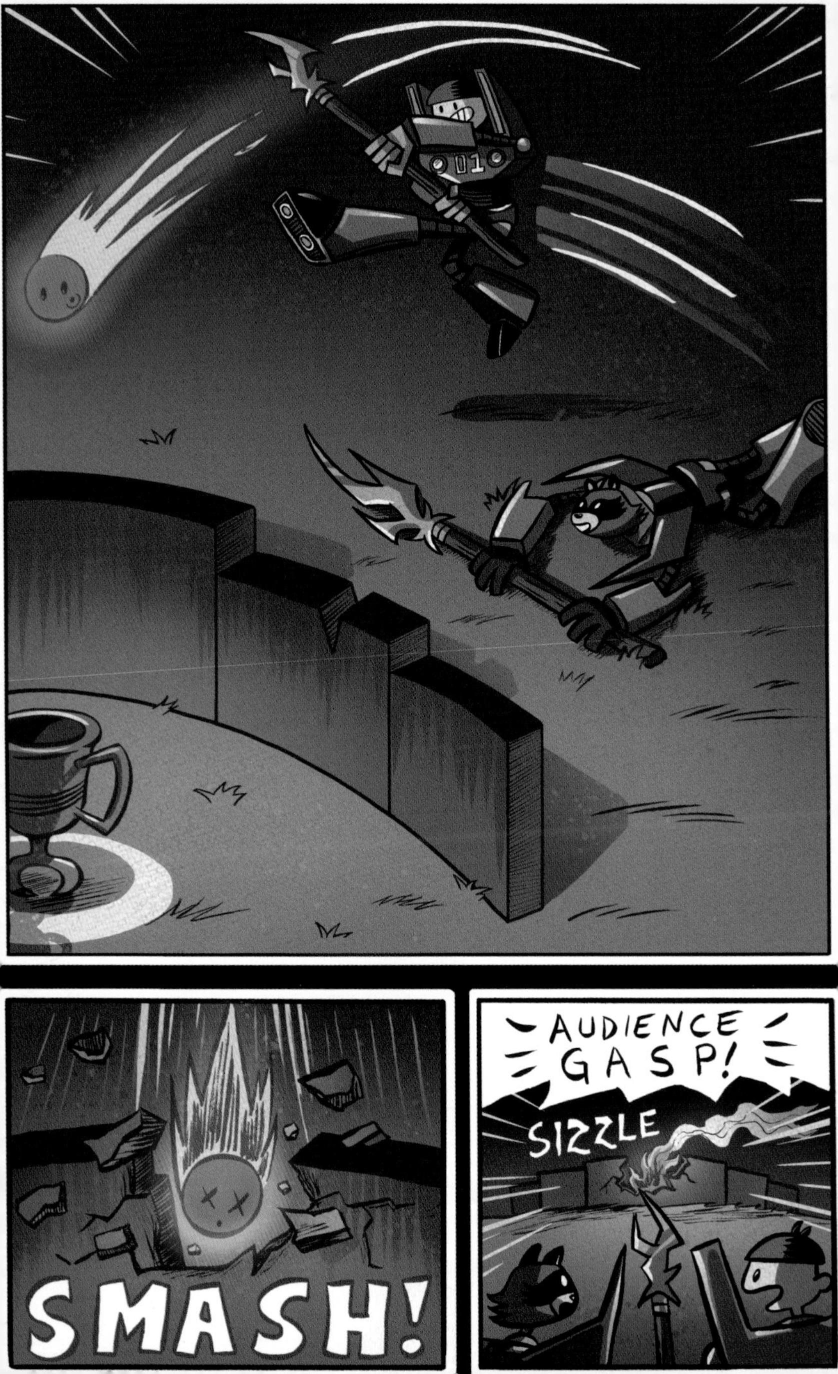
01
SMASH!
AUDIENCE GASP!
SIZZLE

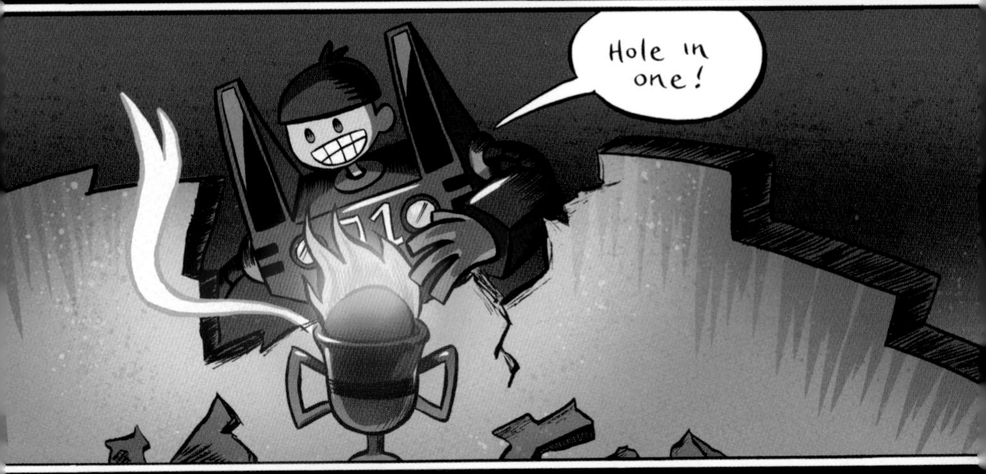
Hole in one!

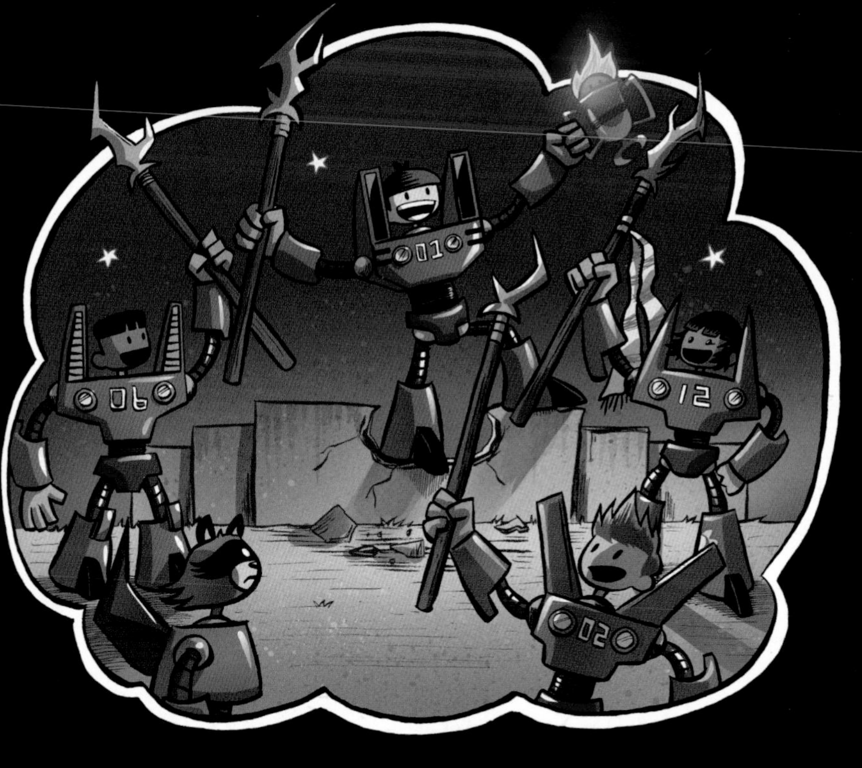

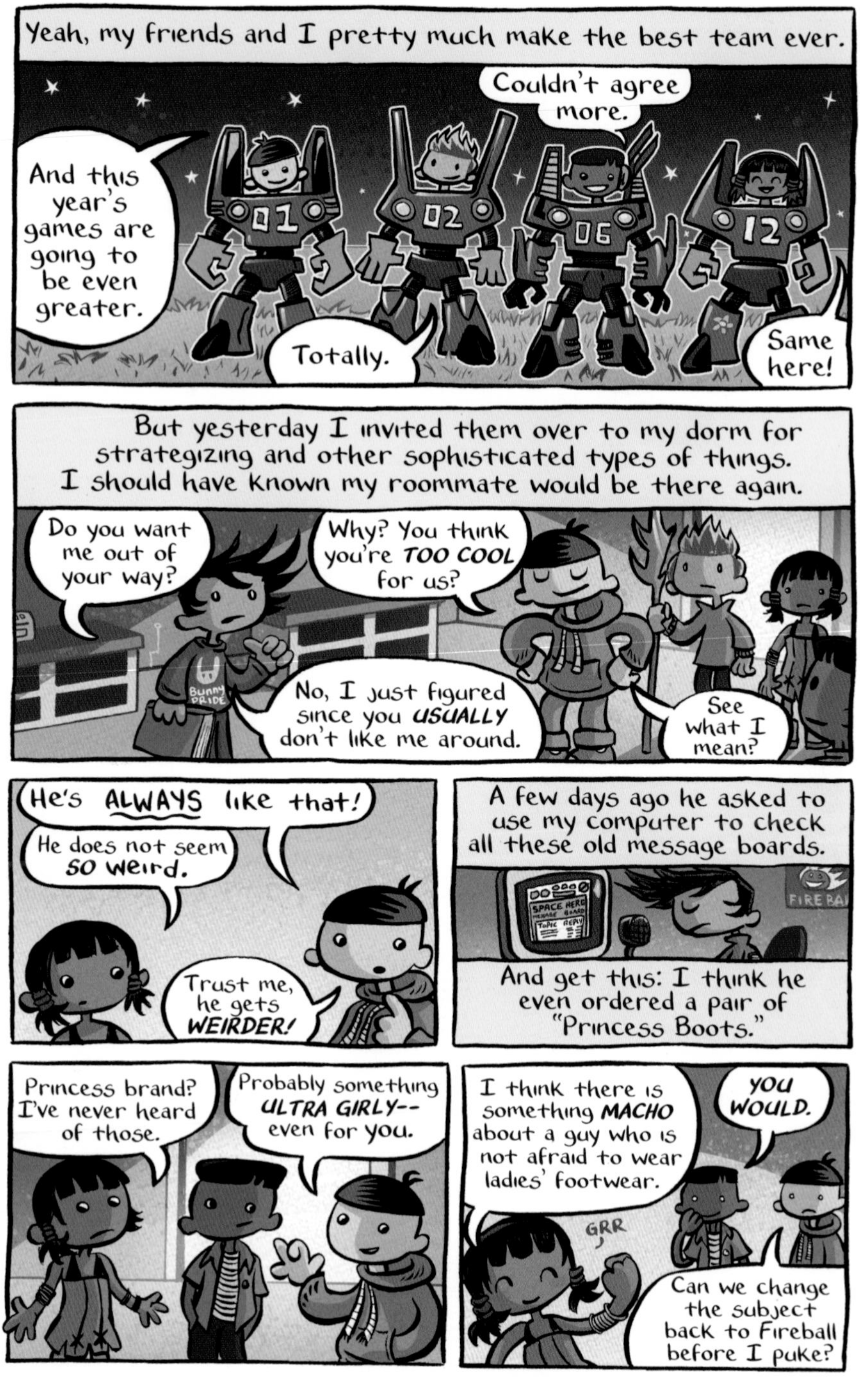

Yeah, my friends and I pretty much make the best team ever.
And this year's games are going to be even greater.
Totally.
Couldn't agree more.
Same here!
01
02
06
12
But yesterday I invited them over to my dorm for strategizing and other sophisticated types of things. I should have known my roommate would be there again.
Do you want me out of your way?
Why? You think you're TOO COOL for us?
BUNNY PRIDE
No, I just figured since you USUALLY don't like me around.
See what I mean?
He's ALWAYS like that!
He does not seem SO weird.
Trust me, he gets WEIRDER!
A few days ago he asked to use my computer to check all these old message boards.
SPACE HERO MESSAGE BOARD
TOPIC REPLY
FIREBA
And get this: I think he even ordered a pair of "Princess Boots."
Princess brand? I've never heard of those.
Probably something ULTRA GIRLY-- even for you.
I think there is something MACHO about a guy who is not afraid to wear ladies' footwear.
YOU WOULD.
GRR
Can we change the subject back to Fireball before I puke?

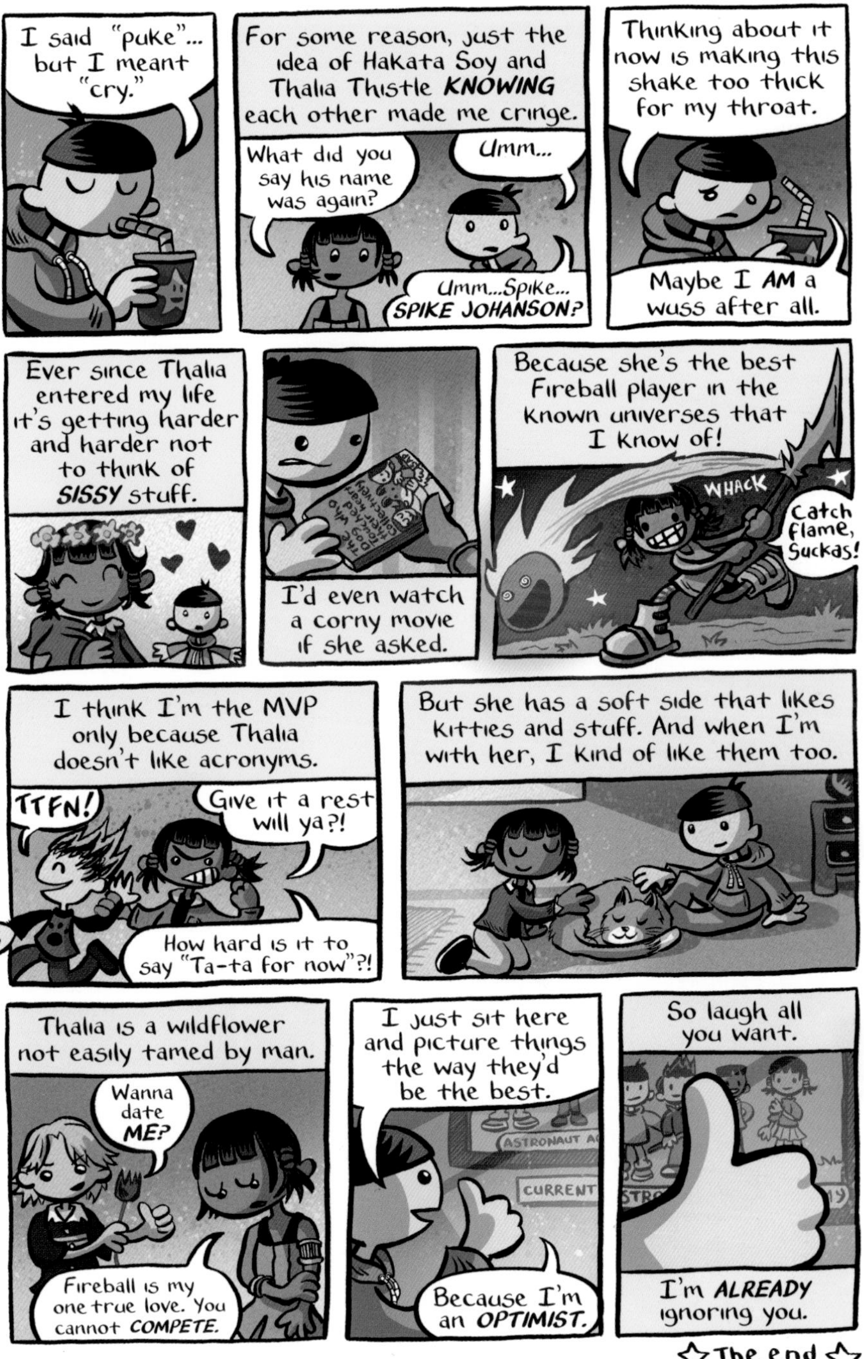
I said "puke"... but I meant "cry."
For some reason, just the idea of Hakata Soy and Thalia Thistle KNOWING each other made me cringe.
What did you say his name was again?
Umm...
Umm...Spike... SPIKE JOHANSON?
Thinking about it now is making this shake too thick for my throat.
Maybe I AM a wuss after all.
Ever since Thalia entered my life it's getting harder and harder not to think of SISSY stuff.
The Dog who Collected their hearts
I'd even watch a corny movie if she asked.
Because she's the best Fireball player in the known universes that I know of!
WHACK
Catch flame, Suckas!
I think I'm the MVP only because Thalia doesn't like acronyms.
TTFN!
Give it a rest will ya?!
How hard is it to say "Ta-ta for now"?!
But she has a soft side that likes kitties and stuff. And when I'm with her, I kind of like them too.
Thalia is a wildflower not easily tamed by man.
Wanna date ME?
Fireball is my one true love. You cannot COMPETE.
I just sit here and picture things the way they'd be the best.
ASTRONAUT A
CURRENT
Because I'm an OPTIMIST.
So laugh all you want.
I'm ALREADY ignoring you.

☆ The end ☆

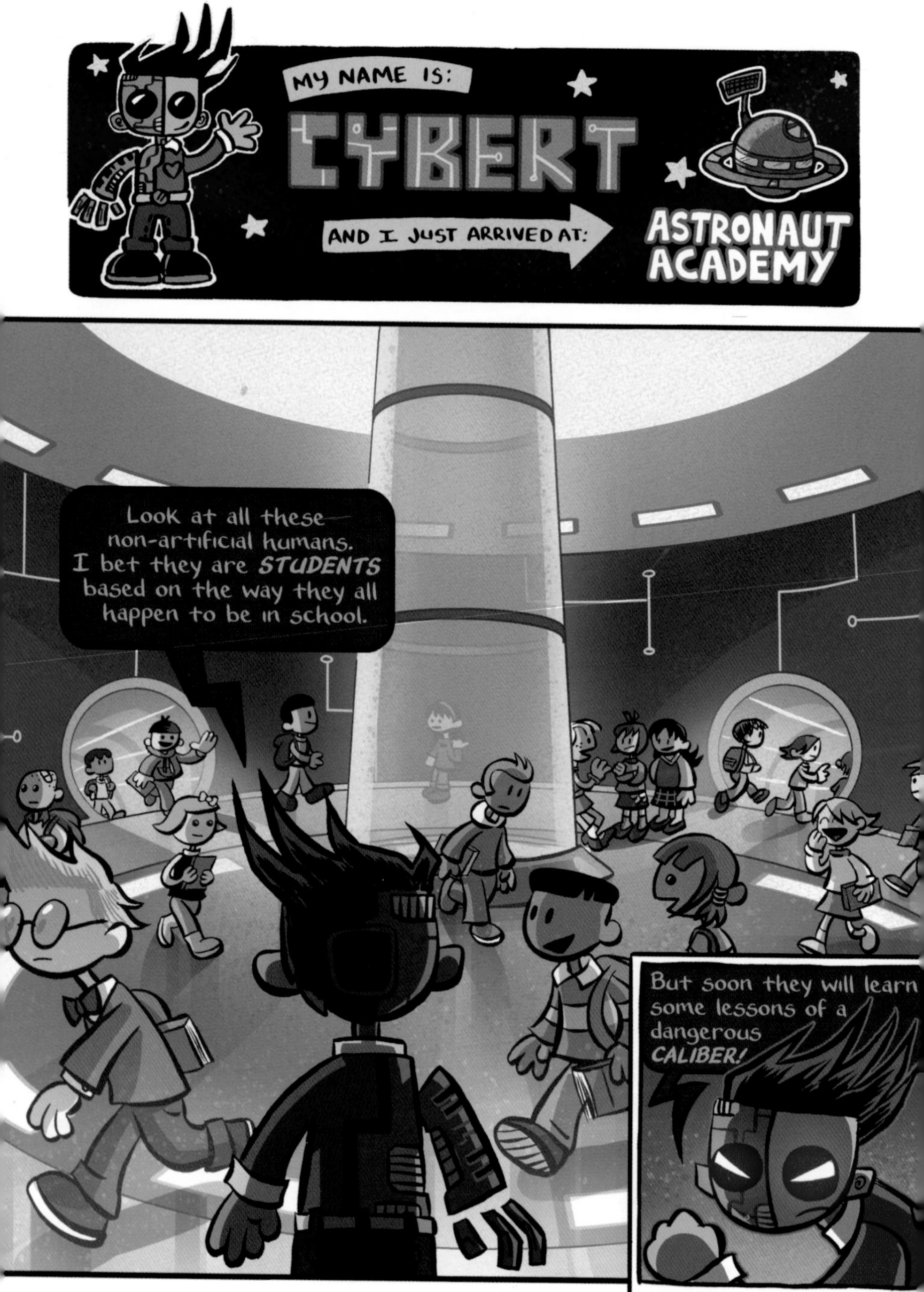
MY NAME IS:
CYBERT
AND I JUST ARRIVED AT:
ASTRONAUT ACADEMY
Look at all these non-artificial humans. I bet they are STUDENTS based on the way they all happen to be in school.
But soon they will learn some lessons of a dangerous CALIBER!

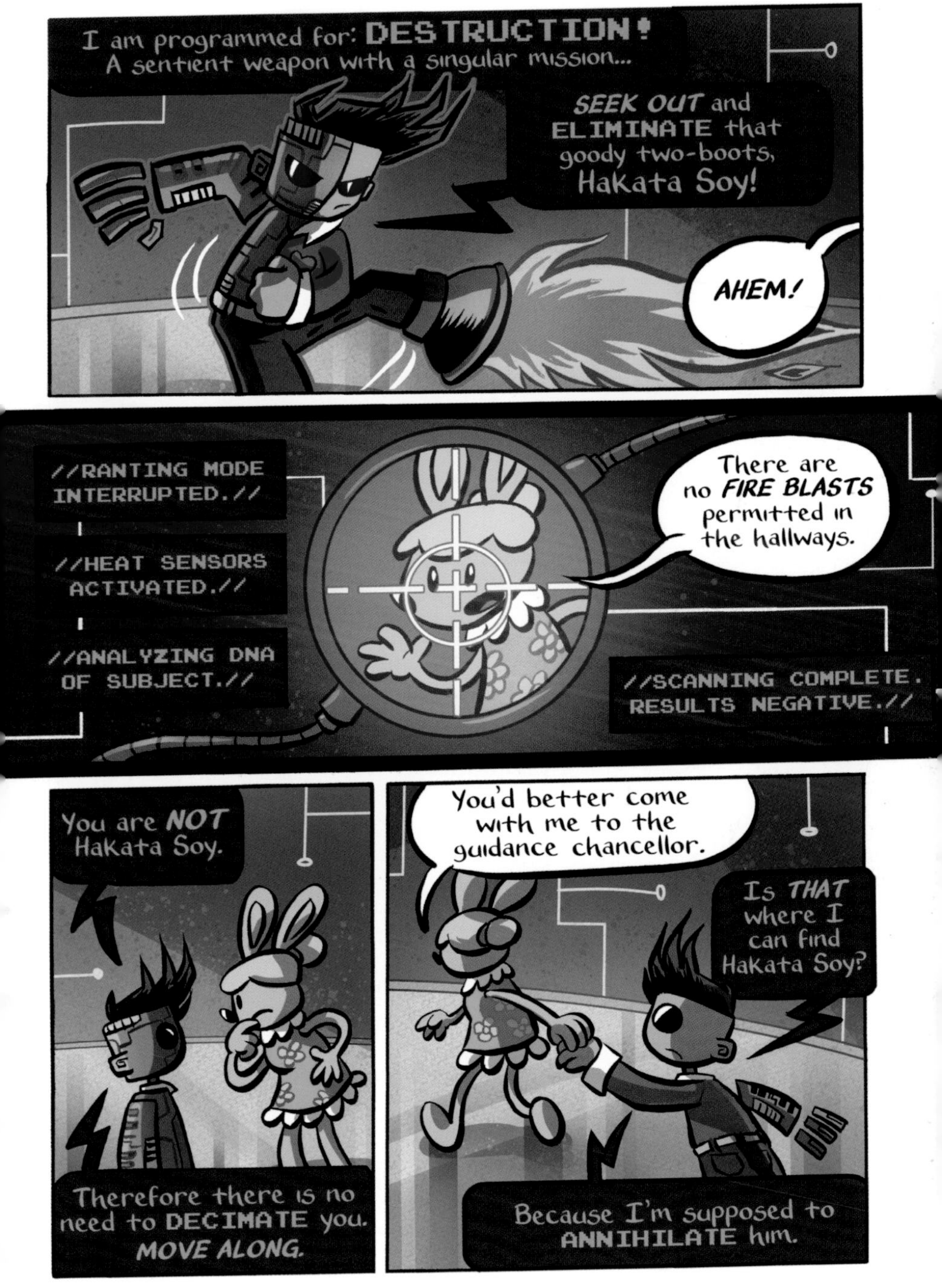
I am programmed for: DESTRUCTION! A sentient weapon with a singular mission...
SEEK OUT and ELIMINATE that goody two-boots, Hakata Soy!
AHEM!
//RANTING MODE INTERRUPTED.//
//HEAT SENSORS ACTIVATED.//
//ANALYZING DNA OF SUBJECT.//
There are no FIRE BLASTS permitted in the hallways.
//SCANNING COMPLETE. RESULTS NEGATIVE.//
You are NOT Hakata Soy.
Therefore there is no need to DECIMATE you. MOVE ALONG.
You'd better come with me to the guidance chancellor.
Is THAT where I can find Hakata Soy?
Because I'm supposed to ANNIHILATE him.

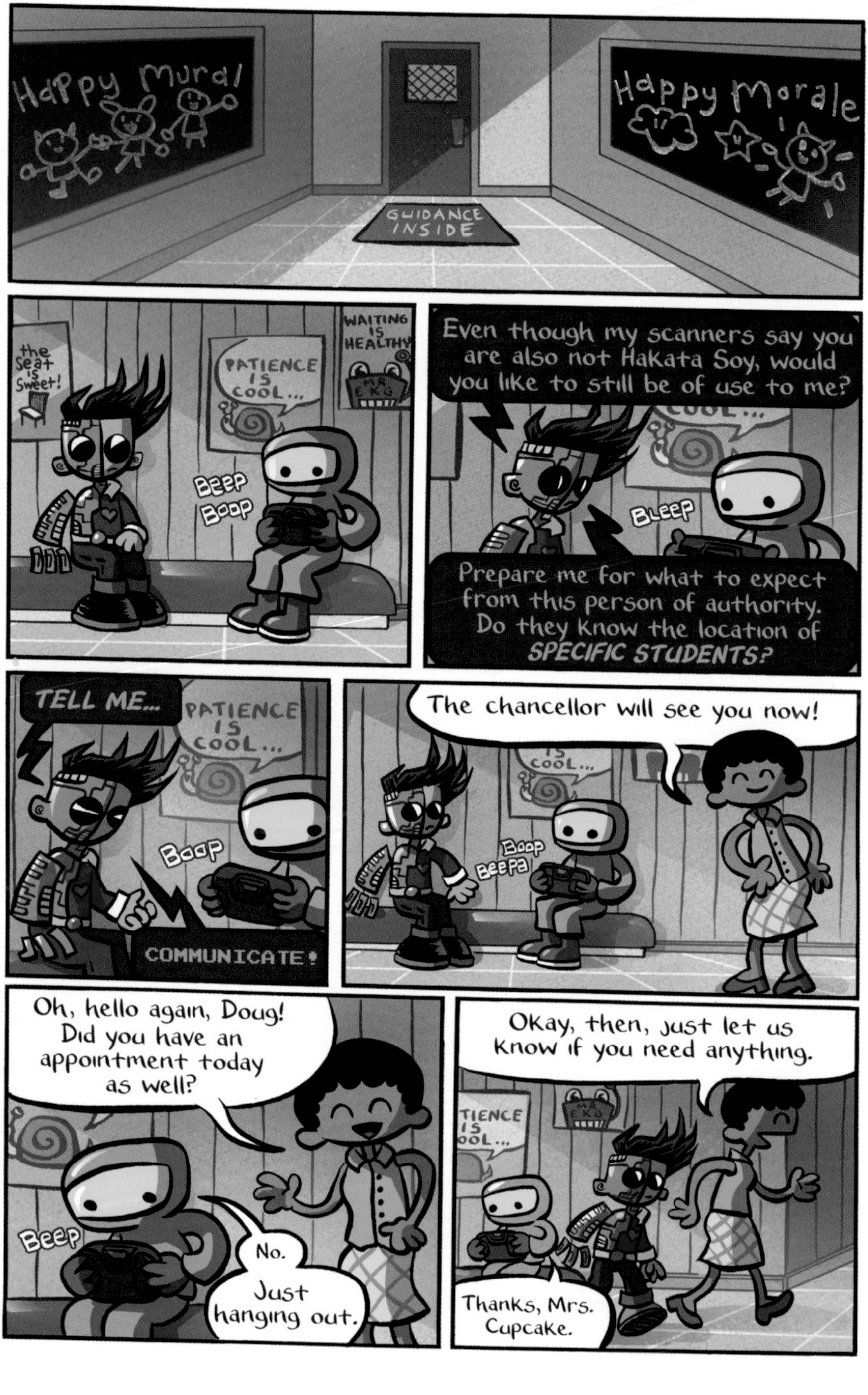
Happy Mural
Happy Morale
GUIDANCE INSIDE
the Seat is Sweet!
PATIENCE IS COOL...
WAITING IS HEALTHY
MR. EKG
BEEP BOOP
Even though my scanners say you are also not Hakata Soy, would you like to still be of use to me?
BLEEP
Prepare me for what to expect from this person of authority. Do they know the location of *SPECIFIC STUDENTS?*
TELL ME...
BOOP
COMMUNICATE!
The chancellor will see you now!
BOOP BEEPA
Oh, hello again, Doug! Did you have an appointment today as well?
BEEP
No.
Just hanging out.
Okay, then, just let us know if you need anything.
Thanks, Mrs. Cupcake.

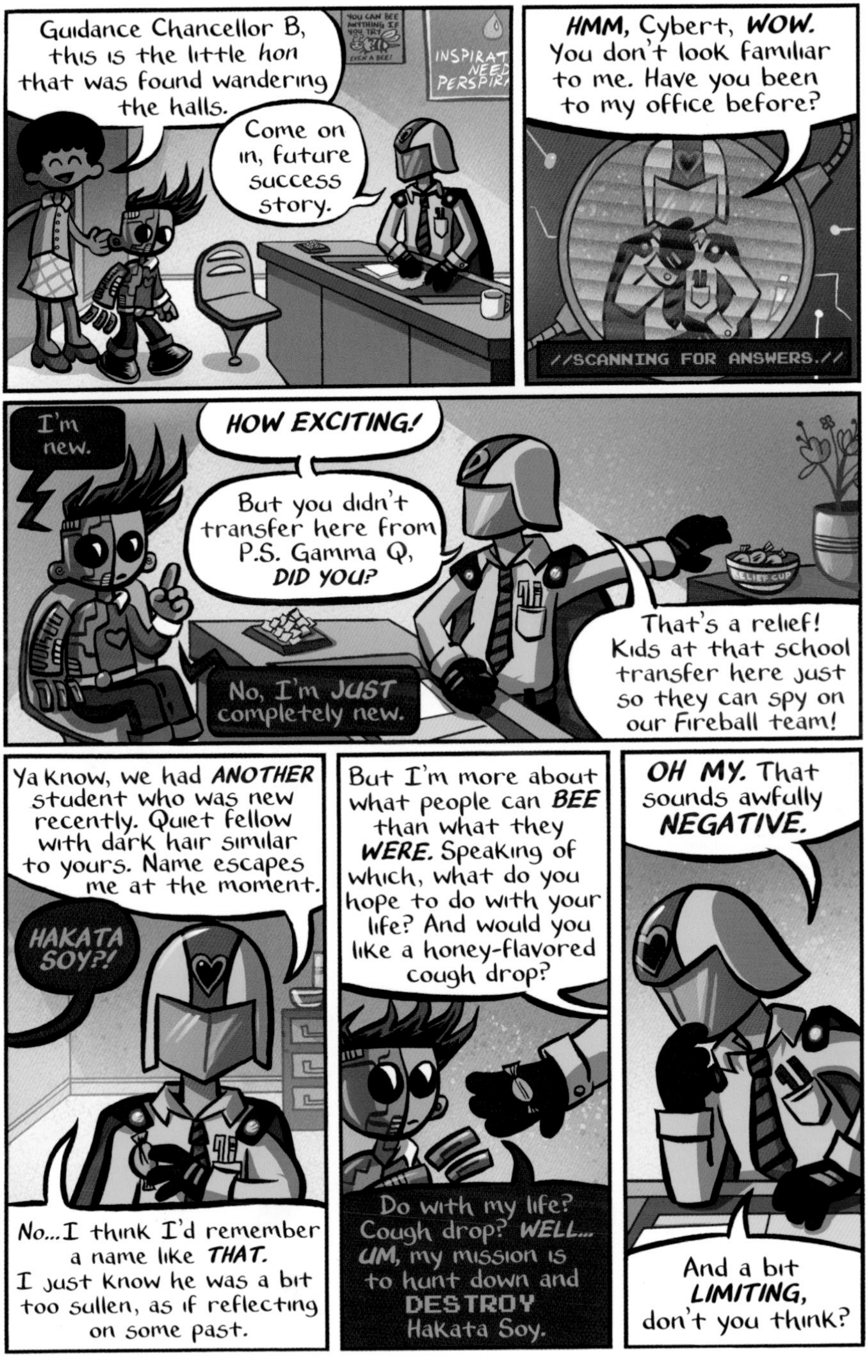

Guidance Chancellor B, this is the little hon that was found wandering the halls.
Come on in, future success story.
YOU CAN BEE ANYTHING IF YOU TRY
INSPIRAT NEED PERSPIR
HMM, Cybert, WOW. You don't look familiar to me. Have you been to my office before?
//SCANNING FOR ANSWERS.//
I'm new.
HOW EXCITING!
But you didn't transfer here from P.S. Gamma Q, DID YOU?
No, I'm JUST completely new.
That's a relief! Kids at that school transfer here just so they can spy on our Fireball team!
Ya know, we had ANOTHER student who was new recently. Quiet fellow with dark hair similar to yours. Name escapes me at the moment.
HAKATA SOY?!
No...I think I'd remember a name like THAT. I just know he was a bit too sullen, as if reflecting on some past.
But I'm more about what people can BEE than what they WERE. Speaking of which, what do you hope to do with your life? And would you like a honey-flavored cough drop?
Do with my life? Cough drop? WELL... UM, my mission is to hunt down and DESTROY Hakata Soy.
OH MY. That sounds awfully NEGATIVE.
And a bit LIMITING, don't you think?

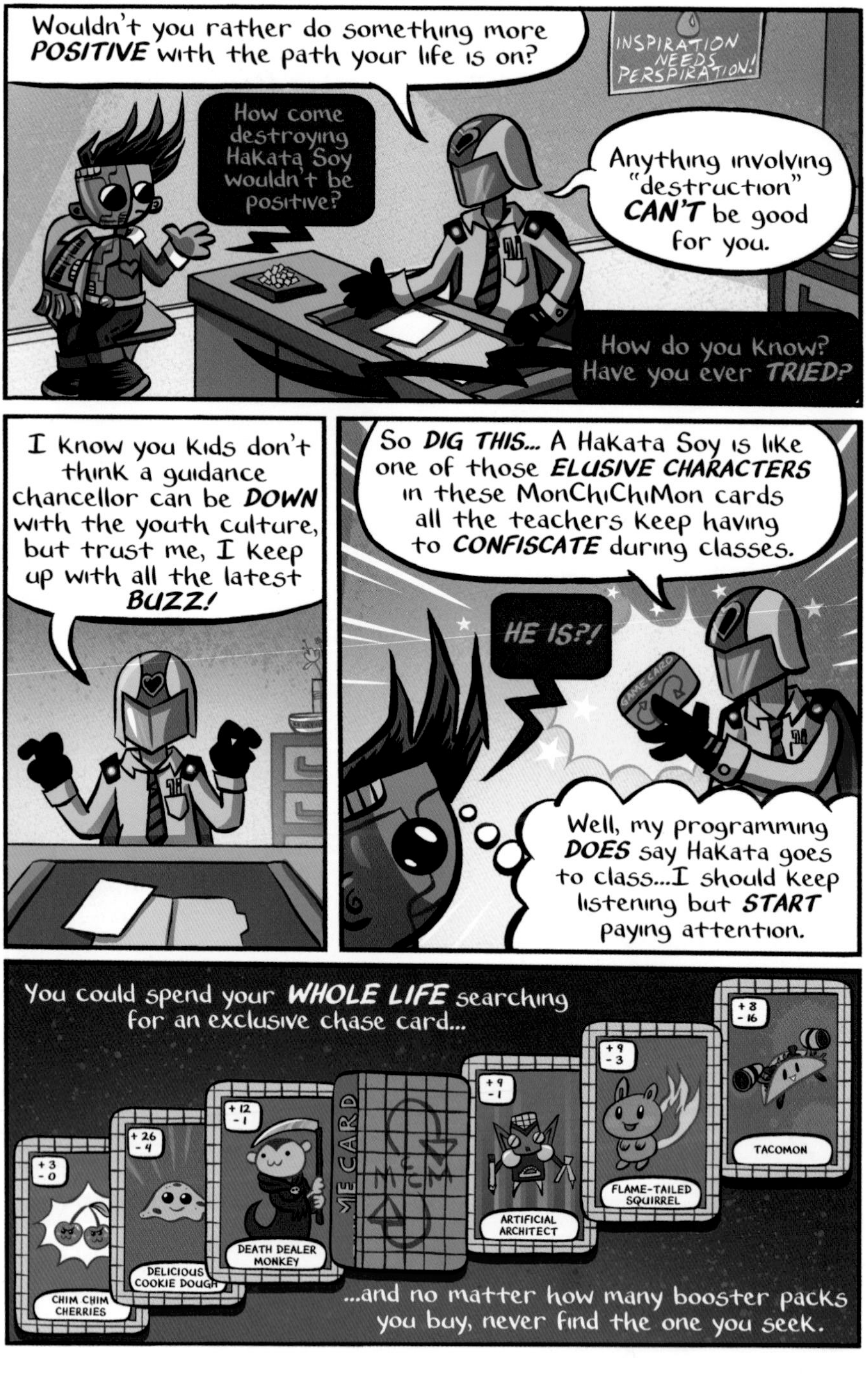

Wouldn't you rather do something more POSITIVE with the path your life is on?
INSPIRATION NEEDS PERSPIRATION!
How come destroying Hakata Soy wouldn't be positive?
Anything involving "destruction" CAN'T be good for you.
How do you know? Have you ever TRIED?
I know you kids don't think a guidance chancellor can be DOWN with the youth culture, but trust me, I keep up with all the latest BUZZ!
So DIG THIS... A Hakata Soy is like one of those ELUSIVE CHARACTERS in these MonChiChiMon cards all the teachers keep having to CONFISCATE during classes.
HE IS?!
GAME CARD
Well, my programming DOES say Hakata goes to class...I should keep listening but START paying attention.
You could spend your WHOLE LIFE searching for an exclusive chase card...
+3 -0
CHIM CHIM CHERRIES
+26 -4
DELICIOUS COOKIE DOUGH
+12 -1
DEATH DEALER MONKEY
ME CARD
MCM
+9 -1
ARTIFICIAL ARCHITECT
+9 -3
FLAME-TAILED SQUIRREL
+8 -16
TACOMON
...and no matter how many booster packs you buy, never find the one you seek.

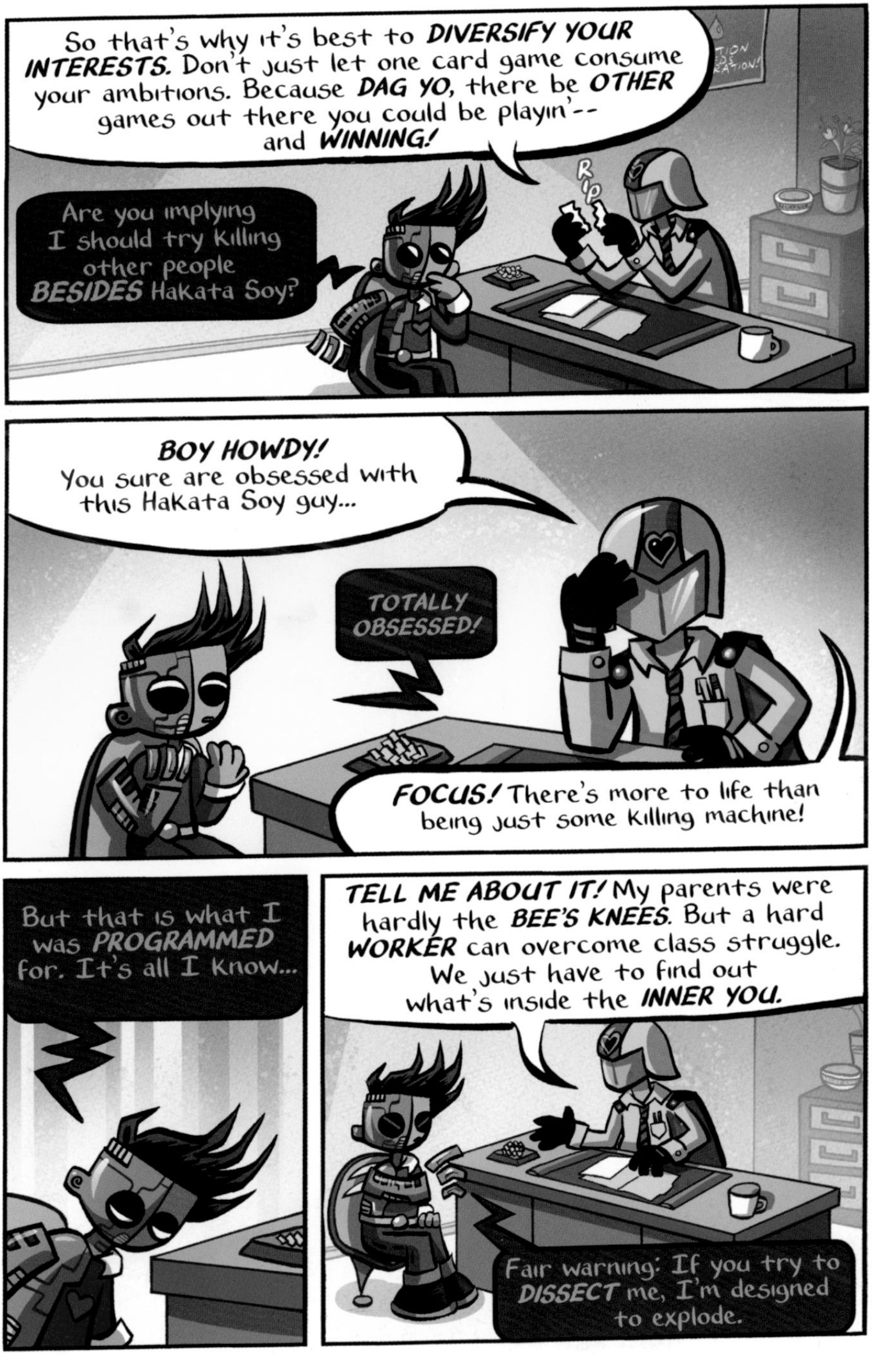
So that's why it's best to DIVERSIFY YOUR INTERESTS. Don't just let one card game consume your ambitions. Because DAG YO, there be OTHER games out there you could be playin'-- and WINNING!
RIP
Are you implying I should try killing other people BESIDES Hakata Soy?
BOY HOWDY! You sure are obsessed with this Hakata Soy guy...
TOTALLY OBSESSED!
FOCUS! There's more to life than being just some killing machine!
But that is what I was PROGRAMMED for. It's all I know...
TELL ME ABOUT IT! My parents were hardly the BEE'S KNEES. But a hard WORKER can overcome class struggle. We just have to find out what's inside the INNER YOU.
Fair warning: If you try to DISSECT me, I'm designed to explode.

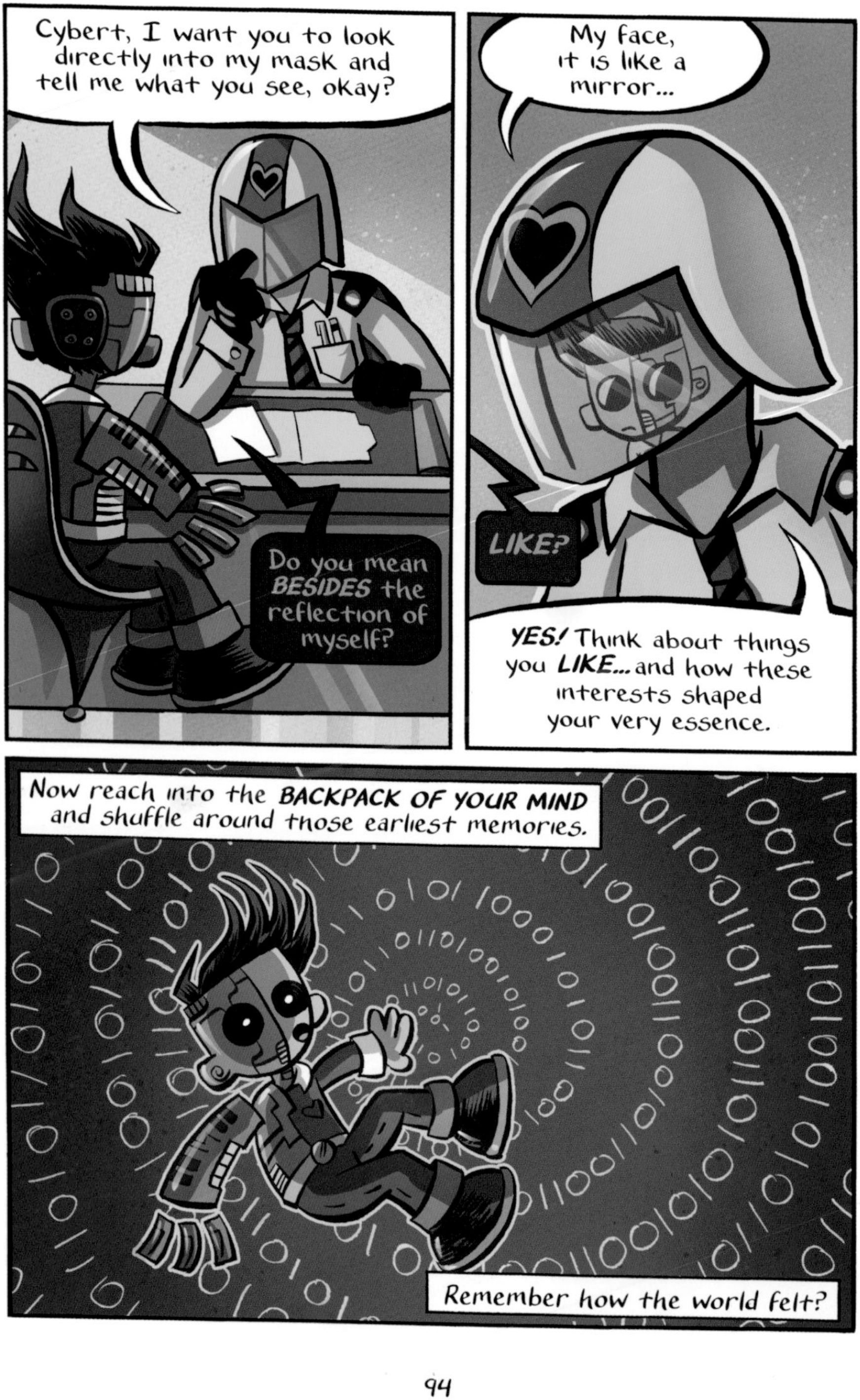
Cybert, I want you to look directly into my mask and tell me what you see, okay?
Do you mean BESIDES the reflection of myself?
My face, it is like a mirror...
LIKE?
YES! Think about things you LIKE... and how these interests shaped your very essence.
Now reach into the BACKPACK OF YOUR MIND and shuffle around those earliest memories.
Remember how the world felt?

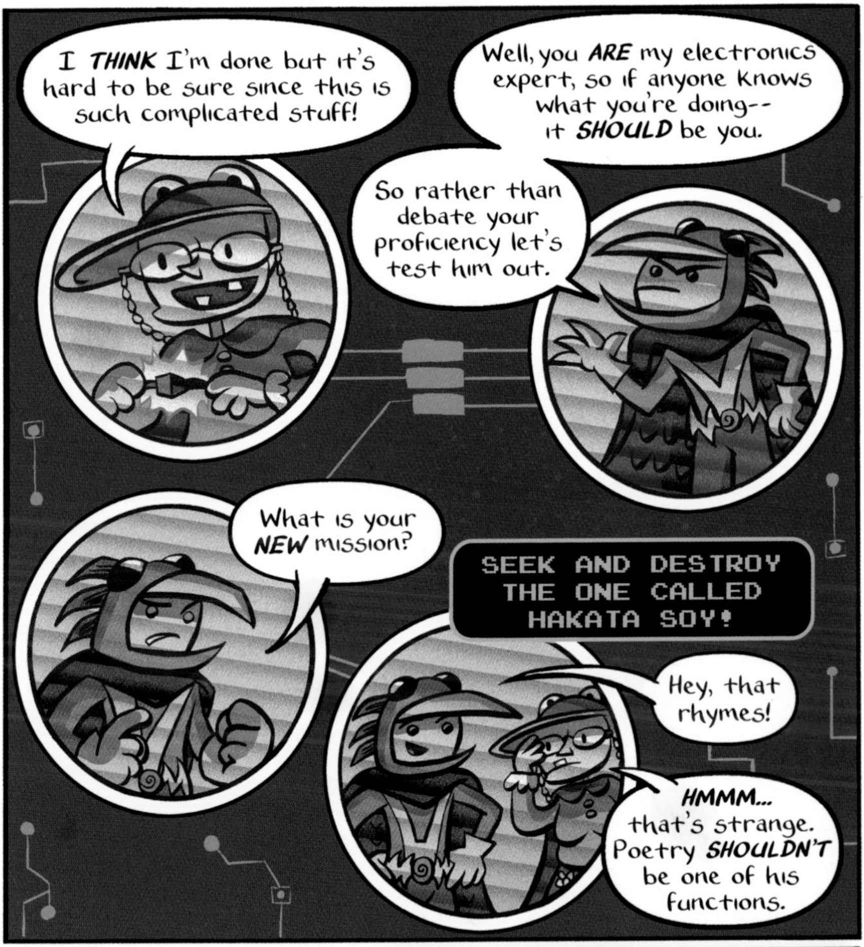
I THINK I'm done but it's hard to be sure since this is such complicated stuff!
Well, you ARE my electronics expert, so if anyone knows what you're doing-- it SHOULD be you.
So rather than debate your proficiency let's test him out.
What is your NEW mission?
SEEK AND DESTROY THE ONE CALLED HAKATA SOY!
Hey, that rhymes!
HMMM... that's strange. Poetry SHOULDN'T be one of his functions.

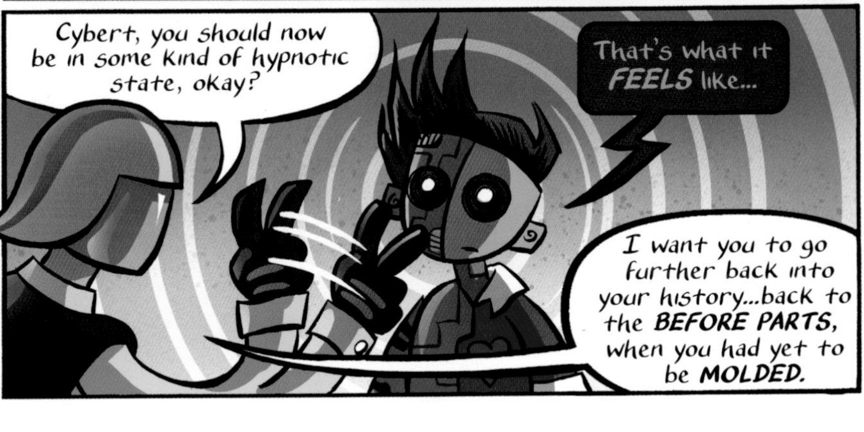
Cybert, you should now be in some kind of hypnotic state, okay?
That's what it FEELS like...
I want you to go further back into your history...back to the BEFORE PARTS, when you had yet to be MOLDED.

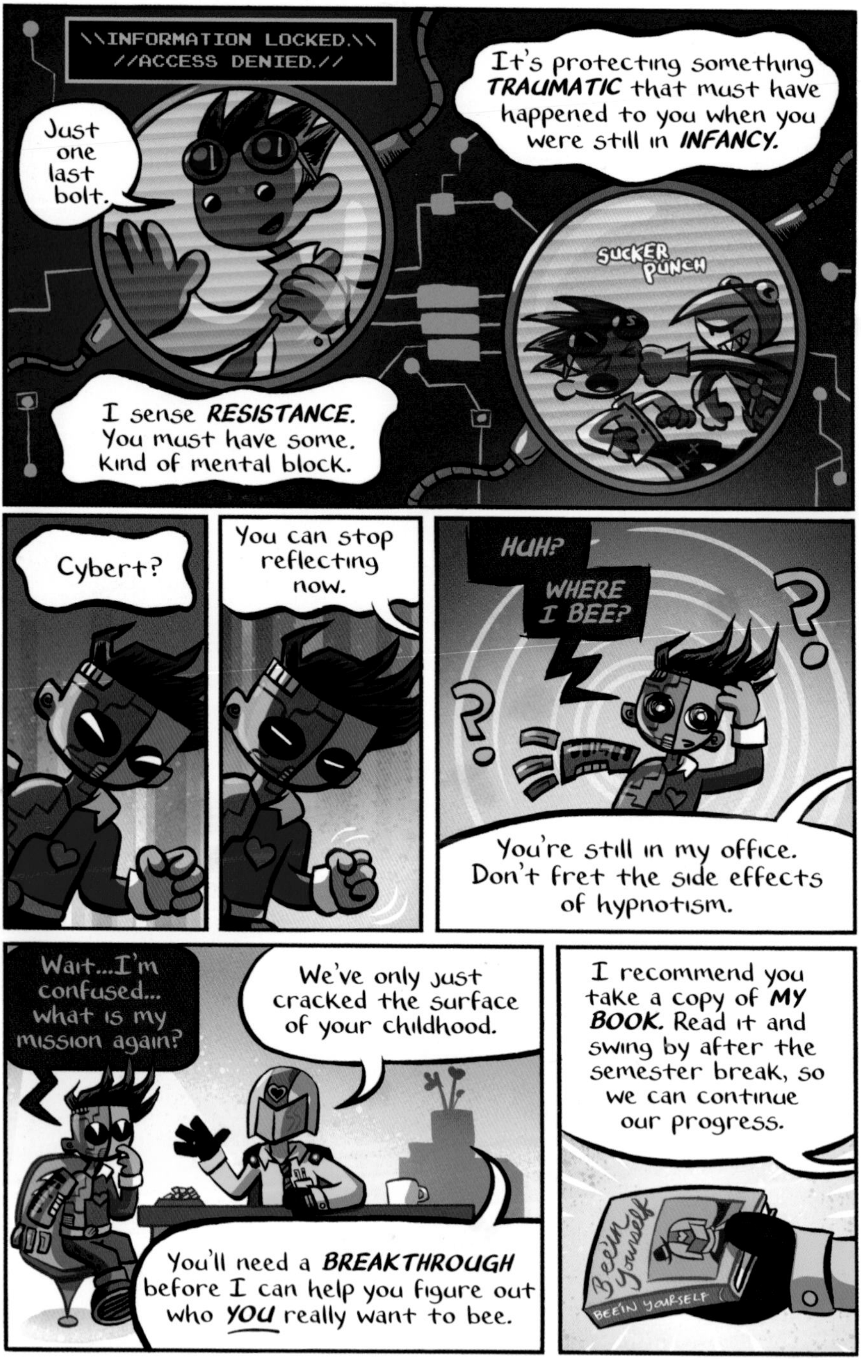
\\INFORMATION LOCKED.\\
//ACCESS DENIED.//
Just one last bolt.
It's protecting something TRAUMATIC that must have happened to you when you were still in INFANCY.
SUCKER PUNCH
I sense RESISTANCE. You must have some. Kind of mental block.
Cybert?
You can stop reflecting now.
HUH?
WHERE I BEE?
You're still in my office. Don't fret the side effects of hypnotism.
Wait...I'm confused... what is my mission again?
We've only just cracked the surface of your childhood.
You'll need a BREAKTHROUGH before I can help you figure out who YOU really want to bee.
I recommend you take a copy of MY BOOK. Read it and swing by after the semester break, so we can continue our progress.
Bee'in Yourself
BEE'IN YOURSELF

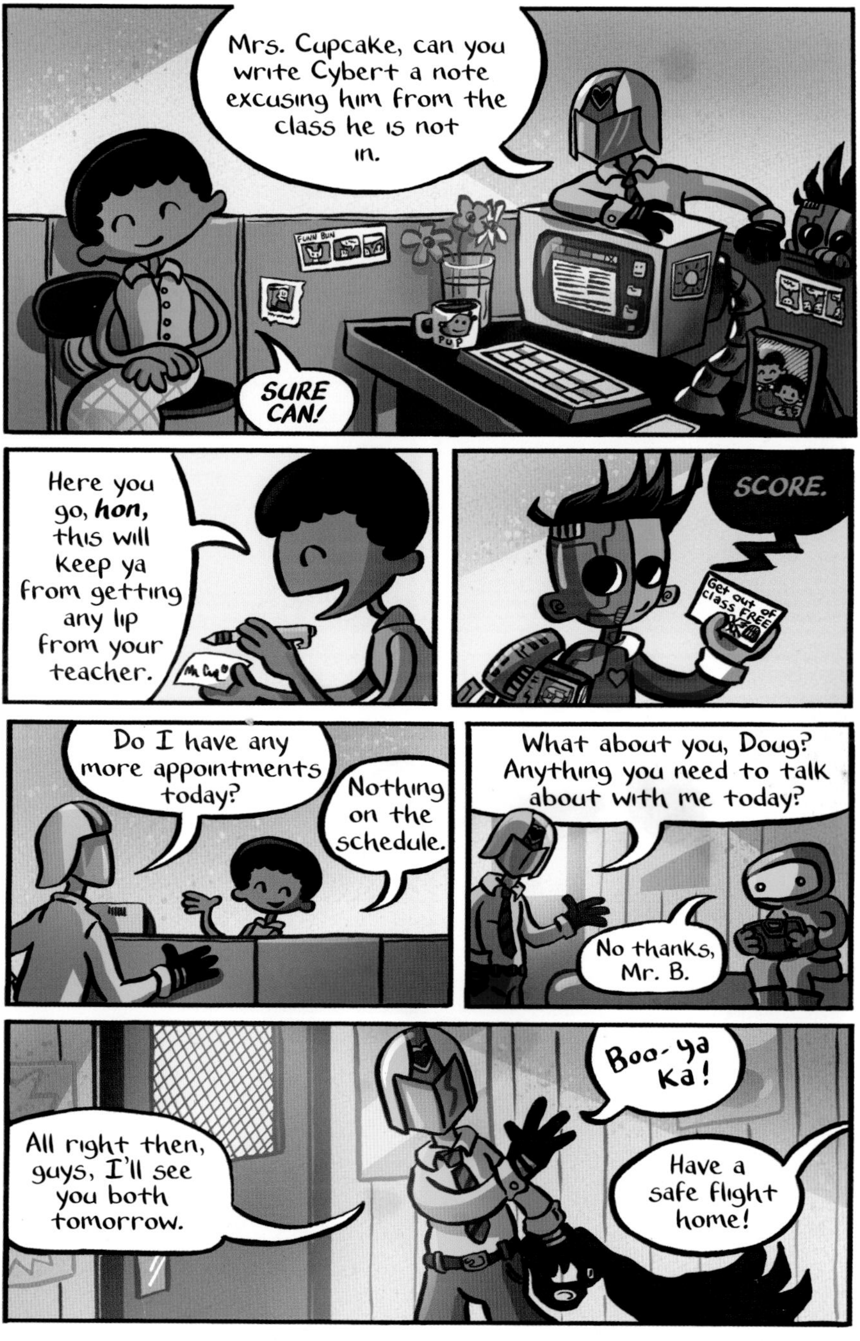
Mrs. Cupcake, can you write Cybert a note excusing him from the class he is not in.
SURE CAN!
Here you go, hon, this will keep ya from getting any lip from your teacher.
SCORE.
Get out of class FREE
Do I have any more appointments today?
Nothing on the schedule.
What about you, Doug? Anything you need to talk about with me today?
No thanks, Mr. B.
All right then, guys, I'll see you both tomorrow.
Boo-ya ka!
Have a safe flight home!

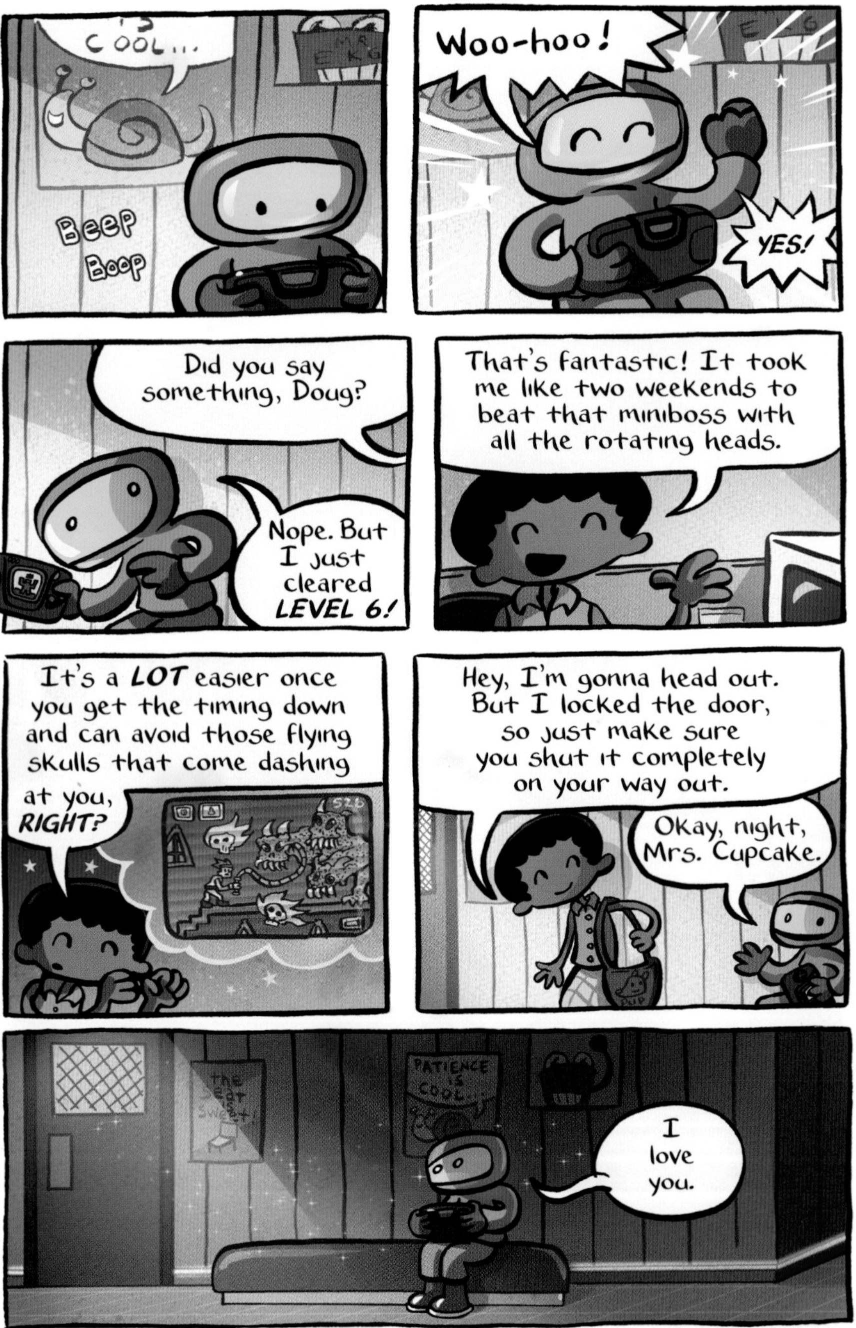

COOL...
Beep
Boop
Woo-hoo!
YES!
Did you say something, Doug?
Nope. But I just cleared LEVEL 6!
That's fantastic! It took me like two weekends to beat that miniboss with all the rotating heads.
It's a LOT easier once you get the timing down and can avoid those flying skulls that come dashing
at you, RIGHT?
Hey, I'm gonna head out. But I locked the door, so just make sure you shut it completely on your way out.
Okay, night, Mrs. Cupcake.
PATIENCE IS COOL...
I love you.

☆ The end ☆

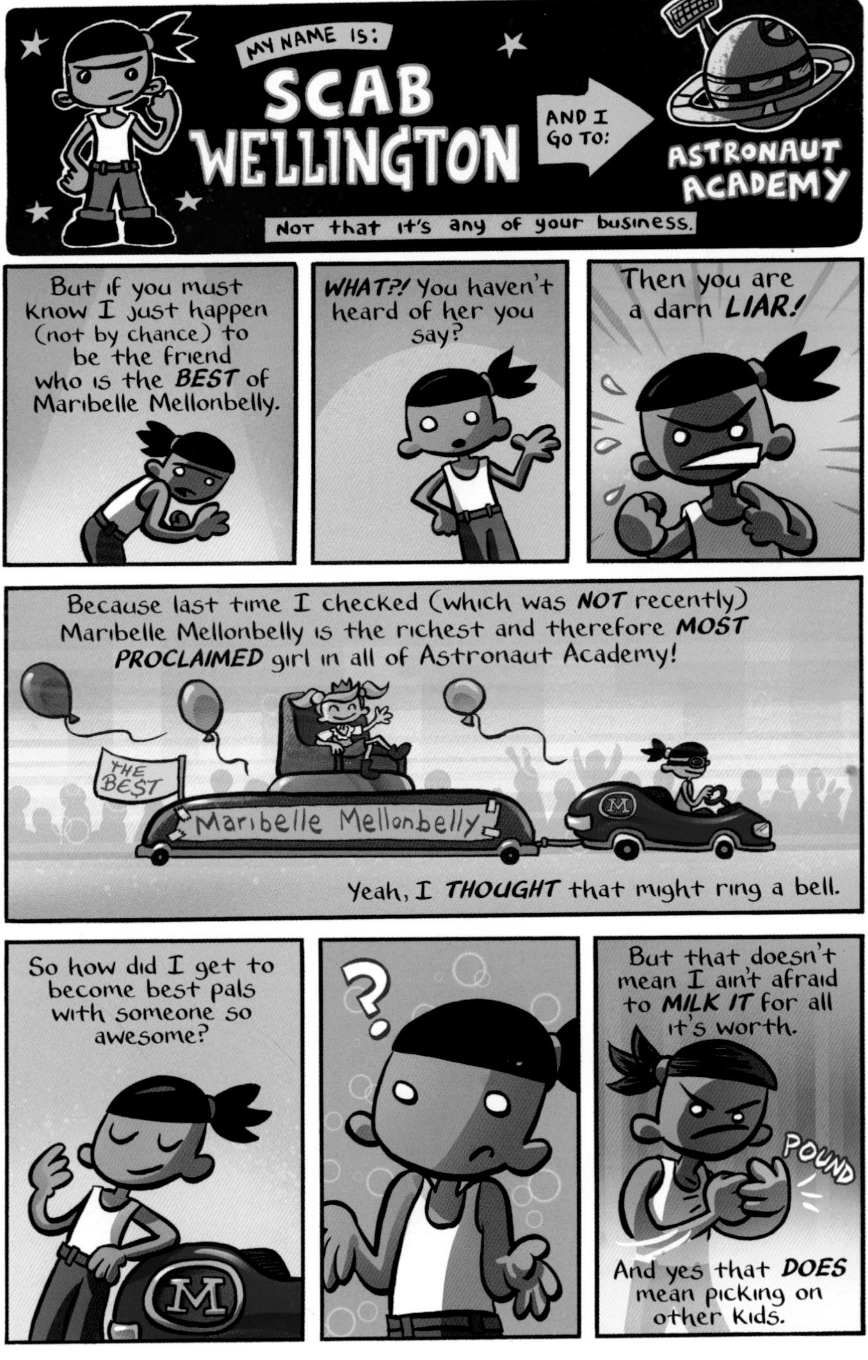
MY NAME IS:
SCAB WELLINGTON
AND I GO TO:
ASTRONAUT ACADEMY
Not that it's any of your business.
But if you must know I just happen (not by chance) to be the friend who is the BEST of Maribelle Mellonbelly.
WHAT?! You haven't heard of her you say?
Then you are a darn LIAR!
Because last time I checked (which was NOT recently) Maribelle Mellonbelly is the richest and therefore MOST PROCLAIMED girl in all of Astronaut Academy!
THE BEST
Maribelle Mellonbelly
M
Yeah, I THOUGHT that might ring a bell.
So how did I get to become best pals with someone so awesome?
M
?
But that doesn't mean I ain't afraid to MILK IT for all it's worth.
POUND
And yes that DOES mean picking on other kids.

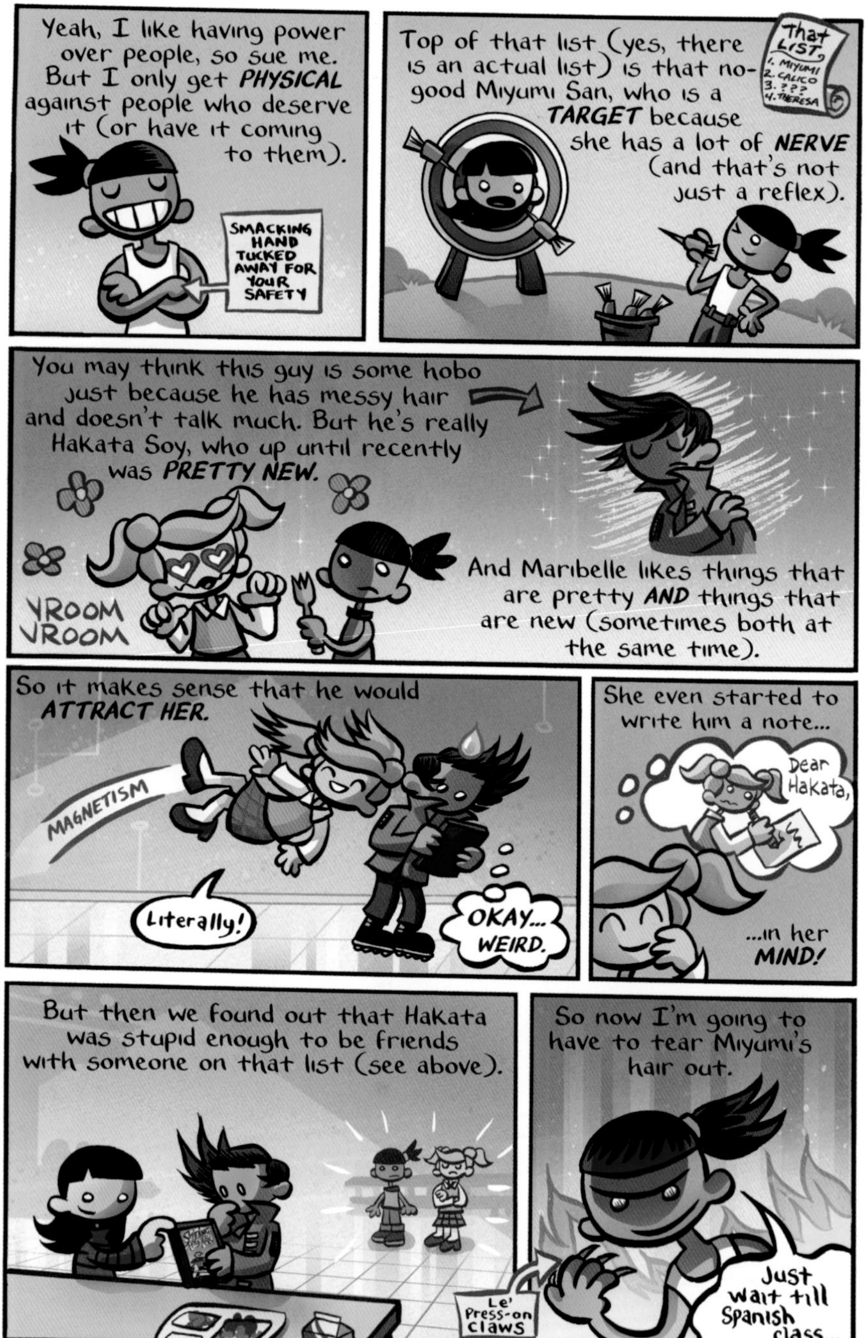

Yeah, I like having power over people, so sue me. But I only get PHYSICAL against people who deserve it (or have it coming to them).
SMACKING HAND TUCKED AWAY FOR YOUR SAFETY
Top of that list (yes, there is an actual list) is that no-good Miyumi San, who is a TARGET because she has a lot of NERVE (and that's not just a reflex).
That LIST,
1. MIYUMI
2. CALICO
3. ???
4. THERESA
You may think this guy is some hobo just because he has messy hair and doesn't talk much. But he's really Hakata Soy, who up until recently was PRETTY NEW.
VROOM VROOM
And Maribelle likes things that are pretty AND things that are new (sometimes both at the same time).
So it makes sense that he would ATTRACT HER.
MAGNETISM
Literally!
OKAY... WEIRD.
She even started to write him a note...
Dear Hakata,
...in her MIND!
But then we found out that Hakata was stupid enough to be friends with someone on that list (see above).
So now I'm going to have to tear Miyumi's hair out.
Le' Press-on claws
Just wait till Spanish class...

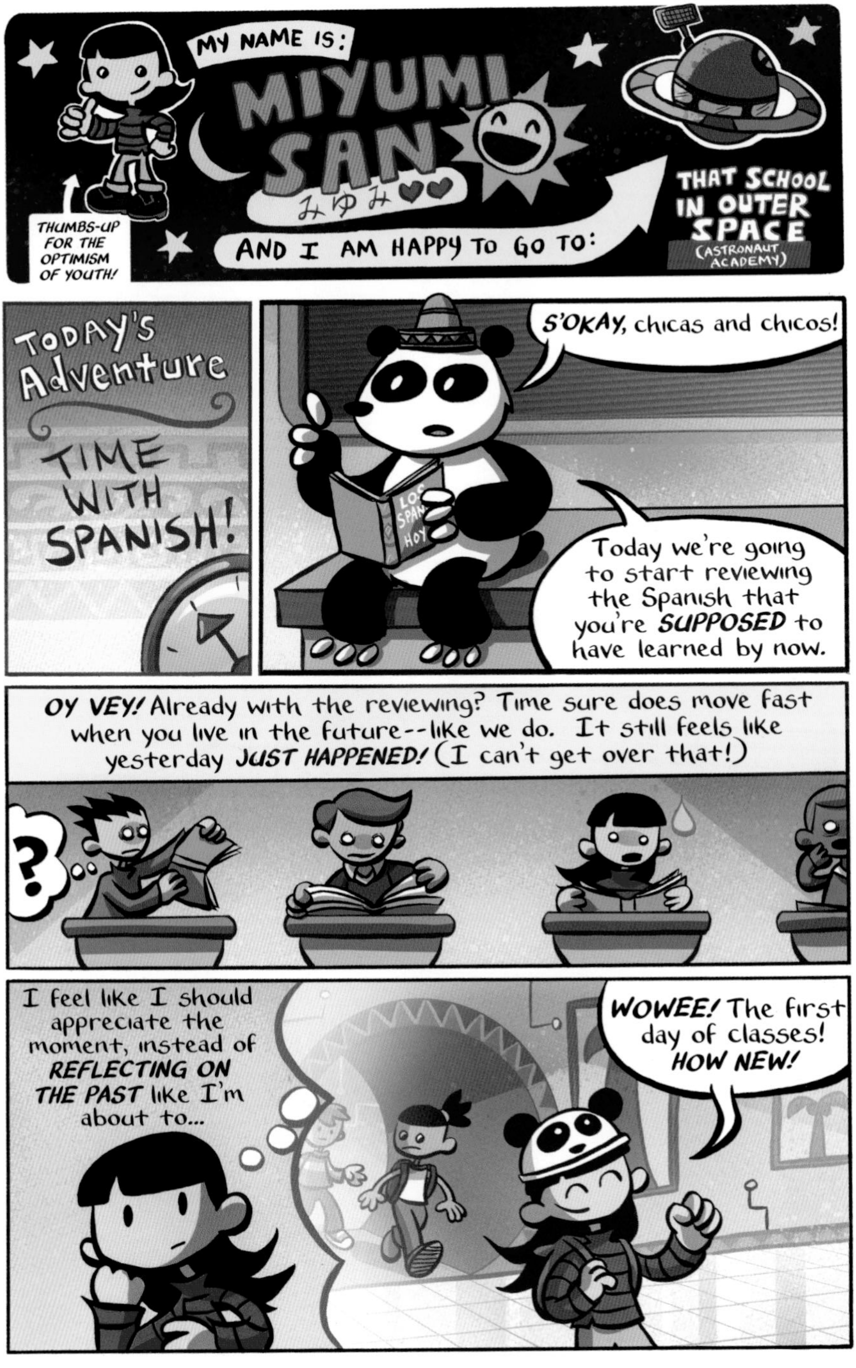
MY NAME IS:
MIYUMI SAN
みゆみ
AND I AM HAPPY TO GO TO:
THAT SCHOOL IN OUTER SPACE
(ASTRONAUT ACADEMY)
THUMBS-UP FOR THE OPTIMISM OF YOUTH!
TODAY'S Adventure
TIME WITH SPANISH!
S'OKAY, chicas and chicos!
LOS SPAN... HOY
Today we're going to start reviewing the Spanish that you're SUPPOSED to have learned by now.
OY VEY! Already with the reviewing? Time sure does move fast when you live in the future--like we do. It still feels like yesterday JUST HAPPENED! (I can't get over that!)
?
I feel like I should appreciate the moment, instead of REFLECTING ON THE PAST like I'm about to...
WOWEE! The first day of classes! HOW NEW!

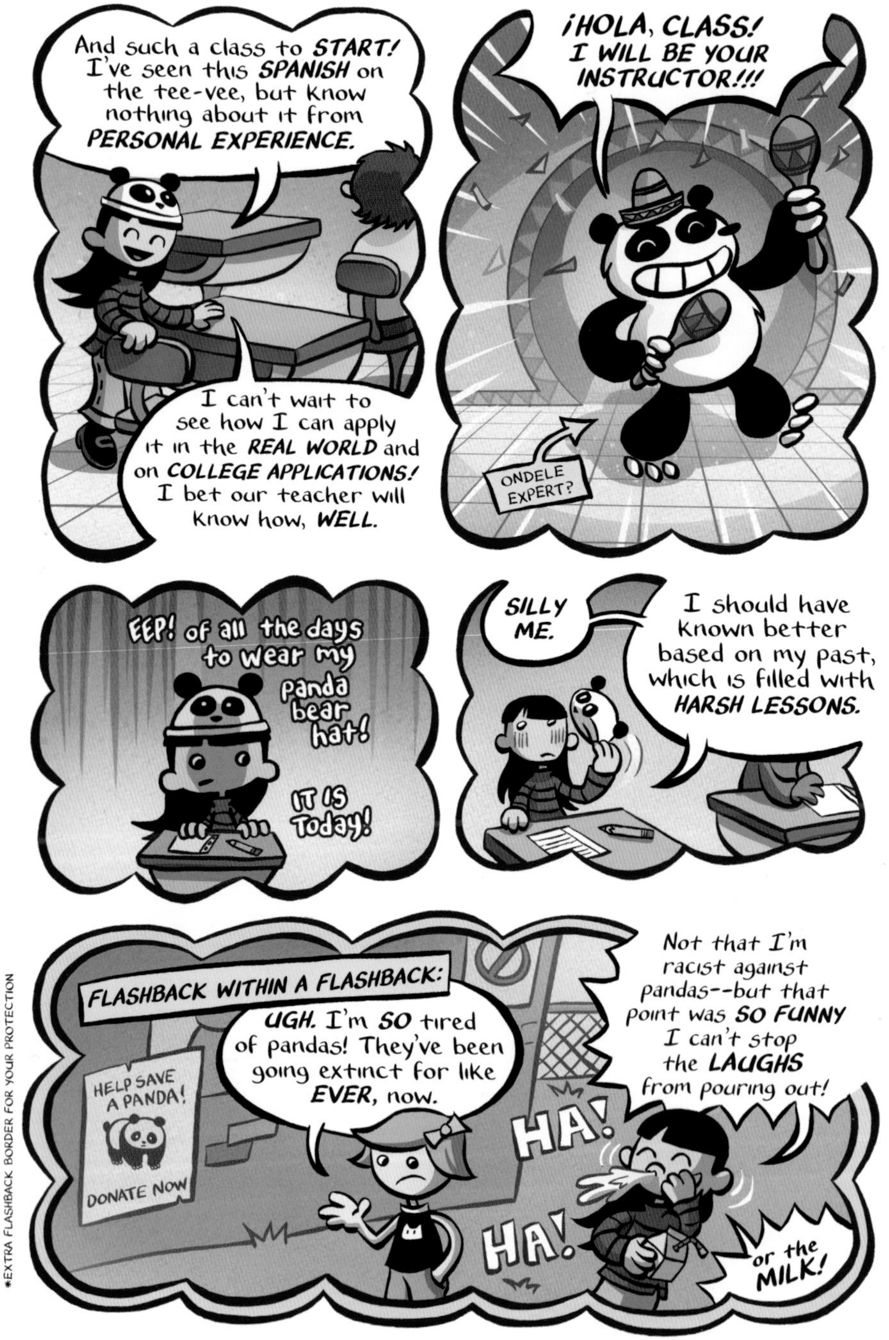
And such a class to START! I've seen this SPANISH on the tee-vee, but know nothing about it from PERSONAL EXPERIENCE.
I can't wait to see how I can apply it in the REAL WORLD and on COLLEGE APPLICATIONS! I bet our teacher will know how, WELL.
¡HOLA, CLASS! I WILL BE YOUR INSTRUCTOR!!!
ONDELE EXPERT?
EEP! of all the days to wear my panda bear hat!
IT IS Today!
SILLY ME.
I should have known better based on my past, which is filled with HARSH LESSONS.
FLASHBACK WITHIN A FLASHBACK:
HELP SAVE A PANDA!
DONATE NOW
UGH. I'm SO tired of pandas! They've been going extinct for like EVER, now.
Not that I'm racist against pandas--but that point was SO FUNNY I can't stop the LAUGHS from pouring out!
HA!
HA!
or the MILK!
*EXTRA FLASHBACK BORDER FOR YOUR PROTECTION

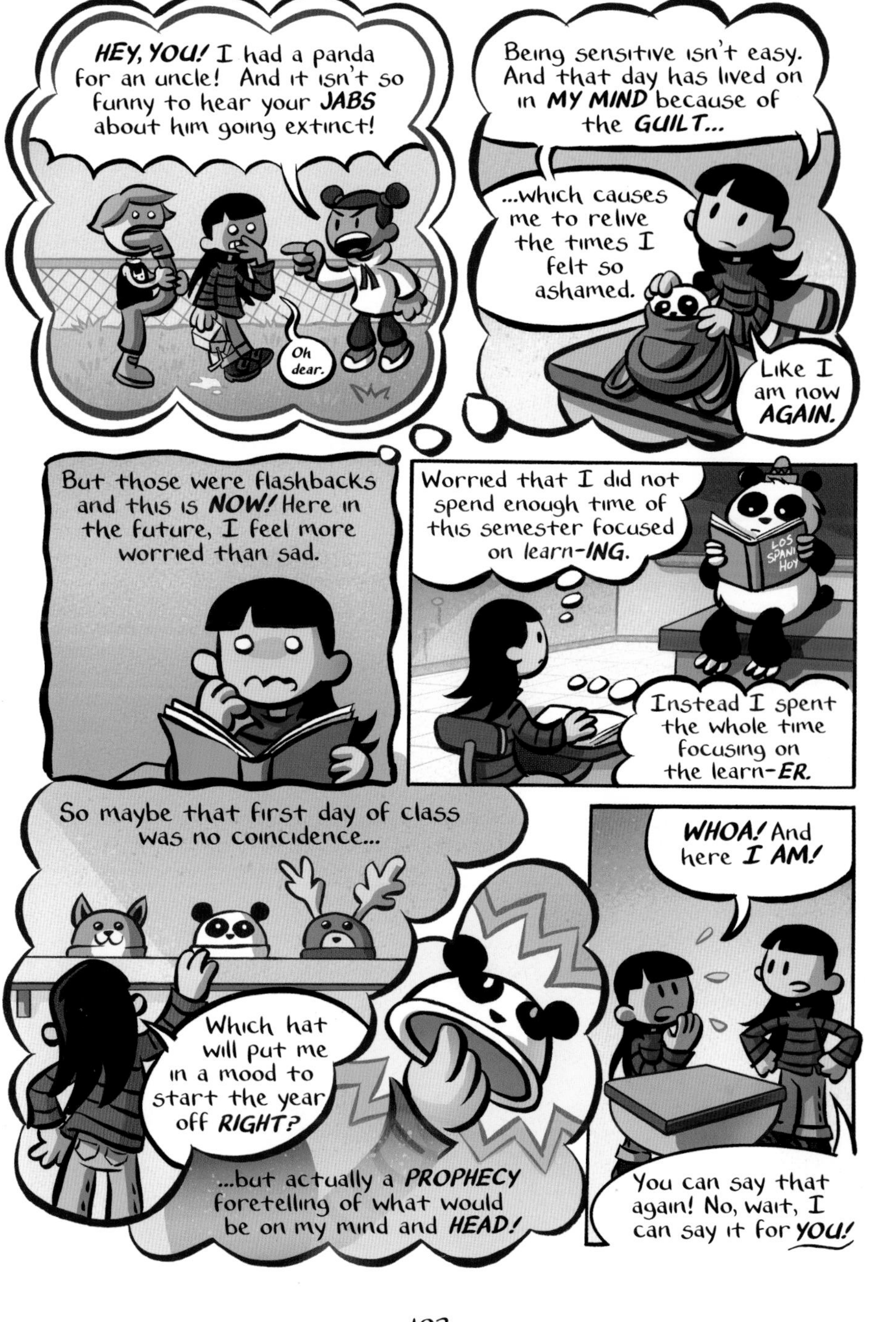

HEY, YOU! I had a panda for an uncle! And it isn't so funny to hear your JABS about him going extinct!
Oh dear.
Being sensitive isn't easy. And that day has lived on in MY MIND because of the GUILT...
...which causes me to relive the times I felt so ashamed.
Like I am now AGAIN.
But those were flashbacks and this is NOW! Here in the future, I feel more worried than sad.
Worried that I did not spend enough time of this semester focused on learn-ING.
LOS SPANI HOY
Instead I spent the whole time focusing on the learn-ER.
So maybe that first day of class was no coincidence...
Which hat will put me in a mood to start the year off RIGHT?
...but actually a PROPHECY foretelling of what would be on my mind and HEAD!
WHOA! And here I AM!
You can say that again! No, wait, I can say it for YOU!

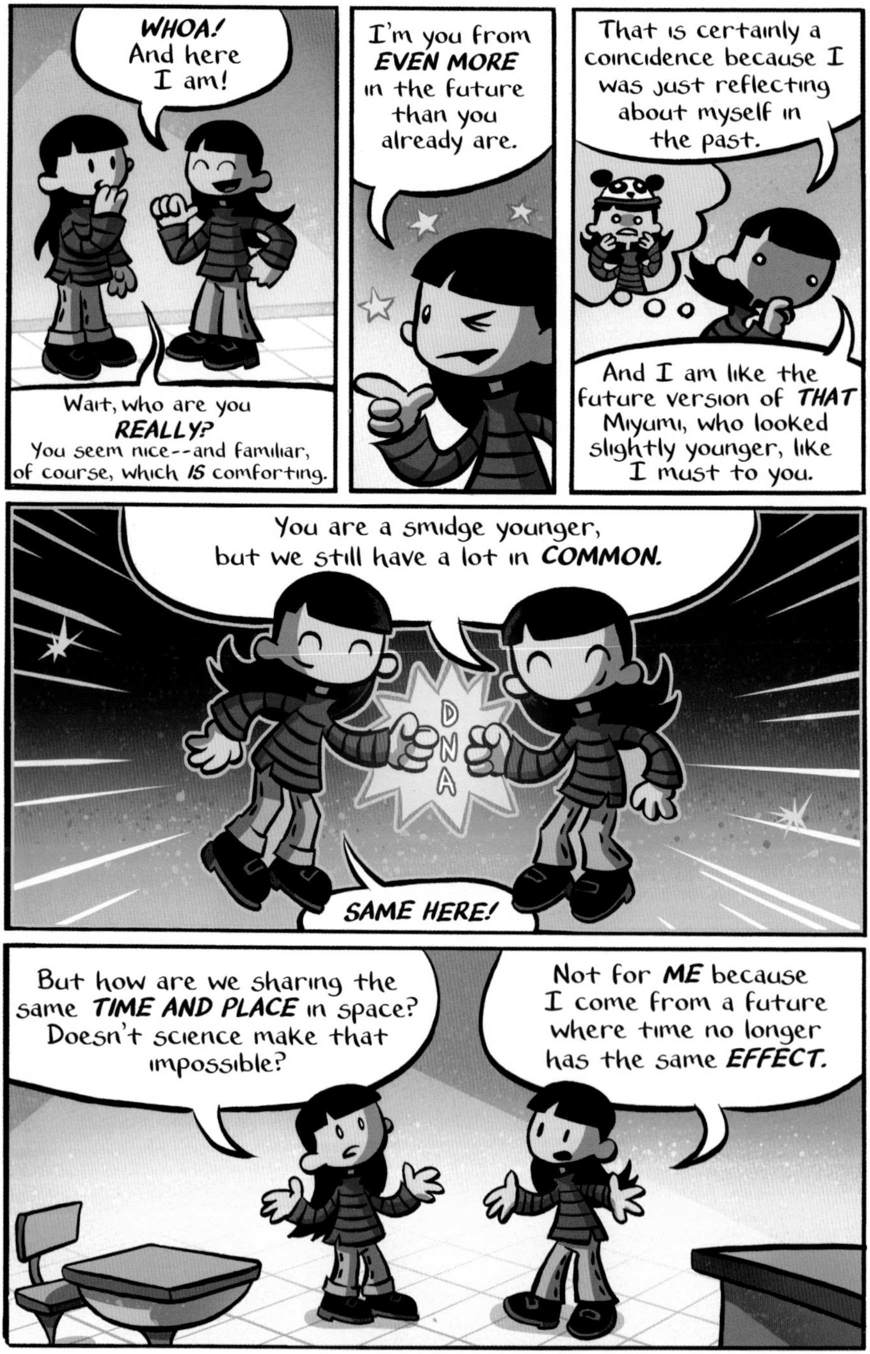
WHOA! And here I am!
Wait, who are you REALLY? You seem nice--and familiar, of course, which IS comforting.
I'm you from EVEN MORE in the future than you already are.
That is certainly a coincidence because I was just reflecting about myself in the past.
And I am like the future version of THAT Miyumi, who looked slightly younger, like I must to you.
You are a smidge younger, but we still have a lot in COMMON.
DNA
SAME HERE!
But how are we sharing the same TIME AND PLACE in space? Doesn't science make that impossible?
Not for ME because I come from a future where time no longer has the same EFFECT.

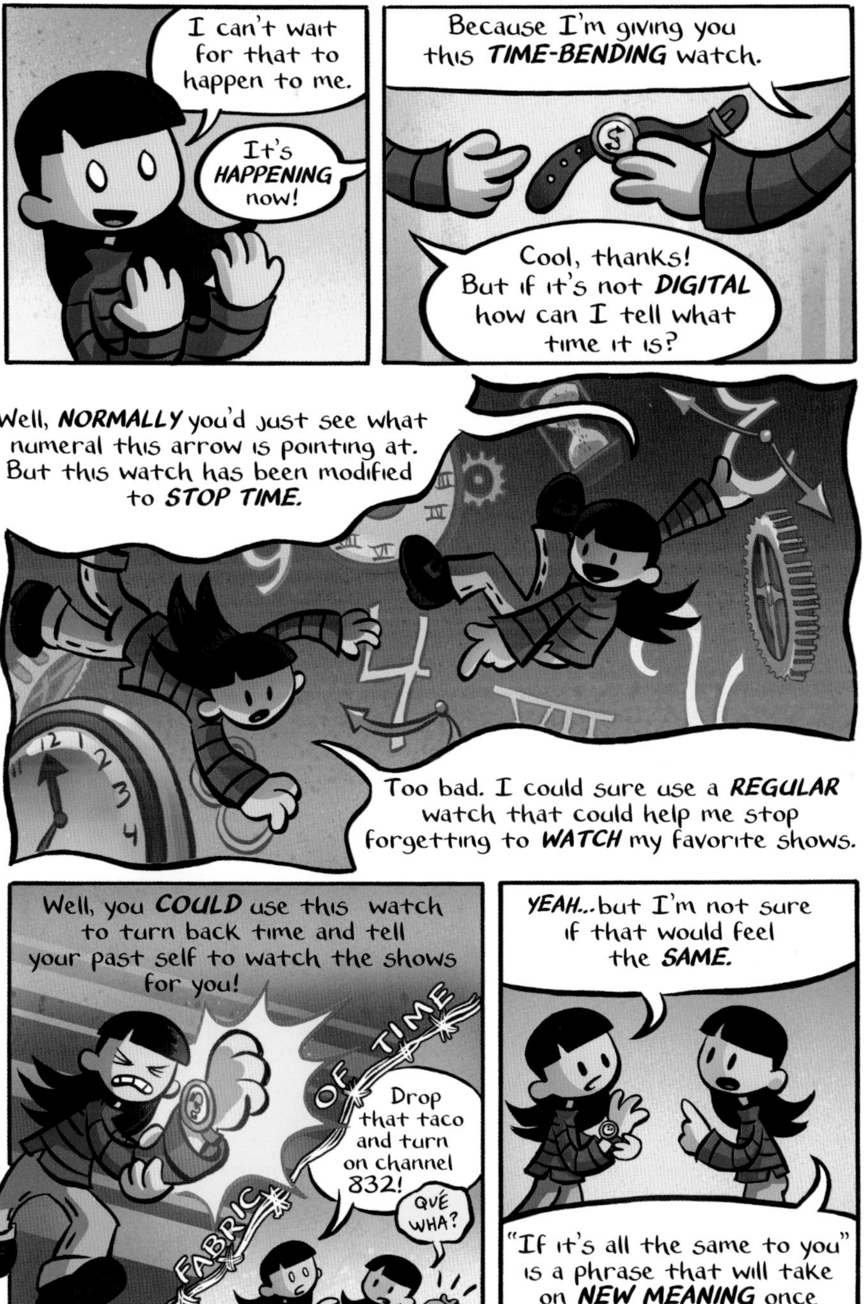
I can't wait for that to happen to me.
It's HAPPENING now!
Because I'm giving you this TIME-BENDING watch.
Cool, thanks! But if it's not DIGITAL how can I tell what time it is?
Well, NORMALLY you'd just see what numeral this arrow is pointing at. But this watch has been modified to STOP TIME.
Too bad. I could sure use a REGULAR watch that could help me stop forgetting to WATCH my favorite shows.
Well, you COULD use this watch to turn back time and tell your past self to watch the shows for you!
FABRIC OF TIME
Drop that taco and turn on channel 832!
QUÉ WHA?
YEAH... but I'm not sure if that would feel the SAME.
"If it's all the same to you" is a phrase that will take on NEW MEANING once you catch up with me.

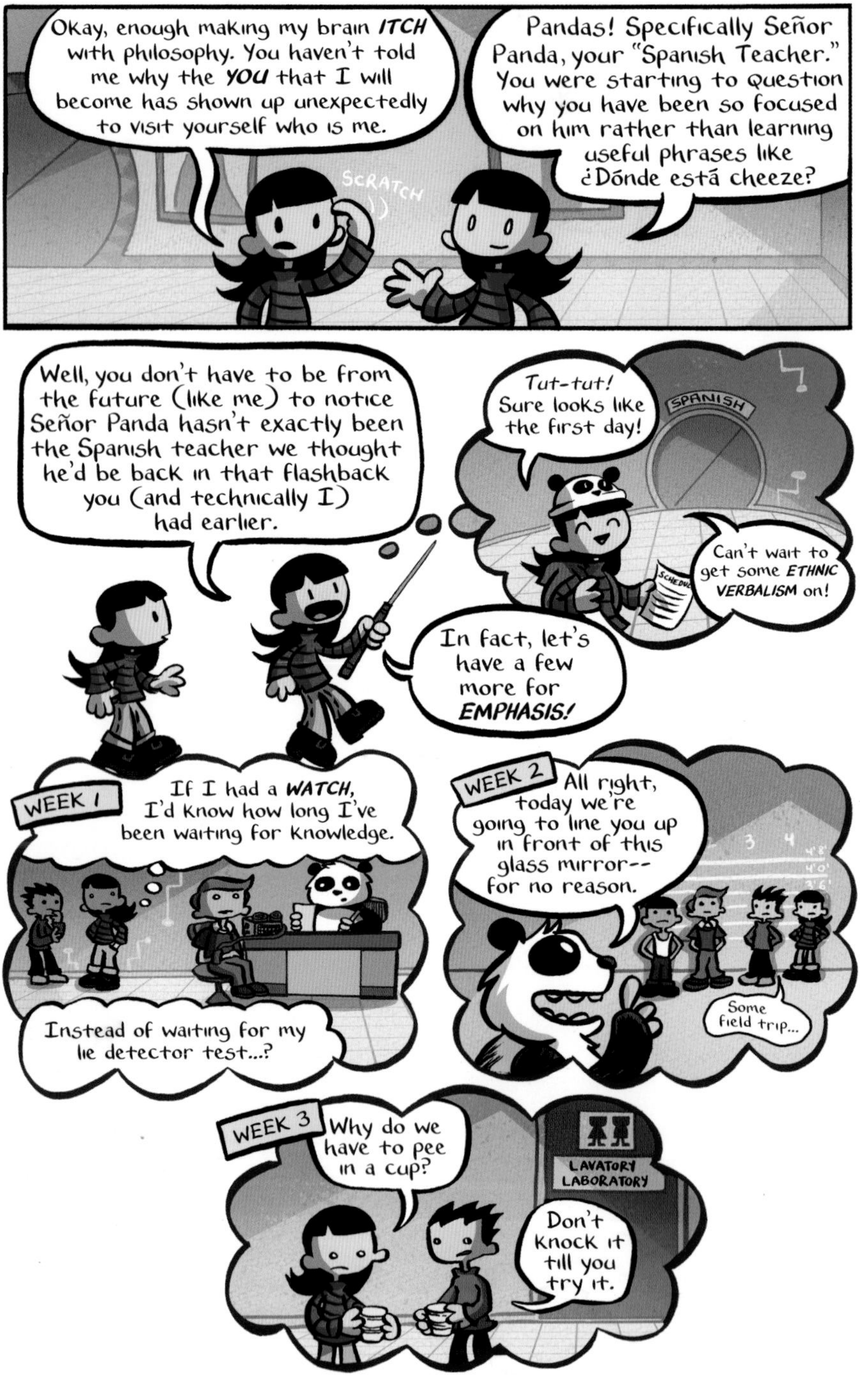
Okay, enough making my brain ITCH with philosophy. You haven't told me why the YOU that I will become has shown up unexpectedly to visit yourself who is me.
SCRATCH
Pandas! Specifically Señor Panda, your "Spanish Teacher." You were starting to question why you have been so focused on him rather than learning useful phrases like ¿Dónde está cheeze?
Well, you don't have to be from the future (like me) to notice Señor Panda hasn't exactly been the Spanish teacher we thought he'd be back in that flashback you (and technically I) had earlier.
SPANISH
Tut-tut! Sure looks like the first day!
Can't wait to get some ETHNIC VERBALISM on!
In fact, let's have a few more for EMPHASIS!
WEEK 1
If I had a WATCH, I'd know how long I've been waiting for knowledge.
Instead of waiting for my lie detector test...?
WEEK 2
All right, today we're going to line you up in front of this glass mirror--for no reason.
Some field trip...
WEEK 3
Why do we have to pee in a cup?
LAVATORY LABORATORY
Don't knock it till you try it.

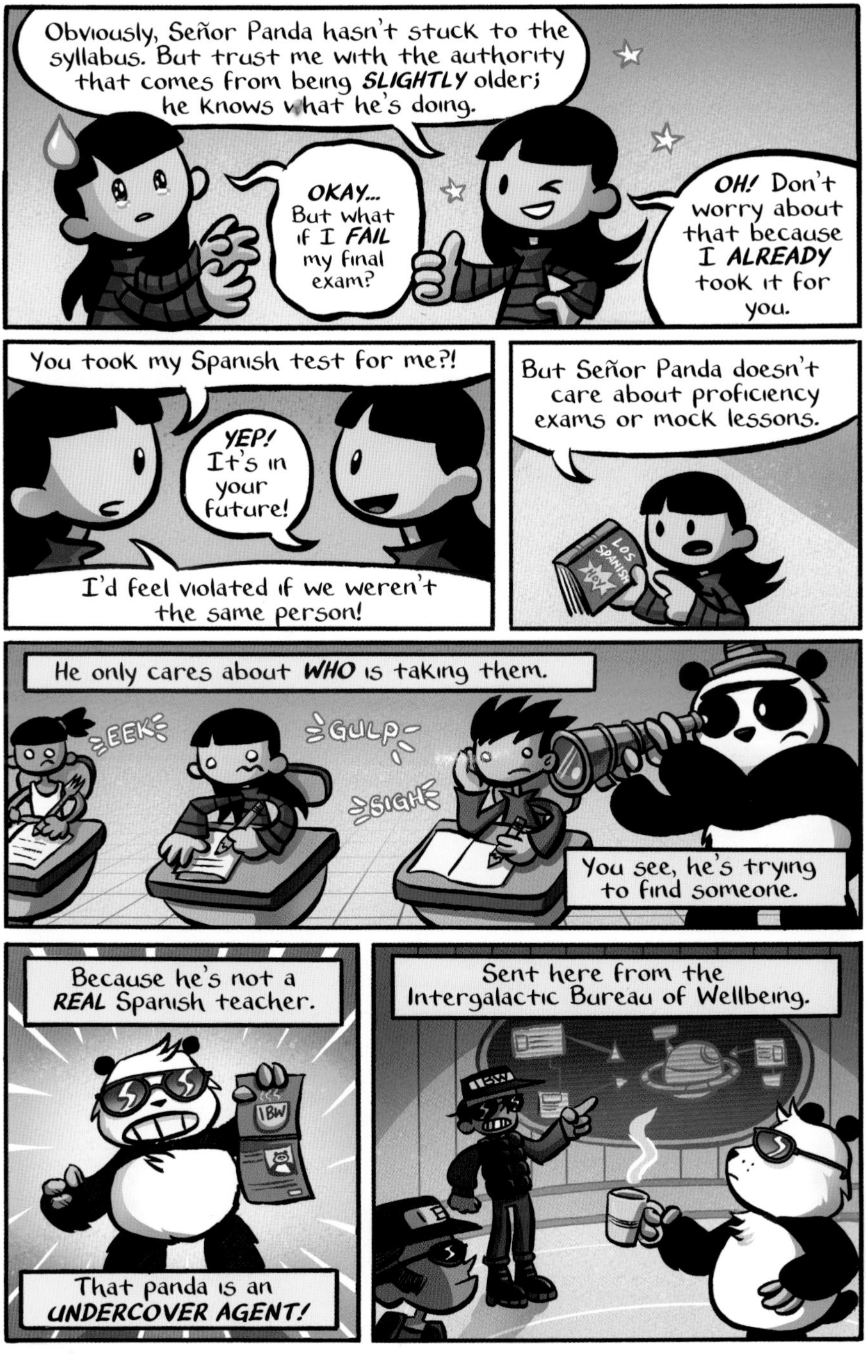

Obviously, Señor Panda hasn't stuck to the syllabus. But trust me with the authority that comes from being SLIGHTLY older; he knows what he's doing.
OKAY... But what if I FAIL my final exam?
OH! Don't worry about that because I ALREADY took it for you.
You took my Spanish test for me?!
YEP! It's in your future!
I'd feel violated if we weren't the same person!
But Señor Panda doesn't care about proficiency exams or mock lessons.
LOS SPANISH
He only cares about WHO is taking them.
EEK
GULP
SIGH
You see, he's trying to find someone.
Because he's not a REAL Spanish teacher.
IBW
That panda is an UNDERCOVER AGENT!
Sent here from the Intergalactic Bureau of Wellbeing.
IBW

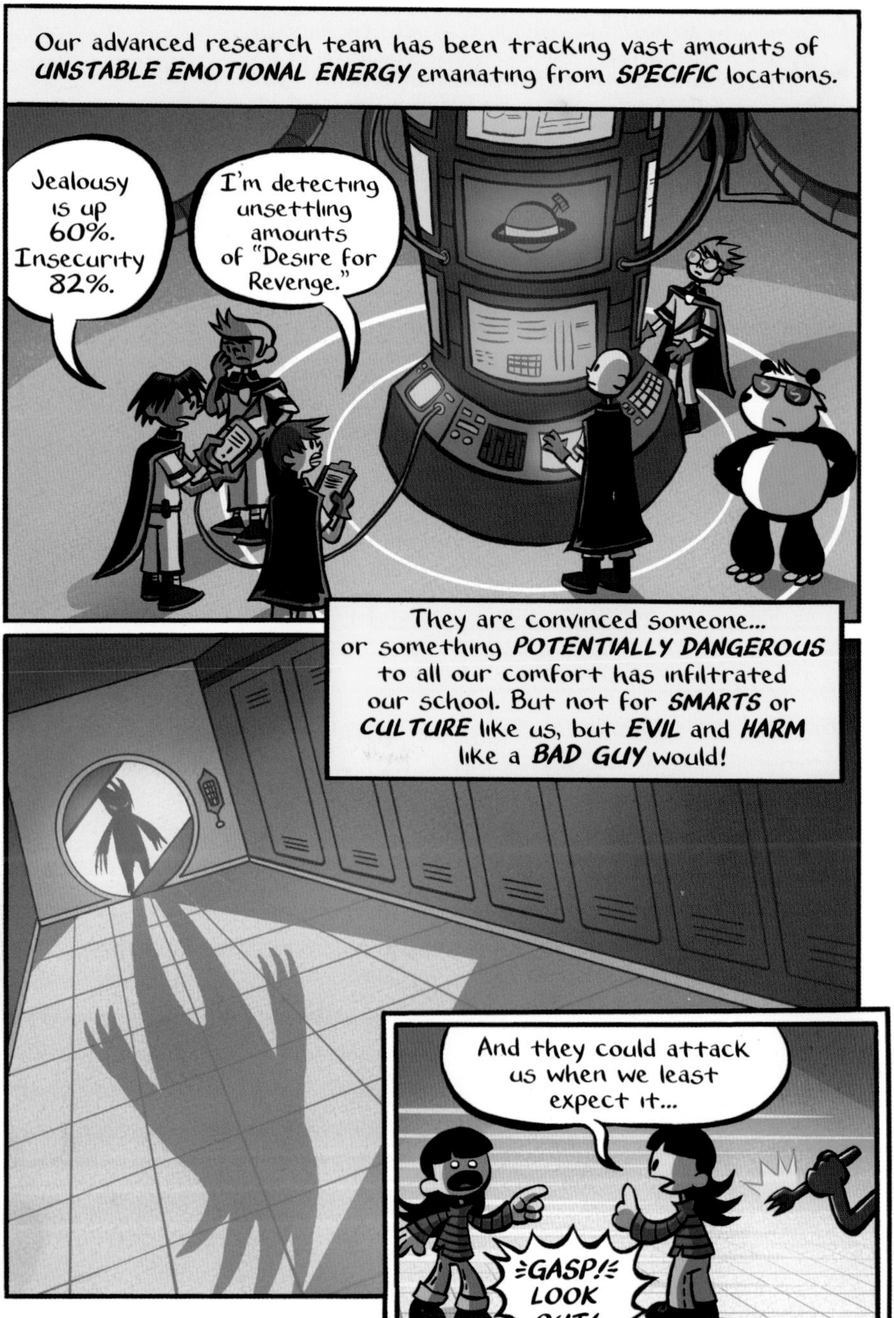

Our advanced research team has been tracking vast amounts of UNSTABLE EMOTIONAL ENERGY emanating from SPECIFIC locations.
Jealousy is up 60%. Insecurity 82%.
I'm detecting unsettling amounts of "Desire for Revenge."
They are convinced someone... or something POTENTIALLY DANGEROUS to all our comfort has infiltrated our school. But not for SMARTS or CULTURE like us, but EVIL and HARM like a BAD GUY would!
And they could attack us when we least expect it...
GASP! LOOK OUT!

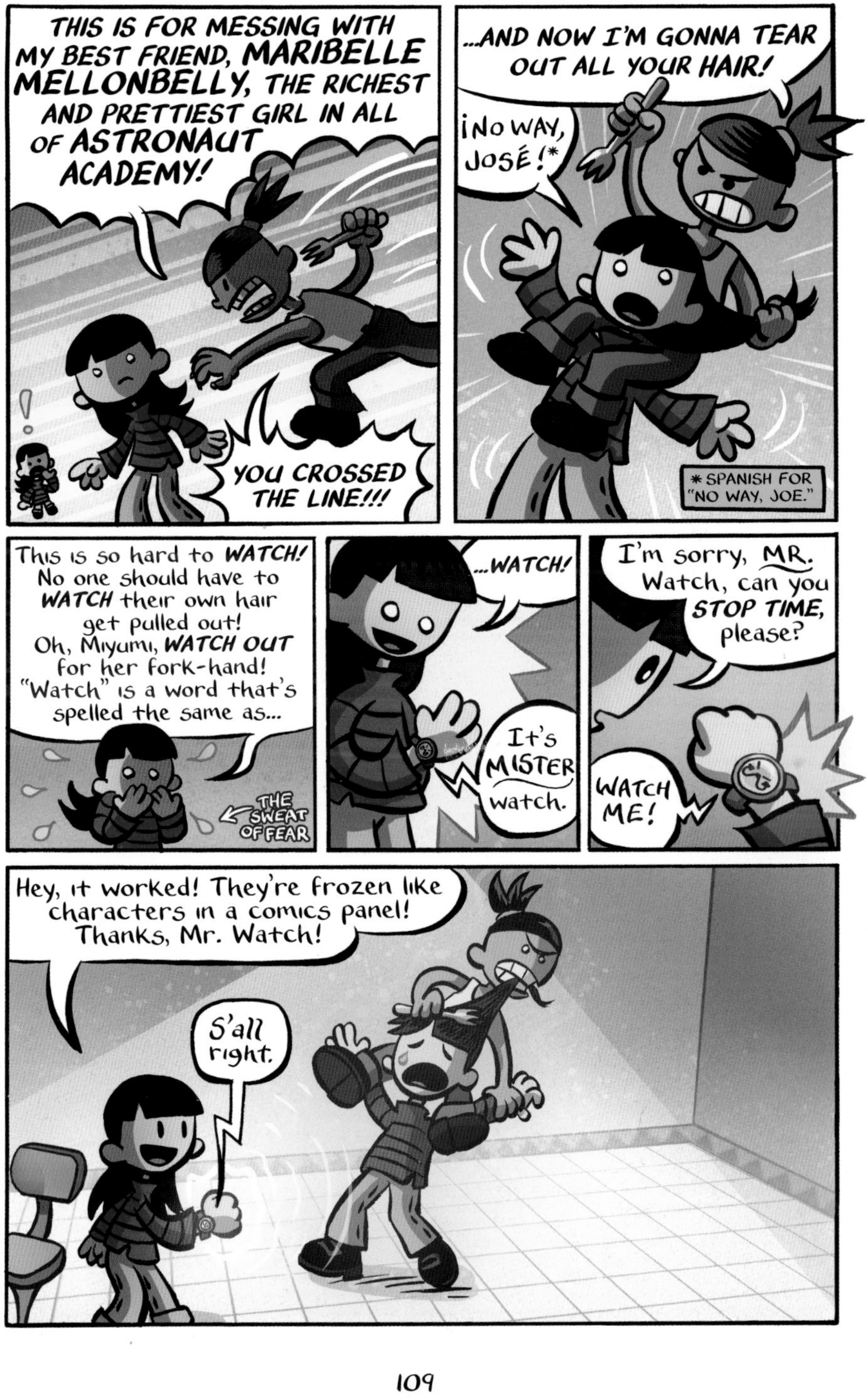
THIS IS FOR MESSING WITH MY BEST FRIEND, MARIBELLE MELLONBELLY, THE RICHEST AND PRETTIEST GIRL IN ALL OF ASTRONAUT ACADEMY!
!
YOU CROSSED THE LINE!!!
...AND NOW I'M GONNA TEAR OUT ALL YOUR HAIR!
¡NO WAY, JOSÉ!*
*SPANISH FOR "NO WAY, JOE."
This is so hard to WATCH! No one should have to WATCH their own hair get pulled out! Oh, Miyumi, WATCH OUT for her fork-hand! "Watch" is a word that's spelled the same as...
THE SWEAT OF FEAR
...WATCH!
It's MISTER watch.
I'm sorry, MR. Watch, can you STOP TIME, please?
WATCH ME!
Hey, it worked! They're frozen like characters in a comics panel! Thanks, Mr. Watch!
S'all right.

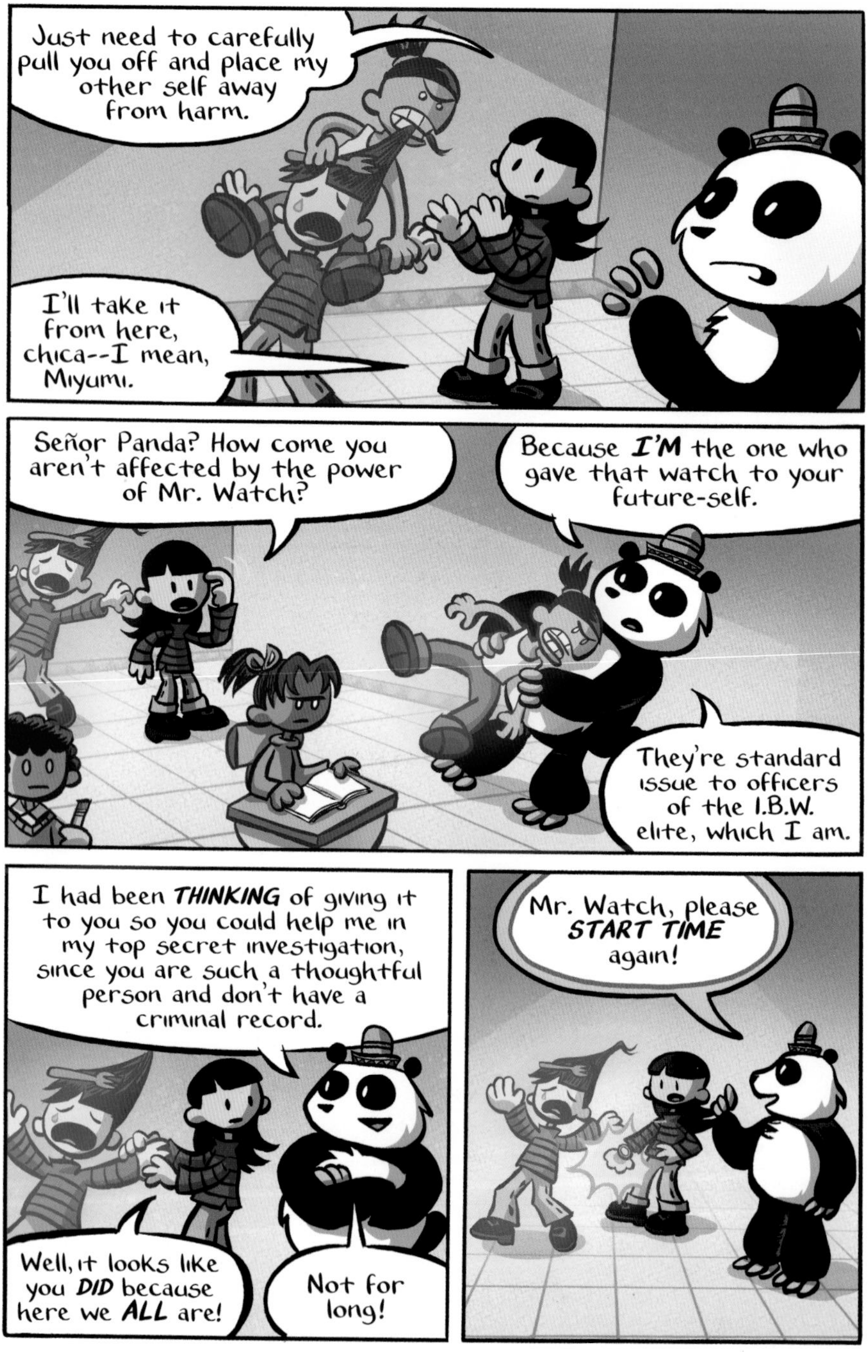

Just need to carefully pull you off and place my other self away from harm.
I'll take it from here, chica--I mean, Miyumi.
Señor Panda? How come you aren't affected by the power of Mr. Watch?
Because I'M the one who gave that watch to your future-self.
They're standard issue to officers of the I.B.W. elite, which I am.
I had been THINKING of giving it to you so you could help me in my top secret investigation, since you are such a thoughtful person and don't have a criminal record.
Well, it looks like you DID because here we ALL are!
Not for long!
Mr. Watch, please START TIME again!

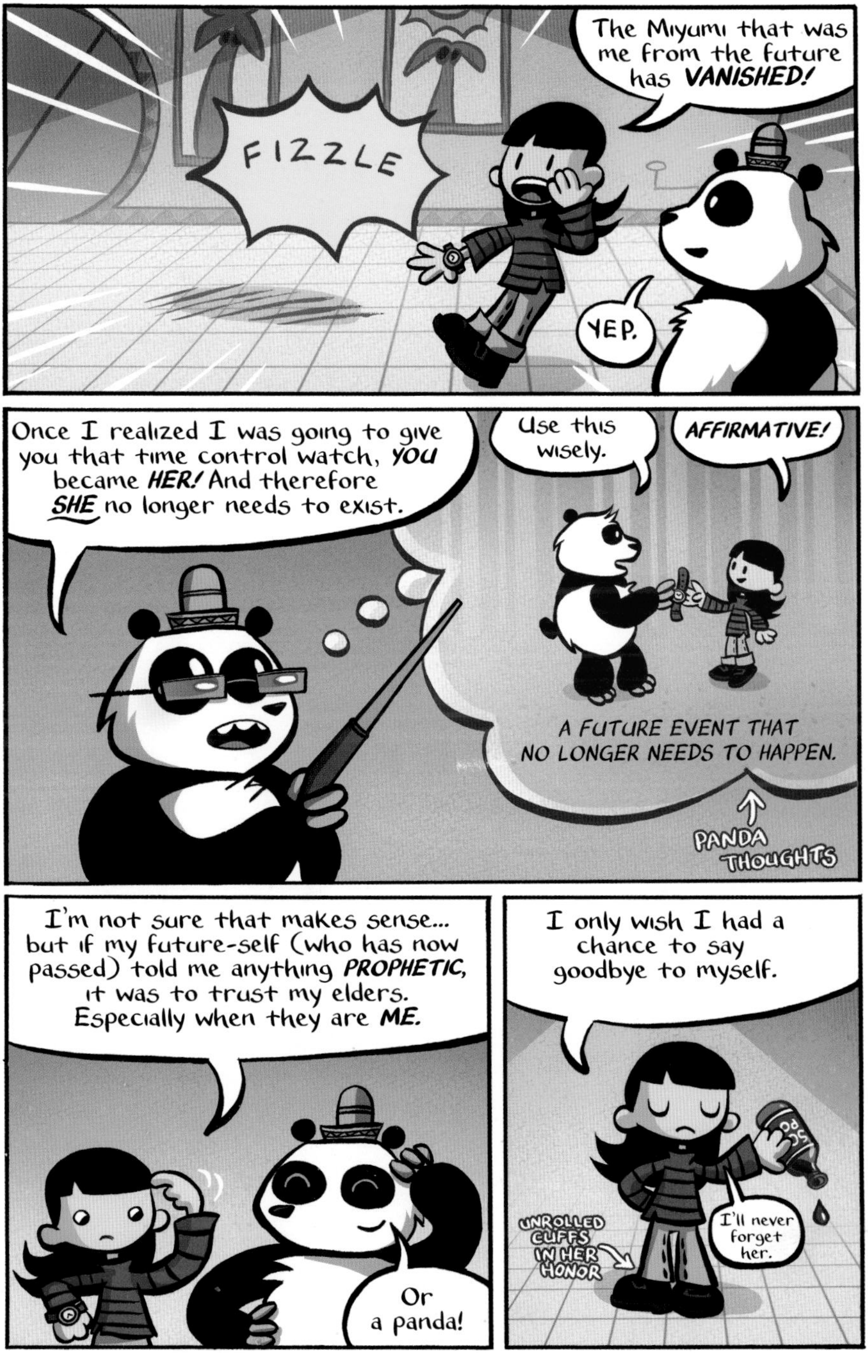
FIZZLE
The Miyumi that was me from the future has VANISHED!
YEP.
Once I realized I was going to give you that time control watch, YOU became HER! And therefore SHE no longer needs to exist.
Use this wisely.
AFFIRMATIVE!
A FUTURE EVENT THAT NO LONGER NEEDS TO HAPPEN.
PANDA THOUGHTS
I'm not sure that makes sense... but if my future-self (who has now passed) told me anything PROPHETIC, it was to trust my elders. Especially when they are ME.
Or a panda!
I only wish I had a chance to say goodbye to myself.
UNROLLED CUFFS IN HER HONOR
I'll never forget her.

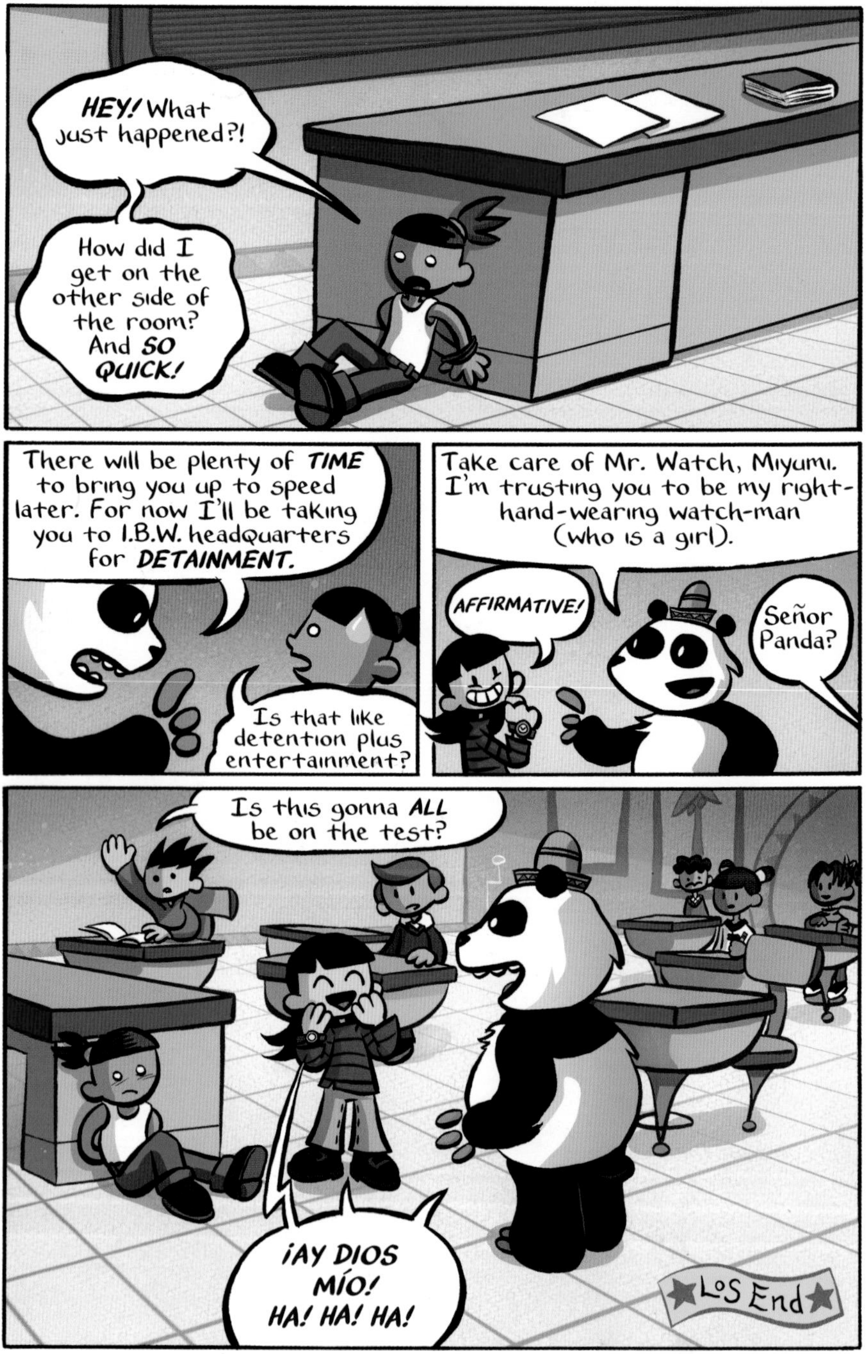
HEY! What just happened?!
How did I get on the other side of the room? And SO QUICK!
There will be plenty of TIME to bring you up to speed later. For now I'll be taking you to I.B.W. headquarters for DETAINMENT.
Is that like detention plus entertainment?
Take care of Mr. Watch, Miyumi. I'm trusting you to be my right-hand-wearing watch-man (who is a girl).
AFFIRMATIVE!
Señor Panda?
Is this gonna ALL be on the test?
¡AY DIOS MÍO! HA! HA! HA!
Los End

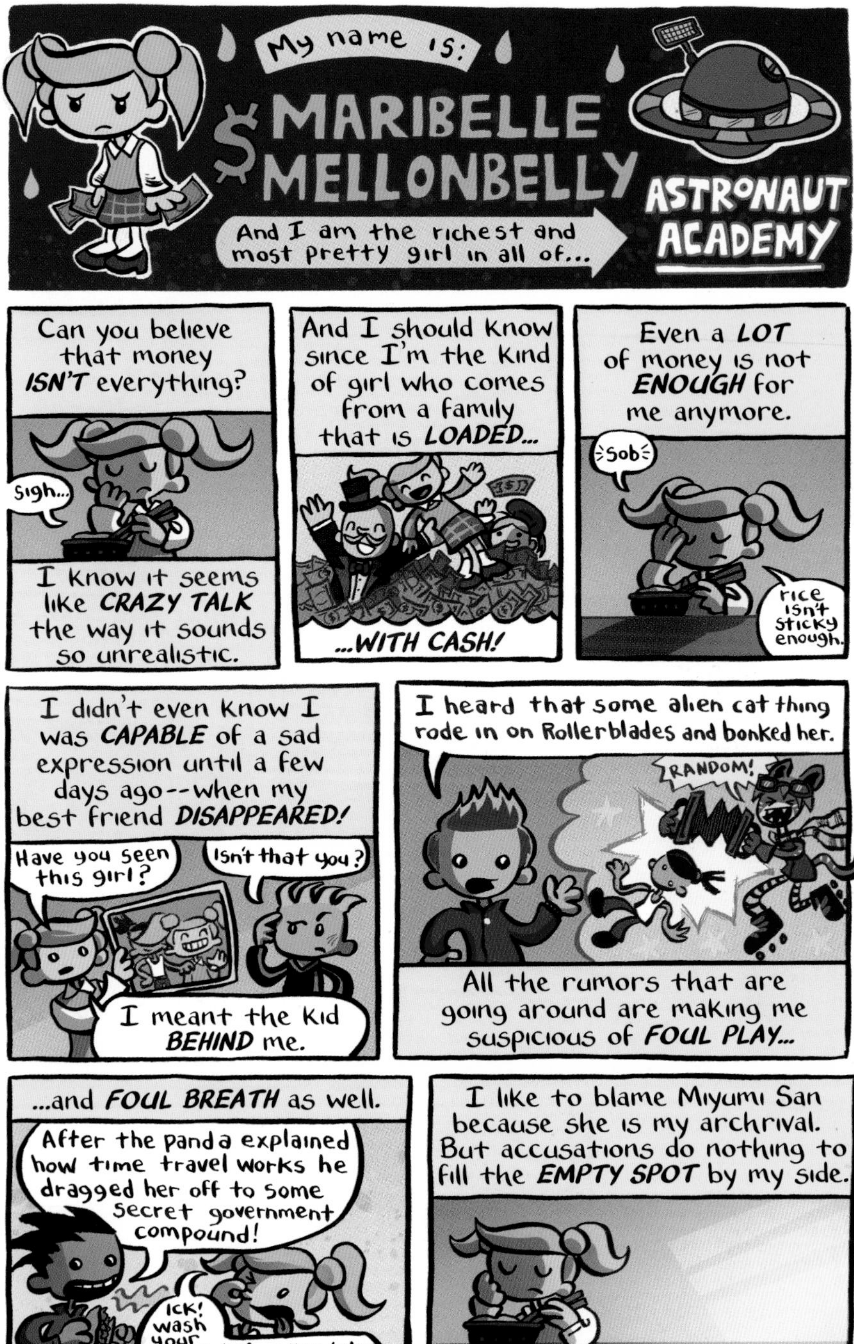

My name is:
$ MARIBELLE MELLONBELLY
And I am the richest and most pretty girl in all of...
ASTRONAUT ACADEMY
Can you believe that money ISN'T everything?
Sigh...
I know it seems like CRAZY TALK the way it sounds so unrealistic.
And I should know since I'm the kind of girl who comes from a family that is LOADED...
...WITH CASH!
Even a LOT of money is not ENOUGH for me anymore.
Sob
rice isn't sticky enough.
I didn't even know I was CAPABLE of a sad expression until a few days ago--when my best friend DISAPPEARED!
Have you seen this girl?
Isn't that you?
I meant the kid BEHIND me.
I heard that some alien cat thing rode in on Rollerblades and bonked her.
RANDOM!
All the rumors that are going around are making me suspicious of FOUL PLAY...
...and FOUL BREATH as well.
After the panda explained how time travel works he dragged her off to some secret government compound!
ICK! wash your mouth before you talk!
I like to blame Miyumi San because she is my archrival. But accusations do nothing to fill the EMPTY SPOT by my side.

The end

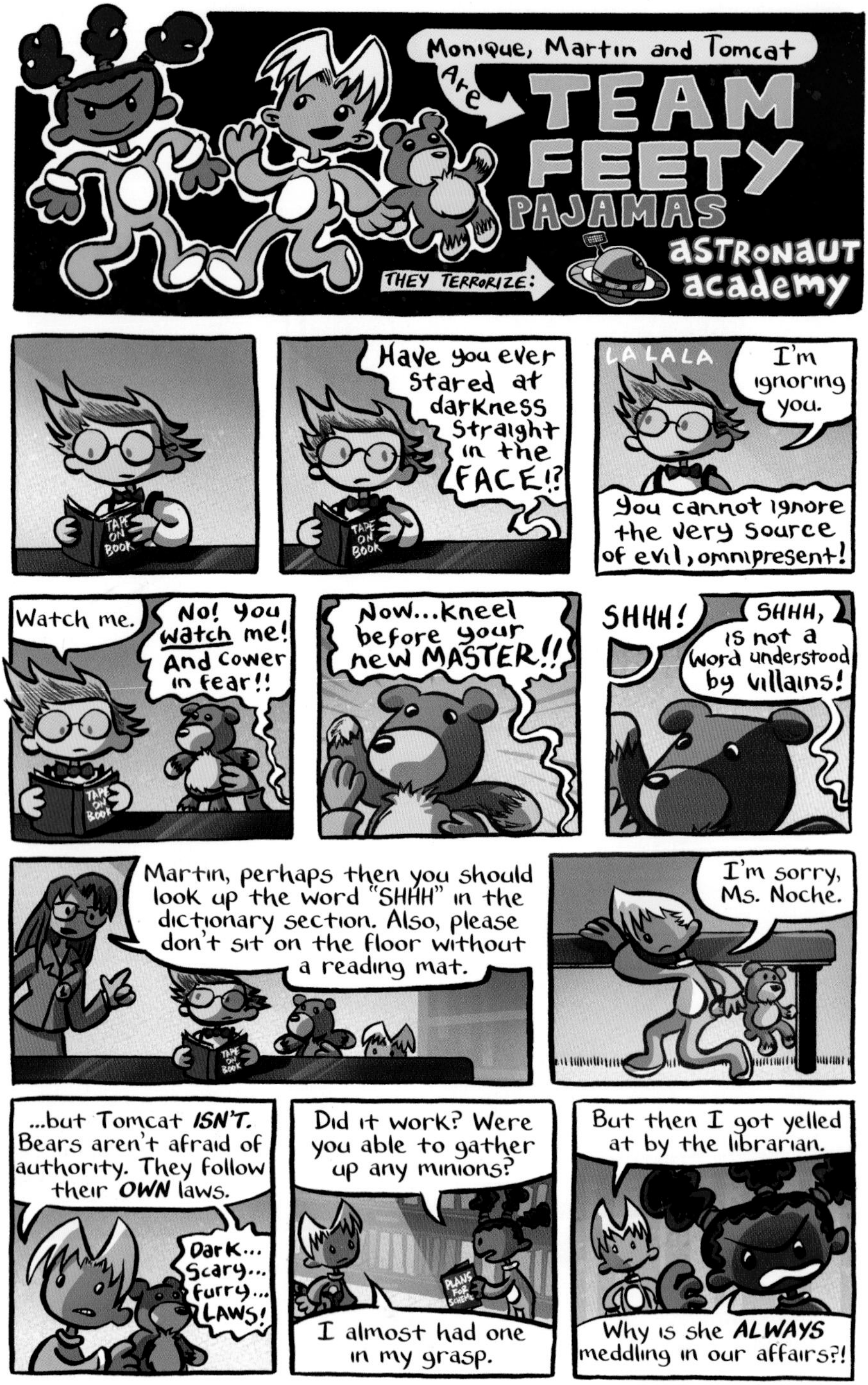

Monique, Martin and Tomcat
Are
TEAM FEETY PAJAMAS
THEY TERRORIZE:
astronaut academy
Have you ever stared at darkness straight in the FACE!?
LA LA LA
I'm ignoring you.
You cannot ignore the very source of evil, omnipresent!
TAPE ON BOOK
Watch me.
No! You watch me! And cower in fear!!
Now...kneel before your new MASTER!!
SHHH!
SHHH, is not a word understood by villains!
Martin, perhaps then you should look up the word "SHHH" in the dictionary section. Also, please don't sit on the floor without a reading mat.
I'm sorry, Ms. Noche.
...but Tomcat ISN'T. Bears aren't afraid of authority. They follow their OWN laws.
Dark... Scary... furry... LAWS!
Did it work? Were you able to gather up any minions?
PLANS FOR SCHEME
I almost had one in my grasp.
But then I got yelled at by the librarian.
Why is she ALWAYS meddling in our affairs?!

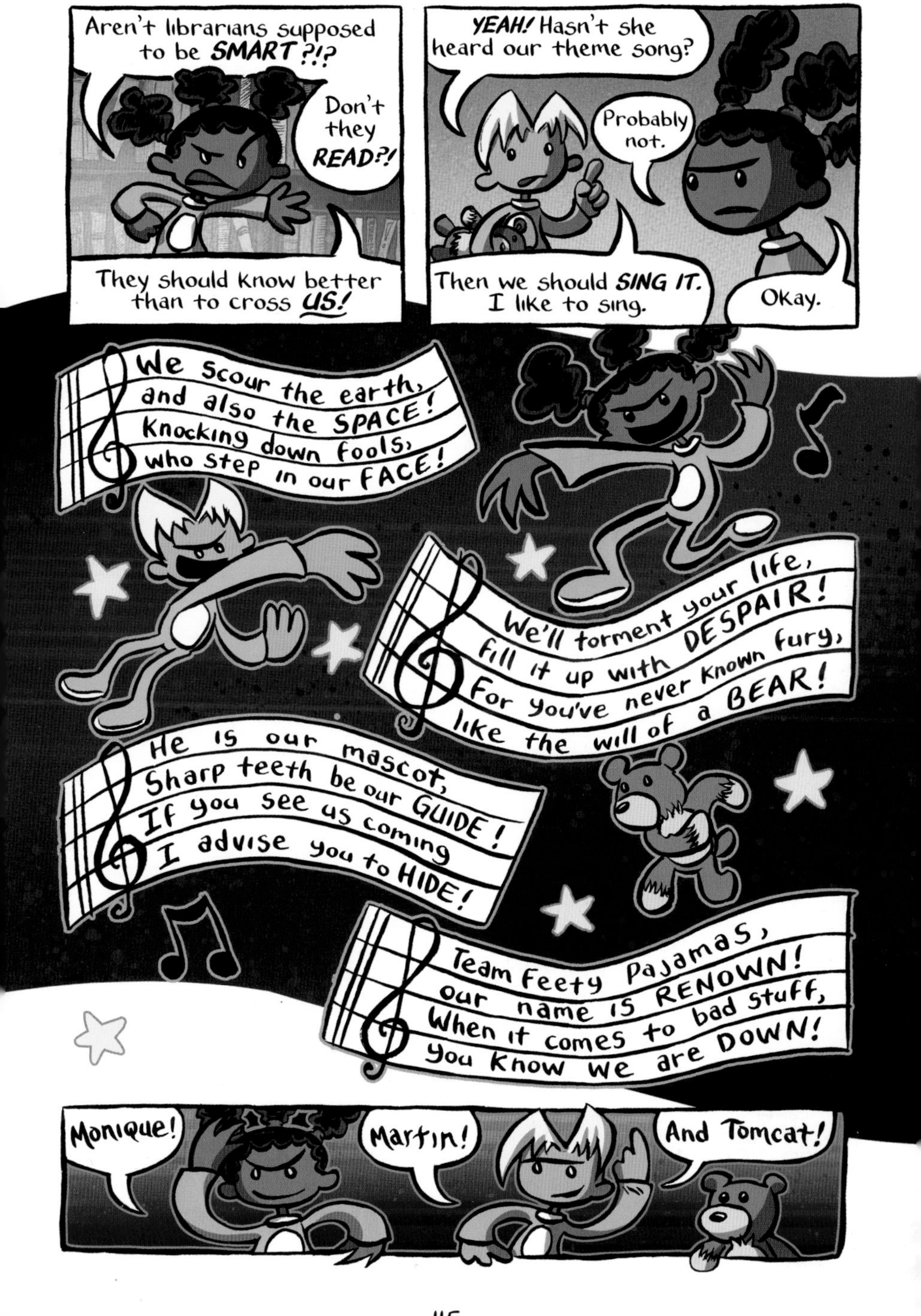

Aren't librarians supposed to be SMART?!?
Don't they READ?!
They should know better than to cross US!
YEAH! Hasn't she heard our theme song?
Probably not.
Then we should SING IT. I like to sing.
Okay.
We scour the earth, and also the SPACE! Knocking down fools, who step in our FACE!
We'll torment your life, fill it up with DESPAIR! For you've never known fury, like the will of a BEAR!
He is our mascot, Sharp teeth be our GUIDE! If you see us coming I advise you to HIDE!
Team Feety Pajamas, our name is RENOWN! When it comes to bad stuff, you know we are DOWN!
Monique!
Martin!
And Tomcat!

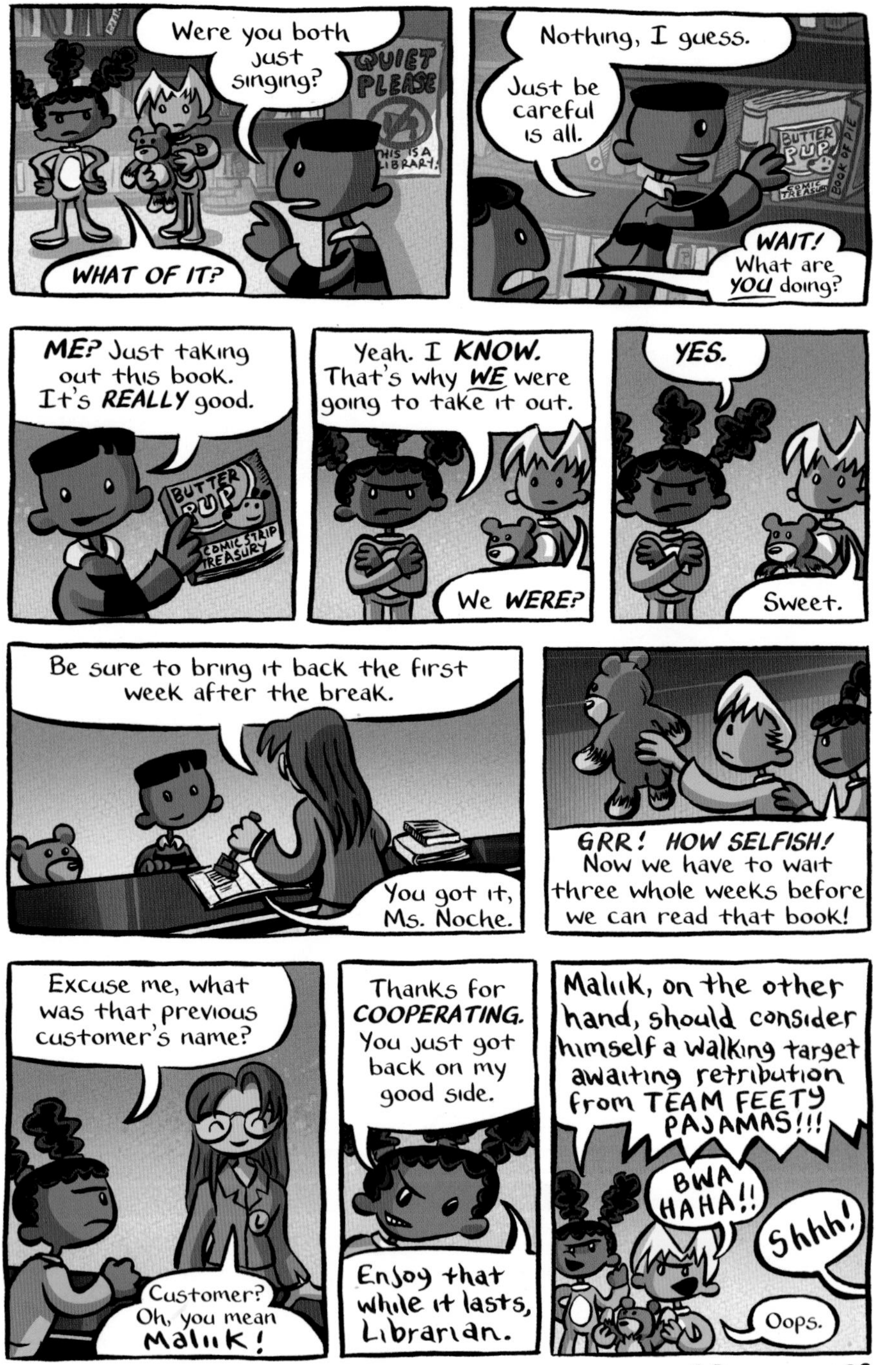
Were you both just singing?
QUIET PLEASE
THIS IS A LIBRARY!
WHAT OF IT?
Nothing, I guess.
Just be careful is all.
BUTTER PUP
COMIC TREASURY
BOOK OF PIE
WAIT! What are YOU doing?
ME? Just taking out this book. It's REALLY good.
BUTTER PUP
COMIC STRIP TREASURY
Yeah. I KNOW. That's why WE were going to take it out.
We WERE?
YES.
Sweet.
Be sure to bring it back the first week after the break.
You got it, Ms. Noche.
GRR! HOW SELFISH! Now we have to wait three whole weeks before we can read that book!
Excuse me, what was that previous customer's name?
Customer? Oh, you mean Maliik!
Thanks for COOPERATING. You just got back on my good side.
Enjoy that while it lasts, Librarian.
Maliik, on the other hand, should consider himself a walking target awaiting retribution from TEAM FEETY PAJAMAS!!!
BWA HAHA!!
Shhh!
Oops.
The end??

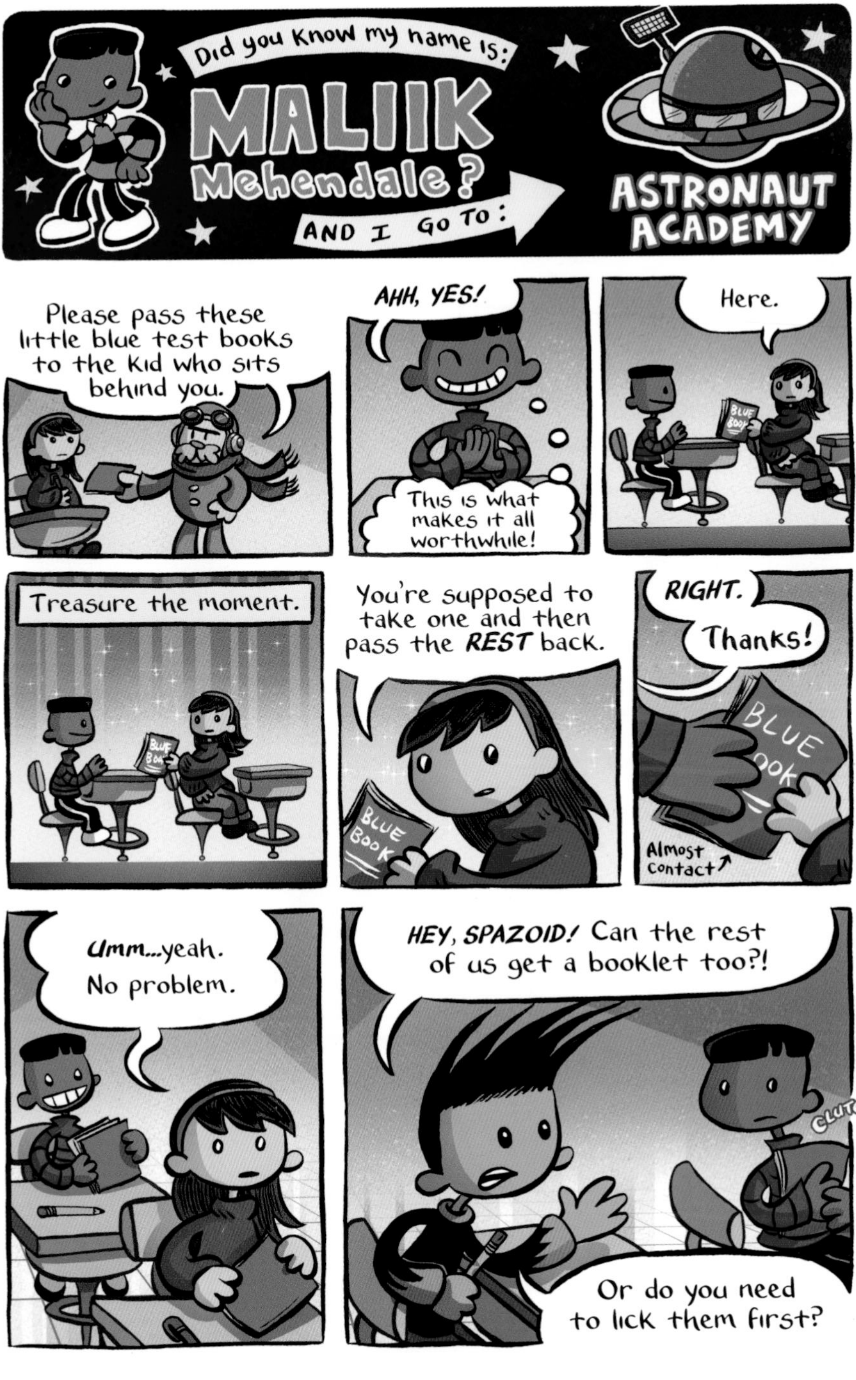
Did you know my name is:
MALIIK Mehendale?
AND I GO TO:
ASTRONAUT ACADEMY
Please pass these little blue test books to the kid who sits behind you.
AHH, YES!
This is what makes it all worthwhile!
Here.
BLUE BOOK
Treasure the moment.
BLUE BOOK
You're supposed to take one and then pass the REST back.
BLUE BOOK
RIGHT.
Thanks!
BLUE BOOK
Almost contact
Umm...yeah. No problem.
HEY, SPAZOID! Can the rest of us get a booklet too?!
CLUTCH
Or do you need to lick them first?

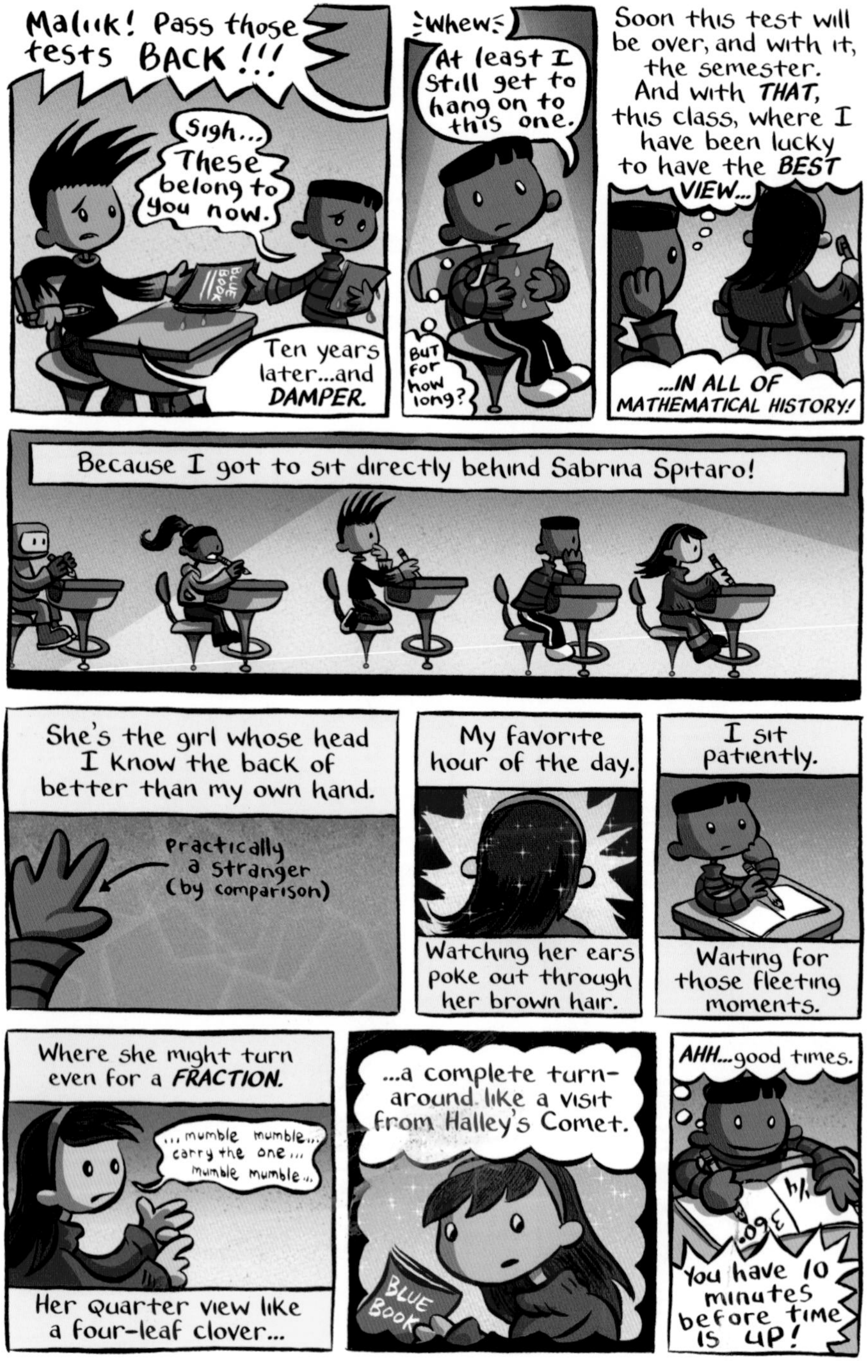
Maliik! Pass those tests BACK!!!
Sigh... These belong to you now.
BLUE BOOK
Ten years later...and DAMPER.
Whew
At least I still get to hang on to this one.
BUT for how long?
Soon this test will be over, and with it, the semester. And with THAT, this class, where I have been lucky to have the BEST VIEW...
...IN ALL OF MATHEMATICAL HISTORY!
Because I got to sit directly behind Sabrina Spitaro!
She's the girl whose head I know the back of better than my own hand.
Practically a stranger (by comparison)
My favorite hour of the day.
Watching her ears poke out through her brown hair.
I sit patiently.
Waiting for those fleeting moments.
Where she might turn even for a FRACTION.
...mumble mumble... carry the one... mumble mumble...
Her quarter view like a four-leaf clover...
...a complete turn-around like a visit from Halley's Comet.
BLUE BOOK
AHH...good times.
1/4
360°
You have 10 minutes before time is up!

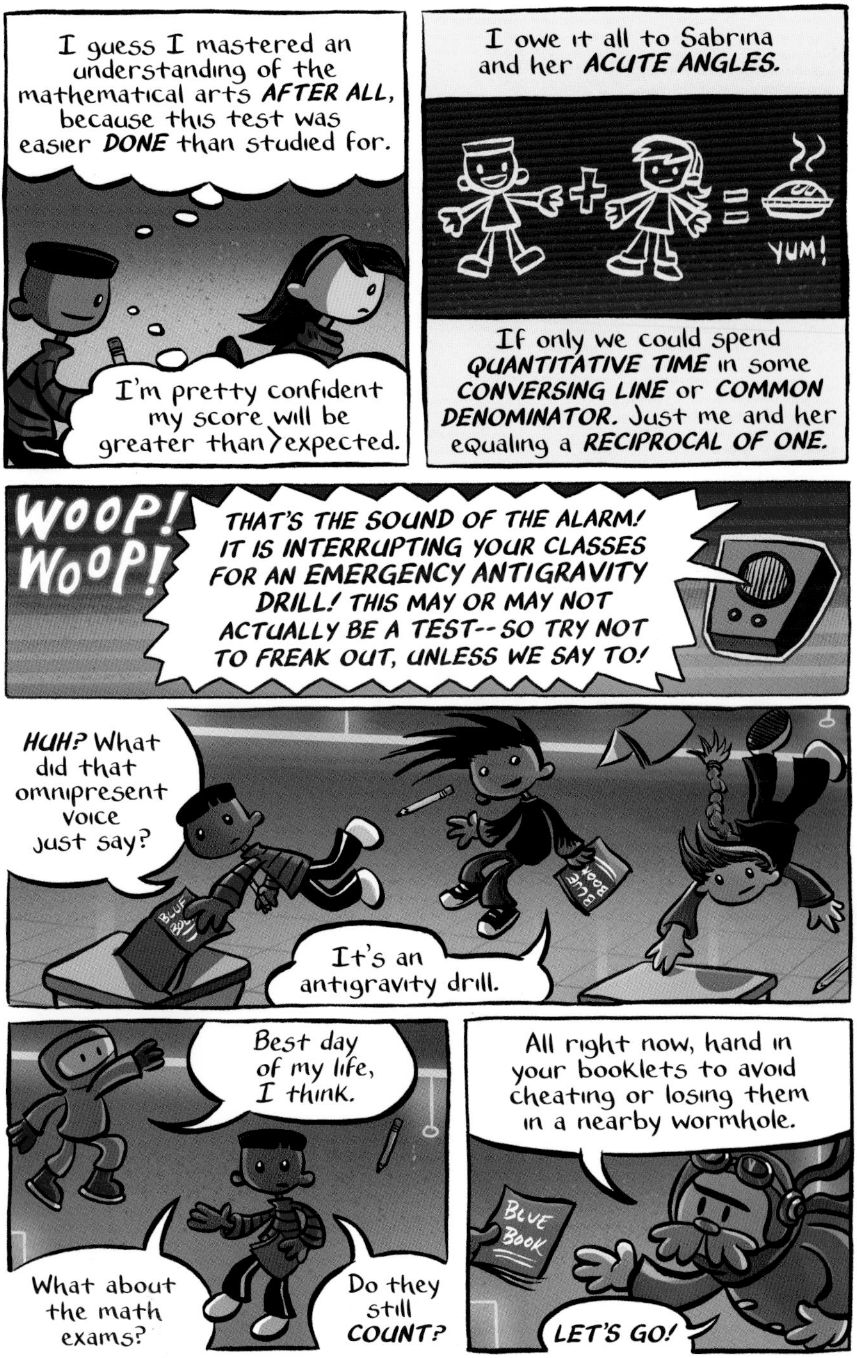

I guess I mastered an understanding of the mathematical arts AFTER ALL, because this test was easier DONE than studied for.
I'm pretty confident my score will be greater than > expected.
I owe it all to Sabrina and her ACUTE ANGLES.
YUM!
If only we could spend QUANTITATIVE TIME in some CONVERSING LINE or COMMON DENOMINATOR. Just me and her equaling a RECIPROCAL OF ONE.
WOOP! WOOP!
THAT'S THE SOUND OF THE ALARM! IT IS INTERRUPTING YOUR CLASSES FOR AN EMERGENCY ANTIGRAVITY DRILL! THIS MAY OR MAY NOT ACTUALLY BE A TEST--SO TRY NOT TO FREAK OUT, UNLESS WE SAY TO!
HUH? What did that omnipresent voice just say?
BLUE BOOK
BLUE BOOK
It's an antigravity drill.
Best day of my life, I think.
What about the math exams?
Do they still COUNT?
All right now, hand in your booklets to avoid cheating or losing them in a nearby wormhole.
BLUE BOOK
LET'S GO!

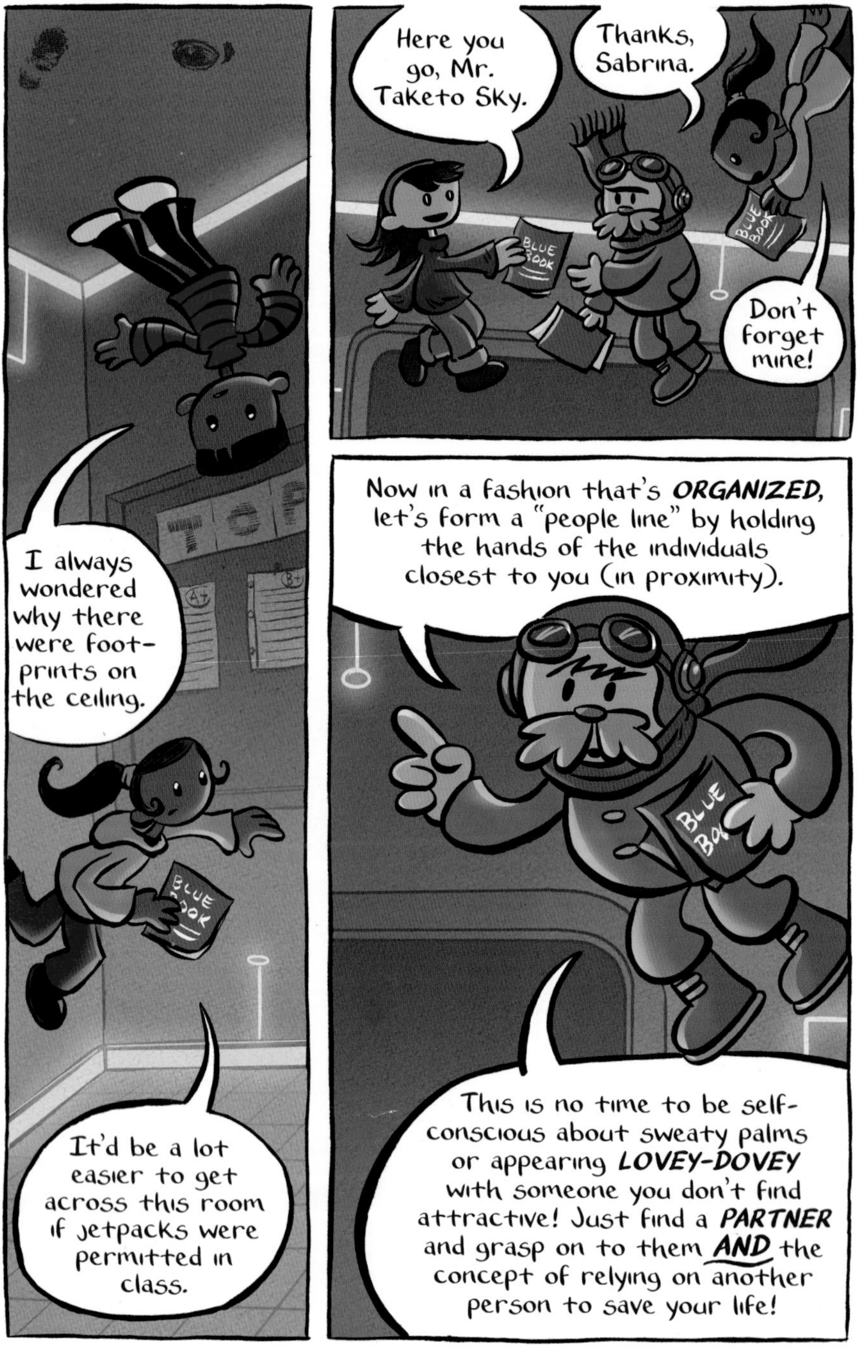
I always wondered why there were foot-prints on the ceiling.
It'd be a lot easier to get across this room if jetpacks were permitted in class.
Here you go, Mr. Taketo Sky.
Thanks, Sabrina.
Don't forget mine!
BLUE BOOK
Now in a fashion that's ORGANIZED, let's form a "people line" by holding the hands of the individuals closest to you (in proximity).
This is no time to be self-conscious about sweaty palms or appearing LOVEY-DOVEY with someone you don't find attractive! Just find a PARTNER and grasp on to them AND the concept of relying on another person to save your life!

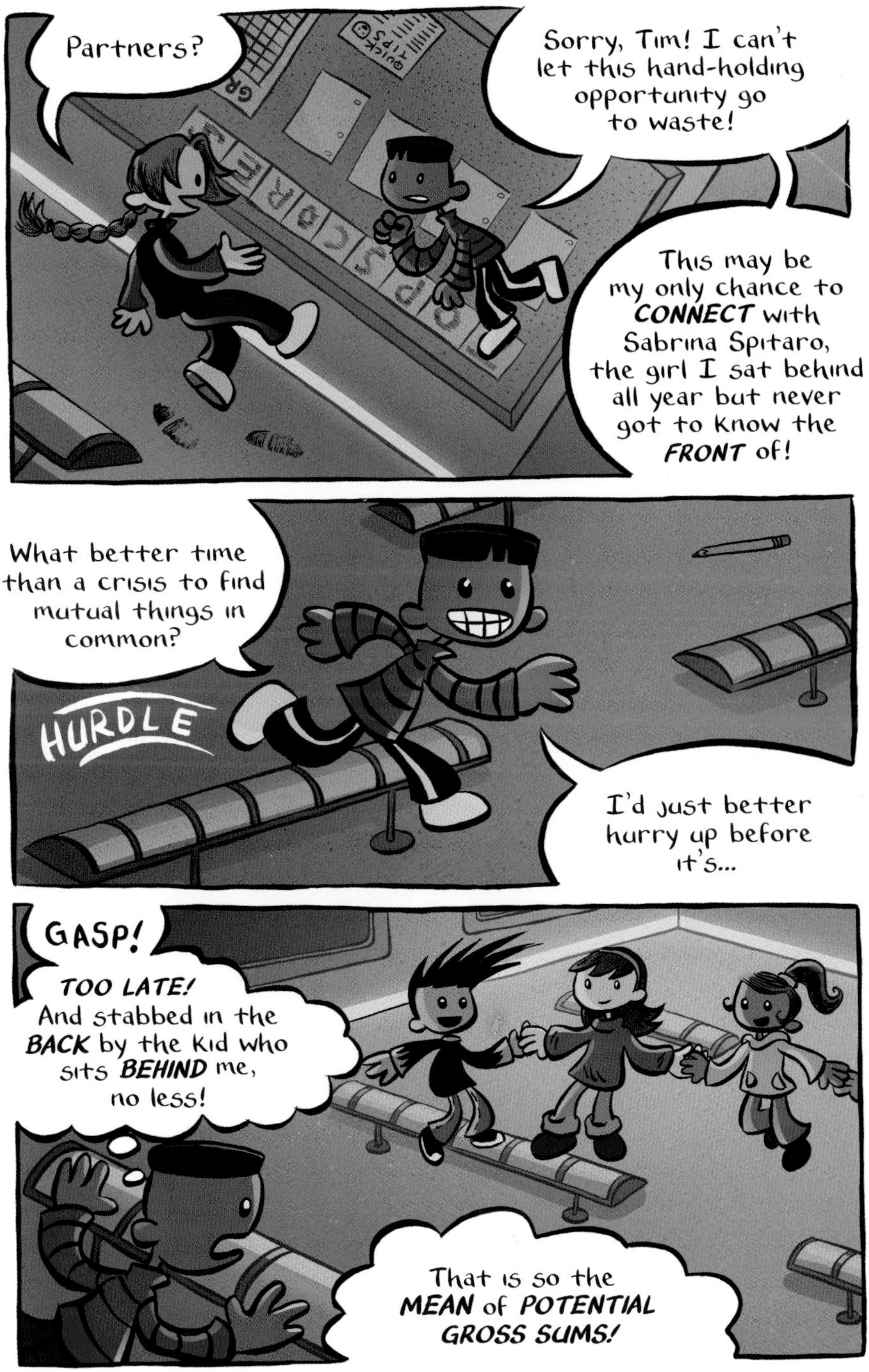
Partners?
Sorry, Tim! I can't let this hand-holding opportunity go to waste!
This may be my only chance to CONNECT with Sabrina Spitaro, the girl I sat behind all year but never got to know the FRONT of!
What better time than a crisis to find mutual things in common?
HURDLE
I'd just better hurry up before it's...
GASP!
TOO LATE! And stabbed in the BACK by the kid who sits BEHIND me, no less!
That is so the MEAN of POTENTIAL GROSS SUMS!

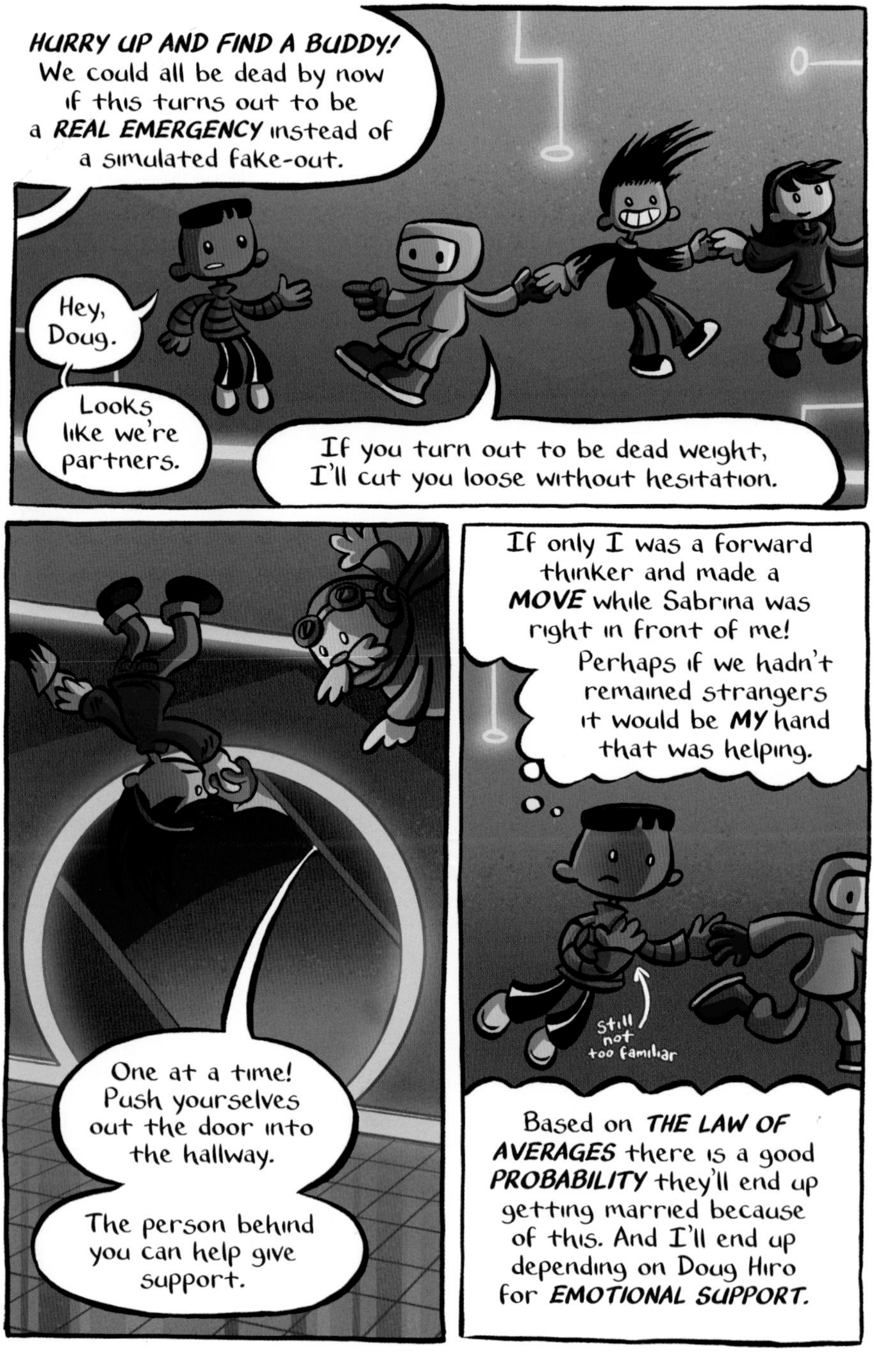
HURRY UP AND FIND A BUDDY! We could all be dead by now if this turns out to be a REAL EMERGENCY instead of a simulated fake-out.
Hey, Doug.
Looks like we're partners.
If you turn out to be dead weight, I'll cut you loose without hesitation.
One at a time! Push yourselves out the door into the hallway.
The person behind you can help give support.
If only I was a forward thinker and made a MOVE while Sabrina was right in front of me!
Perhaps if we hadn't remained strangers it would be MY hand that was helping.
Still not too familiar
Based on THE LAW OF AVERAGES there is a good PROBABILITY they'll end up getting married because of this. And I'll end up depending on Doug Hiro for EMOTIONAL SUPPORT.

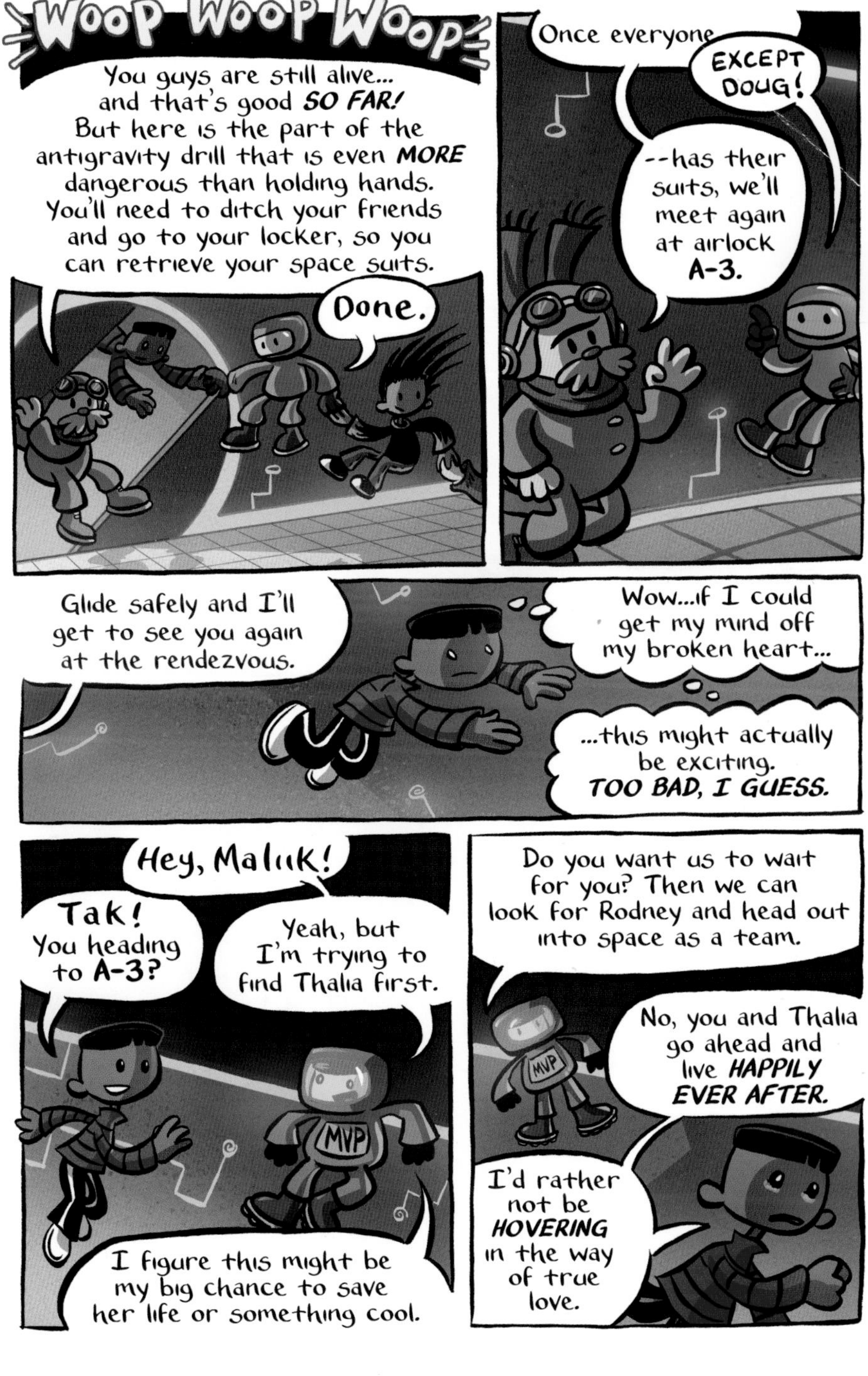
WOOP WOOP WOOP
You guys are still alive... and that's good SO FAR! But here is the part of the antigravity drill that is even MORE dangerous than holding hands. You'll need to ditch your friends and go to your locker, so you can retrieve your space suits.
Done.
Once everyone
EXCEPT DOUG!
--has their suits, we'll meet again at airlock A-3.
Glide safely and I'll get to see you again at the rendezvous.
Wow...if I could get my mind off my broken heart...
...this might actually be exciting. TOO BAD, I GUESS.
Hey, Maliik!
Tak! You heading to A-3?
Yeah, but I'm trying to find Thalia first.
I figure this might be my big chance to save her life or something cool.
Do you want us to wait for you? Then we can look for Rodney and head out into space as a team.
No, you and Thalia go ahead and live HAPPILY EVER AFTER.
I'd rather not be HOVERING in the way of true love.

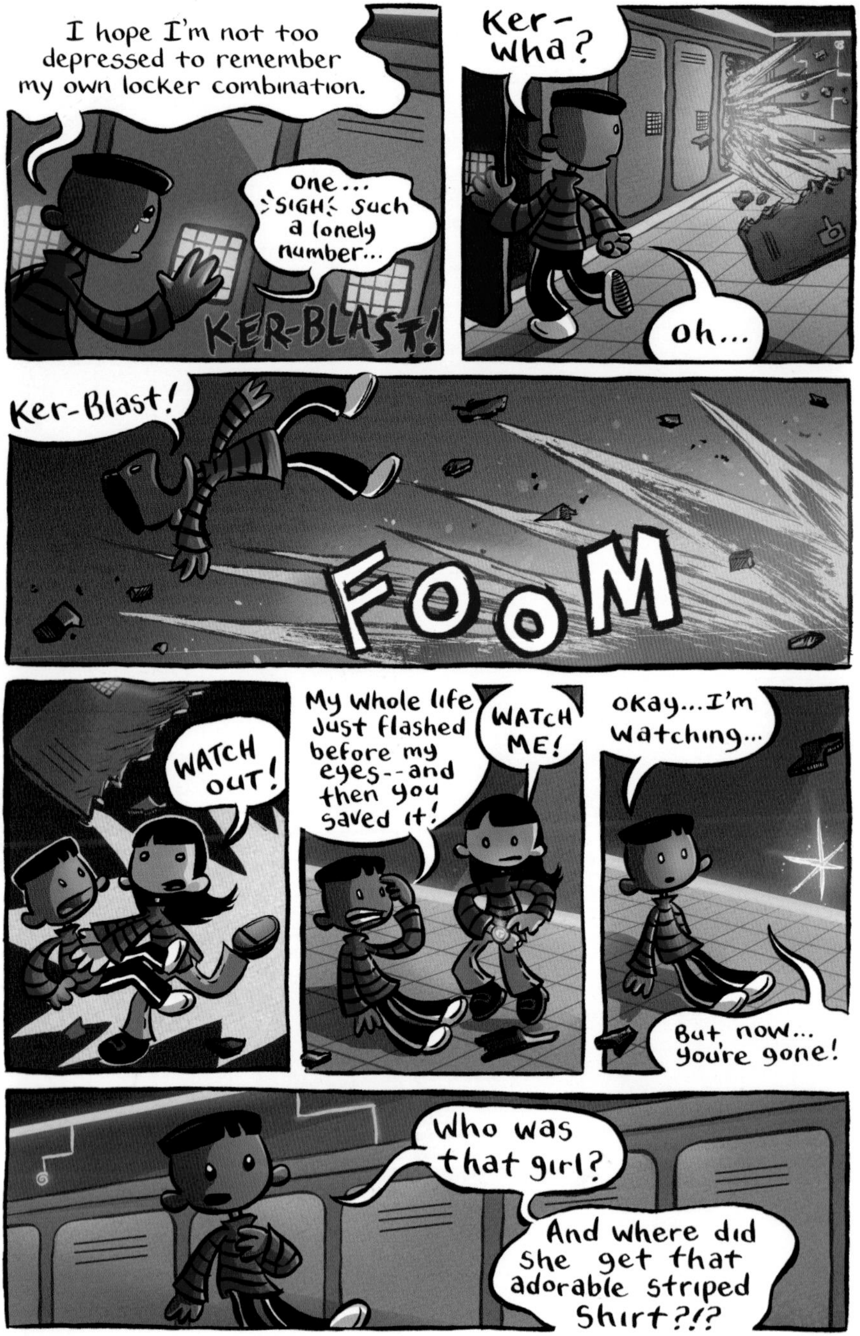
I hope I'm not too depressed to remember my own locker combination.
One... SIGH Such a lonely number...
KER-BLAST!
Ker-Wha?
Oh...
Ker-Blast!
FOOM
WATCH OUT!
My whole life just flashed before my eyes--and then you saved it!
WATCH ME!
Okay... I'm watching...
But, now... you're gone!
Who was that girl?
And where did she get that adorable striped shirt?!?

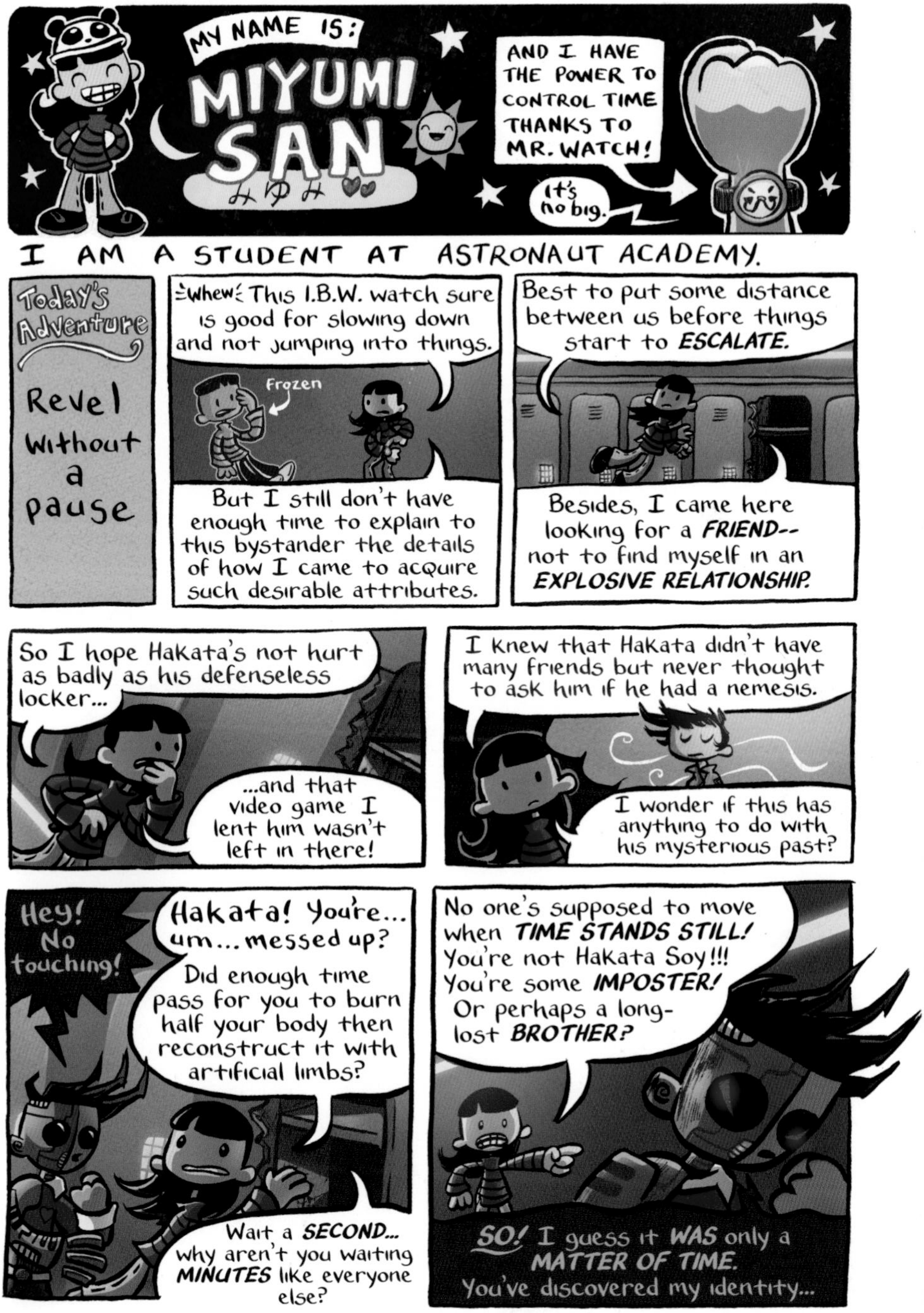
MY NAME IS:
MIYUMI SAN
みゆみ
AND I HAVE THE POWER TO CONTROL TIME THANKS TO MR. WATCH!
It's no big.
I AM A STUDENT AT ASTRONAUT ACADEMY.
Today's Adventure
Revel Without a pause
Whew! This I.B.W. watch sure is good for slowing down and not jumping into things.
Frozen
But I still don't have enough time to explain to this bystander the details of how I came to acquire such desirable attributes.
Best to put some distance between us before things start to ESCALATE.
Besides, I came here looking for a FRIEND-- not to find myself in an EXPLOSIVE RELATIONSHIP.
So I hope Hakata's not hurt as badly as his defenseless locker...
...and that video game I lent him wasn't left in there!
I knew that Hakata didn't have many friends but never thought to ask him if he had a nemesis.
I wonder if this has anything to do with his mysterious past?
Hey! No touching!
Hakata! You're... um... messed up?
Did enough time pass for you to burn half your body then reconstruct it with artificial limbs?
Wait a SECOND... why aren't you waiting MINUTES like everyone else?
No one's supposed to move when TIME STANDS STILL! You're not Hakata Soy!!! You're some IMPOSTER! Or perhaps a long-lost BROTHER?
SO! I guess it WAS only a MATTER OF TIME. You've discovered my identity...

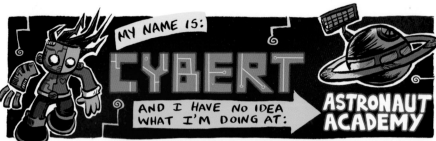

MY NAME IS: **CYBERT**

AND I HAVE NO IDEA WHAT I'M DOING AT: → **ASTRONAUT ACADEMY**

Cybert What? Sounds ethnic. What are your origins?

Well, I *THOUGHT* I was programmed for **DESTRUCTION**.

scratchy scratchy

But now I'm not sure.

I'm really good at blowing stuff up. Even from a distance.

But what does *SAY* about a person?

It says "stay away from me," I think.

chop chop

HEY! You don't play MonChiChiMon, do you?

I found this Charbroil Czar.

CHARBROIL CZAR

It says that he's a level 3 King Chef with Mediterranean side dish attacks.

ALSO... he's got a +3 digestive and +6 intimidation.

I'm not sure what kind of scale those are graded on. Do you have any cards I could compare stats with?

Never really got into card games. Do you mind if I leave now? You're kind of freaking me out with the obsessive personality.

Sure.

Thanks for talking to me.

grasp grasp

Nice girl... Too bad she's aligned with my mortal enemy.

I guess I should detonate her locker *TOO*, just in case I *AM* still supposed to be evil.

What'd my sensors say her name was again?

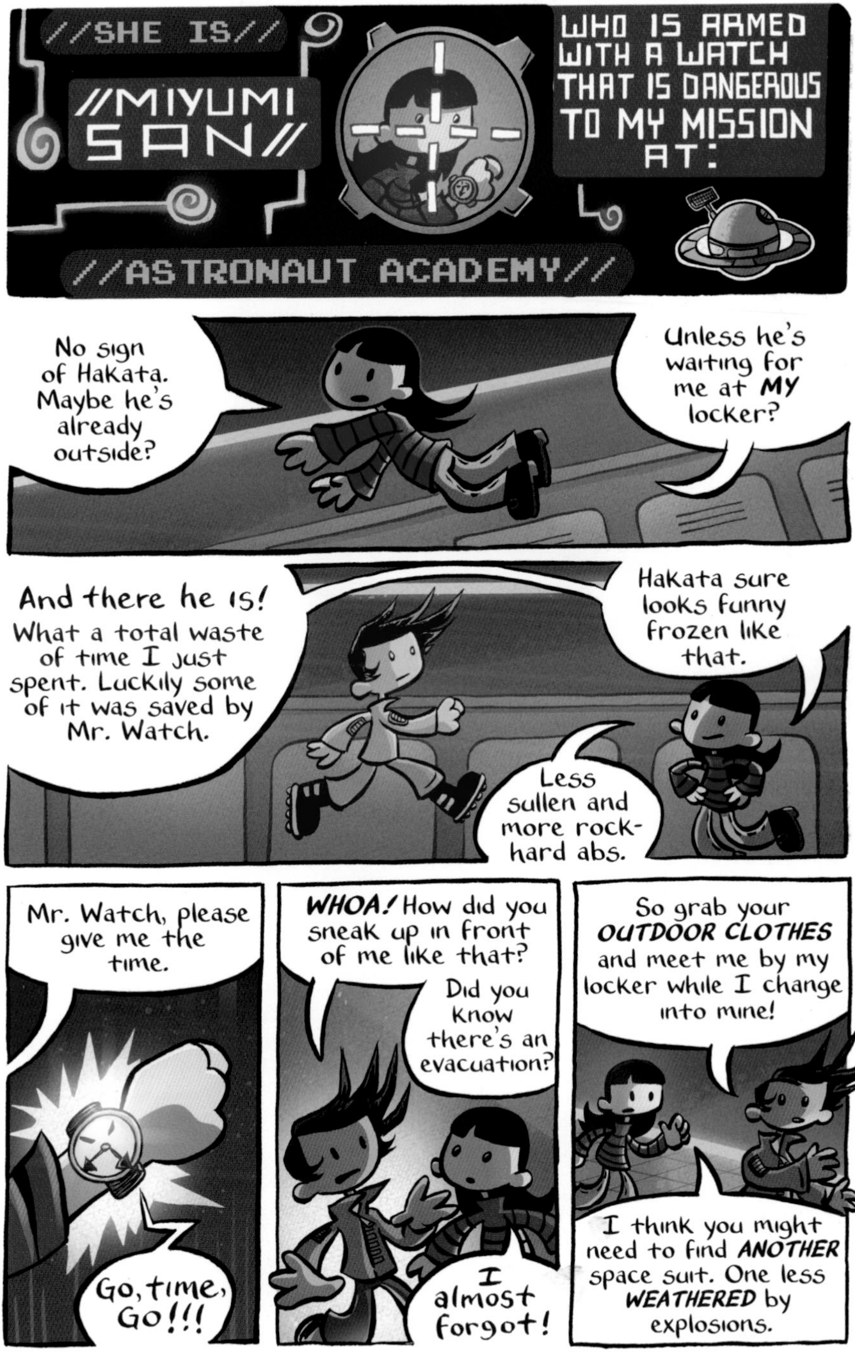

//SHE IS//
//MIYUMI SAN//
WHO IS ARMED WITH A WATCH THAT IS DANGEROUS TO MY MISSION AT:
//ASTRONAUT ACADEMY//
No sign of Hakata. Maybe he's already outside?
Unless he's waiting for me at MY locker?
And there he is! What a total waste of time I just spent. Luckily some of it was saved by Mr. Watch.
Hakata sure looks funny frozen like that.
Less sullen and more rock-hard abs.
Mr. Watch, please give me the time.
Go, time, Go!!!
WHOA! How did you sneak up in front of me like that?
Did you know there's an evacuation?
I almost forgot!
So grab your OUTDOOR CLOTHES and meet me by my locker while I change into mine!
I think you might need to find ANOTHER space suit. One less WEATHERED by explosions.

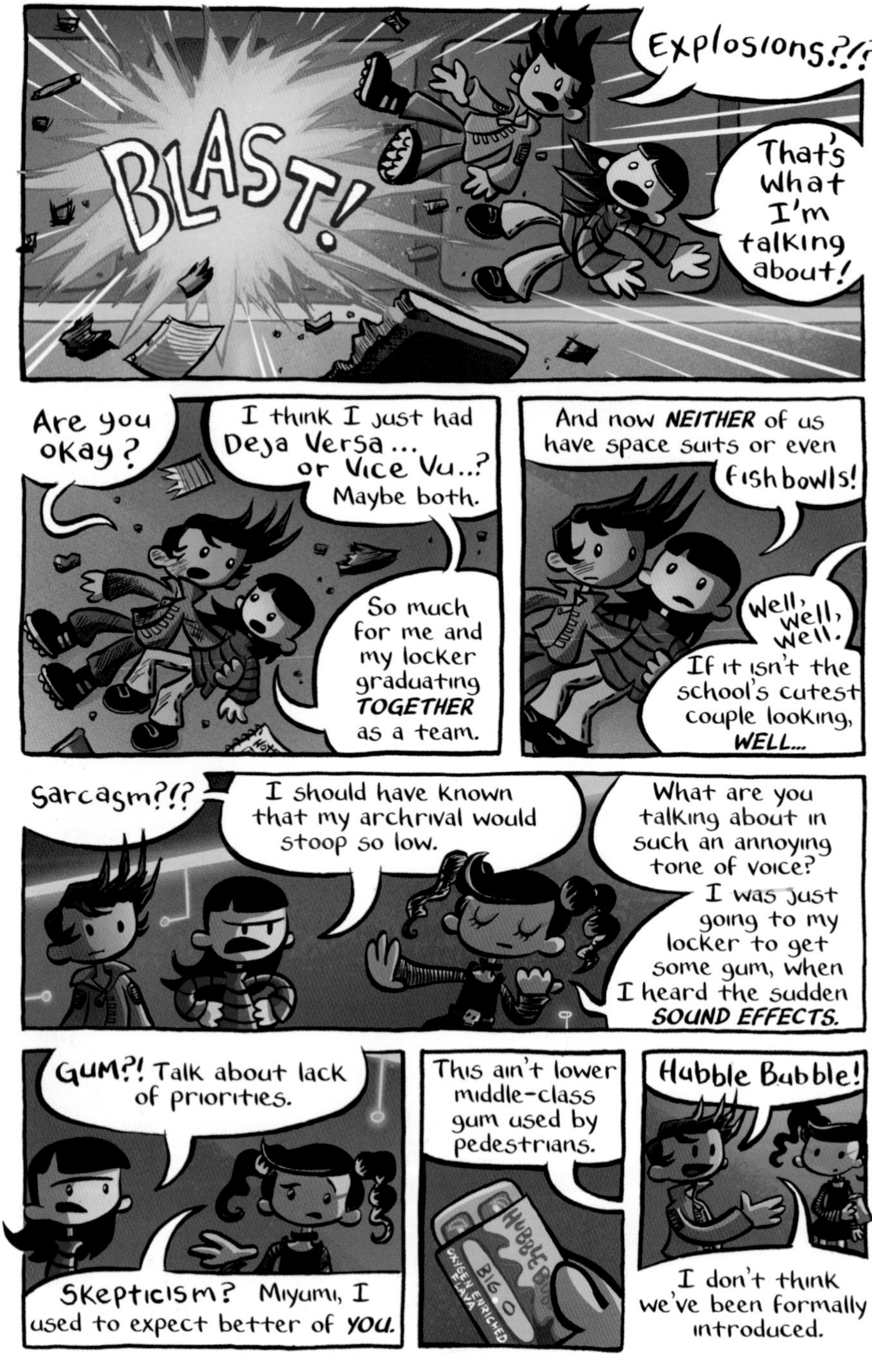
BLAST!
Explosions?!?
That's What I'm talking about!
Are you okay?
I think I just had Deja Versa... or Vice Vu...? Maybe both.
So much for me and my locker graduating TOGETHER as a team.
And now NEITHER of us have space suits or even fishbowls!
Well, well, well.
If it isn't the school's cutest couple looking, WELL...
Sarcasm?!?
I should have known that my archrival would stoop so low.
What are you talking about in such an annoying tone of voice?
I was just going to my locker to get some gum, when I heard the sudden SOUND EFFECTS.
GUM?! Talk about lack of priorities.
Skepticism? Miyumi, I used to expect better of YOU.
This ain't lower middle-class gum used by pedestrians.
HUBBLE BUB
BIG O
OXYGEN ENRICHED FLAVA
Hubble Bubble!
I don't think we've been formally introduced.

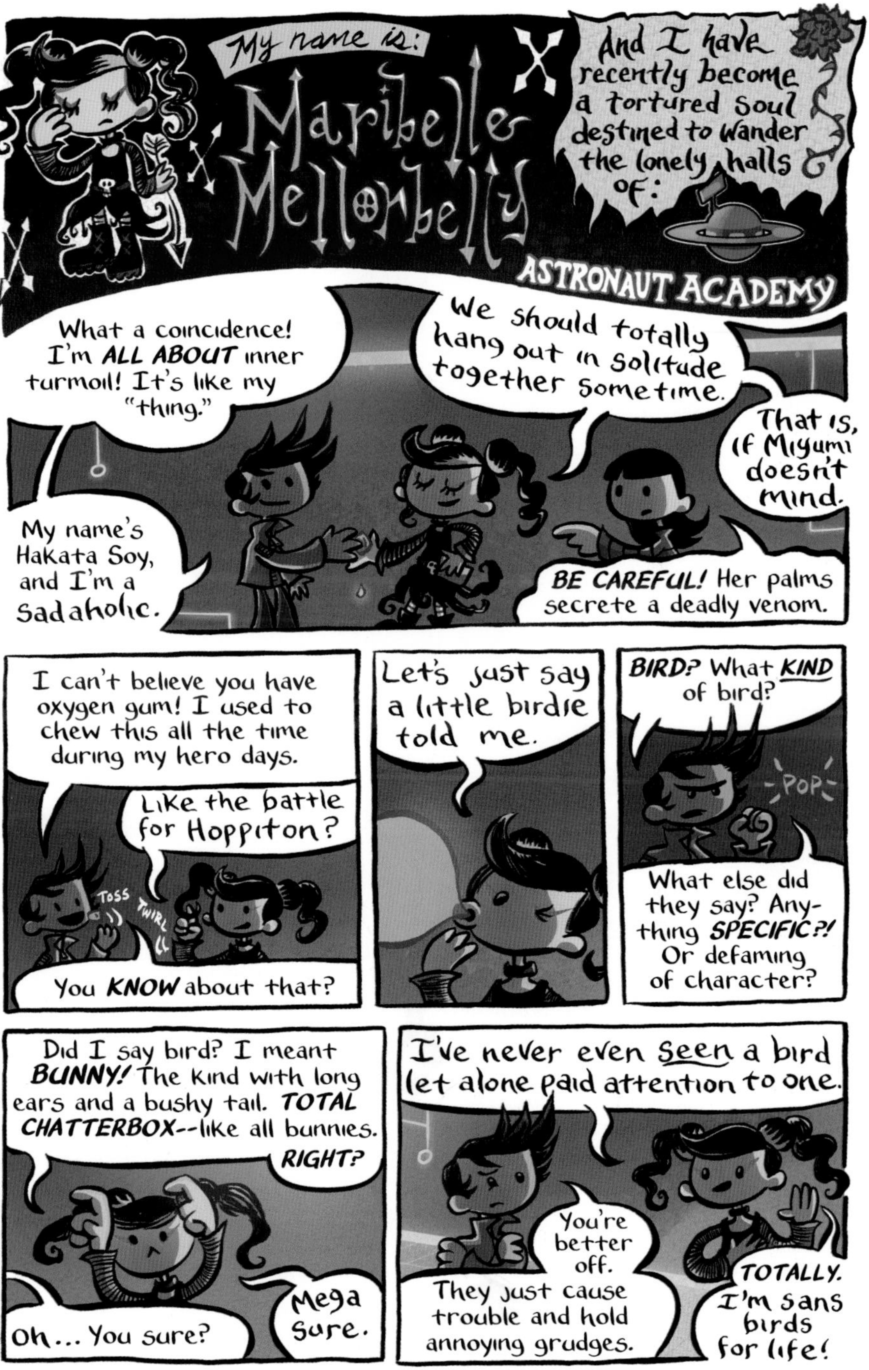
My name is:
Maribelle Mellonbelly
And I have recently become a tortured soul destined to wander the lonely halls of:
ASTRONAUT ACADEMY
What a coincidence! I'm ALL ABOUT inner turmoil! It's like my "thing."
We should totally hang out in solitude together sometime.
That is, if Miyumi doesn't mind.
My name's Hakata Soy, and I'm a sadaholic.
BE CAREFUL! Her palms secrete a deadly venom.
I can't believe you have oxygen gum! I used to chew this all the time during my hero days.
Like the battle for Hoppiton?
TOSS
TWIRL
You KNOW about that?
Let's just say a little birdie told me.
BIRD? What KIND of bird?
POP
What else did they say? Anything SPECIFIC?! Or defaming of character?
Did I say bird? I meant BUNNY! The kind with long ears and a bushy tail. TOTAL CHATTERBOX--like all bunnies. RIGHT?
Oh... You sure?
Mega sure.
I've never even seen a bird let alone paid attention to one.
You're better off.
They just cause trouble and hold annoying grudges.
TOTALLY. I'm sans birds for life!

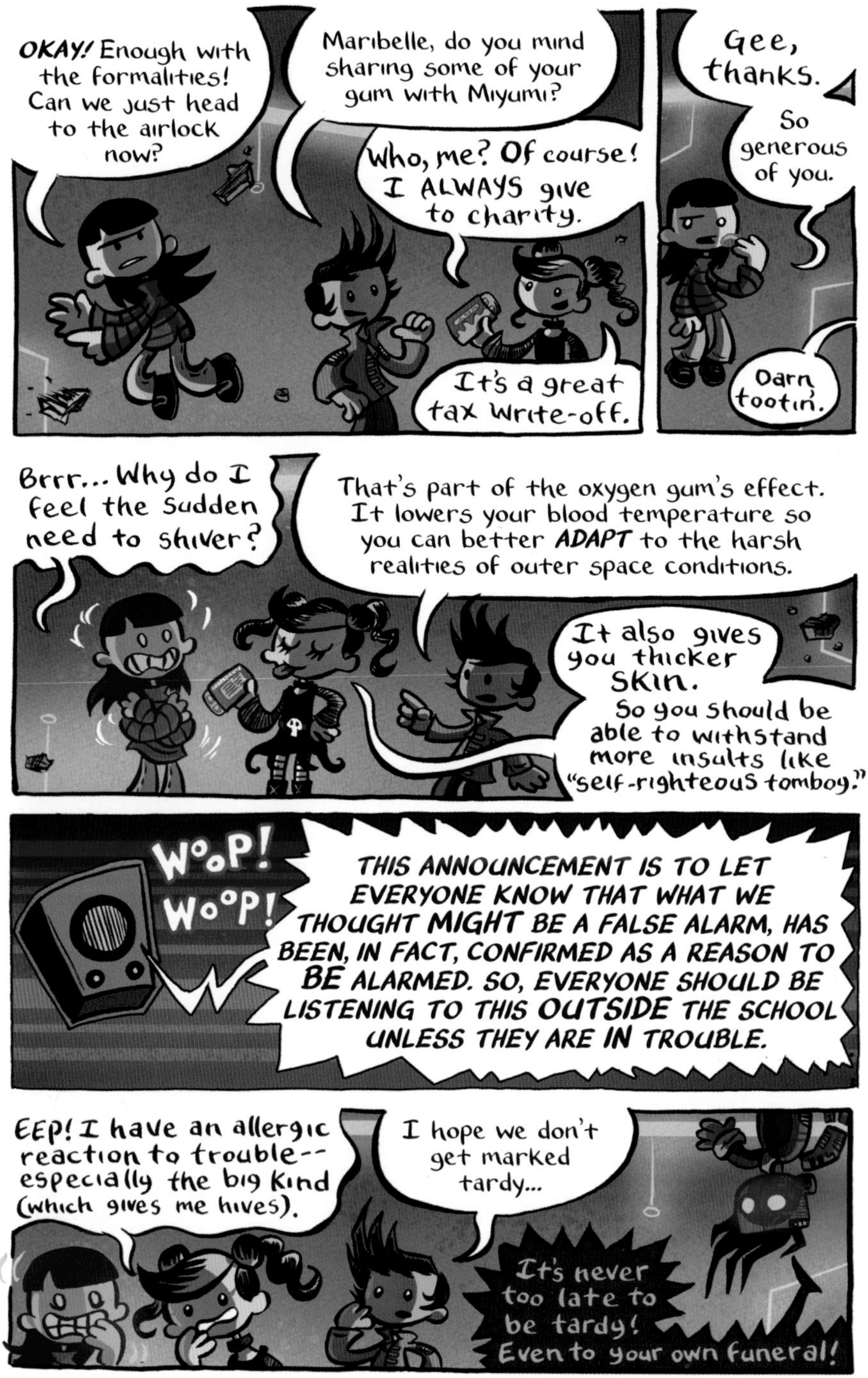
OKAY! Enough with the formalities! Can we just head to the airlock now?
Maribelle, do you mind sharing some of your gum with Miyumi?
Who, me? Of course! I ALWAYS give to charity.
It's a great tax write-off.
Gee, thanks.
So generous of you.
Darn tootin'.
Brrr... Why do I feel the sudden need to shiver?
That's part of the oxygen gum's effect. It lowers your blood temperature so you can better ADAPT to the harsh realities of outer space conditions.
It also gives you thicker SKIN.
So you should be able to withstand more insults like "self-righteous tomboy."
WOOP! WOOP!
THIS ANNOUNCEMENT IS TO LET EVERYONE KNOW THAT WHAT WE THOUGHT MIGHT BE A FALSE ALARM, HAS BEEN, IN FACT, CONFIRMED AS A REASON TO BE ALARMED. SO, EVERYONE SHOULD BE LISTENING TO THIS OUTSIDE THE SCHOOL UNLESS THEY ARE IN TROUBLE.
EEP! I have an allergic reaction to trouble-- especially the big kind (which gives me hives).
I hope we don't get marked tardy...
It's never too late to be tardy! Even to your own funeral!

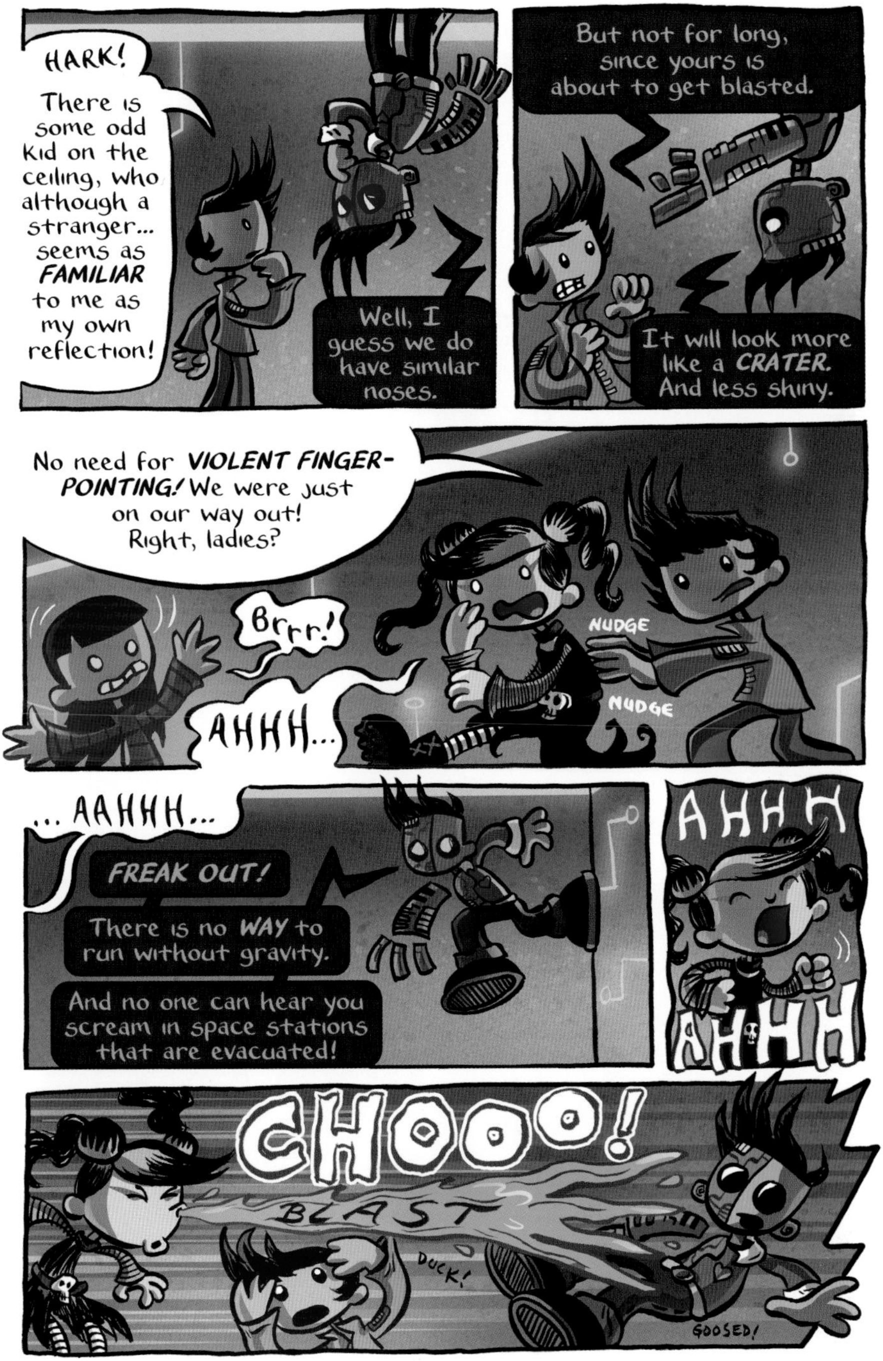
HARK!
There is some odd kid on the ceiling, who although a stranger... seems as FAMILIAR to me as my own reflection!
Well, I guess we do have similar noses.
But not for long, since yours is about to get blasted.
It will look more like a CRATER. And less shiny.
No need for VIOLENT FINGER-POINTING! We were just on our way out! Right, ladies?
Brrr!
NUDGE
NUDGE
AHHH...
...AAHHH...
FREAK OUT!
There is no WAY to run without gravity.
And no one can hear you scream in space stations that are evacuated!
AHHH
AHHH
CHOOO!
BLAST
DUCK!
GOOSED!

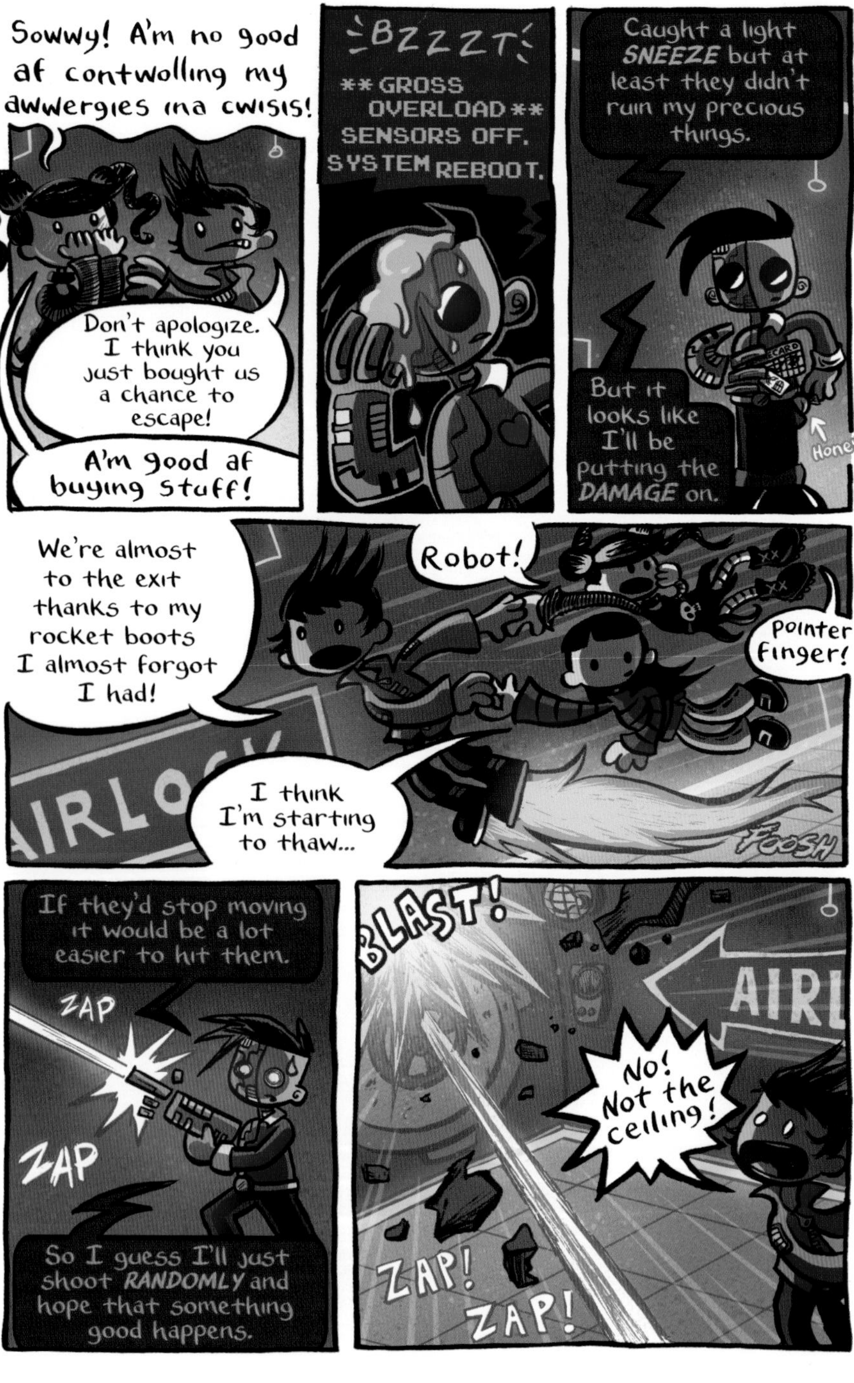

Sowwy! A'm no good af contwolling my awwergies ina cwisis!
Don't apologize. I think you just bought us a chance to escape!
A'm good af buying stuff!
BZZZT
** GROSS OVERLOAD ** SENSORS OFF. SYSTEM REBOOT.
Caught a light SNEEZE but at least they didn't ruin my precious things.
But it looks like I'll be putting the DAMAGE on.
Honey
We're almost to the exit thanks to my rocket boots I almost forgot I had!
Robot!
Pointer finger!
I think I'm starting to thaw...
AIRLOC
FOOSH
If they'd stop moving it would be a lot easier to hit them.
ZAP
ZAP
So I guess I'll just shoot RANDOMLY and hope that something good happens.
BLAST!
AIRL
No! Not the ceiling!
ZAP!
ZAP!

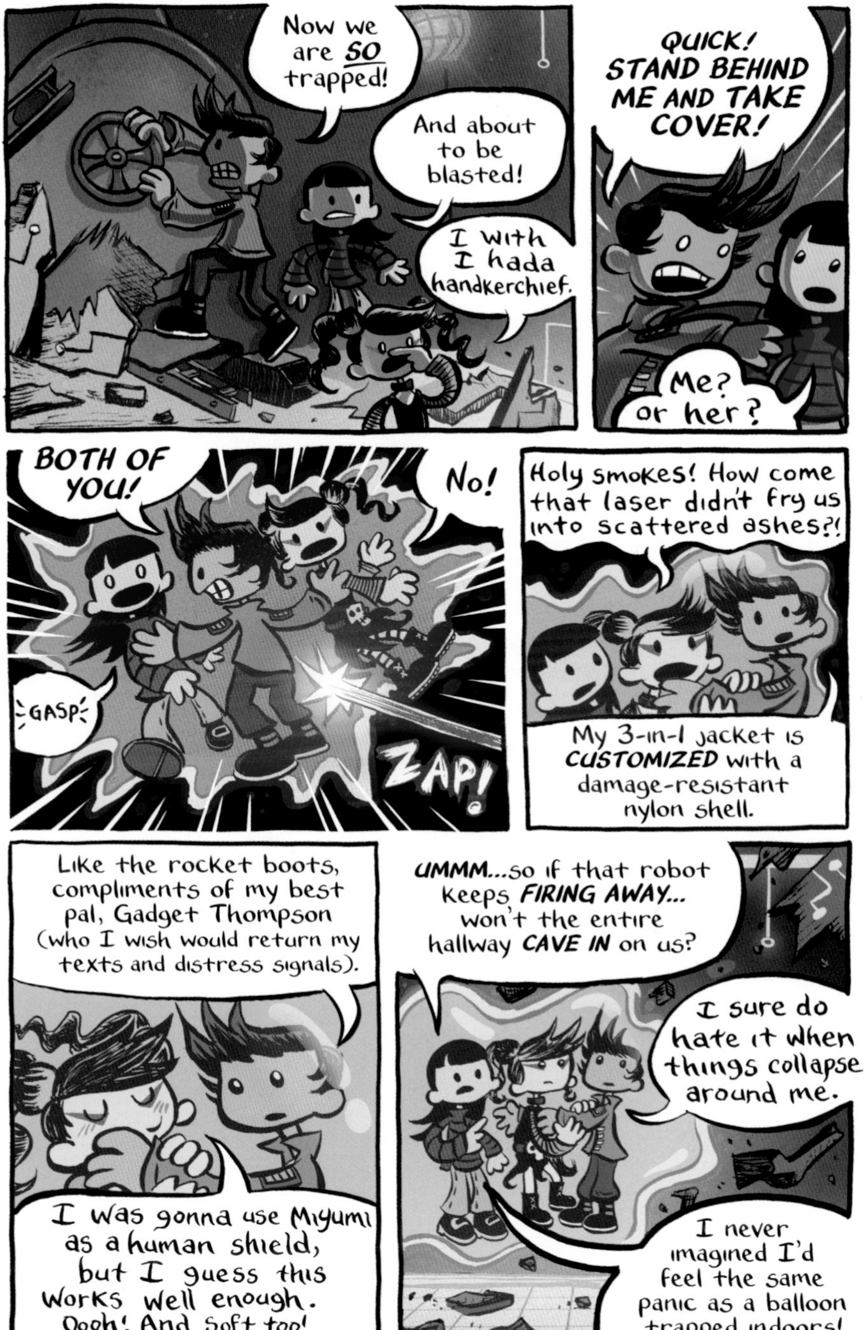
Now we are SO trapped!
And about to be blasted!
I with I hada handkerchief.
QUICK! STAND BEHIND ME AND TAKE COVER!
Me? or her?
BOTH OF YOU!
No!
GASP
ZAP!
Holy smokes! How come that laser didn't fry us into scattered ashes?!
My 3-in-1 jacket is CUSTOMIZED with a damage-resistant nylon shell.
Like the rocket boots, compliments of my best pal, Gadget Thompson (who I wish would return my texts and distress signals).
I was gonna use Miyumi as a human shield, but I guess this works well enough. Oooh! And soft too!
UMMM...so if that robot keeps FIRING AWAY... won't the entire hallway CAVE IN on us?
I sure do hate it when things collapse around me.
I never imagined I'd feel the same panic as a balloon trapped indoors!

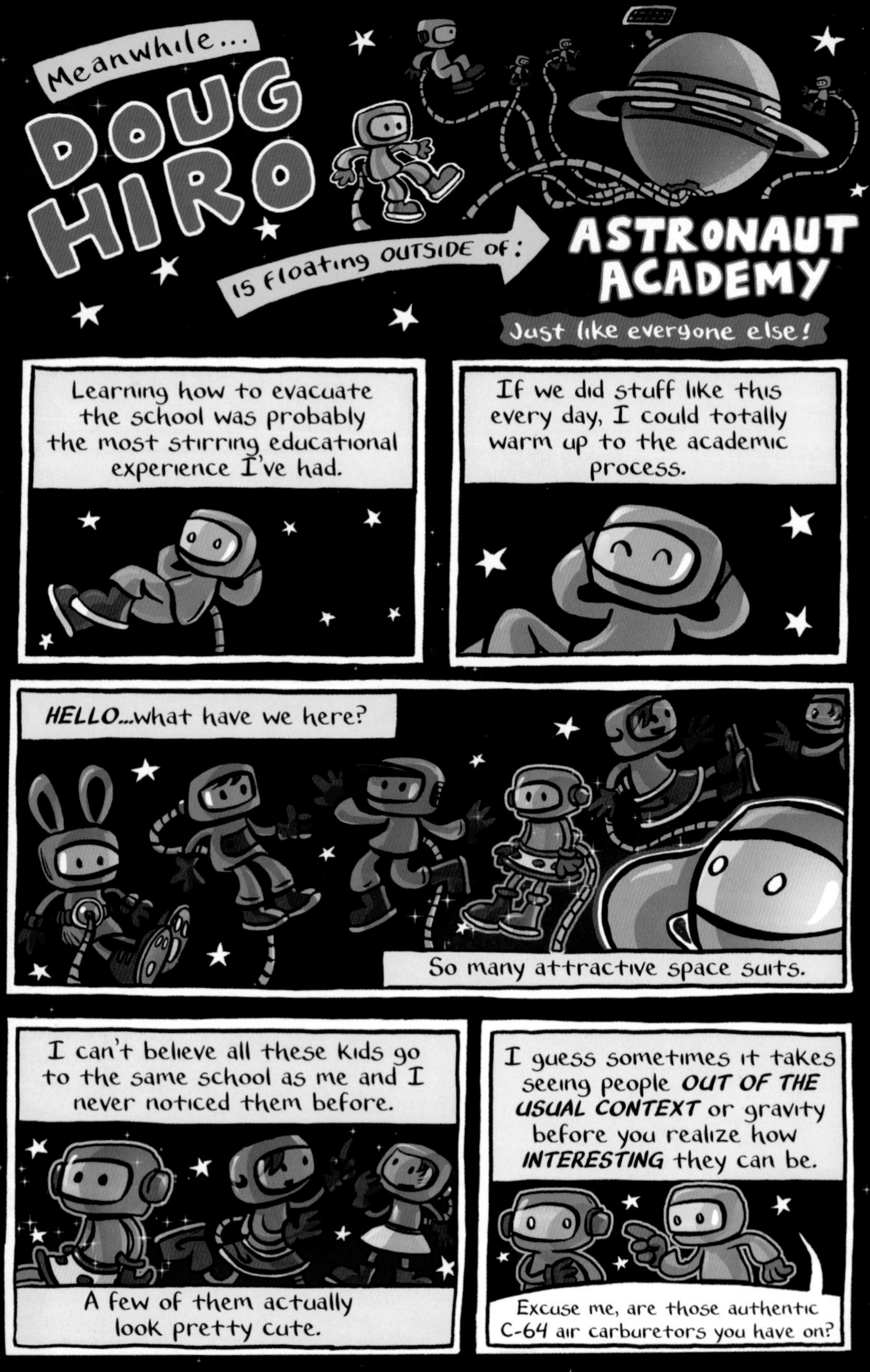
Meanwhile...
DOUG HIRO
IS Floating OUTSIDE OF:
ASTRONAUT ACADEMY
Just like everyone else!
Learning how to evacuate the school was probably the most stirring educational experience I've had.
If we did stuff like this every day, I could totally warm up to the academic process.
HELLO...what have we here?
So many attractive space suits.
I can't believe all these kids go to the same school as me and I never noticed them before.
A few of them actually look pretty cute.
I guess sometimes it takes seeing people OUT OF THE USUAL CONTEXT or gravity before you realize how INTERESTING they can be.
Excuse me, are those authentic C-64 air carburetors you have on?

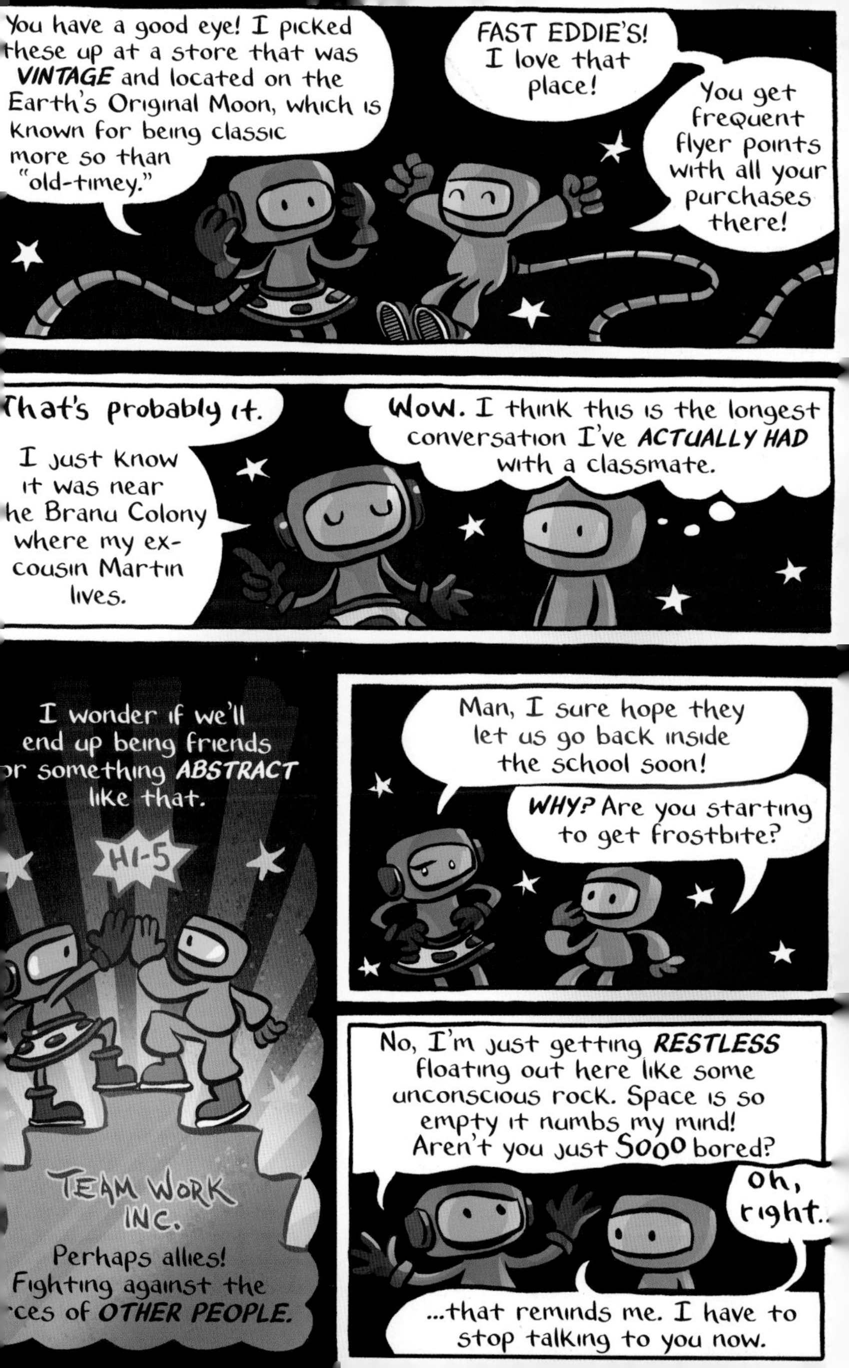

You have a good eye! I picked these up at a store that was VINTAGE and located on the Earth's Original Moon, which is known for being classic more so than "old-timey."
FAST EDDIE'S! I love that place!
You get frequent flyer points with all your purchases there!
That's probably it.
I just know it was near he Branu Colony where my ex-cousin Martin lives.
Wow. I think this is the longest conversation I've ACTUALLY HAD with a classmate.
I wonder if we'll end up being friends or something ABSTRACT like that.
HI-5
TEAM WORK INC.
Perhaps allies! Fighting against the rces of OTHER PEOPLE.
Man, I sure hope they let us go back inside the school soon!
WHY? Are you starting to get frostbite?
No, I'm just getting RESTLESS floating out here like some unconscious rock. Space is so empty it numbs my mind! Aren't you just SOOO bored?
Oh, right.
...that reminds me. I have to stop talking to you now.

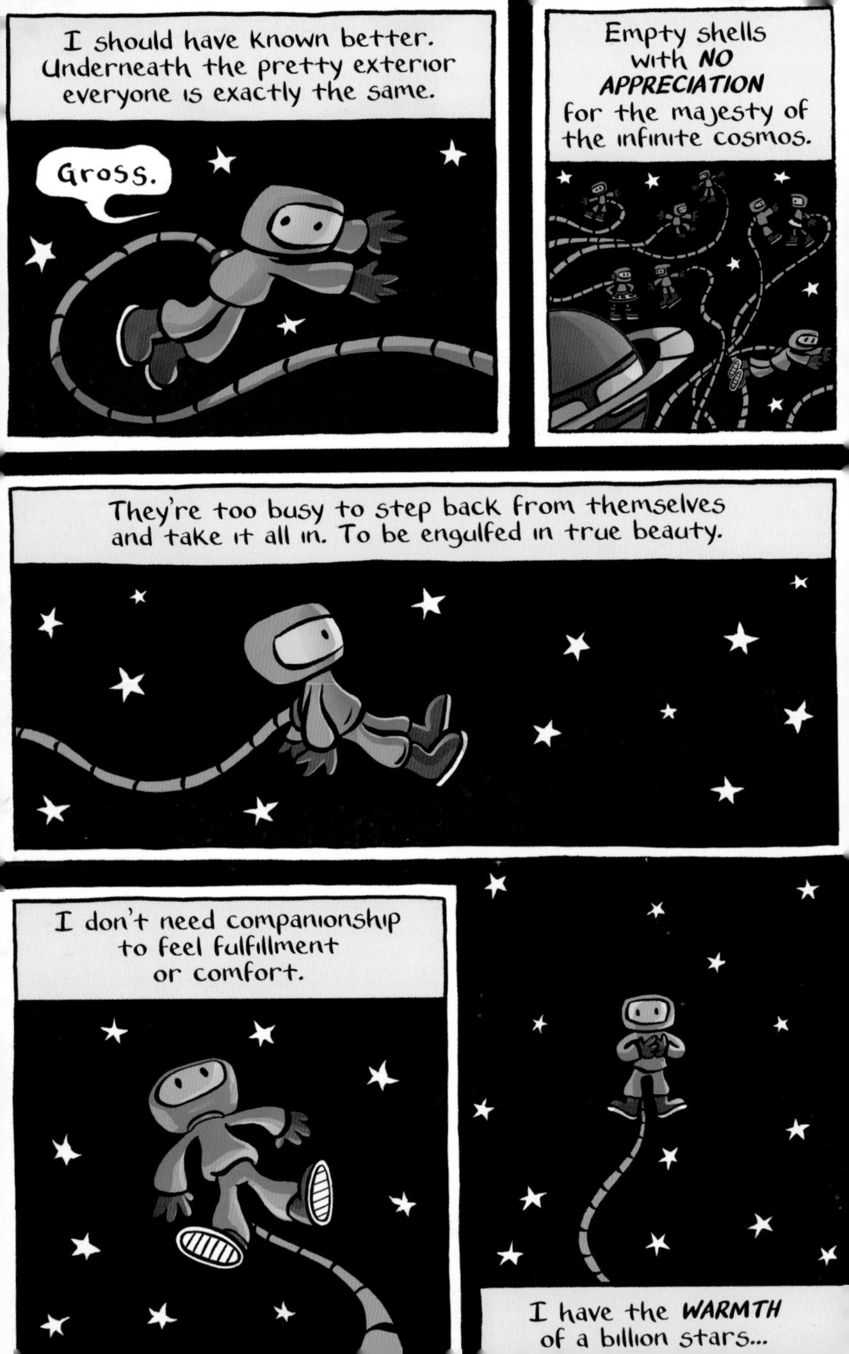
I should have known better. Underneath the pretty exterior everyone is exactly the same.
Gross.
Empty shells with NO APPRECIATION for the majesty of the infinite cosmos.
They're too busy to step back from themselves and take it all in. To be engulfed in true beauty.
I don't need companionship to feel fulfillment or comfort.
I have the WARMTH of a billion stars...

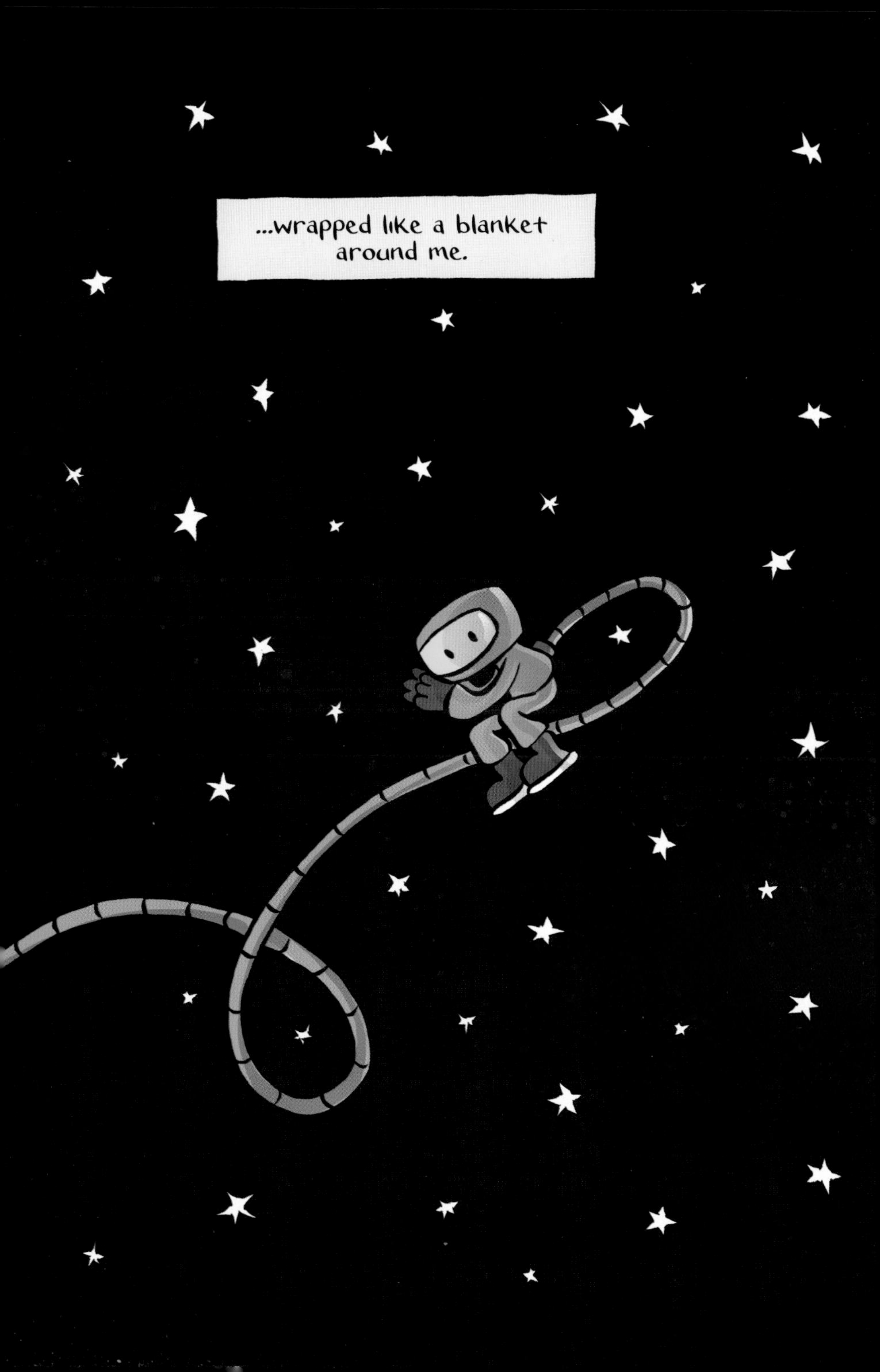
...wrapped like a blanket around me.

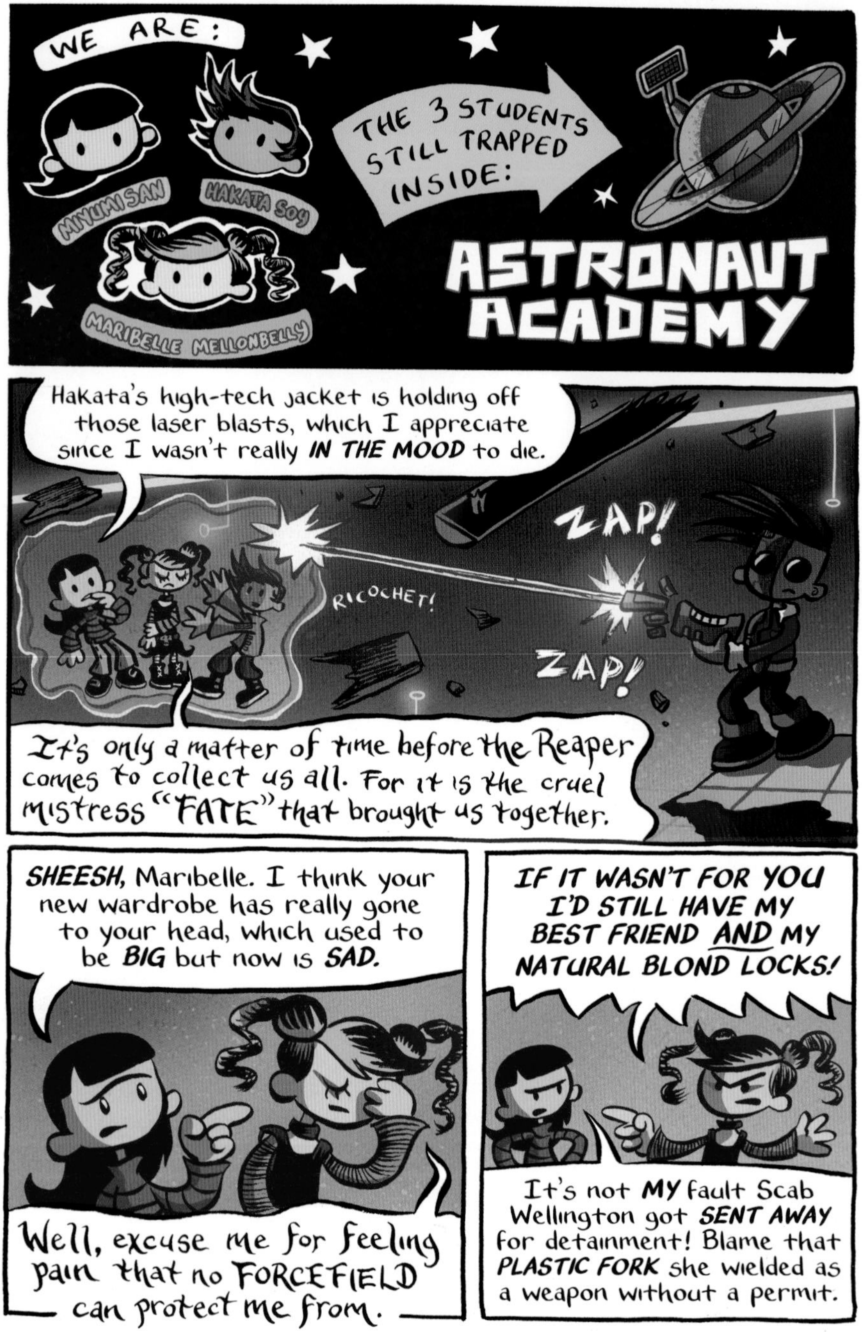
WE ARE:
MIYUMI SAN
HAKATA SOY
MARIBELLE MELLONBELLY
THE 3 STUDENTS STILL TRAPPED INSIDE:
ASTRONAUT ACADEMY
Hakata's high-tech jacket is holding off those laser blasts, which I appreciate since I wasn't really IN THE MOOD to die.
ZAP!
RICOCHET!
ZAP!
It's only a matter of time before the Reaper comes to collect us all. For it is the cruel mistress "FATE" that brought us together.
SHEESH, Maribelle. I think your new wardrobe has really gone to your head, which used to be BIG but now is SAD.
Well, excuse me for feeling pain that no FORCEFIELD can protect me from.
IF IT WASN'T FOR YOU I'D STILL HAVE MY BEST FRIEND AND MY NATURAL BLOND LOCKS!
It's not MY fault Scab Wellington got SENT AWAY for detainment! Blame that PLASTIC FORK she wielded as a weapon without a permit.

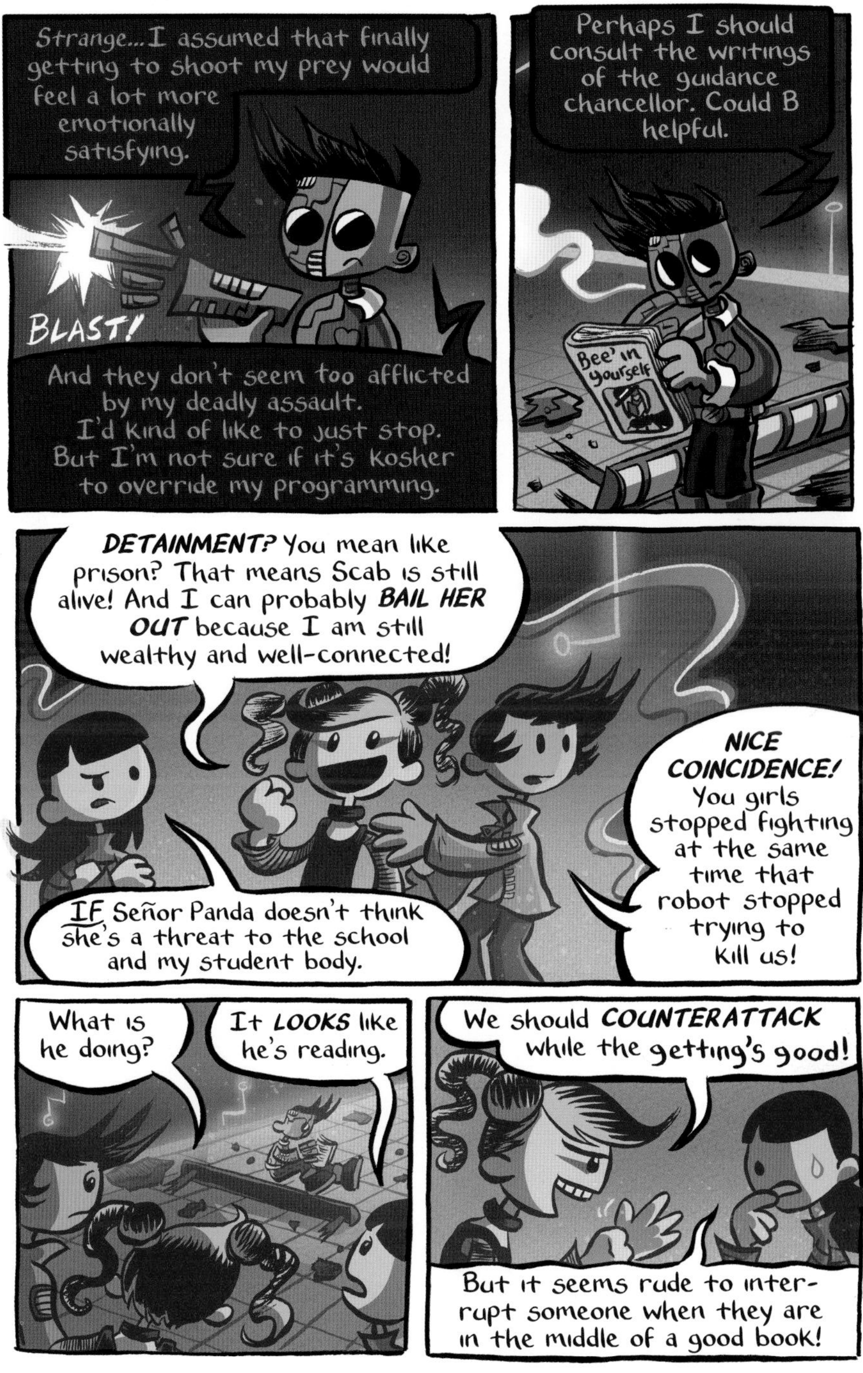
Strange...I assumed that finally getting to shoot my prey would feel a lot more emotionally satisfying.
BLAST!
And they don't seem too afflicted by my deadly assault. I'd kind of like to just stop. But I'm not sure if it's kosher to override my programming.
Perhaps I should consult the writings of the guidance chancellor. Could B helpful.
Bee' in yourself
DETAINMENT? You mean like prison? That means Scab is still alive! And I can probably BAIL HER OUT because I am still wealthy and well-connected!
IF Señor Panda doesn't think she's a threat to the school and my student body.
NICE COINCIDENCE! You girls stopped fighting at the same time that robot stopped trying to kill us!
What is he doing?
It LOOKS like he's reading.
We should COUNTERATTACK while the getting's good!
But it seems rude to interrupt someone when they are in the middle of a good book!

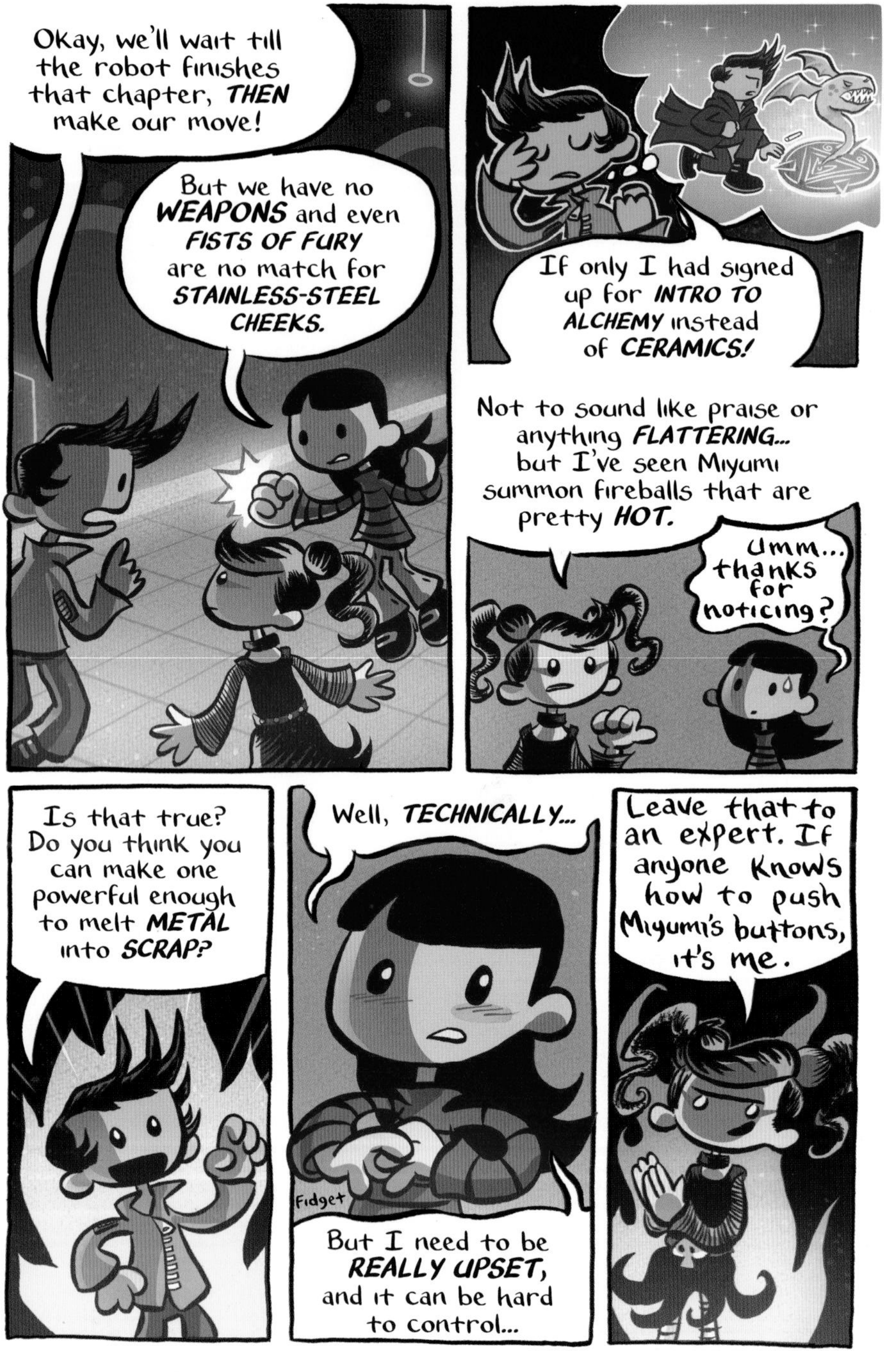

Okay, we'll wait till the robot finishes that chapter, THEN make our move!
But we have no WEAPONS and even FISTS OF FURY are no match for STAINLESS-STEEL CHEEKS.
If only I had signed up for INTRO TO ALCHEMY instead of CERAMICS!
Not to sound like praise or anything FLATTERING... but I've seen Miyumi summon fireballs that are pretty HOT.
Umm... thanks for noticing?
Is that true? Do you think you can make one powerful enough to melt METAL into SCRAP?
Well, TECHNICALLY...
Fidget
But I need to be REALLY UPSET, and it can be hard to control...
Leave that to an expert. If anyone knows how to push Miyumi's buttons, it's me.

MIYUMI and I ARE WORST FRIENDS AT: ASTRONAUT ACADEMY

That's certainly true...

...but so far *EVEN* being trapped here with you hasn't produced enough anger or flint to get me

Fired up!

Maybe we've grown *TOO MUCH* as people.

Perhaps a **FLASHBACK** will rekindle that *PAST* anger and instigate the spark we need!

You keep your flashbacks in your belly button?

Doesn't *EVERYONE*?

Think back... all the way to the Bouncing Ball party I had in nursery school...

Hoot!

Hoot!

... Remember what a bouncyful hootenanny it was?

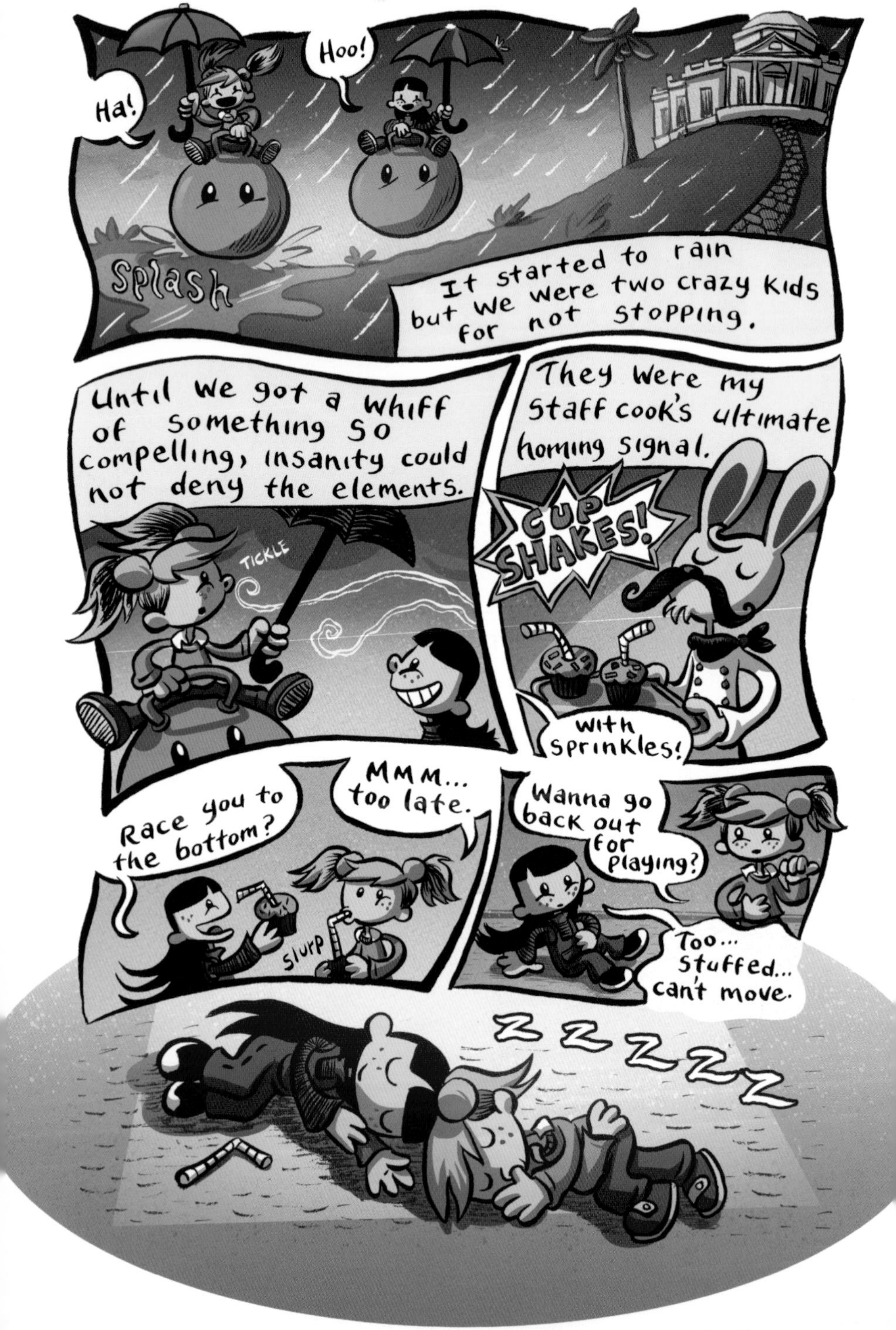
Ha!
Hoo!
Splash
It started to rain but we were two crazy kids for not stopping.
Until we got a whiff of something so compelling, insanity could not deny the elements.
TICKLE
They were my staff cook's ultimate homing signal.
CUP SHAKES!
With sprinkles!
Race you to the bottom?
MMM... too late.
slurp
Wanna go back out for playing?
Too... stuffed... can't move.
Z Z Z Z Z Z

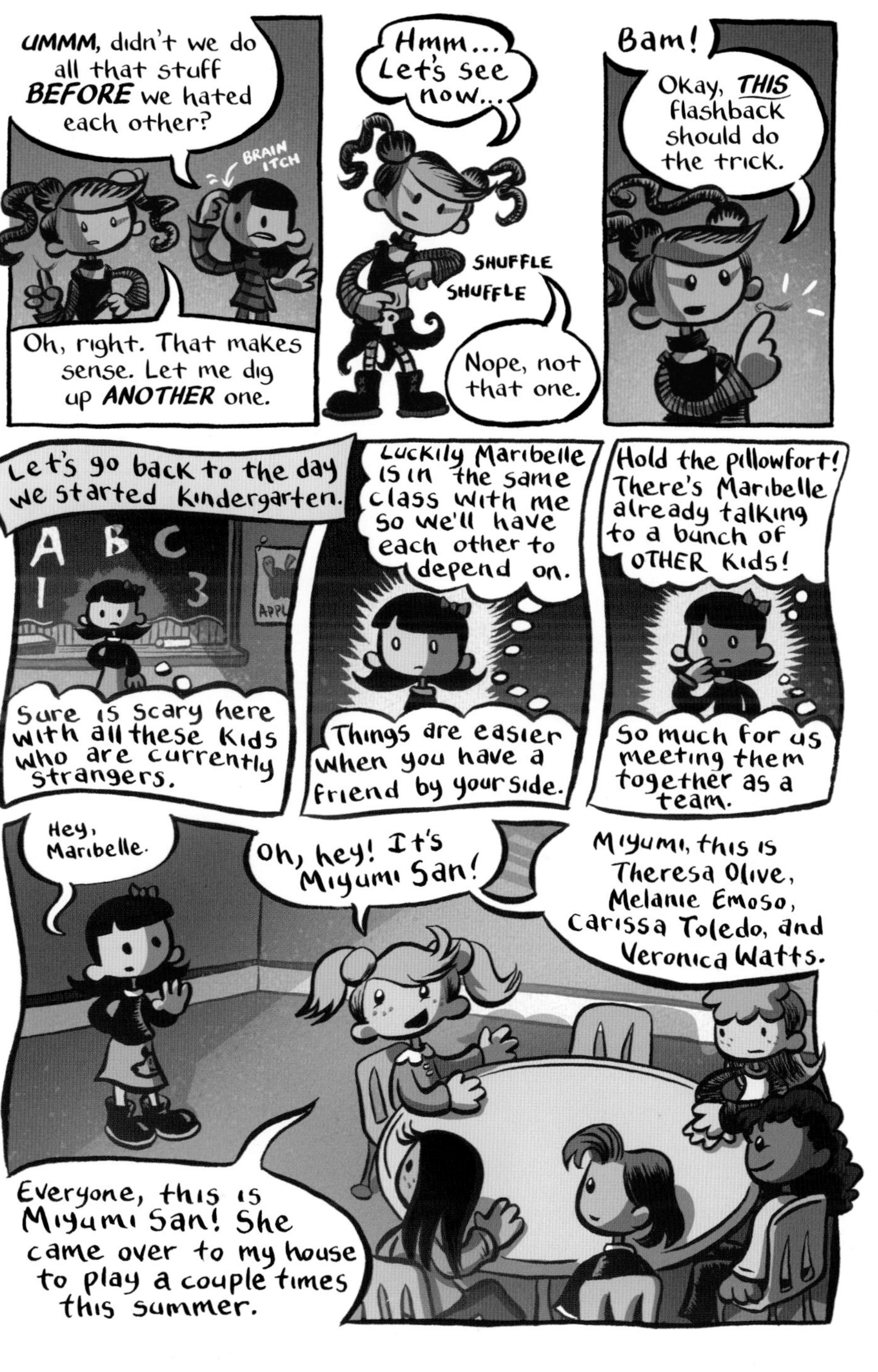

UMMM, didn't we do all that stuff BEFORE we hated each other?
BRAIN ITCH
Oh, right. That makes sense. Let me dig up ANOTHER one.
Hmm... Let's see now...
SHUFFLE
SHUFFLE
Nope, not that one.
Bam!
Okay, THIS flashback should do the trick.
Let's go back to the day we started Kindergarten.
A B C
1 3
APPL
Sure is scary here with all these kids who are currently strangers.
Luckily Maribelle is in the same class with me so we'll have each other to depend on.
Things are easier when you have a friend by your side.
Hold the pillowfort! There's Maribelle already talking to a bunch of OTHER kids!
So much for us meeting them together as a team.
Hey, Maribelle.
Oh, hey! It's Miyumi San!
Miyumi, this is Theresa Olive, Melanie Emoso, Carissa Toledo, and Veronica Watts.
Everyone, this is Miyumi San! She came over to my house to play a couple times this summer.

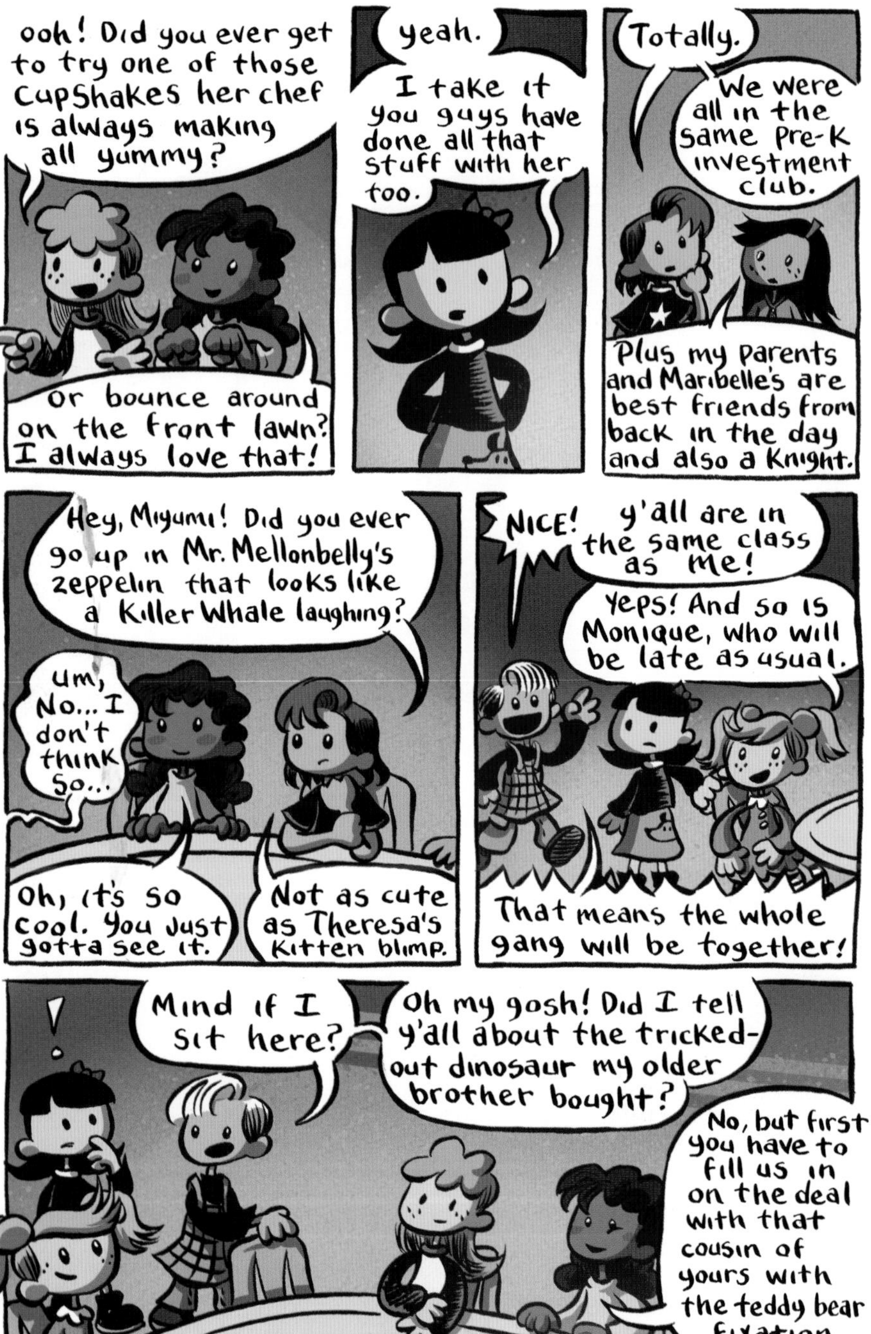
ooh! Did you ever get to try one of those CupShakes her chef is always making all yummy?
Or bounce around on the front lawn? I always love that!
yeah.
I take it you guys have done all that stuff with her too.
Totally.
We were all in the same Pre-K investment club.
Plus my parents and Maribelle's are best friends from back in the day and also a Knight.
Hey, Miyumi! Did you ever go up in Mr. Mellonbelly's zeppelin that looks like a Killer Whale laughing?
Um, No... I don't think So...
Oh, it's so cool. You just gotta see it.
Not as cute as Theresa's Kitten blimp.
NICE!
y'all are in the same class as me!
Yeps! And so is Monique, who will be late as usual.
That means the whole gang will be together!
!
Mind if I sit here?
Oh my gosh! Did I tell y'all about the tricked-out dinosaur my older brother bought?
No, but first you have to fill us in on the deal with that cousin of yours with the teddy bear fixation.

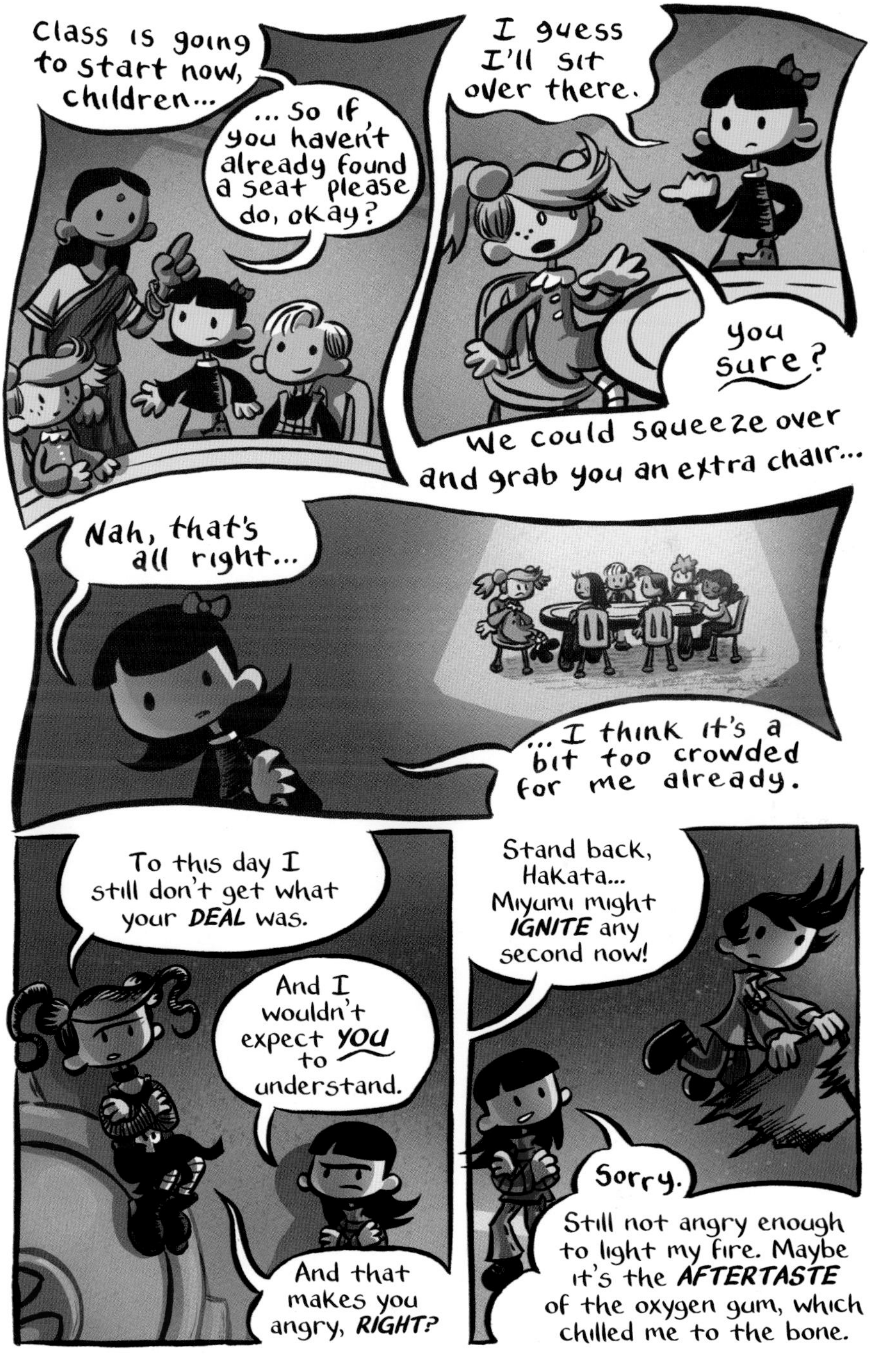

Class is going to start now, children...
...So if you haven't already found a seat please do, okay?
I guess I'll sit over there.
You sure?
We could squeeze over and grab you an extra chair...
Nah, that's all right...
...I think it's a bit too crowded for me already.
To this day I still don't get what your DEAL was.
And I wouldn't expect YOU to understand.
And that makes you angry, RIGHT?
Stand back, Hakata... Miyumi might IGNITE any second now!
Sorry.
Still not angry enough to light my fire. Maybe it's the AFTERTASTE of the oxygen gum, which chilled me to the bone.

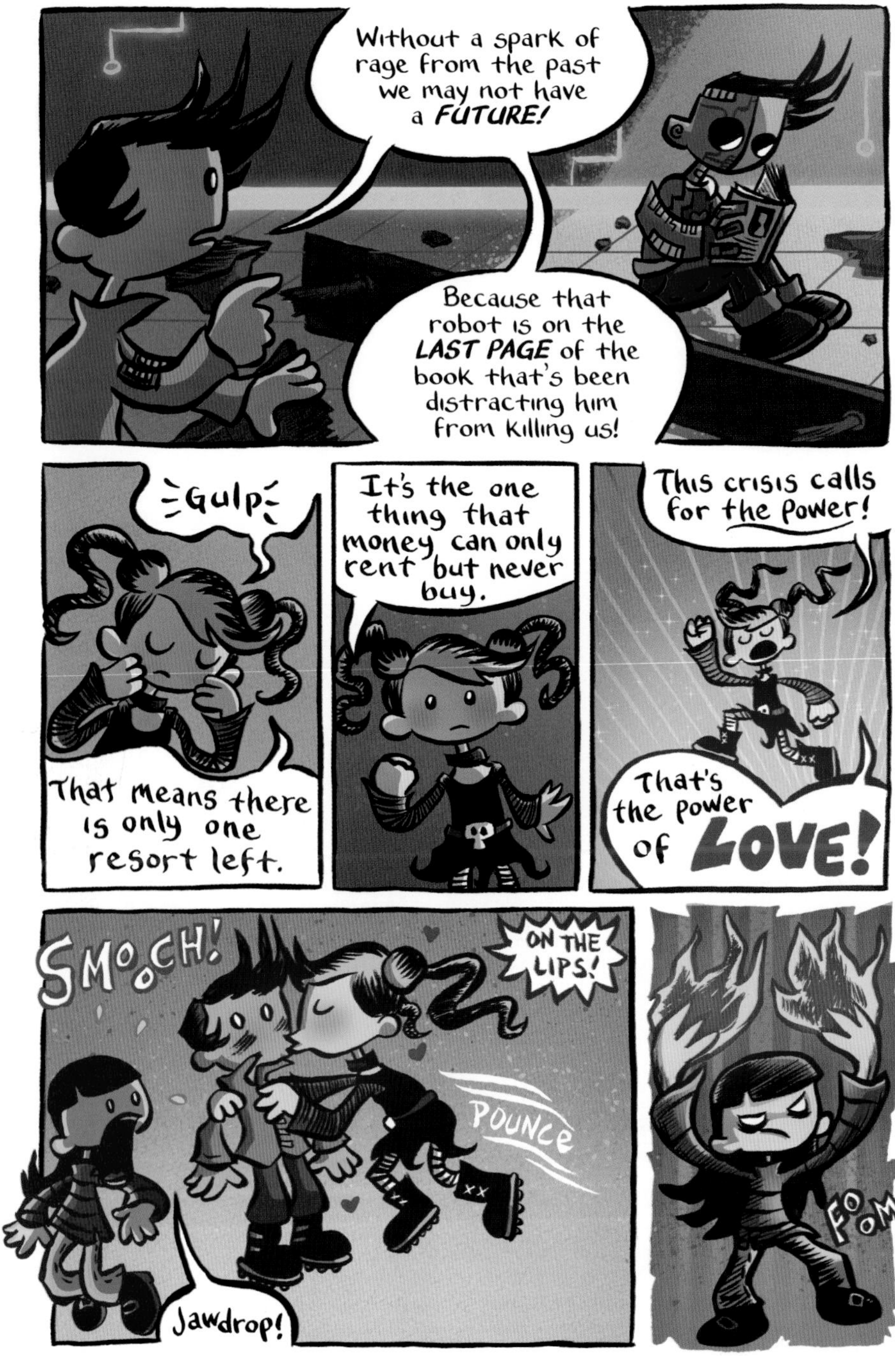
Without a spark of rage from the past we may not have a FUTURE!
Because that robot is on the LAST PAGE of the book that's been distracting him from killing us!
Gulp
That means there is only one resort left.
It's the one thing that money can only rent but never buy.
This crisis calls for the power!
That's the power of LOVE!
SMOOCH!
ON THE LIPS!
POUNCE
Jawdrop!
FOOM!

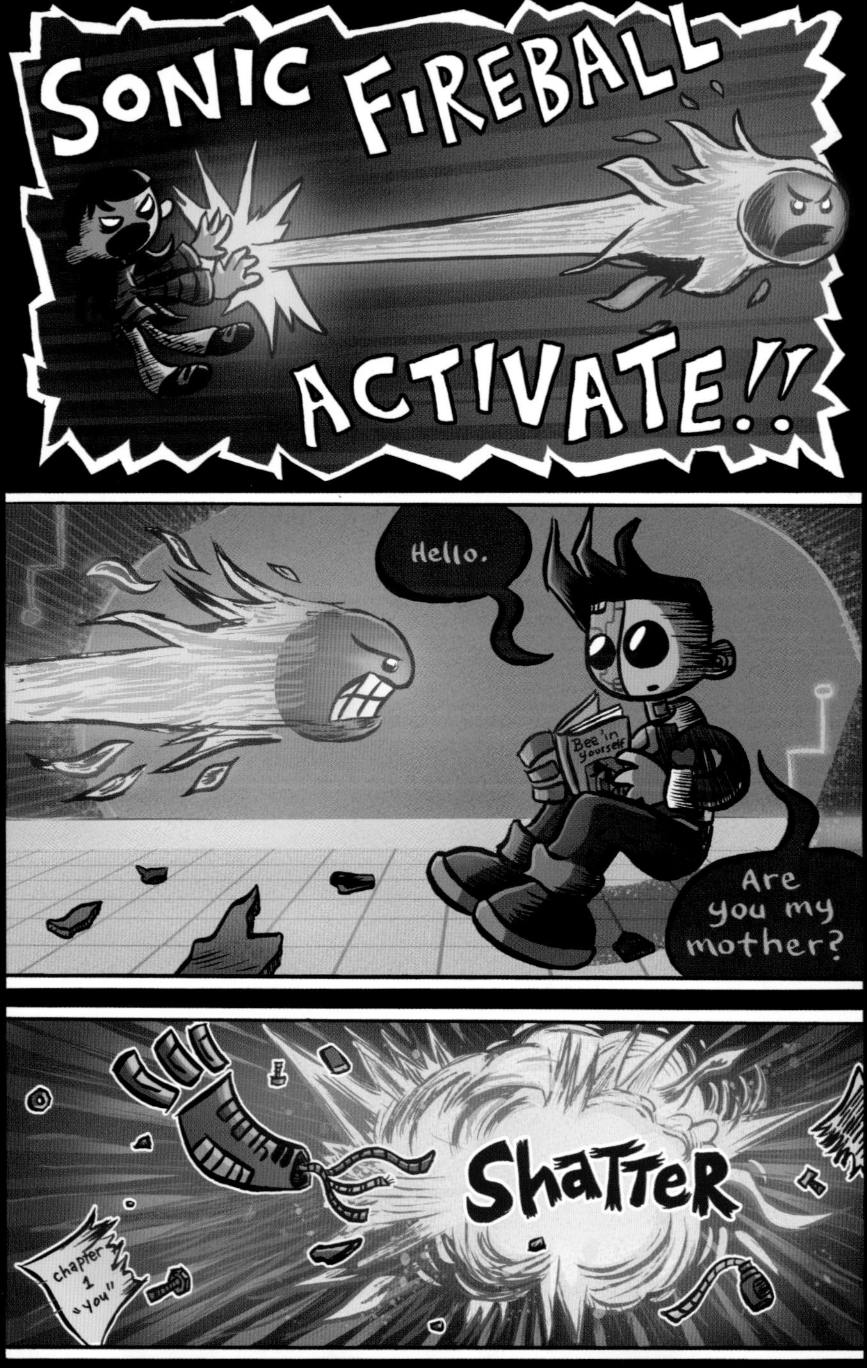
SONIC FIREBALL
ACTIVATE!!
Hello.
Bee 'in yourself
Are you my mother?
SHATTER
chapter 1 "You"

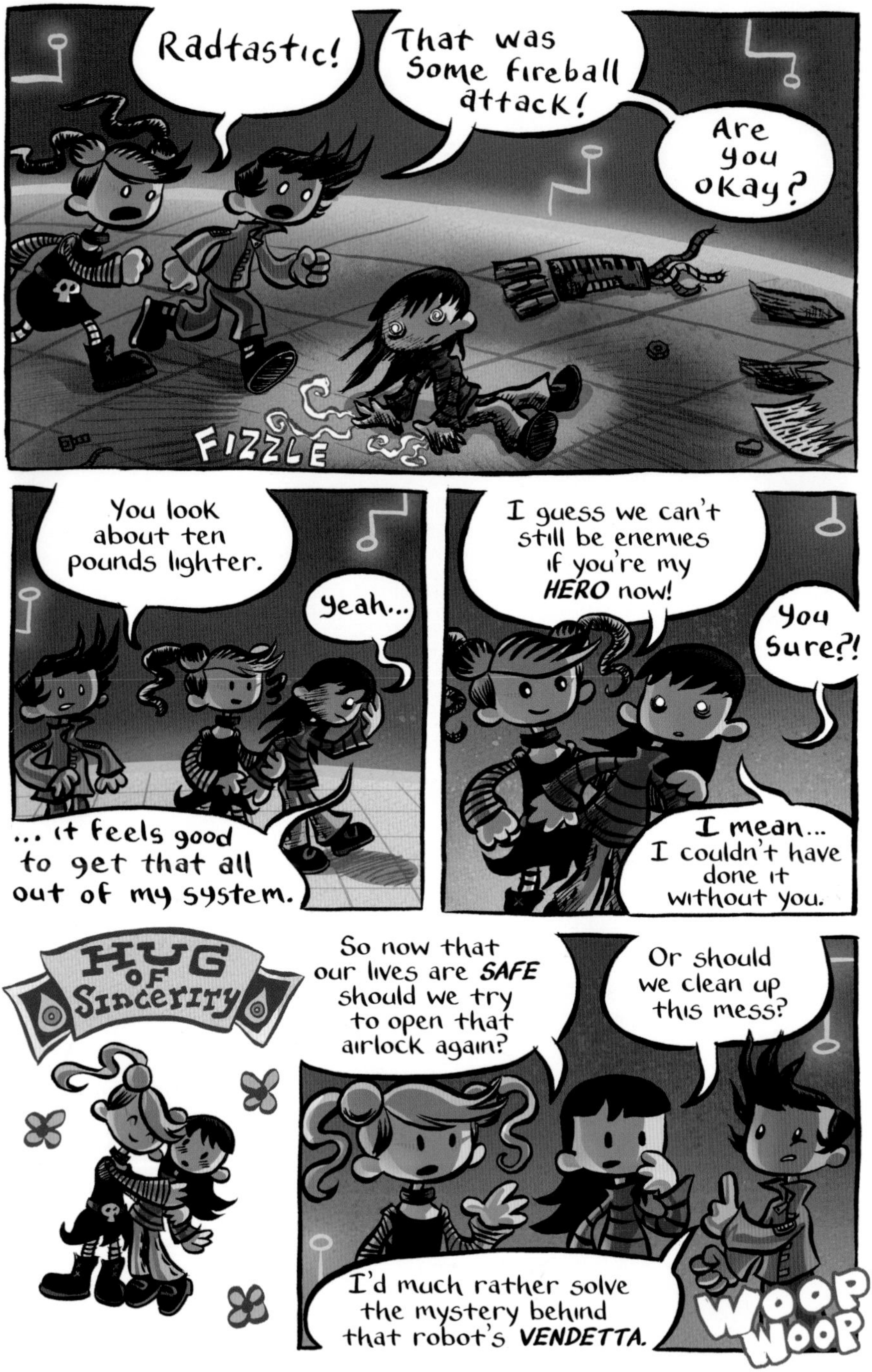

Radtastic!
That was Some fireball attack!
Are you okay?
FIZZLE
You look about ten pounds lighter.
Yeah...
... it feels good to get that all out of my system.
I guess we can't still be enemies if you're my HERO now!
You Sure?!
I mean... I couldn't have done it without you.
HUG OF Sincerity
So now that our lives are SAFE should we try to open that airlock again?
Or should we clean up this mess?
I'd much rather solve the mystery behind that robot's VENDETTA.
WOOP WOOP

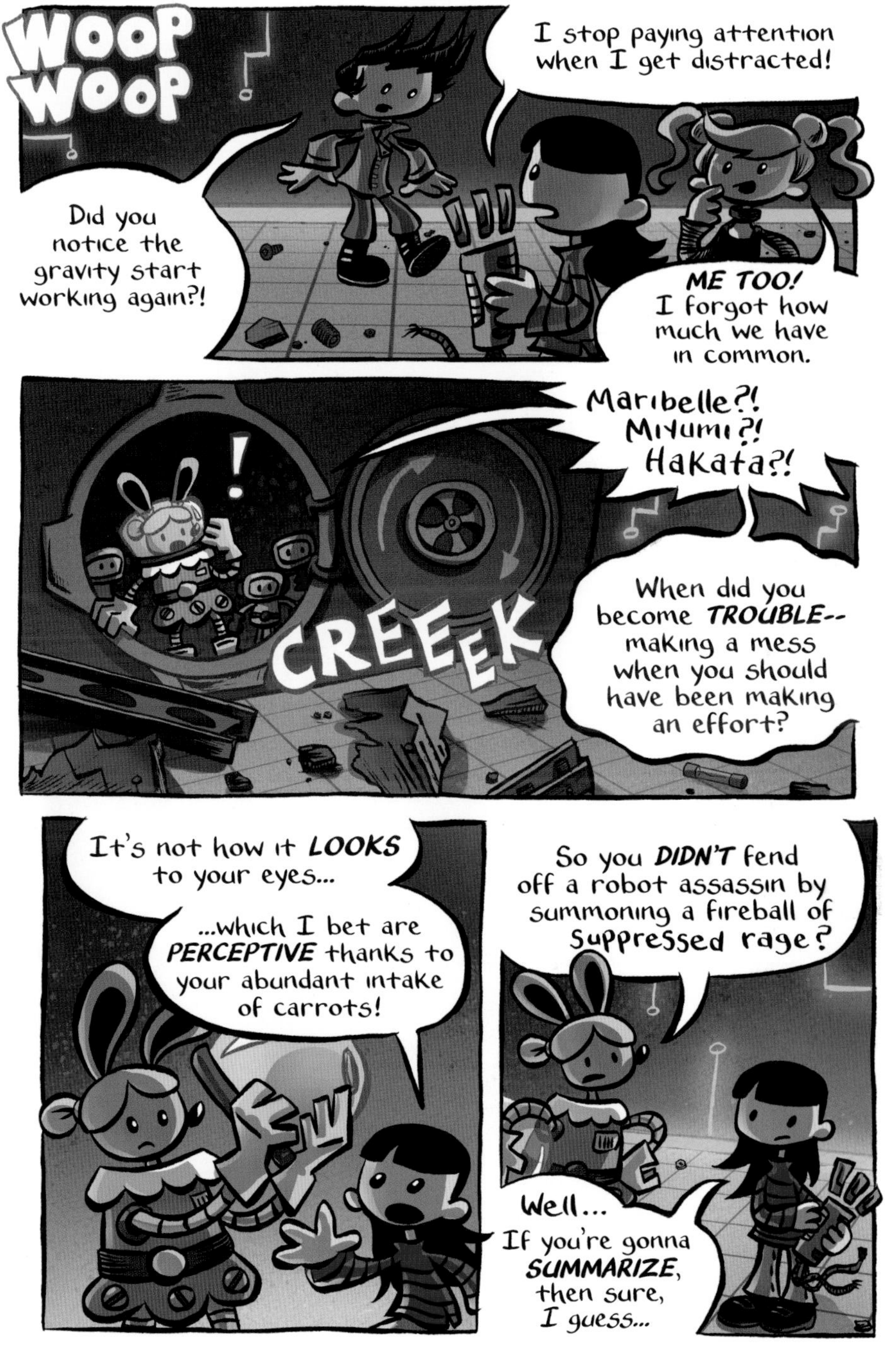
WOOP WOOP
I stop paying attention when I get distracted!
Did you notice the gravity start working again?!
ME TOO! I forgot how much we have in common.
Maribelle?! Miyumi?! Hakata?!
CREEEK
When did you become TROUBLE-- making a mess when you should have been making an effort?
It's not how it LOOKS to your eyes...
...which I bet are PERCEPTIVE thanks to your abundant intake of carrots!
So you DIDN'T fend off a robot assassin by summoning a fireball of suppressed rage?
Well... If you're gonna SUMMARIZE, then sure, I guess...

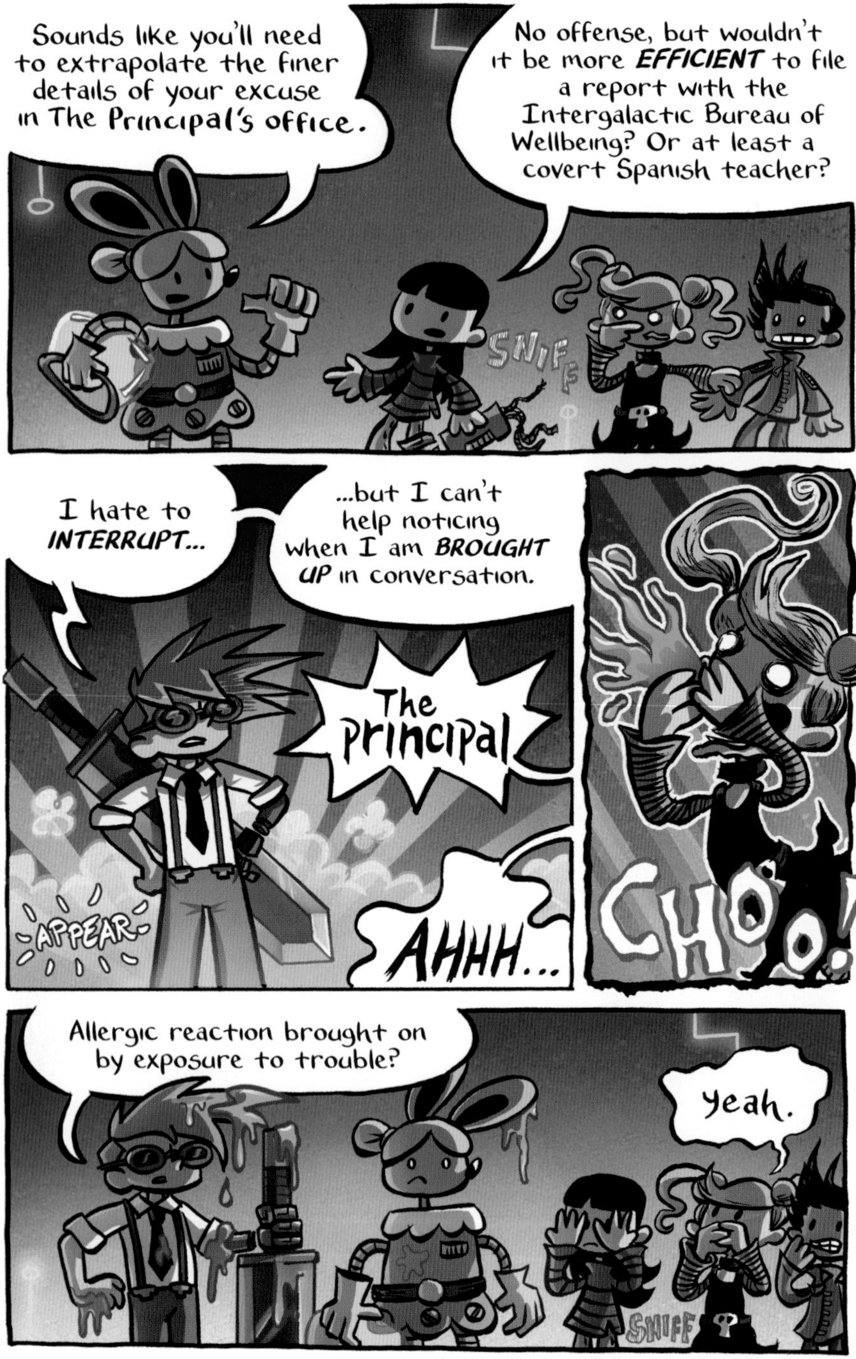
Sounds like you'll need to extrapolate the finer details of your excuse in The Principal's office.
No offense, but wouldn't it be more EFFICIENT to file a report with the Intergalactic Bureau of Wellbeing? Or at least a covert Spanish teacher?
SNIFF
I hate to INTERRUPT...
...but I can't help noticing when I am BROUGHT UP in conversation.
The Principal
APPEAR
AHHH...
CHOO!
Allergic reaction brought on by exposure to trouble?
Yeah.
SNIFF
The End!

SCHOOL'S OUT!
But don't head home just yet...

Parent-Teacher Conferences are tonight!
Followed by the Universal Holiday Party!

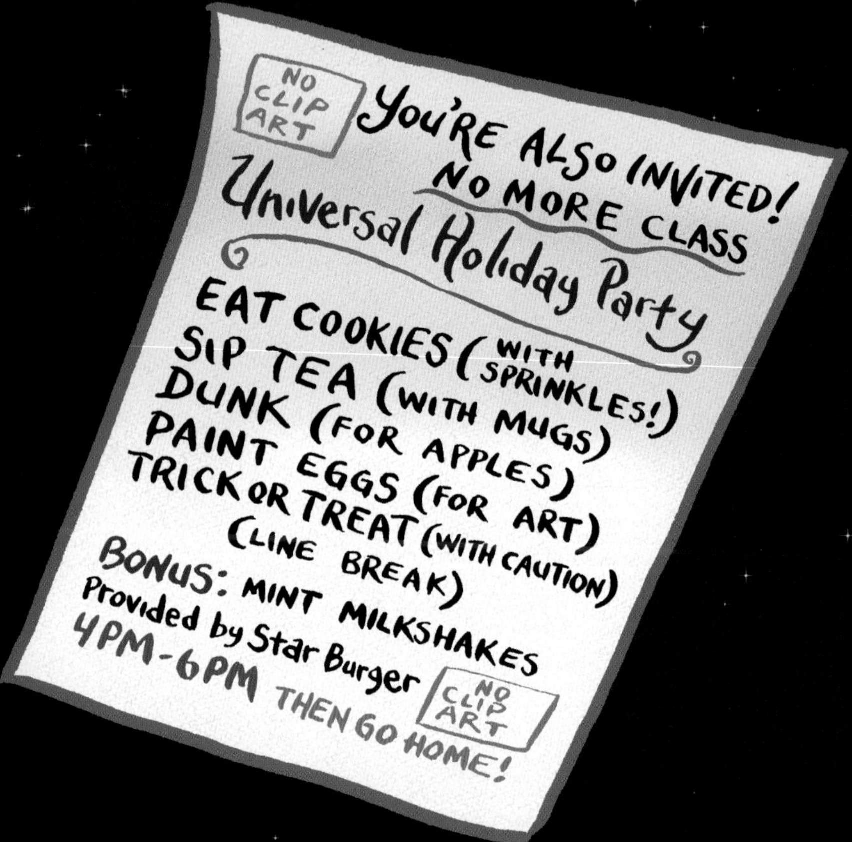
NO CLIP ART
You're ALSO INVITED!
NO MORE CLASS
Universal Holiday Party
EAT COOKIES (WITH SPRINKLES!)
SIP TEA (WITH MUGS)
DUNK (FOR APPLES)
PAINT EGGS (FOR ART)
TRICK OR TREAT (WITH CAUTION)
(LINE BREAK)
BONUS: MINT MILKSHAKES
Provided by Star Burger
4PM-6PM THEN GO HOME!
NO CLIP ART

Don't forget The Principal's farewell
or your epilogues!

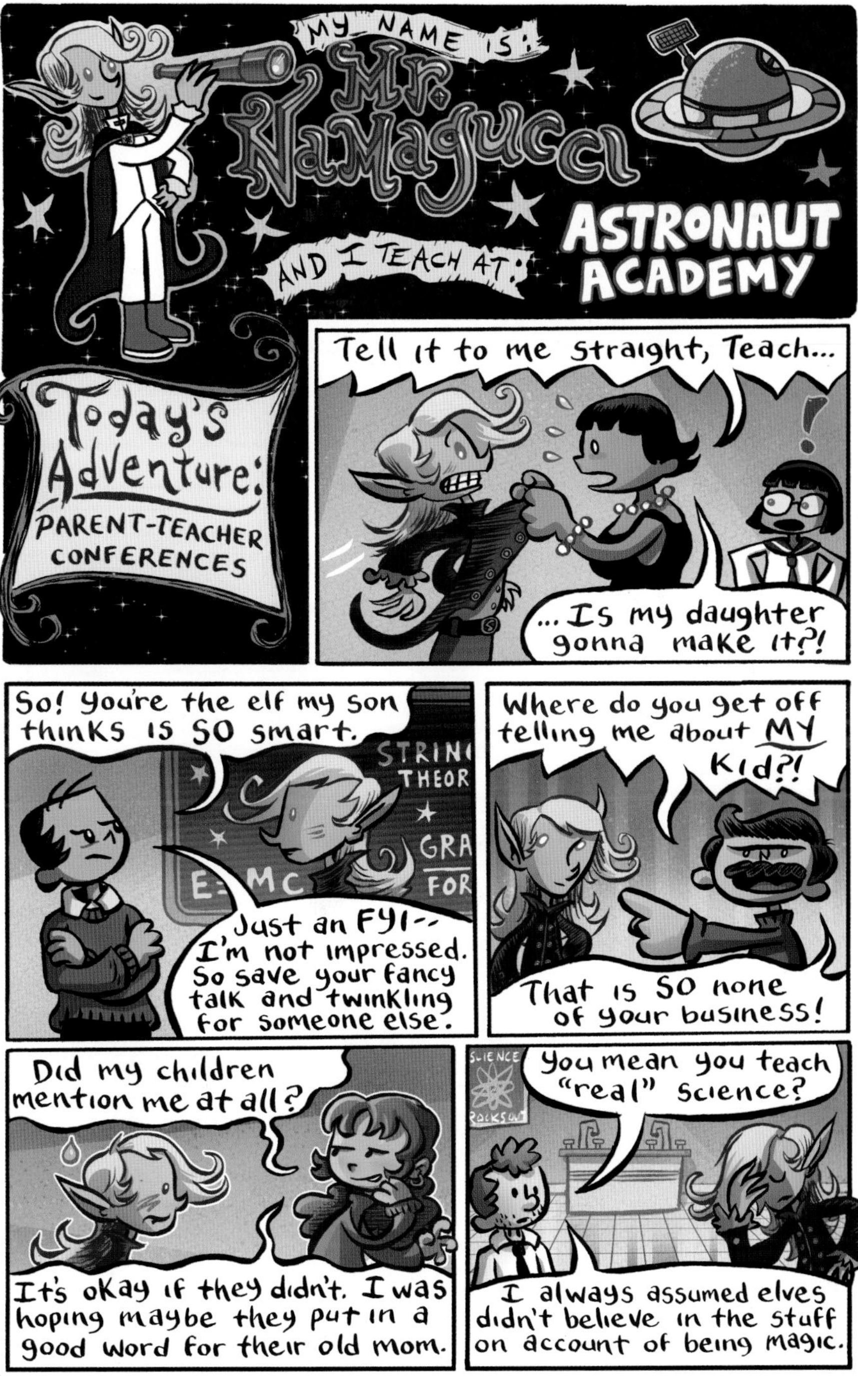
MY NAME IS:
Mr. Namagucci
AND I TEACH AT:
ASTRONAUT ACADEMY
Today's Adventure:
PARENT-TEACHER CONFERENCES
Tell it to me straight, Teach...
!
...Is my daughter gonna make it?!
So! You're the elf my son thinks is SO smart.
STRING THEOR
GRA
E=MC
FOR
Just an FYI-- I'm not impressed. So save your fancy talk and twinkling for someone else.
Where do you get off telling me about MY kid?!
That is SO none of your business!
Did my children mention me at all?
It's okay if they didn't. I was hoping maybe they put in a good word for their old mom.
SCIENCE ROCKS OUT
You mean you teach "real" science?
I always assumed elves didn't believe in the stuff on account of being magic.

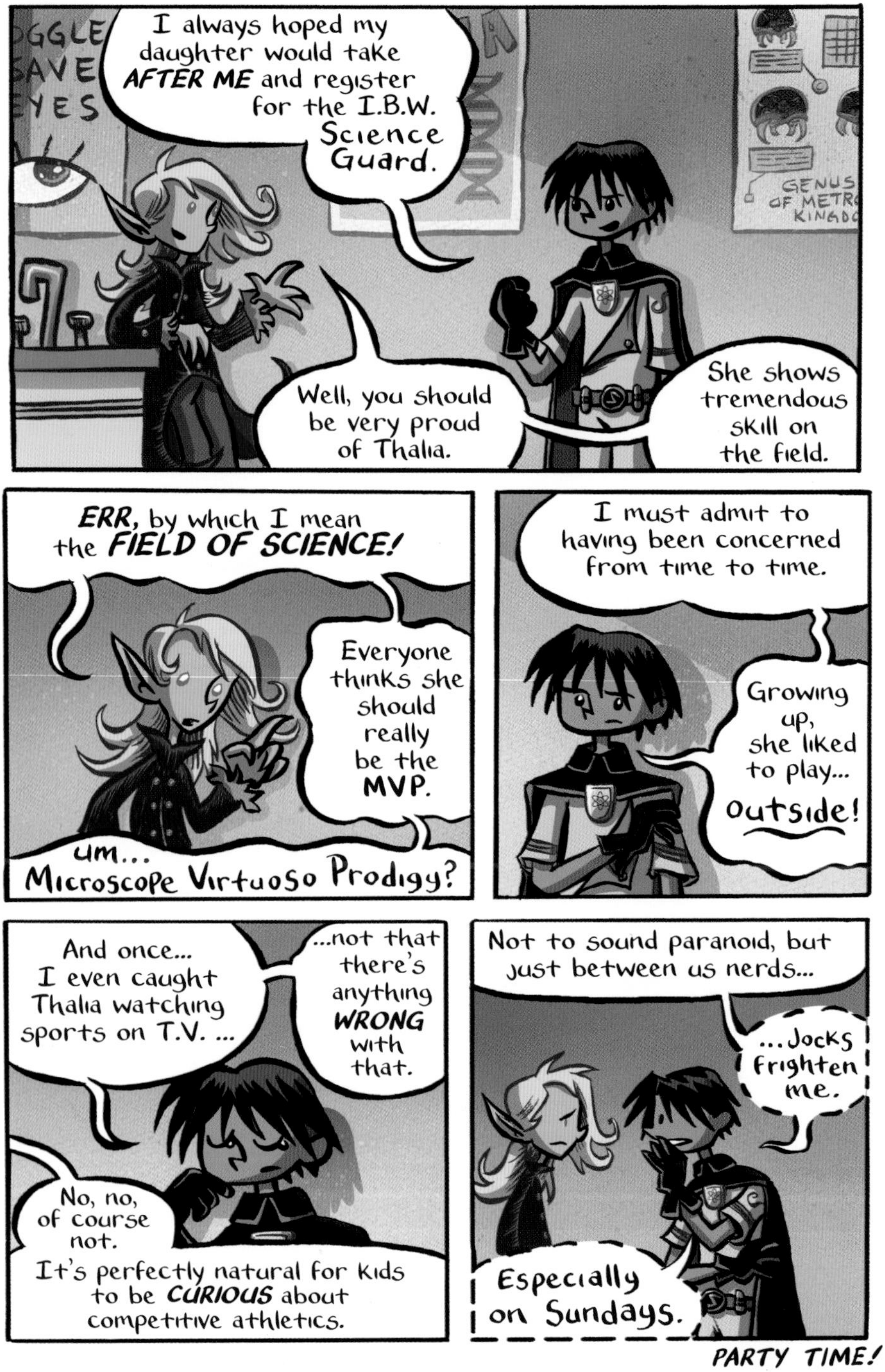
I always hoped my daughter would take AFTER ME and register for the I.B.W. Science Guard.
Well, you should be very proud of Thalia.
She shows tremendous skill on the field.
ERR, by which I mean the FIELD OF SCIENCE!
Everyone thinks she should really be the MVP.
um... Microscope Virtuoso Prodigy?
I must admit to having been concerned from time to time.
Growing up, she liked to play... outside!
And once... I even caught Thalia watching sports on T.V. ...
...not that there's anything WRONG with that.
No, no, of course not.
It's perfectly natural for kids to be CURIOUS about competitive athletics.
Not to sound paranoid, but just between us nerds...
...Jocks frighten me.
Especially on Sundays.
GENUS OF METRO KINGDO
PARTY TIME!

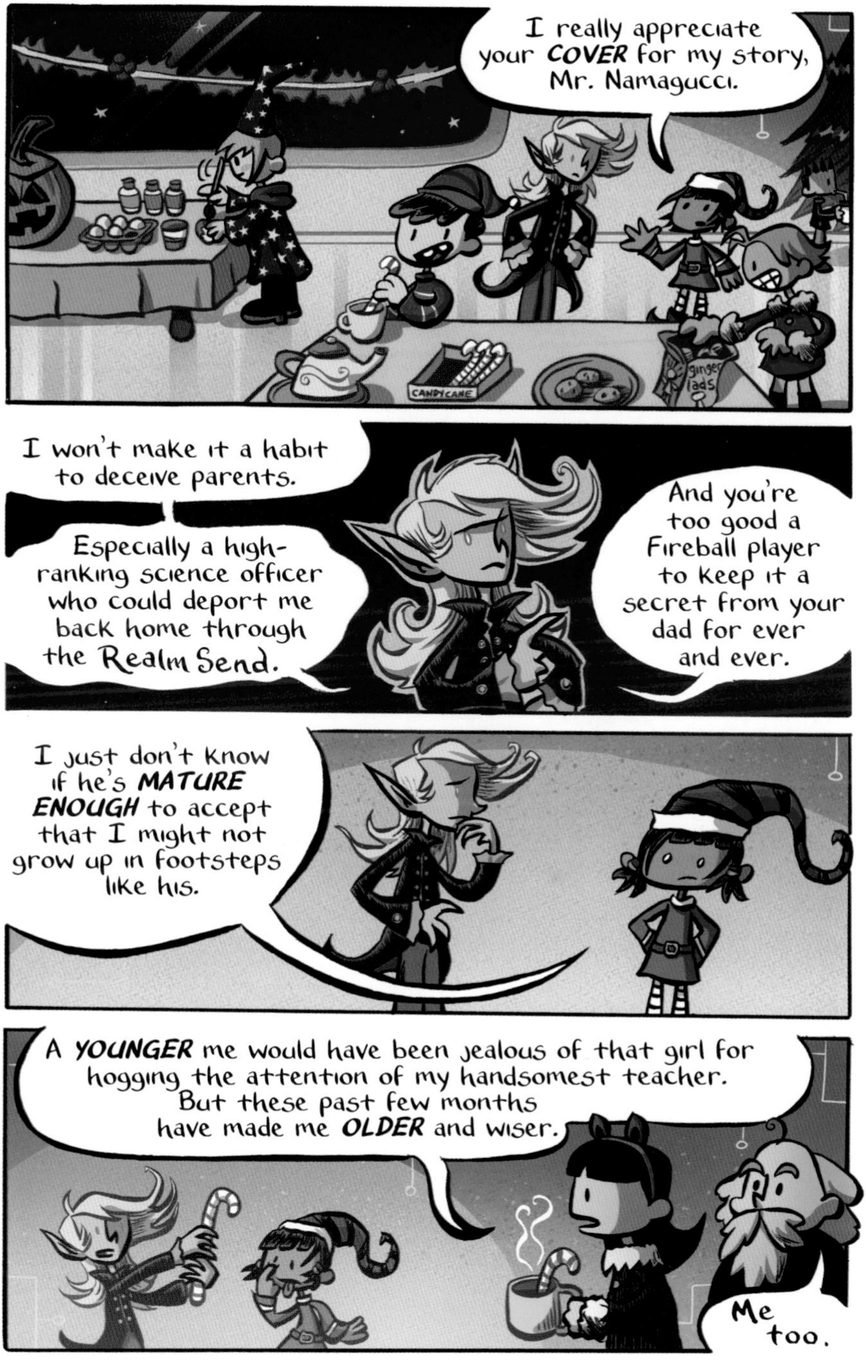
I really appreciate your COVER for my story, Mr. Namagucci.
CANDY CANE
ginger lads
I won't make it a habit to deceive parents.
Especially a high-ranking science officer who could deport me back home through the Realm Send.
And you're too good a Fireball player to keep it a secret from your dad for ever and ever.
I just don't know if he's MATURE ENOUGH to accept that I might not grow up in footsteps like his.
A YOUNGER me would have been jealous of that girl for hogging the attention of my handsomest teacher. But these past few months have made me OLDER and wiser.
Me too.

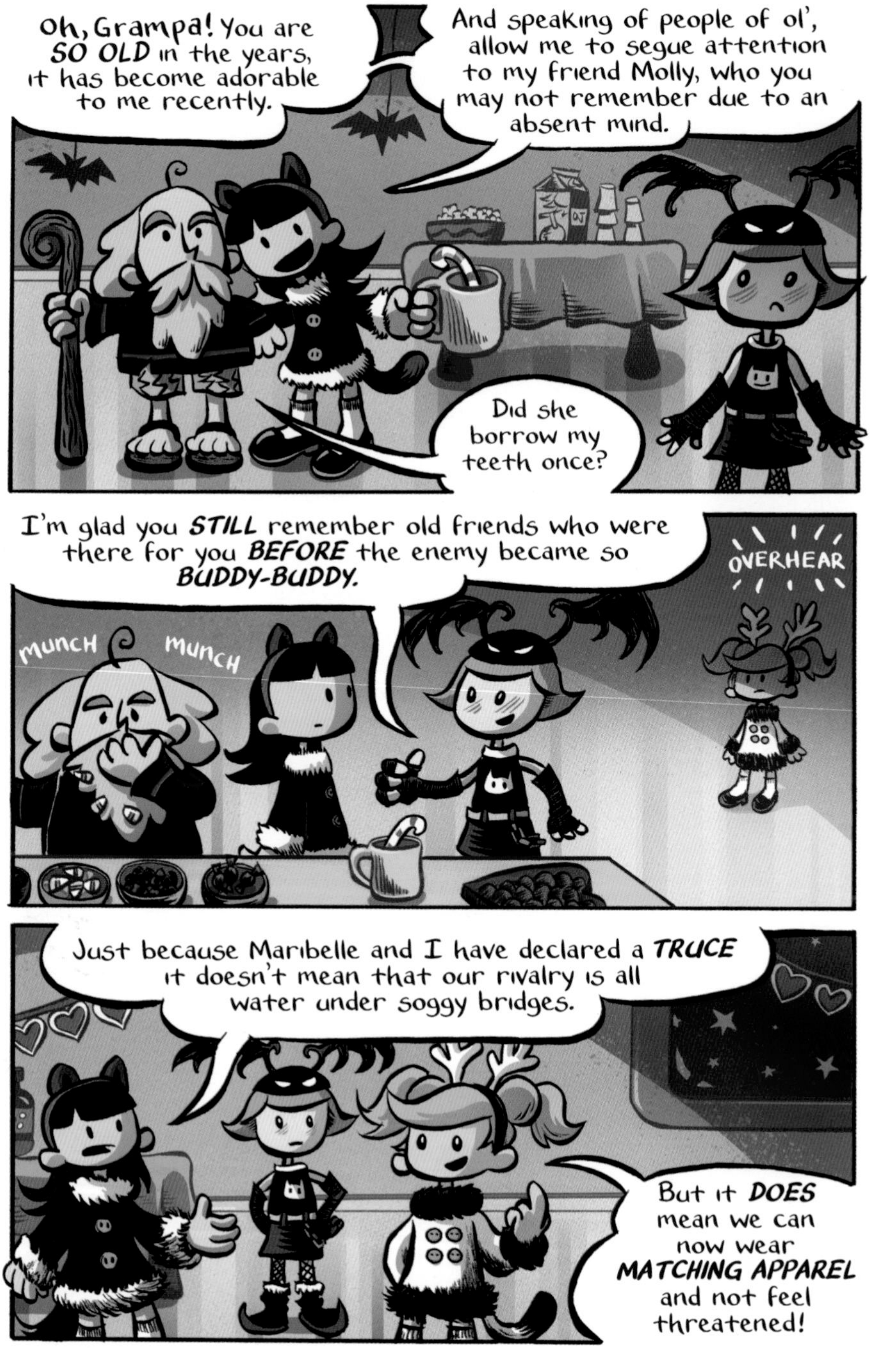
Oh, Grampa! You are SO OLD in the years, it has become adorable to me recently.
And speaking of people of ol', allow me to segue attention to my friend Molly, who you may not remember due to an absent mind.
Did she borrow my teeth once?
I'm glad you STILL remember old friends who were there for you BEFORE the enemy became so BUDDY-BUDDY.
OVERHEAR
MUNCH
MUNCH
Just because Maribelle and I have declared a TRUCE it doesn't mean that our rivalry is all water under soggy bridges.
But it DOES mean we can now wear MATCHING APPAREL and not feel threatened!

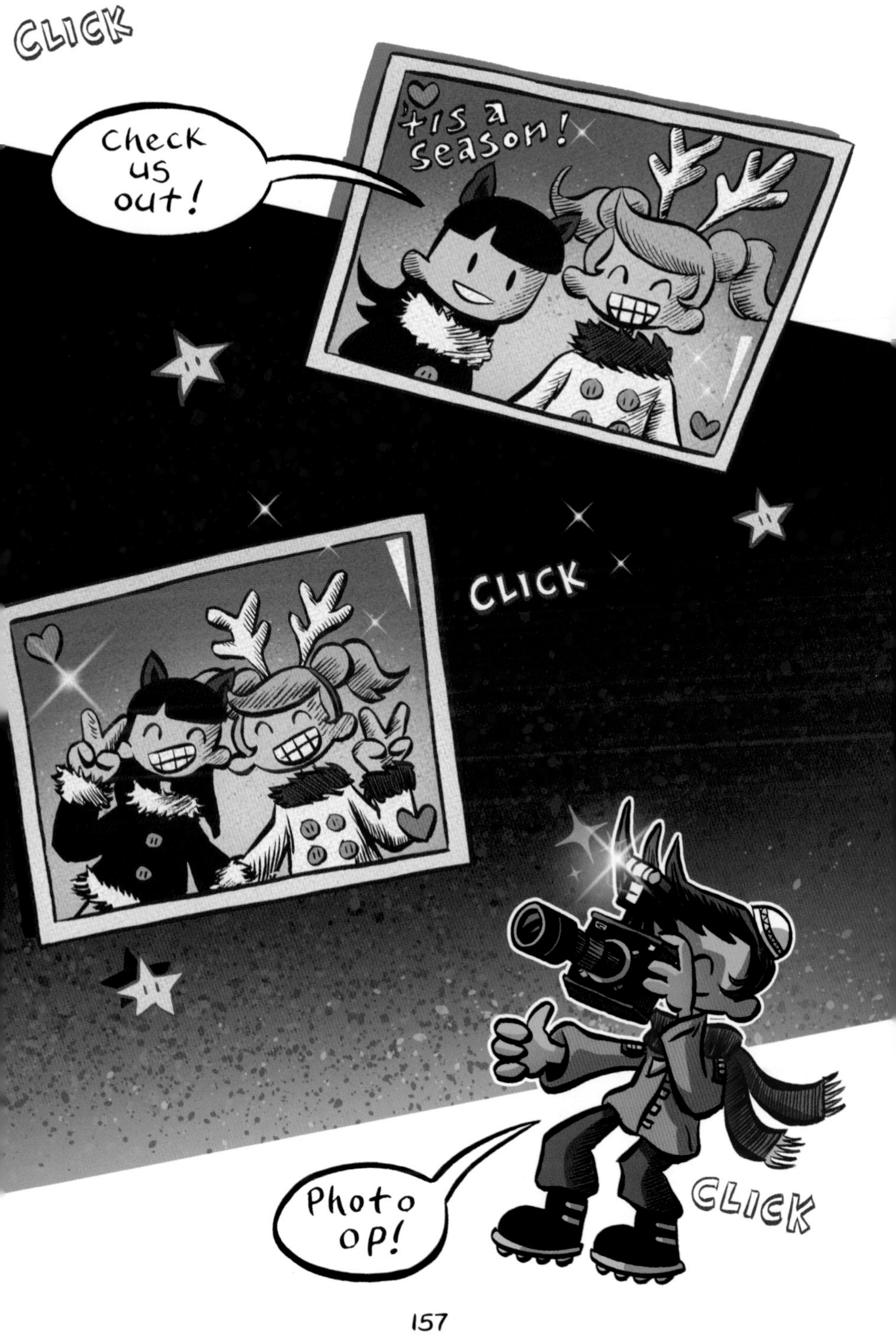
CLICK
Check us out!
'tis a season!
CLICK
Photo op!
CLICK

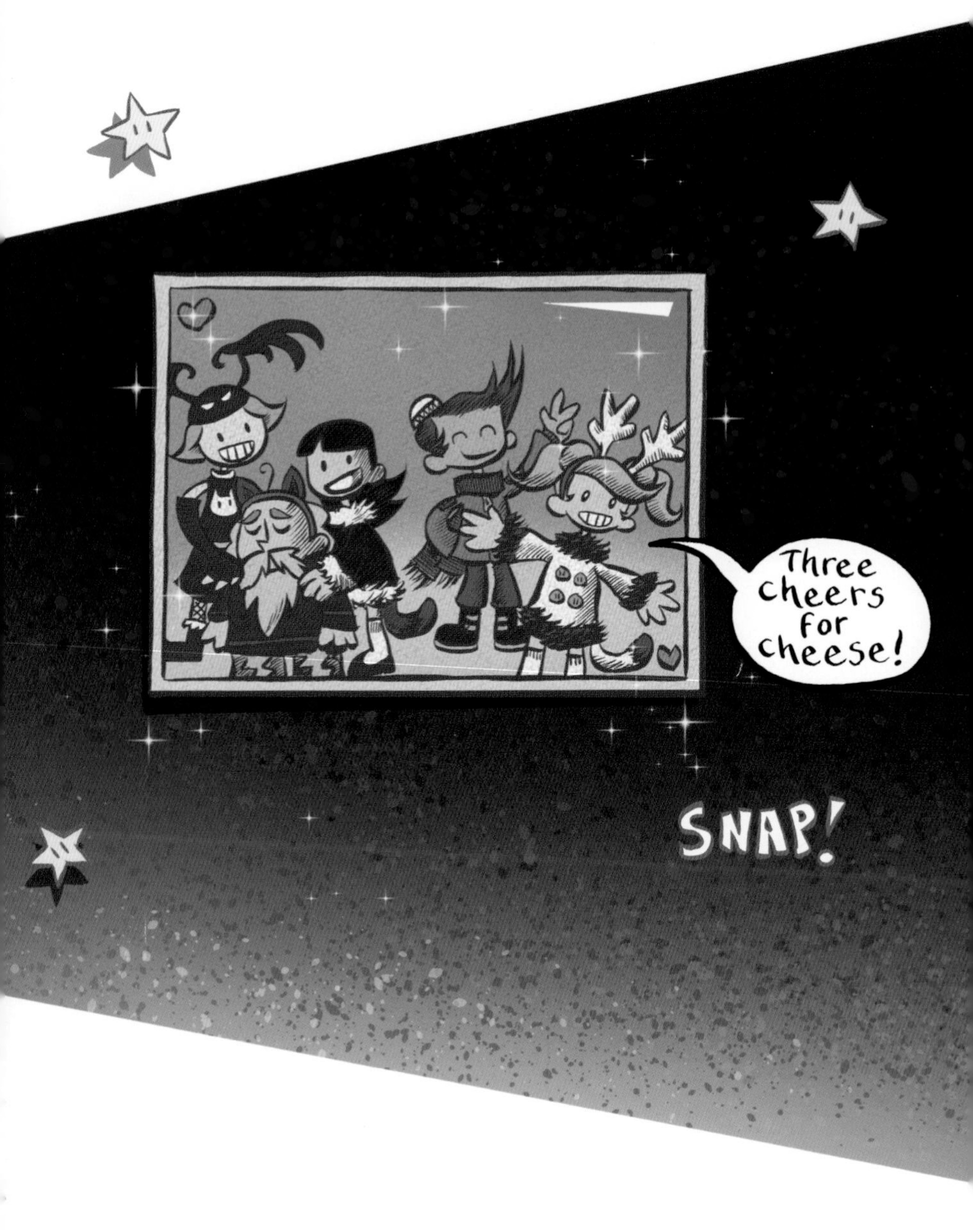
Three cheers for cheese!
SNAP!

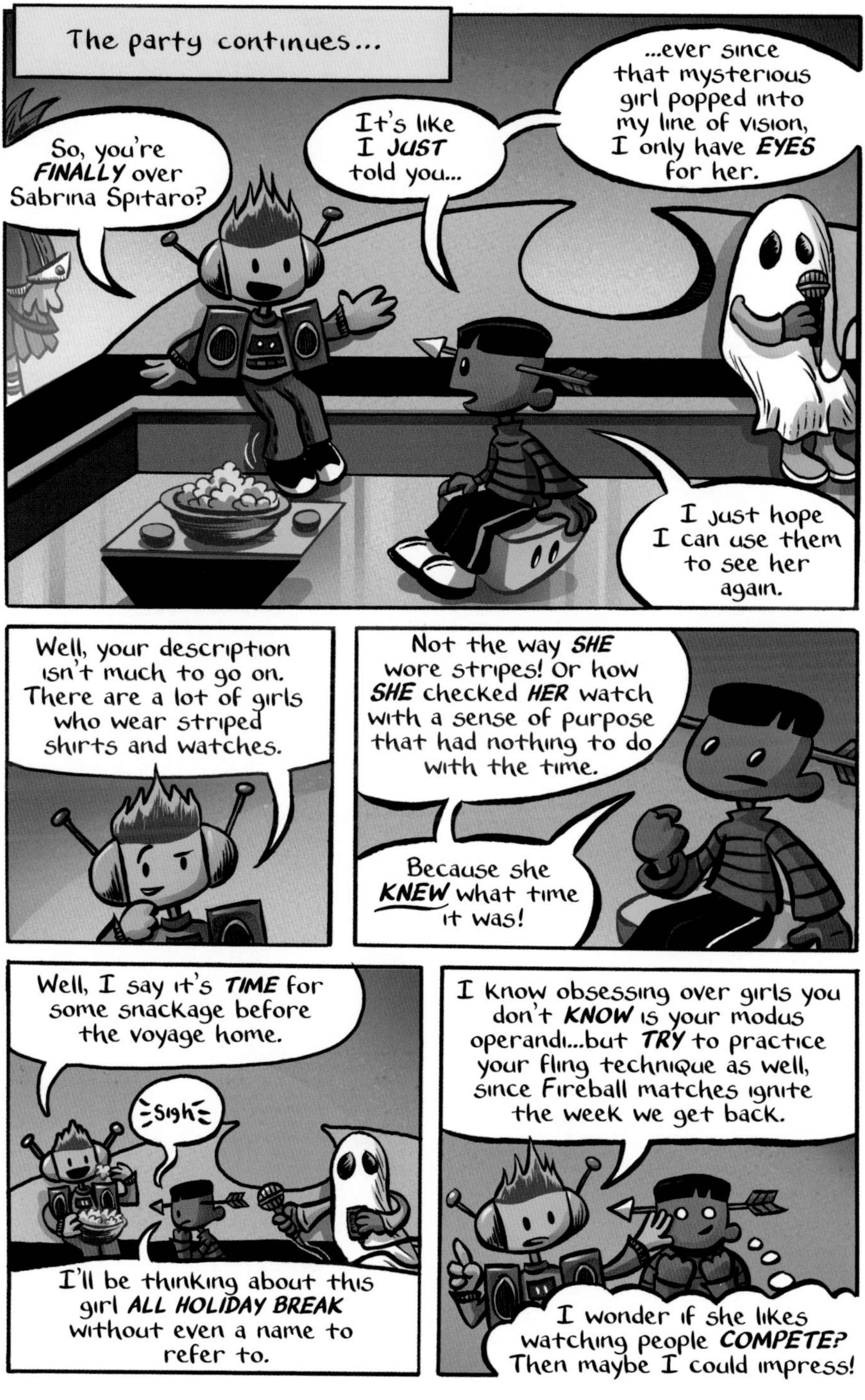
The party continues...
So, you're FINALLY over Sabrina Spitaro?
It's like I JUST told you...
...ever since that mysterious girl popped into my line of vision, I only have EYES for her.
I just hope I can use them to see her again.
Well, your description isn't much to go on. There are a lot of girls who wear striped shirts and watches.
Not the way SHE wore stripes! Or how SHE checked HER watch with a sense of purpose that had nothing to do with the time.
Because she KNEW what time it was!
Well, I say it's TIME for some snackage before the voyage home.
Sigh
I'll be thinking about this girl ALL HOLIDAY BREAK without even a name to refer to.
I know obsessing over girls you don't KNOW is your modus operandi...but TRY to practice your fling technique as well, since Fireball matches ignite the week we get back.
I wonder if she likes watching people COMPETE? Then maybe I could impress!

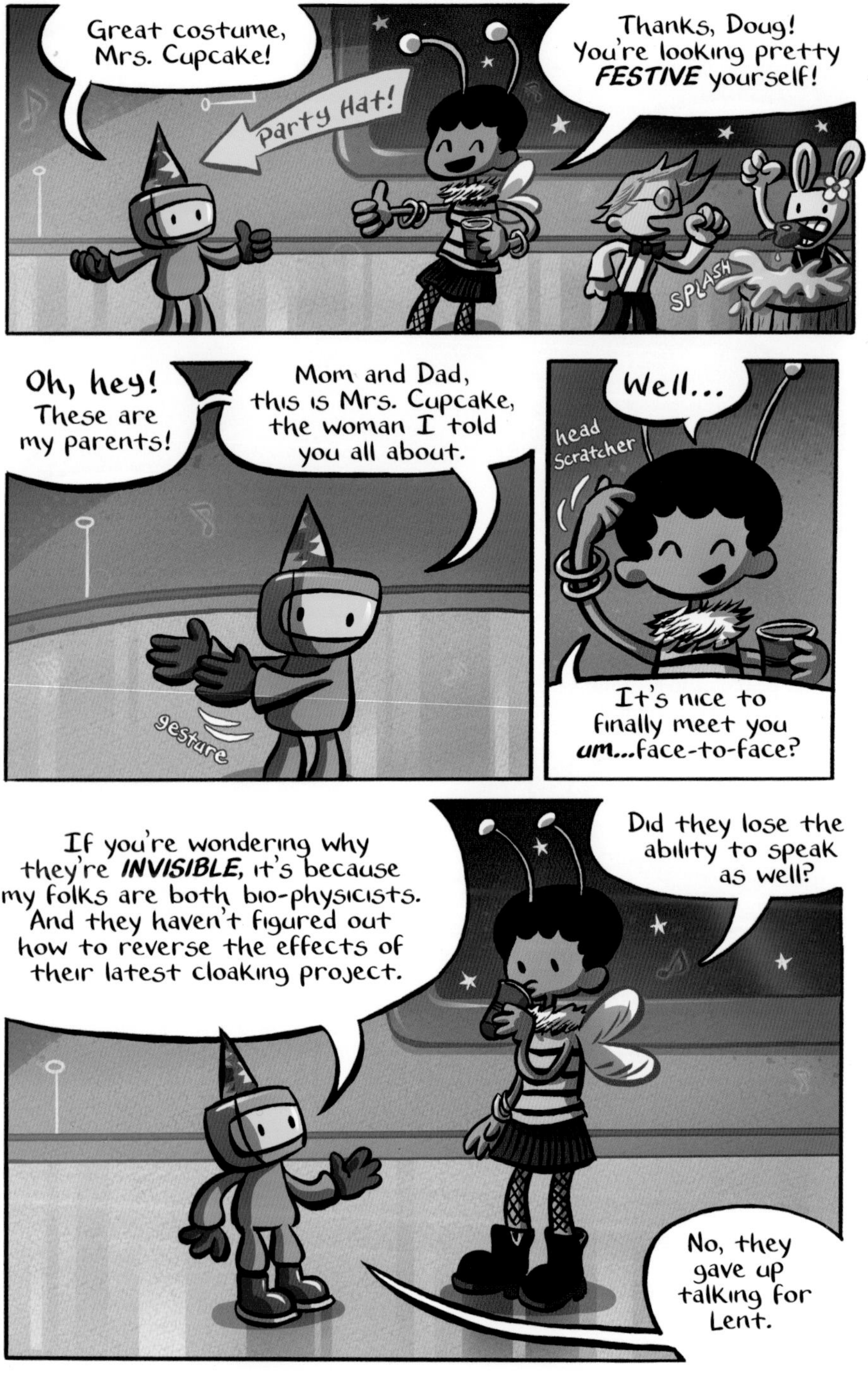
Great costume, Mrs. Cupcake!
Party Hat!
Thanks, Doug! You're looking pretty FESTIVE yourself!
SPLASH
Oh, hey! These are my parents!
Mom and Dad, this is Mrs. Cupcake, the woman I told you all about.
gesture
Well...
head Scratcher
It's nice to finally meet you um...face-to-face?
If you're wondering why they're INVISIBLE, it's because my folks are both bio-physicists. And they haven't figured out how to reverse the effects of their latest cloaking project.
Did they lose the ability to speak as well?
No, they gave up talking for Lent.

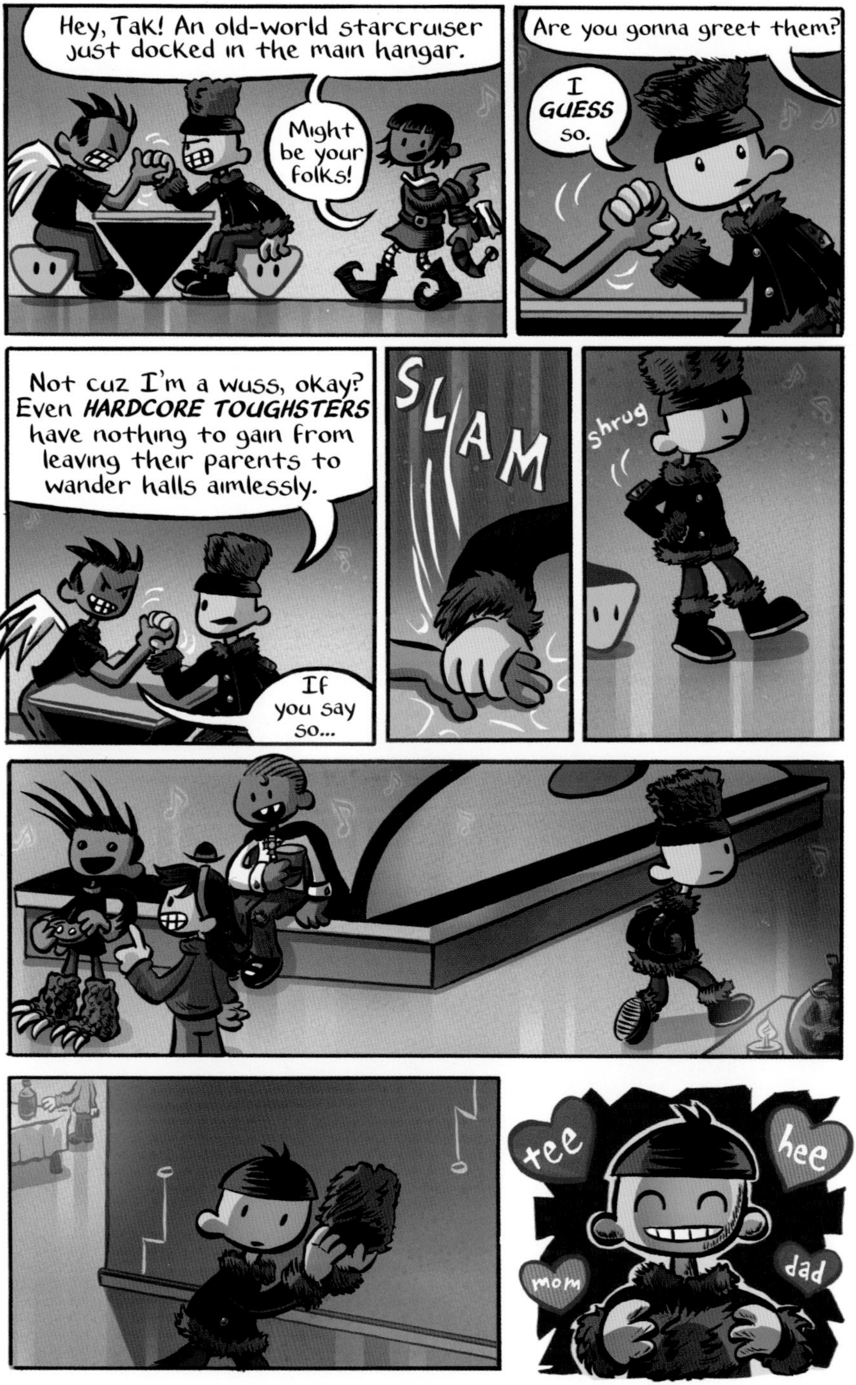
Hey, Tak! An old-world starcruiser just docked in the main hangar.
Might be your folks!
Are you gonna greet them?
I GUESS so.
Not cuz I'm a wuss, okay? Even HARDCORE TOUGHSTERS have nothing to gain from leaving their parents to wander halls aimlessly.
If you say so...
SLAM
shrug
tee
hee
mom
dad

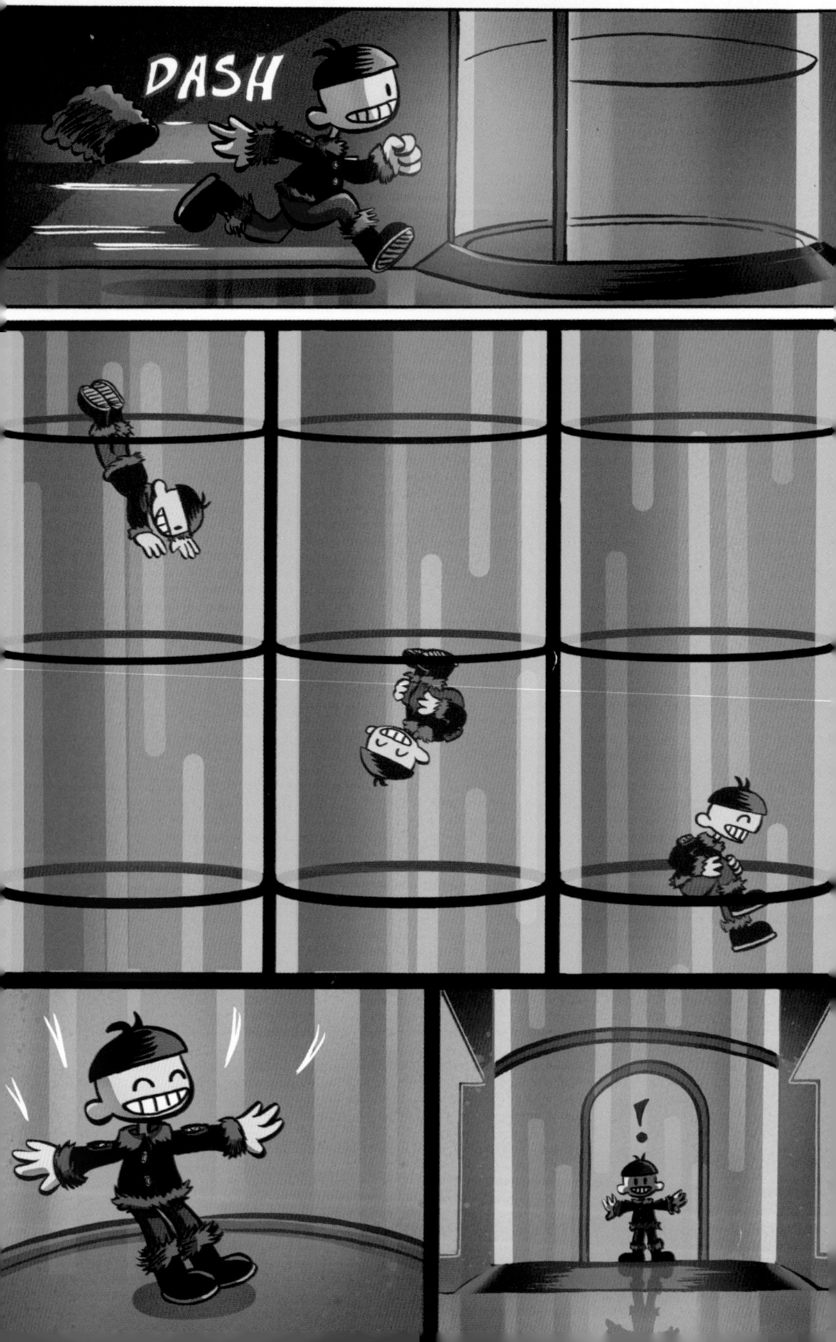
DASH
!

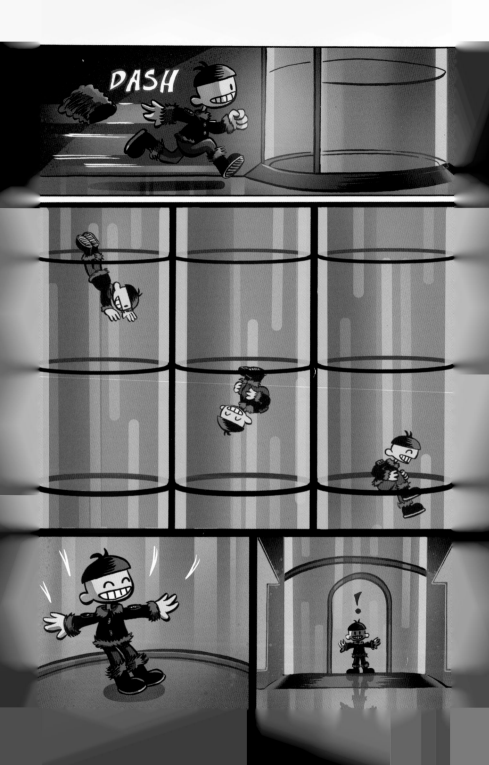

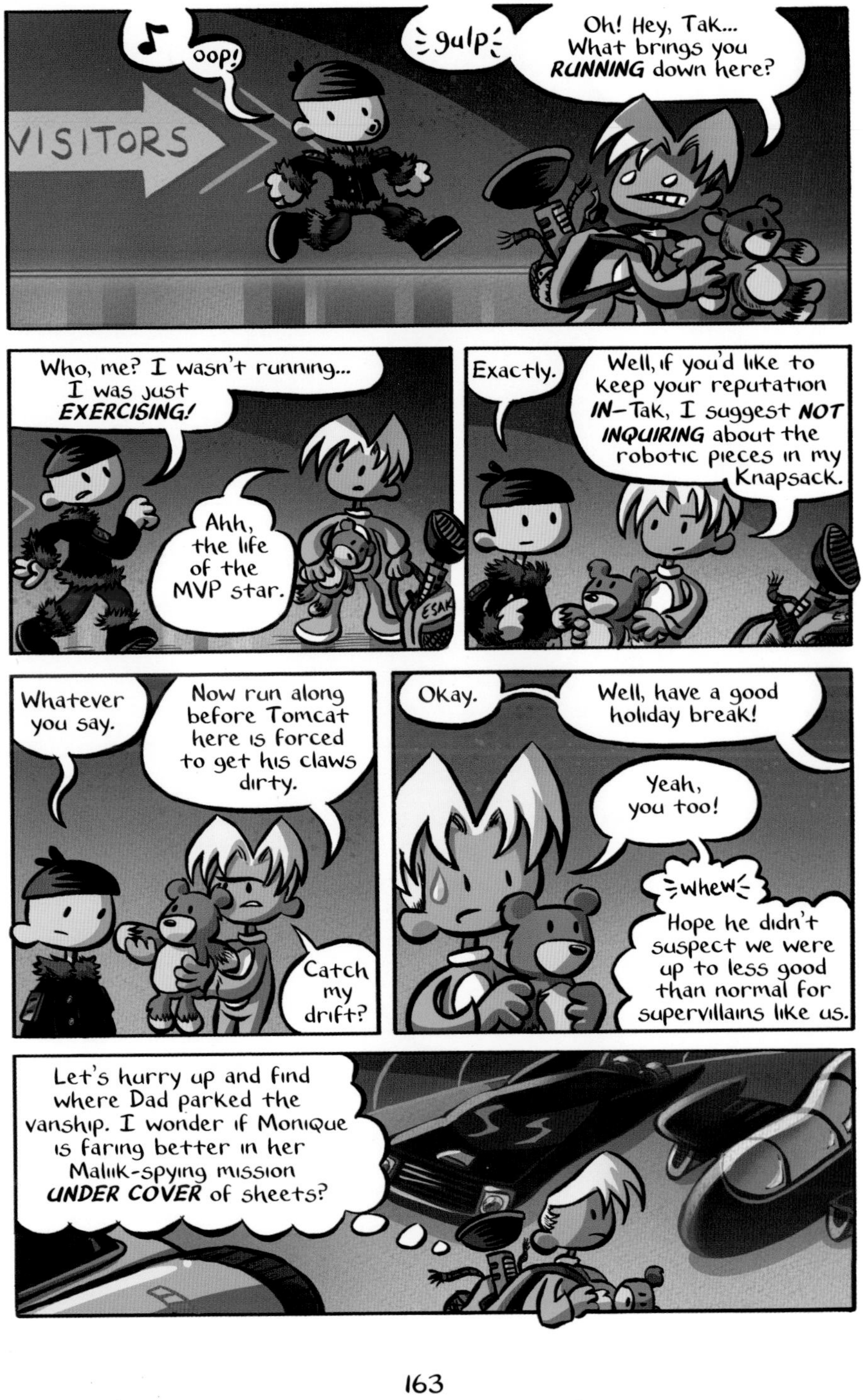
VISITORS
oop!
gulp
Oh! Hey, Tak... What brings you RUNNING down here?
Who, me? I wasn't running... I was just EXERCISING!
Ahh, the life of the MVP star.
ESAK
Exactly.
Well, if you'd like to keep your reputation IN–Tak, I suggest NOT INQUIRING about the robotic pieces in my Knapsack.
Whatever you say.
Now run along before Tomcat here is forced to get his claws dirty.
Catch my drift?
Okay.
Well, have a good holiday break!
Yeah, you too!
whew
Hope he didn't suspect we were up to less good than normal for supervillains like us.
Let's hurry up and find where Dad parked the vanship. I wonder if Monique is faring better in her Maliik-spying mission UNDER COVER of sheets?

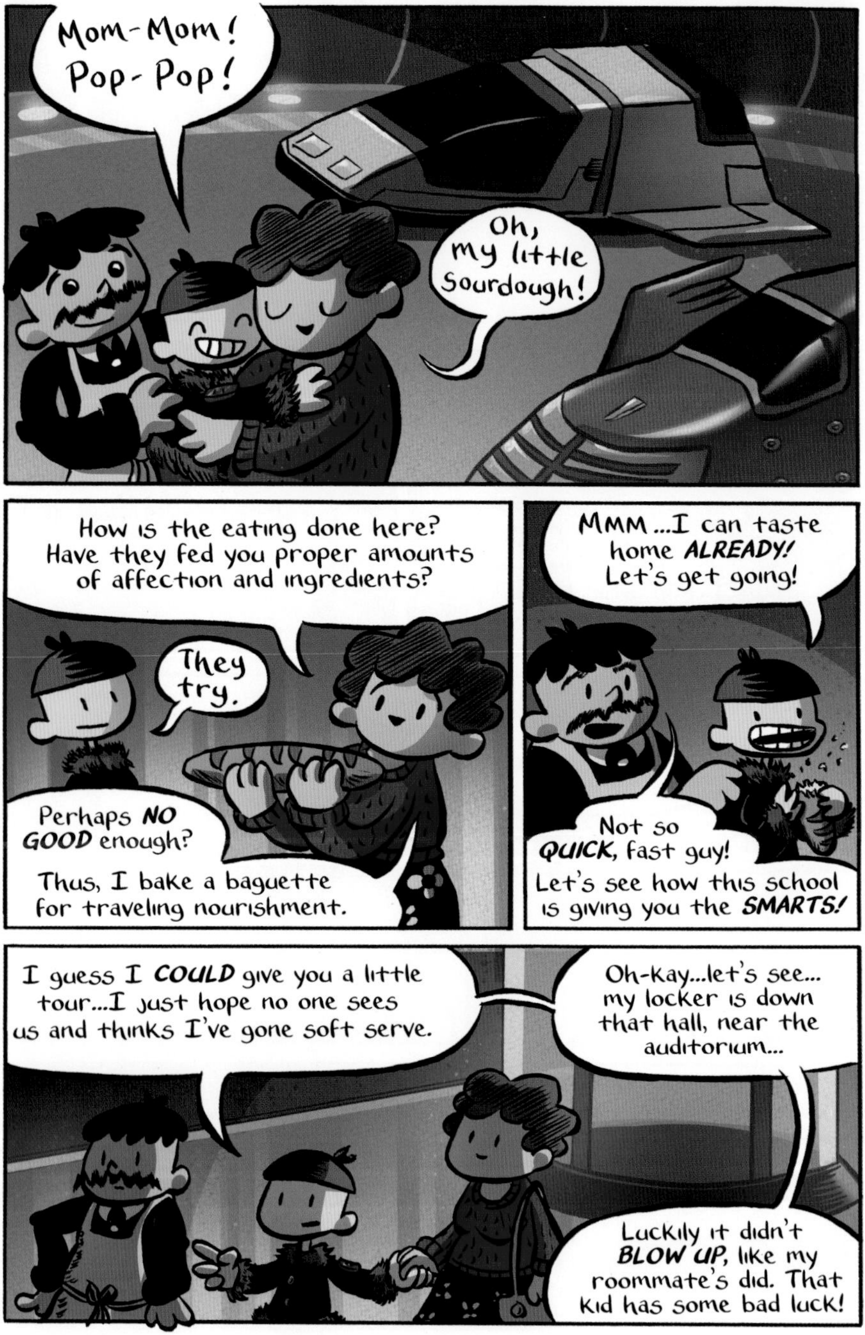
Mom-Mom! Pop-Pop!
Oh, my little Sourdough!
How is the eating done here? Have they fed you proper amounts of affection and ingredients?
They try.
Perhaps NO GOOD enough?
Thus, I bake a baguette for traveling nourishment.
MMM...I can taste home ALREADY! Let's get going!
Not so QUICK, fast guy!
Let's see how this school is giving you the SMARTS!
I guess I COULD give you a little tour...I just hope no one sees us and thinks I've gone soft serve.
Oh-kay...let's see... my locker is down that hall, near the auditorium...
Luckily it didn't BLOW UP, like my roommate's did. That kid has some bad luck!

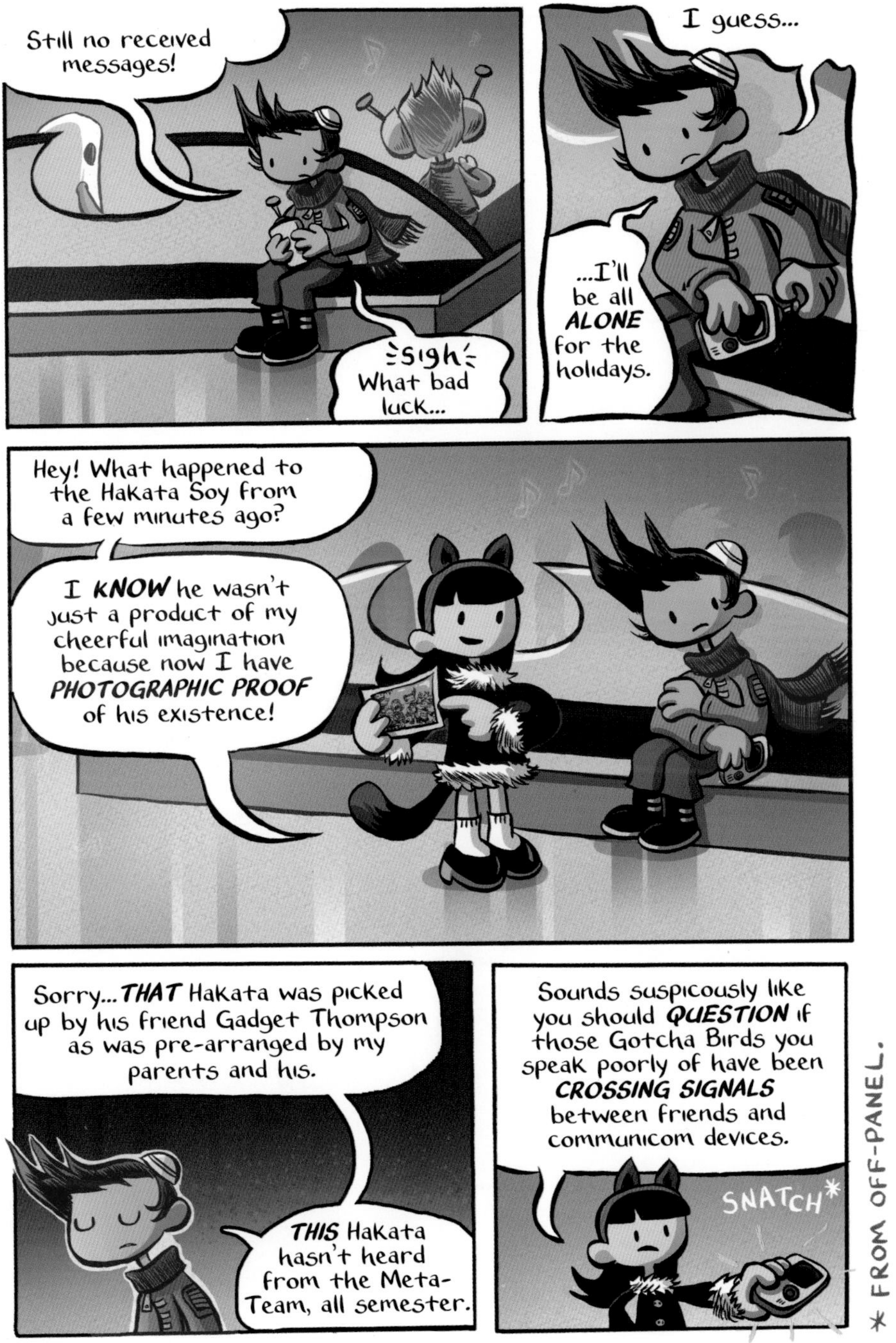
Still no received messages!
SIGH What bad luck...
I guess...
...I'll be all ALONE for the holidays.
Hey! What happened to the Hakata Soy from a few minutes ago?
I KNOW he wasn't just a product of my cheerful imagination because now I have PHOTOGRAPHIC PROOF of his existence!
Sorry... THAT Hakata was picked up by his friend Gadget Thompson as was pre-arranged by my parents and his.
THIS Hakata hasn't heard from the Meta-Team, all semester.
Sounds suspicously like you should QUESTION if those Gotcha Birds you speak poorly of have been CROSSING SIGNALS between friends and communicom devices.
SNATCH*
* FROM OFF-PANEL.

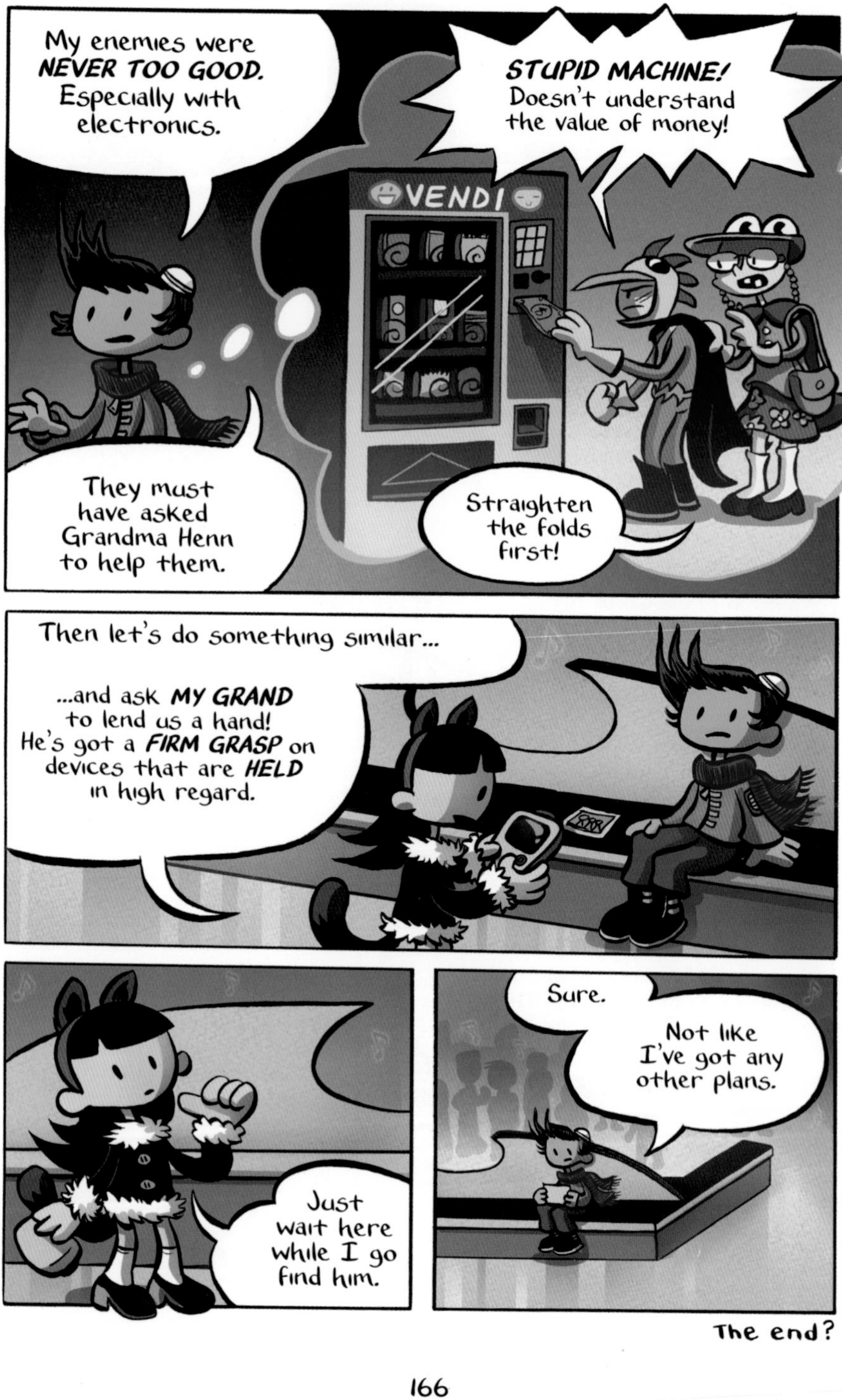
My enemies were NEVER TOO GOOD. Especially with electronics.
STUPID MACHINE! Doesn't understand the value of money!
VENDI
They must have asked Grandma Henn to help them.
Straighten the folds first!
Then let's do something similar...
...and ask MY GRAND to lend us a hand! He's got a FIRM GRASP on devices that are HELD in high regard.
Just wait here while I go find him.
Sure.
Not like I've got any other plans.
The end?

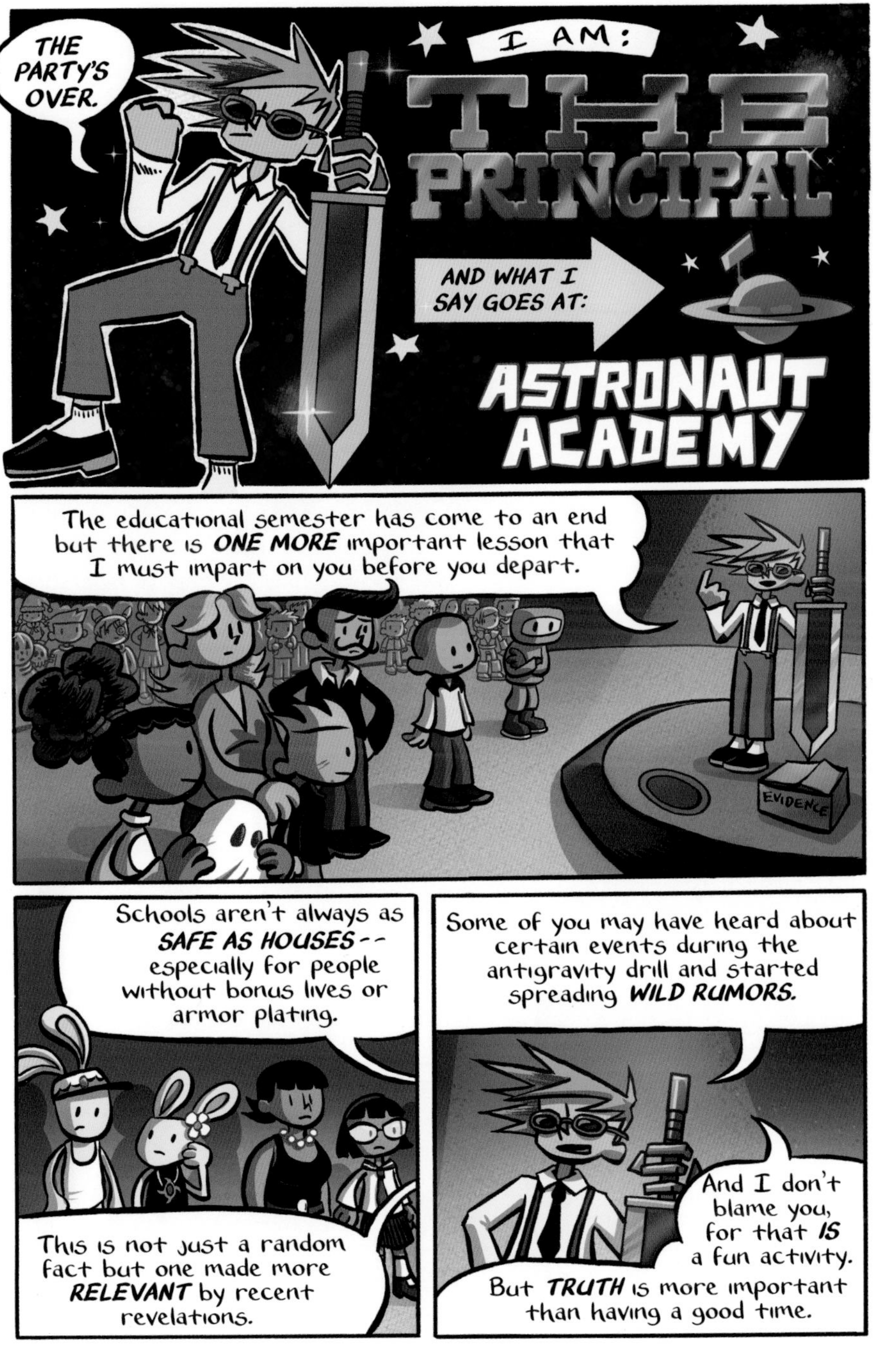
THE PARTY'S OVER.
I AM:
THE PRINCIPAL
AND WHAT I SAY GOES AT:
ASTRONAUT ACADEMY
The educational semester has come to an end but there is ONE MORE important lesson that I must impart on you before you depart.
EVIDENCE
Schools aren't always as SAFE AS HOUSES-- especially for people without bonus lives or armor plating.
This is not just a random fact but one made more RELEVANT by recent revelations.
Some of you may have heard about certain events during the antigravity drill and started spreading WILD RUMORS.
And I don't blame you, for that IS a fun activity.
But TRUTH is more important than having a good time.

Three students (two of which were archrivals and one of which was a boy) were attacked in the hallway near airlock A-3.

ATTACKING is something frowned upon by people because someone may get hurt in the process.

But SOMETIMES...people are ROBOTS -- who may not be programmed to care.

Take it from someone who has a mechanical arm and is holding ANOTHER mechanical arm for emphasis...

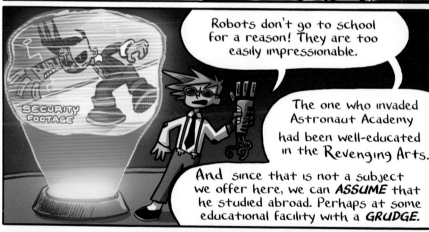

SECURITY FOOTAGE

Robots don't go to school for a reason! They are too easily impressionable.

The one who invaded Astronaut Academy had been well-educated in the Revenging Arts.

And since that is not a subject we offer here, we can ASSUME that he studied abroad. Perhaps at some educational facility with a GRUDGE.

;GASP!; If I were to jump to a CONCLUSION I would think that maybe our rival school had something to do with all that you are IMPLYING!

P.S. GAMMA Q!

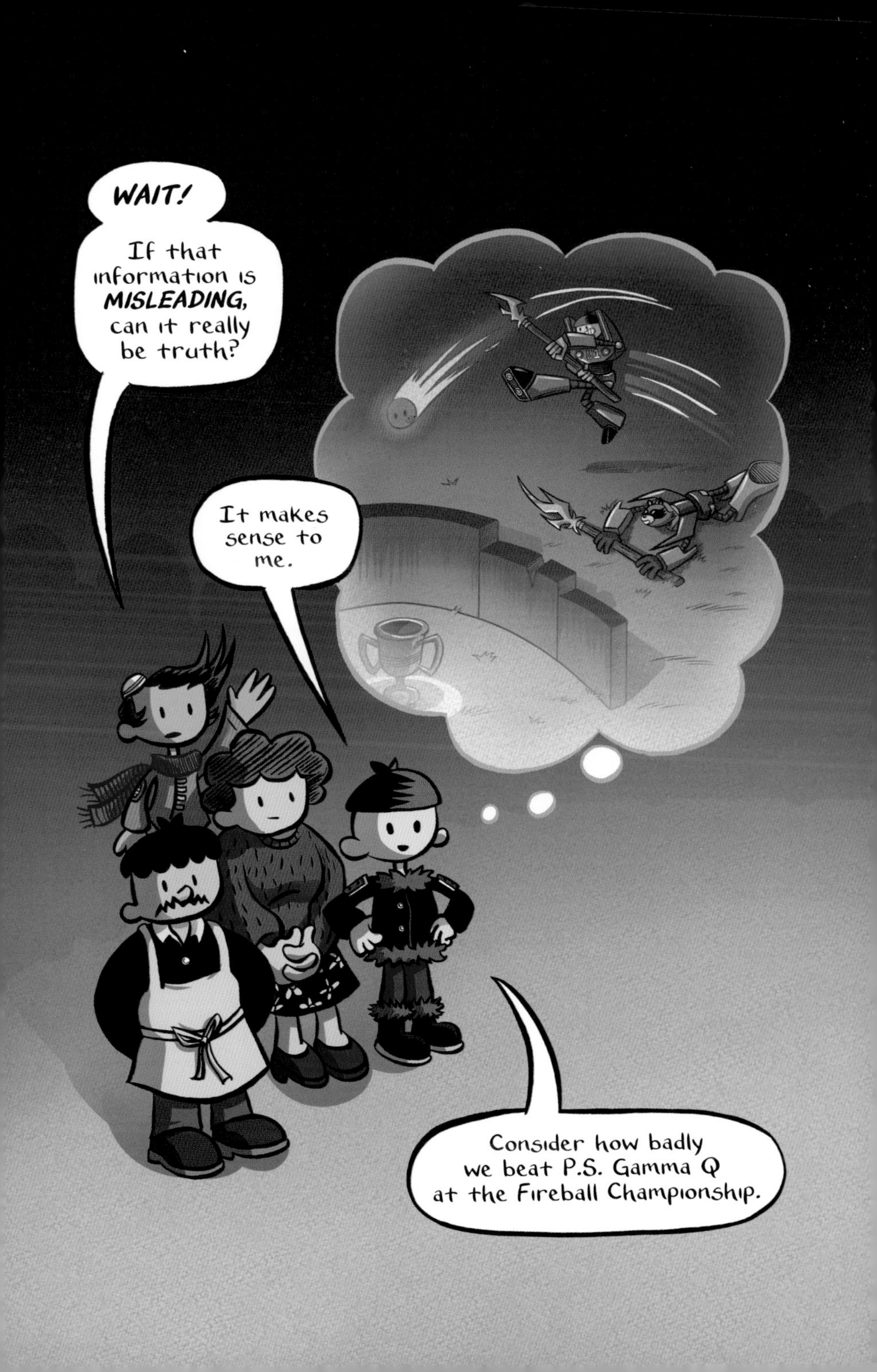
WAIT!
If that information is MISLEADING, can it really be truth?
It makes sense to me.
Consider how badly we beat P.S. Gamma Q at the Fireball Championship.

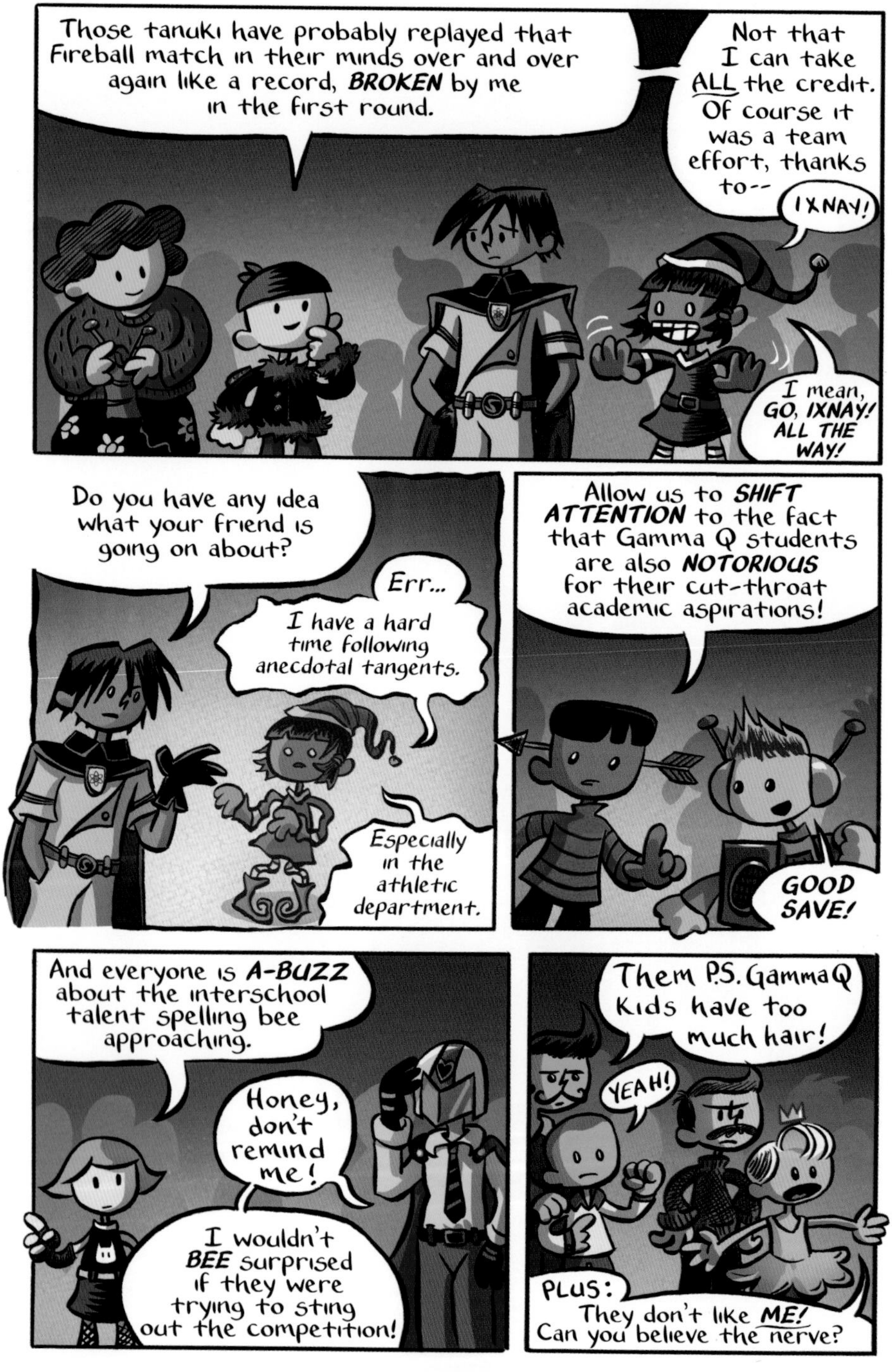

Those tanuki have probably replayed that Fireball match in their minds over and over again like a record, BROKEN by me in the first round.
Not that I can take ALL the credit. Of course it was a team effort, thanks to--
IXNAY!
I mean, GO, IXNAY! ALL THE WAY!
Do you have any idea what your friend is going on about?
Err...
I have a hard time following anecdotal tangents.
Especially in the athletic department.
Allow us to SHIFT ATTENTION to the fact that Gamma Q students are also NOTORIOUS for their cut-throat academic aspirations!
GOOD SAVE!
And everyone is A-BUZZ about the interschool talent spelling bee approaching.
Honey, don't remind me!
I wouldn't BEE surprised if they were trying to sting out the competition!
Them P.S. Gamma Q Kids have too much hair!
YEAH!
PLUS:
They don't like ME! Can you believe the nerve?

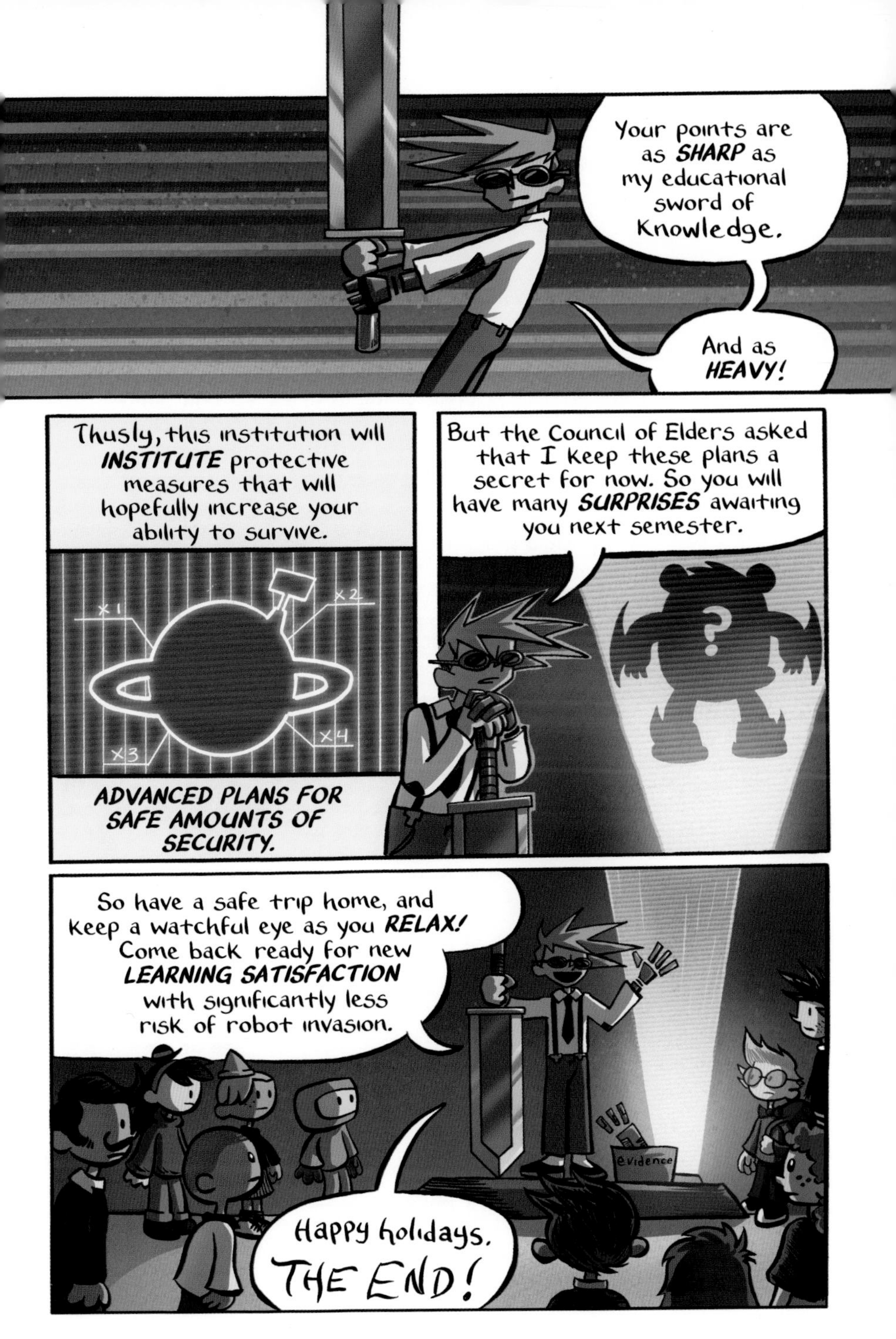
Your points are as SHARP as my educational sword of Knowledge.
And as HEAVY!
Thusly, this institution will INSTITUTE protective measures that will hopefully increase your ability to survive.
x1
x2
x3
x4
ADVANCED PLANS FOR SAFE AMOUNTS OF SECURITY.
But the Council of Elders asked that I keep these plans a secret for now. So you will have many SURPRISES awaiting you next semester.
?
So have a safe trip home, and keep a watchful eye as you RELAX! Come back ready for new LEARNING SATISFACTION with significantly less risk of robot invasion.
evidence
Happy holidays.
THE END!

MY NAME IS:
CALICO HOPPS
AND IT'S TIME TO LEAVE:
ASTRONAUT ACADEMY

Watching the crowd shuffle away, I tried to find some last-minute **COURAGE** to do something **LOUDER** than **WIGGLE MY NOSE** like a bunny with no confidence.

There he is! Now is your chance to take!

≥gulp≤

All semester, I've tried to think of things to say that would make me sound like I was someone worth **KNOWING**--ya know?

And it would be so much easier if he was **JUST** some attractive boy with **UNREALISTICALLY COOL HAIR.**

But this one in particular happens to be Hakata Soy, the boy who **SAVED MY LIFE!**

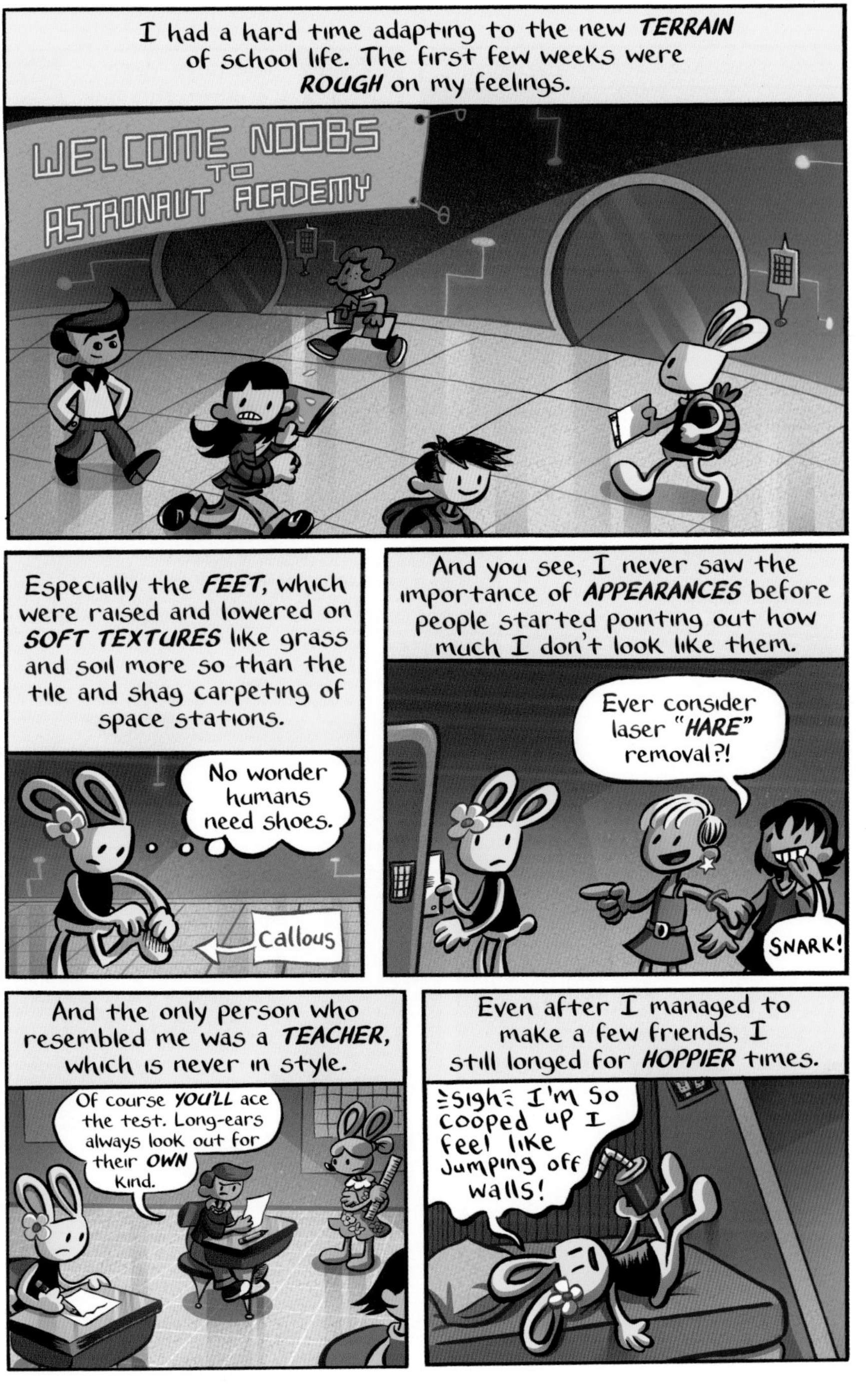
I had a hard time adapting to the new TERRAIN of school life. The first few weeks were ROUGH on my feelings.
WELCOME NOOBS TO ASTRONAUT ACADEMY
Especially the FEET, which were raised and lowered on SOFT TEXTURES like grass and soil more so than the tile and shag carpeting of space stations.
No wonder humans need shoes.
Callous
And you see, I never saw the importance of APPEARANCES before people started pointing out how much I don't look like them.
Ever consider laser "HARE" removal?!
SNARK!
And the only person who resembled me was a TEACHER, which is never in style.
Of course YOU'LL ace the test. Long-ears always look out for their OWN kind.
Even after I managed to make a few friends, I still longed for HOPPIER times.
=Sigh= I'm so cooped up I feel like jumping off walls!

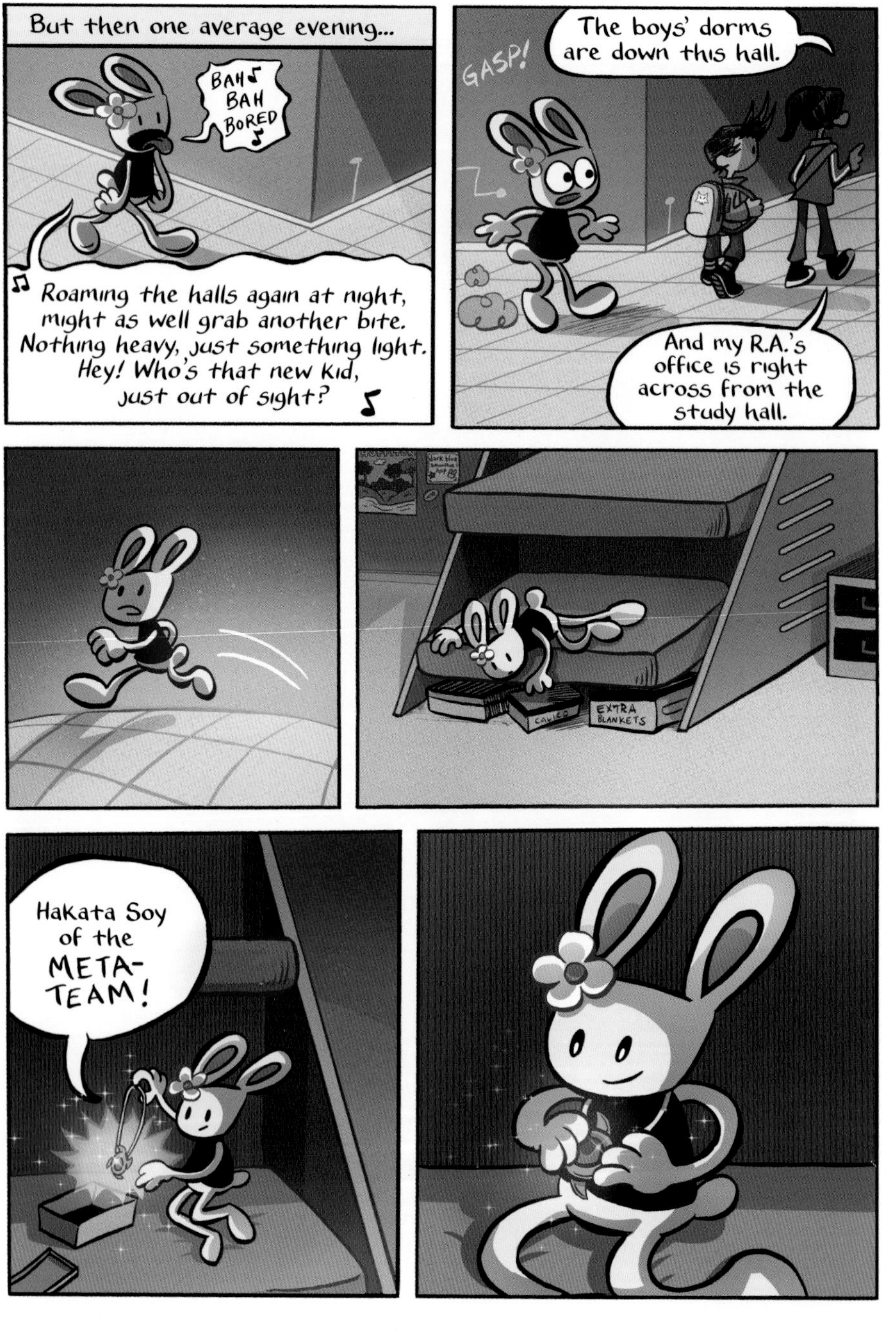
But then one average evening...
BAH BAH BORED
Roaming the halls again at night, might as well grab another bite. Nothing heavy, just something light. Hey! Who's that new kid, just out of sight?
GASP!
The boys' dorms are down this hall.
And my R.A.'s office is right across from the study hall.
EXTRA BLANKETS
Hakata Soy of the META-TEAM!

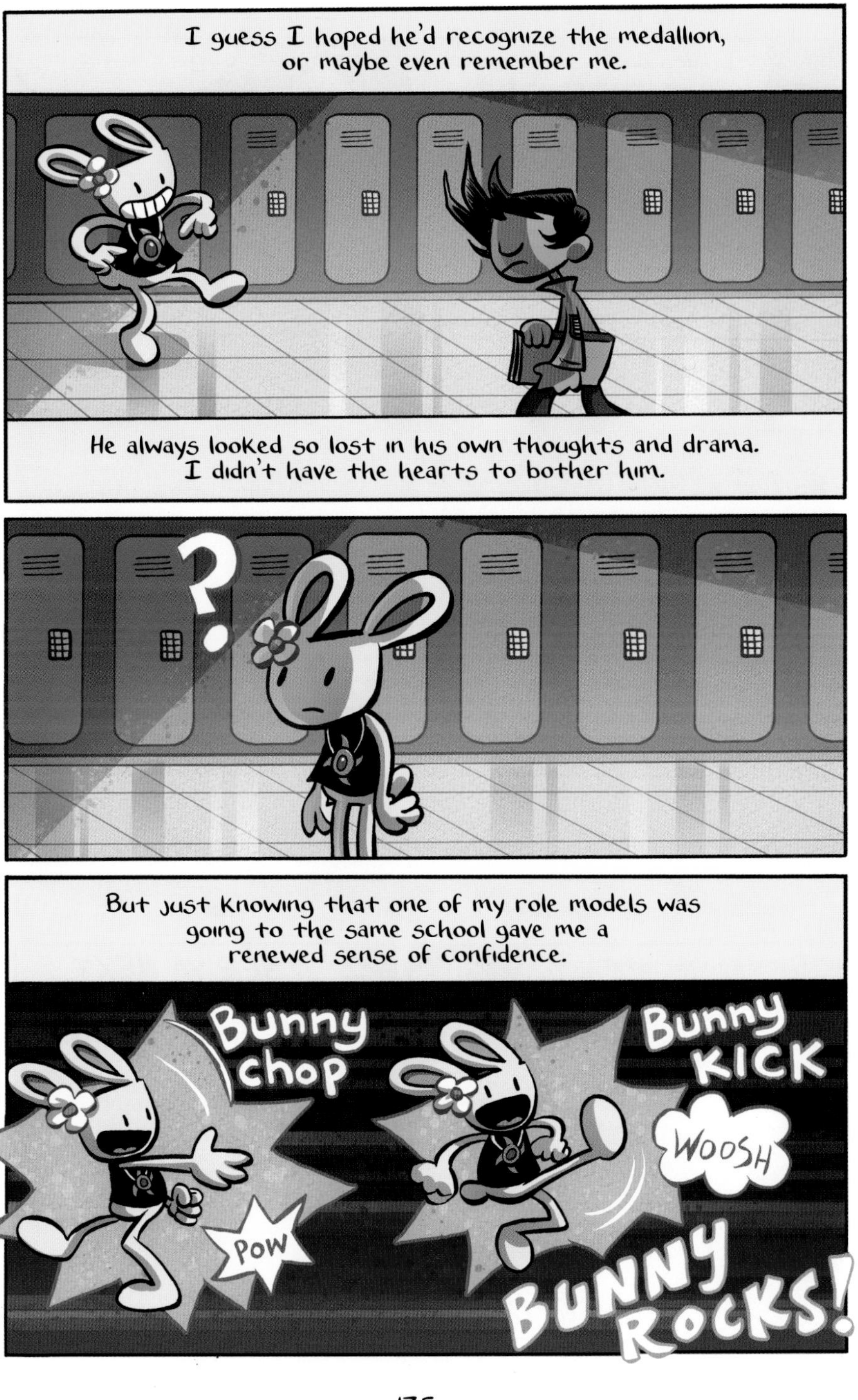
I guess I hoped he'd recognize the medallion, or maybe even remember me.
He always looked so lost in his own thoughts and drama. I didn't have the hearts to bother him.
?
But just knowing that one of my role models was going to the same school gave me a renewed sense of confidence.
Bunny chop
POW
Bunny KICK
WOOSH
BUNNY ROCKS!

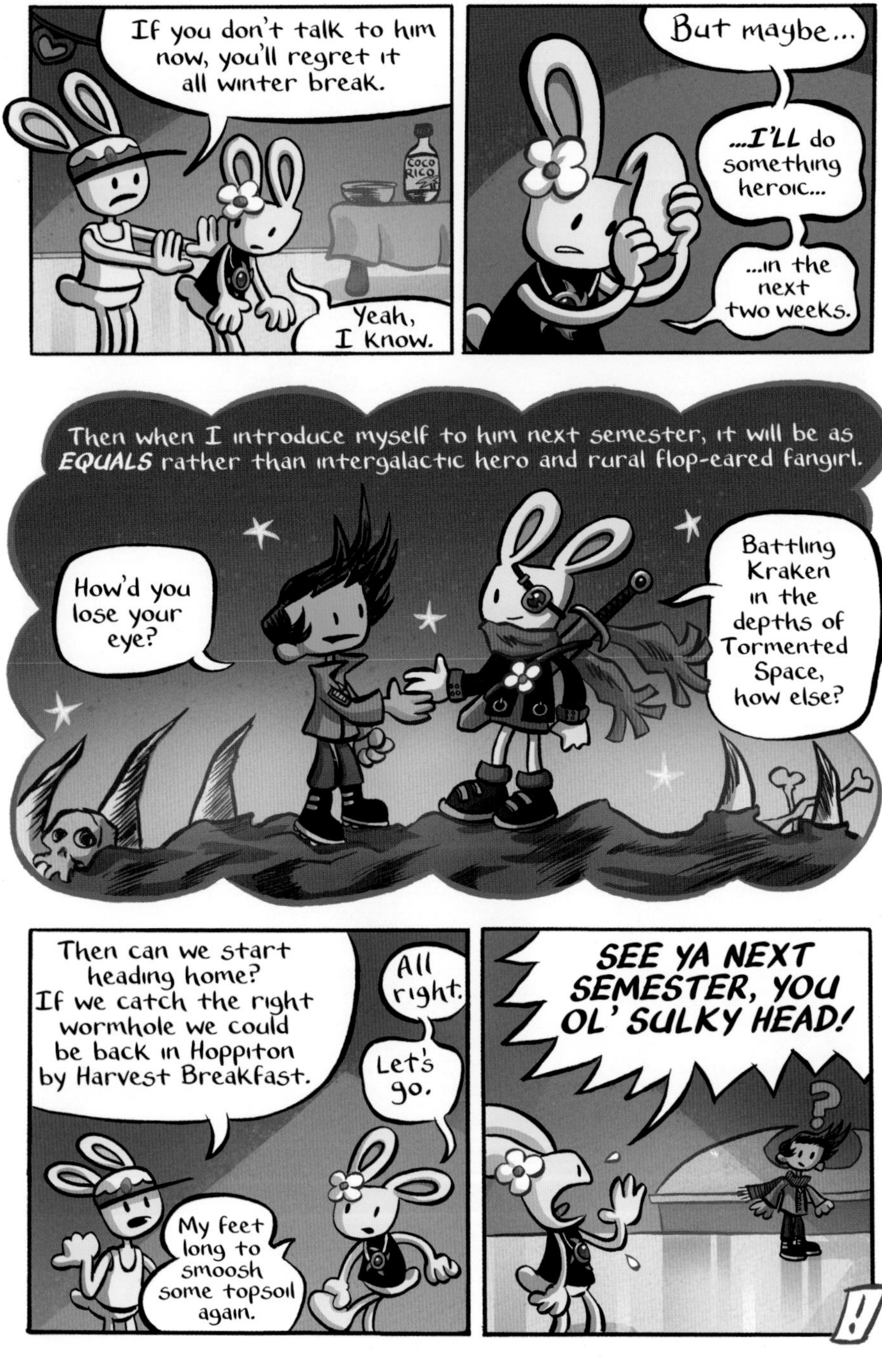
If you don't talk to him now, you'll regret it all winter break.
Yeah, I know.
COCO RICO
But maybe...
...I'LL do something heroic...
...in the next two weeks.
Then when I introduce myself to him next semester, it will be as EQUALS rather than intergalactic hero and rural flop-eared fangirl.
How'd you lose your eye?
Battling Kraken in the depths of Tormented Space, how else?
Then can we start heading home? If we catch the right wormhole we could be back in Hoppiton by Harvest Breakfast.
My feet long to smoosh some topsoil again.
All right.
Let's go.
SEE YA NEXT SEMESTER, YOU OL' SULKY HEAD!
?
!

MY NAME IS:

HAKATA SOY

はかた

AND I'M STILL HERE AT: →

ASTRONAUT ACADEMY

The Gotcha Birds don't even **GO** to school. Why does The Principal think P.S. Gamma Q has anything to do with that robot who wanted to destroy us?

Things aren't always **BLACK AND WHITE** like pandas.

That's why I think the Spanish teacher will better **TRANSLATE** what we've been trying to tell people.

LIQUIDS

BARBER ROOM SNACKS

SUBSTANC

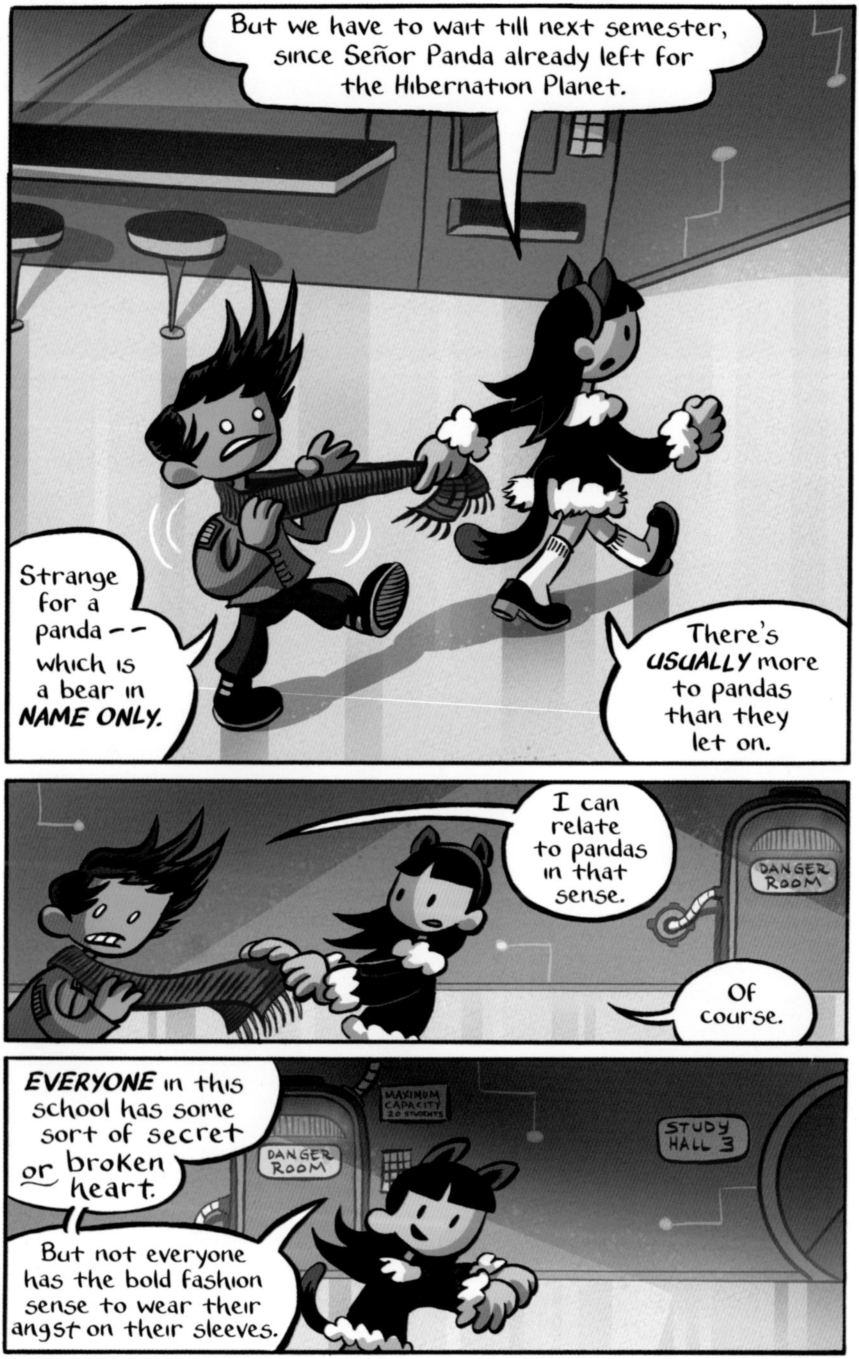

But we have to wait till next semester, since Señor Panda already left for the Hibernation Planet.
Strange for a panda -- which is a bear in NAME ONLY.
There's USUALLY more to pandas than they let on.
I can relate to pandas in that sense.
DANGER ROOM
Of course.
EVERYONE in this school has some sort of secret or broken heart.
MAXIMUM CAPACITY 20 STUDENTS
DANGER ROOM
STUDY HALL 3
But not everyone has the bold fashion sense to wear their angst on their sleeves.

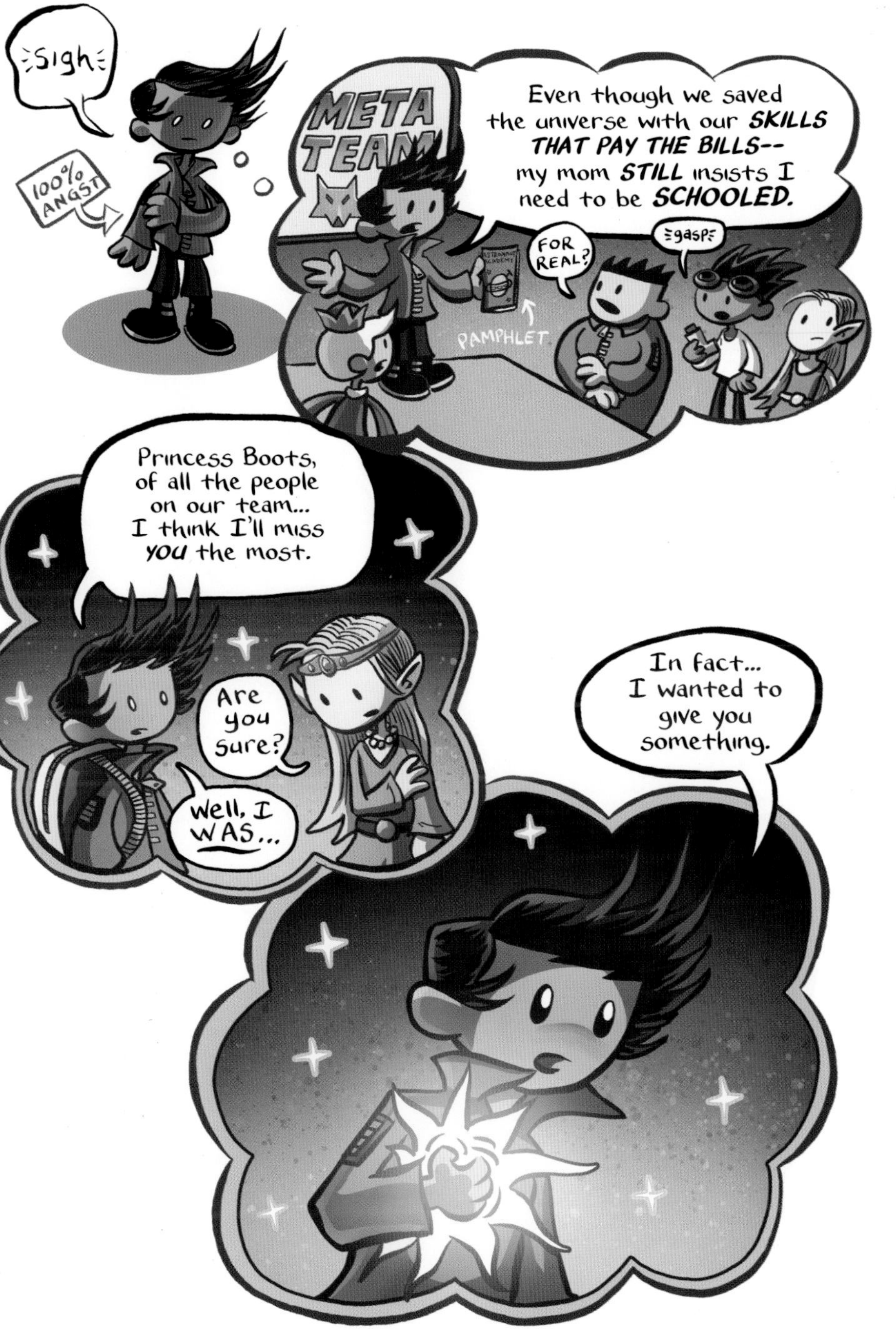
Sigh
100% ANGST
META TEAM
Even though we saved the universe with our SKILLS THAT PAY THE BILLS-- my mom STILL insists I need to be SCHOOLED.
FOR REAL?
gasp
PAMPHLET
Princess Boots, of all the people on our team... I think I'll miss YOU the most.
Are you sure?
Well, I WAS...
In fact... I wanted to give you something.

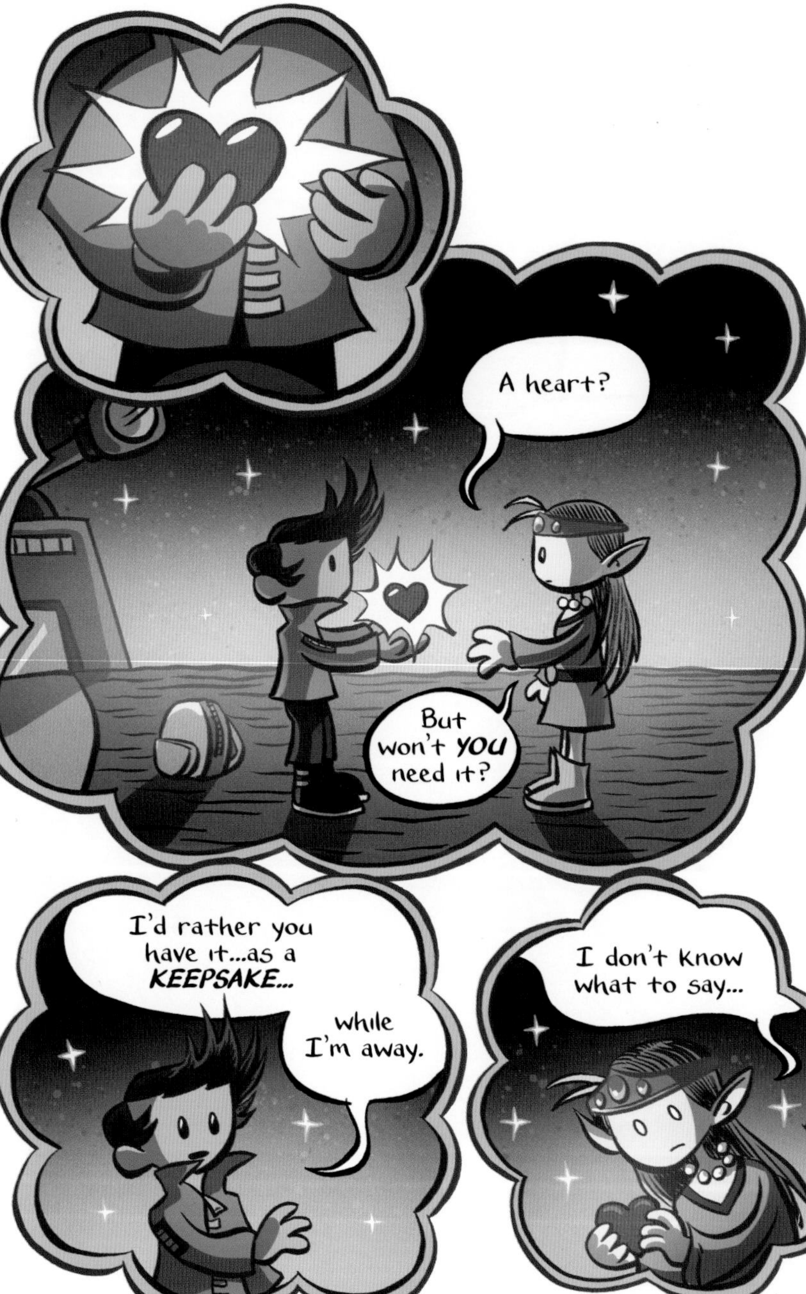
A heart?
But won't YOU need it?
I'd rather you have it...as a KEEPSAKE...
while I'm away.
I don't know what to say...

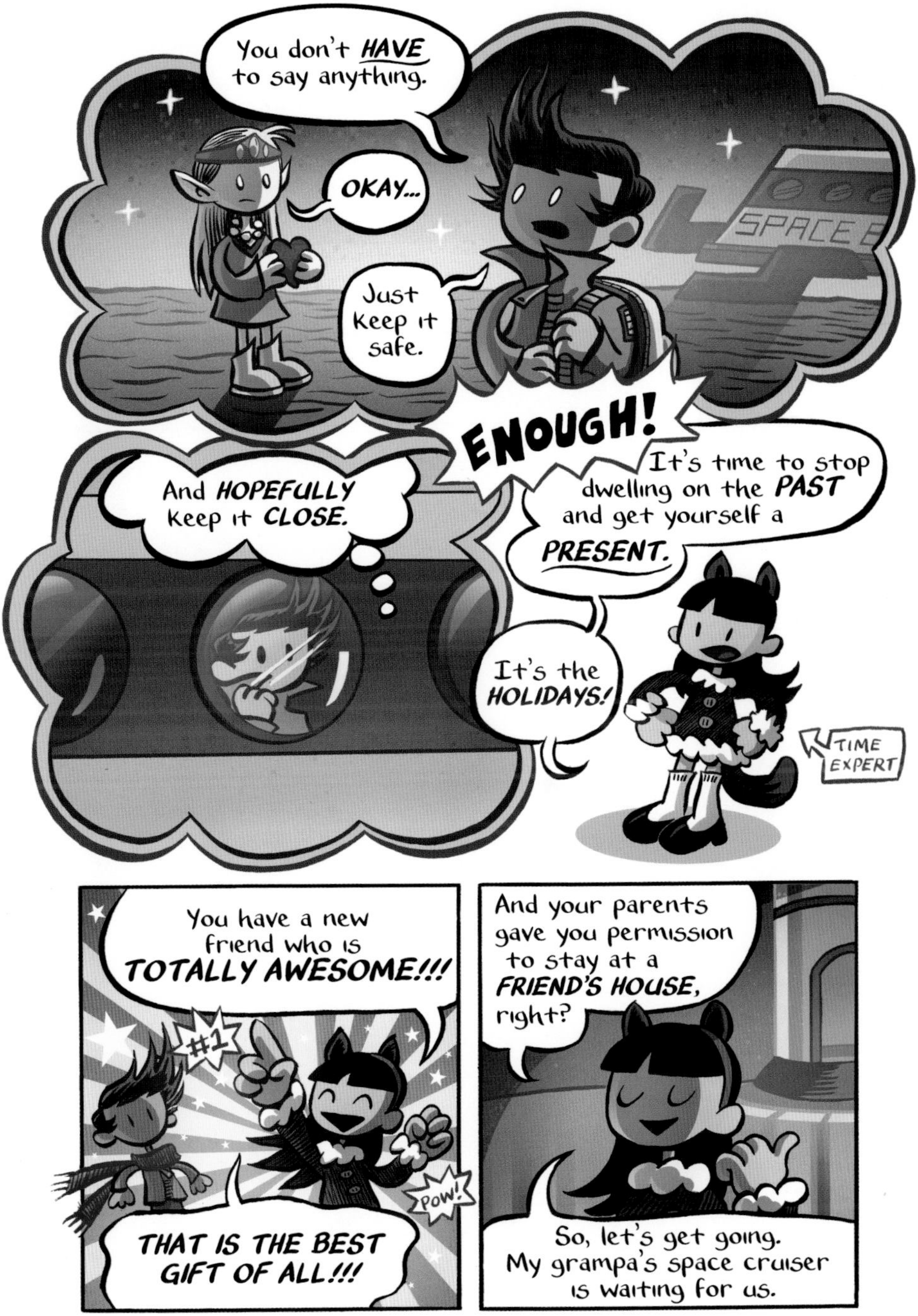

You don't HAVE to say anything.
OKAY...
Just keep it safe.
SPACE
And HOPEFULLY keep it CLOSE.
ENOUGH!
It's time to stop dwelling on the PAST and get yourself a PRESENT.
It's the HOLIDAYS!
TIME EXPERT
You have a new friend who is TOTALLY AWESOME!!!
#1
POW!
THAT IS THE BEST GIFT OF ALL!!!
And your parents gave you permission to stay at a FRIEND'S HOUSE, right?
So, let's get going. My grampa's space cruiser is waiting for us.

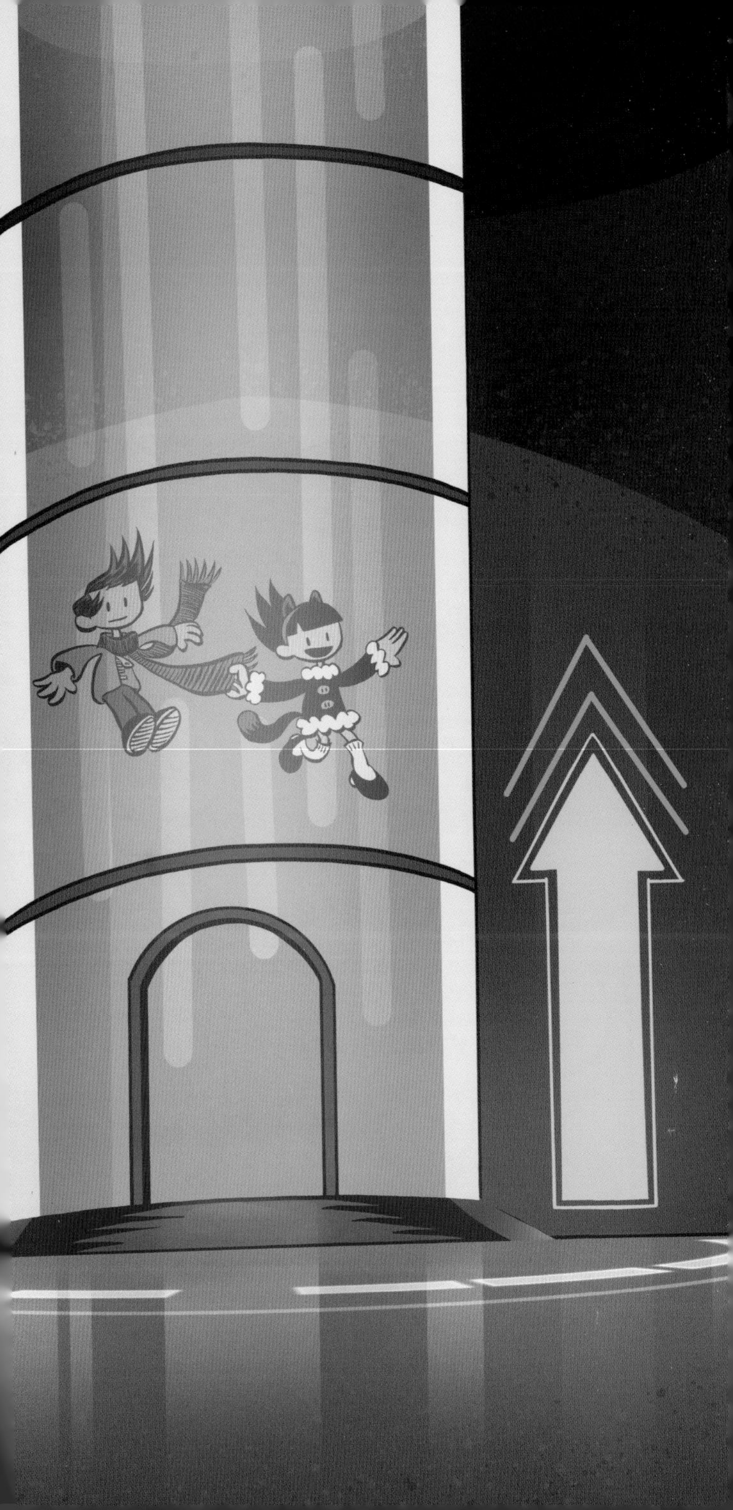

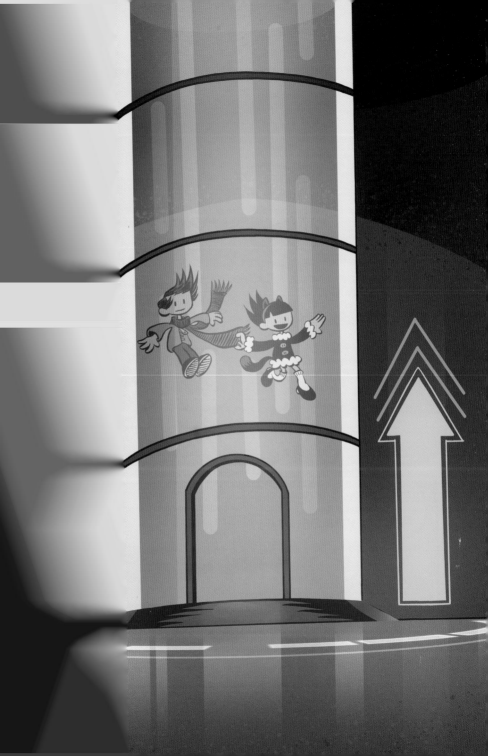

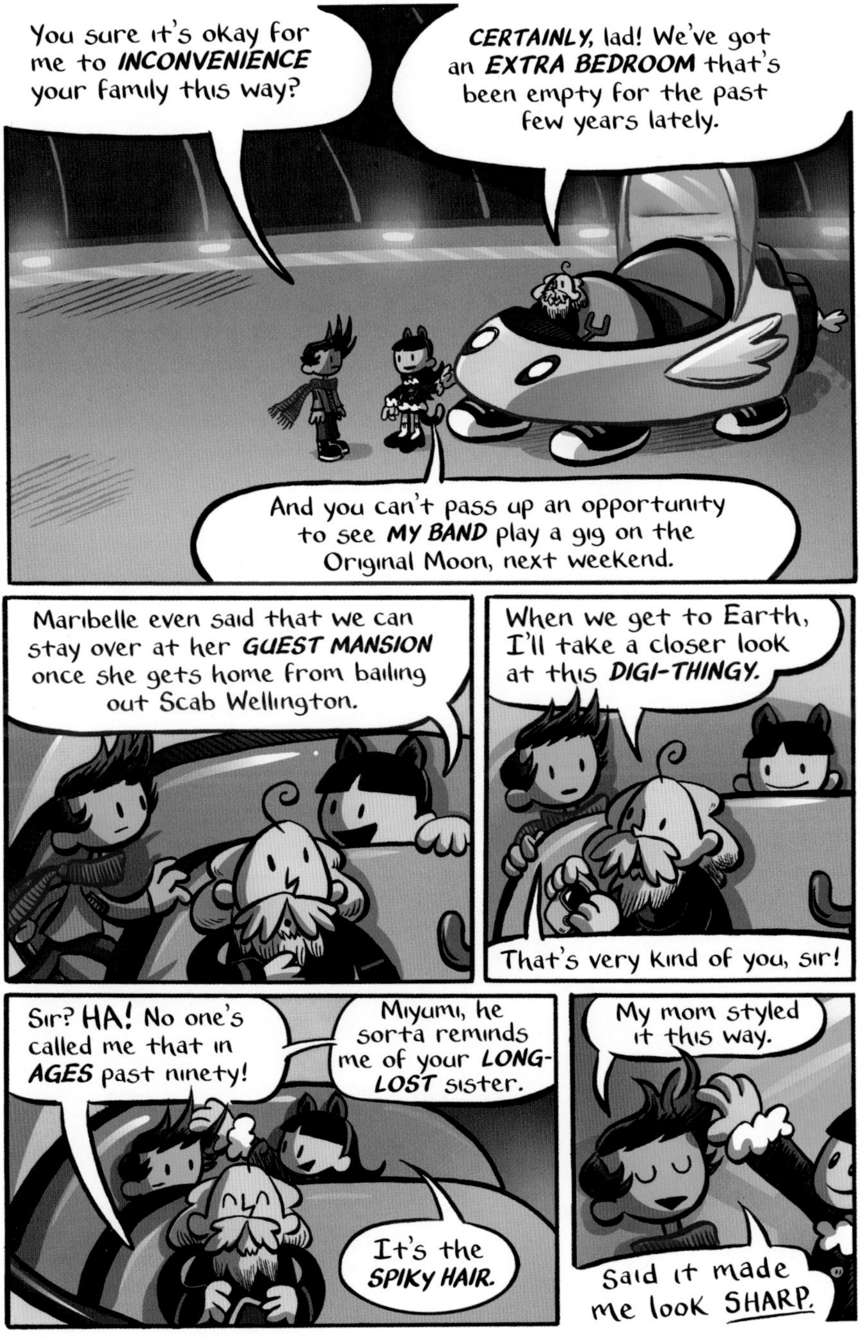
You sure it's okay for me to INCONVENIENCE your family this way?
CERTAINLY, lad! We've got an EXTRA BEDROOM that's been empty for the past few years lately.
And you can't pass up an opportunity to see MY BAND play a gig on the Original Moon, next weekend.
Maribelle even said that we can stay over at her GUEST MANSION once she gets home from bailing out Scab Wellington.
When we get to Earth, I'll take a closer look at this DIGI-THINGY.
That's very kind of you, sir!
Sir? HA! No one's called me that in AGES past ninety!
Miyumi, he sorta reminds me of your LONG-LOST sister.
It's the SPIKY HAIR.
My mom styled it this way.
Said it made me look SHARP.

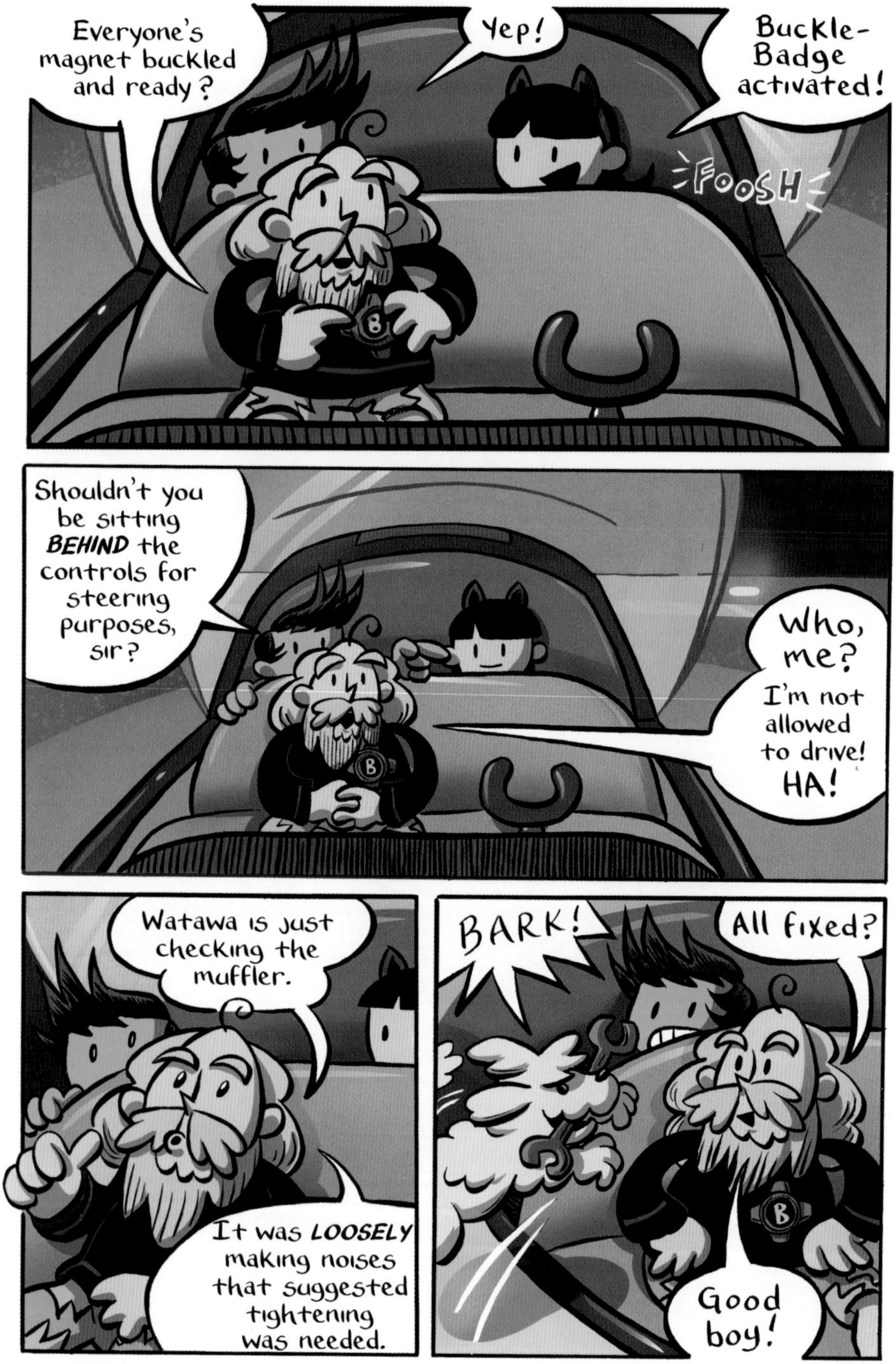
Everyone's magnet buckled and ready?
Yep!
Buckle-Badge activated!
FOOSH
Shouldn't you be sitting BEHIND the controls for steering purposes, sir?
Who, me?
I'm not allowed to drive! HA!
Watawa is just checking the muffler.
It was LOOSELY making noises that suggested tightening was needed.
BARK!
All fixed?
Good boy!

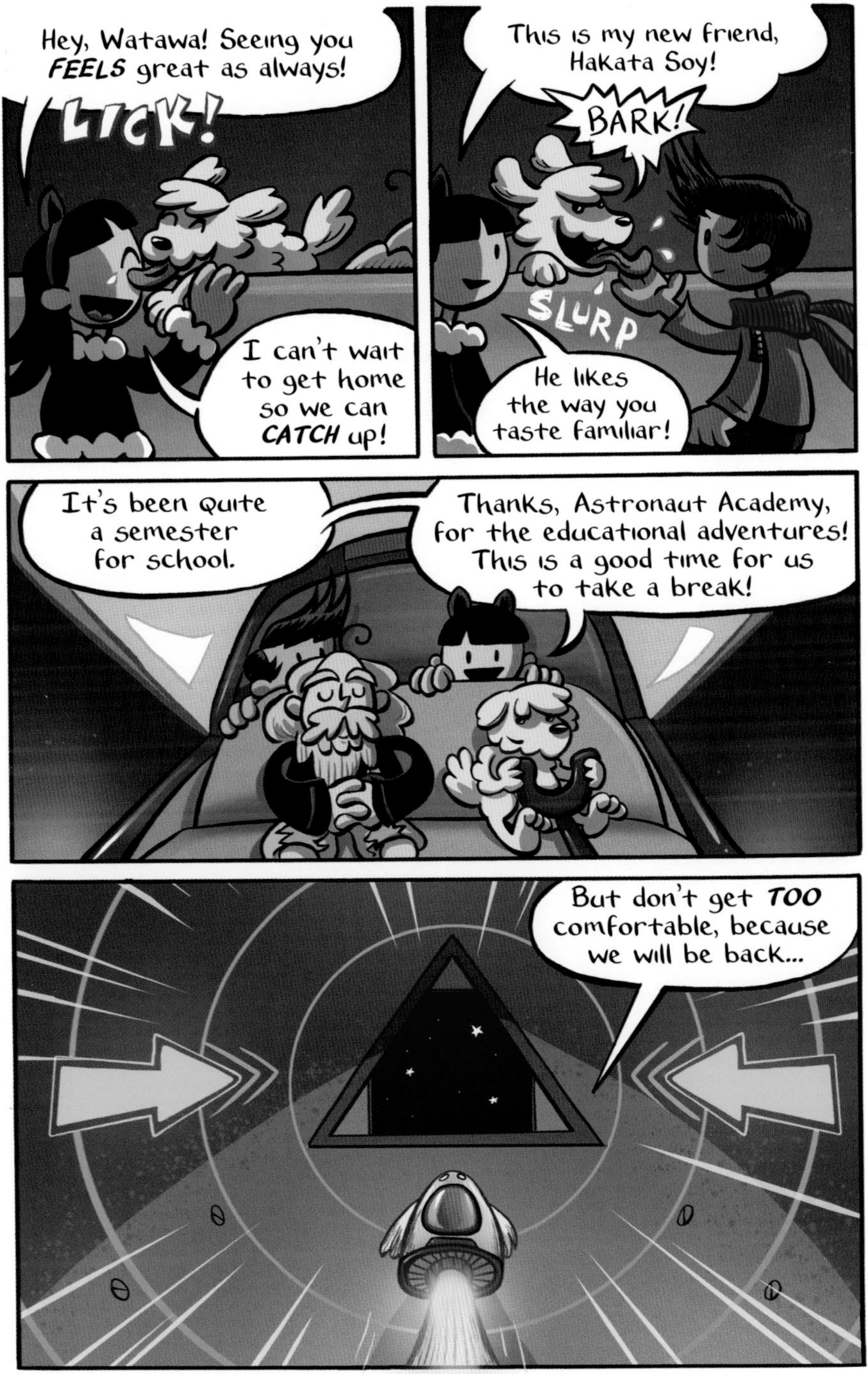
Hey, Watawa! Seeing you FEELS great as always!
LICK!
I can't wait to get home so we can CATCH up!
This is my new friend, Hakata Soy!
BARK!
SLURP
He likes the way you taste familiar!
It's been quite a semester for school.
Thanks, Astronaut Academy, for the educational adventures! This is a good time for us to take a break!
But don't get TOO comfortable, because we will be back...

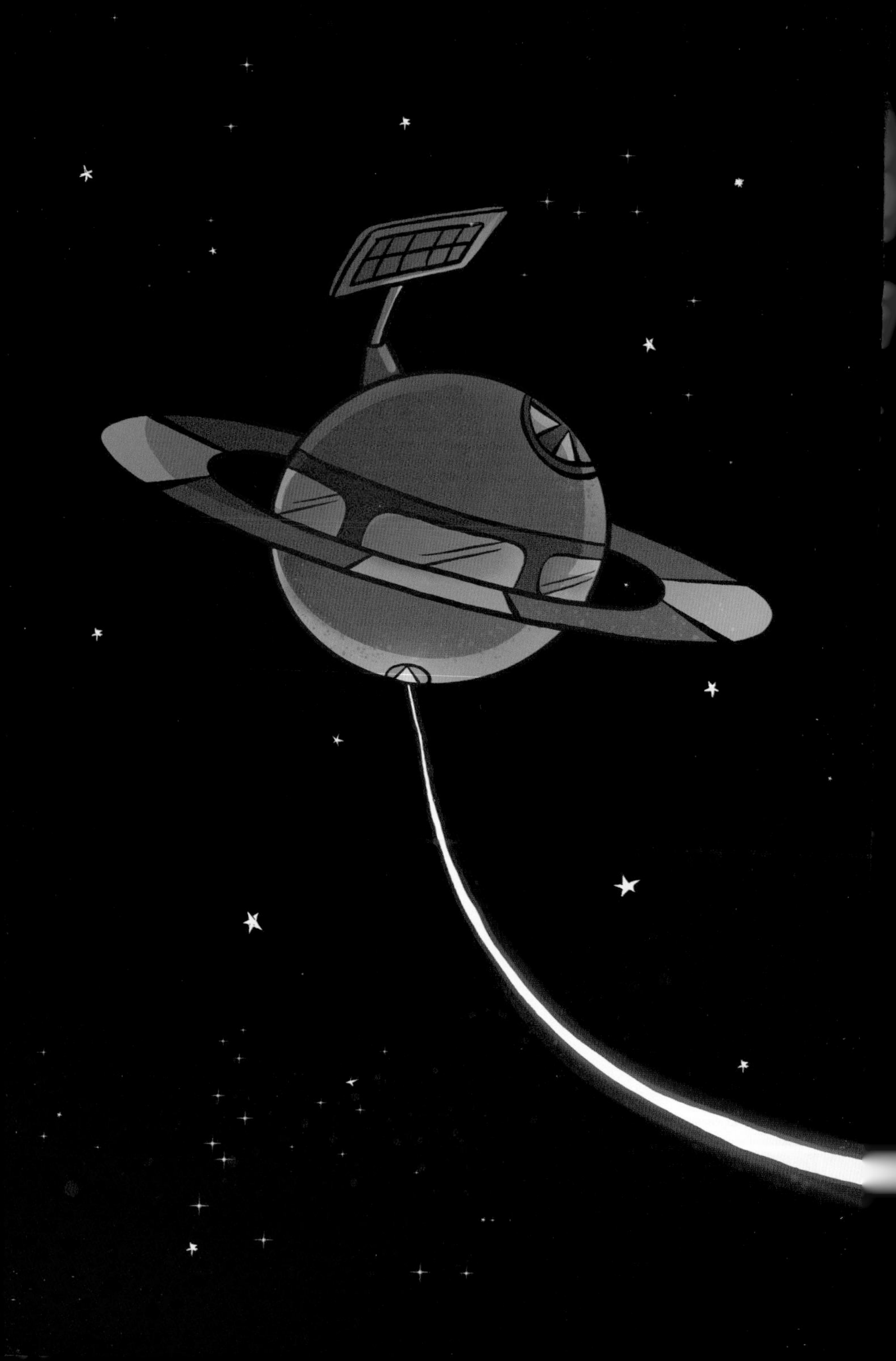

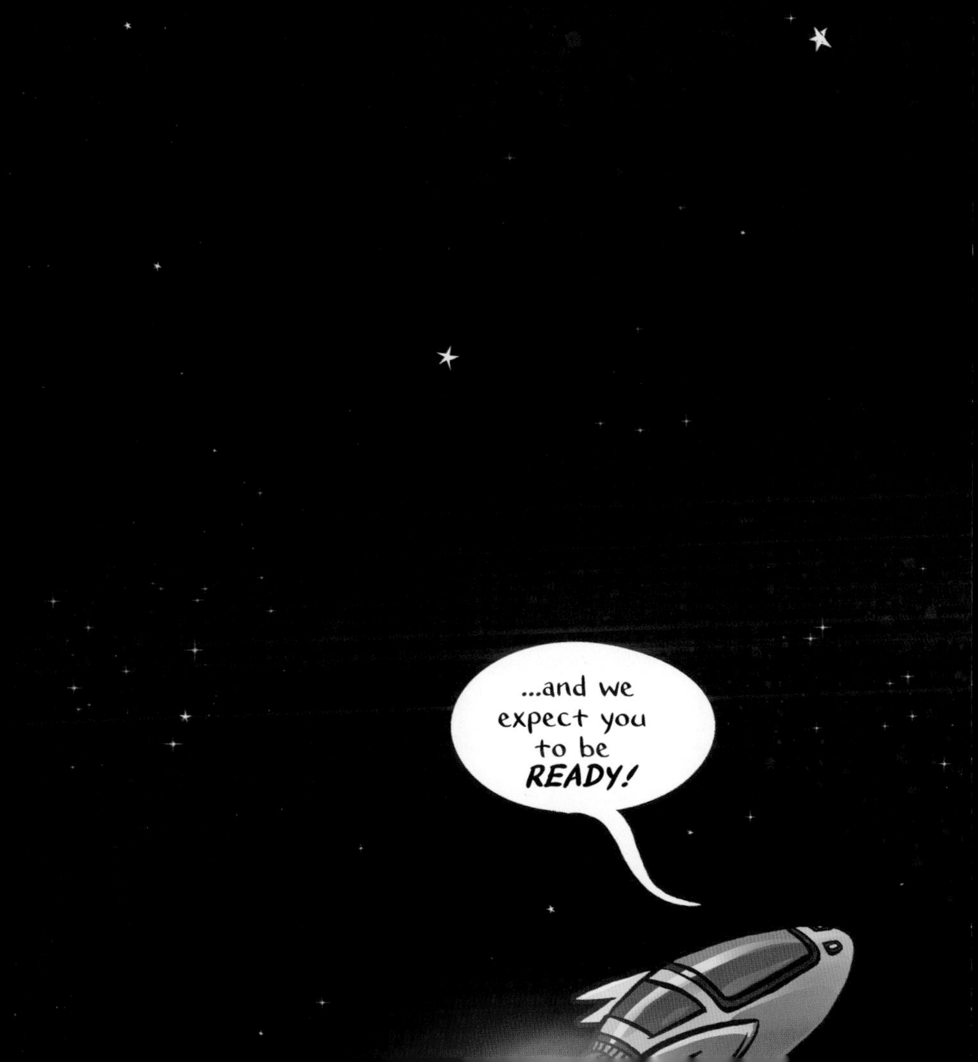
...and we expect you to be READY!

look for

ASTRONAUT ACADEMY

RE-ENTRY

ROCK YOUR SOCKS OFF AT
The Sock Factory
(on the Original Moon)
GORDY PRESENTS...
A TRIPLE BILL OF HANGAR ROCK/ SYNTH/ TWEE-POP
FEATURING:
LEE OF THE STONE
PLAYING ALL HIS HITS!
Auto Gyro
Special holiday-themed set!
PLUS: Local Band
The SUPERCUTES!
$10 $8 W/FLYER
Doors open at 7PM
ALL-AGES SHOW
* Complimentary Apple Juice

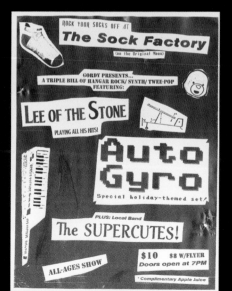

Color flatting assists by David Luna Hernandez, Laura Escodebo, and Miguel Mora. Original gray color assists by Craig Arndt, Rosemary Travale, and Naseem Hrab. Additional crunch help from Jeremy Arambulo, Jordyn Bochon, John Green, Alisa Harris, Yuko Ota, Colleen MacIssac, Marion Vitus, and Dalton Webb.

new edition thanks to:

Emmy Hernández for bringing dynamic color into this formerly gray world! Kiara Valdez, Rachel Stark, Molly Johanson, and Kirk Benshoff, for being the perfect team to help relaunch this series.

original edition thanks to:

Raina Telgemeier—this book would not be possible without you.

My parents and family, for letting me get away with being a full-time cartoonist even when I was just a kid.

Chris Duffy, Laura Galen, and everyone at Nickelodeon Magazine, for eleven years of encouragement, inspiration, and camaraderie.

John Green, for being a great friend and comics-making teammate. Matt Hawkins, Zack Giallongo, Debbie Huey, and all my friends and fellow cartoonists who help make the world so much fun.

Everyone who was a supporter of the Astronaut Elementary webcomic. Tintin Pantoja, for asking me to contribute to her SVA manga anthology. Lea Hernandez and Joey Manley, for giving me an online home. Everyone at Lunchbox Funnies. Erin Houlihan, for designing the early mini-comics.

Judy Hansen, for taking even my silliest ideas so seriously.

Calista Brill, Mark Siegel, Colleen Venable, Gina Gagliano, and everyone else at First Second, for being amazing people to work with and welcoming me with such open arms.

:01
First Second
New York

Text and illustrations copyright © 2011 by Dave Roman
Published by First Second
First Second is an imprint of Roaring Brook Press,
a division of Holtzbrinck Publishing Holdings Limited Partnership
120 Broadway, New York, NY 10271

Don't miss your next favorite book from First Second!
For the latest updates go to firstsecondnewsletter.com
and sign up for our enewsletter.

Library of Congress Control Number: 2020911187
Paperback ISBN: 978-1-250-22589-4
Hardcover ISBN: 978-1-250-22592-4

Our books may be purchased in bulk for
promotional, educational, or business use.
Please contact your local bookseller or the Macmillan
Corporate and Premium Sales Department
at (800) 221-7945 ext. 5442 or by email at
MacmillanSpecialMarkets@macmillan.com.

Edited by Calista Brill and Rachel Stark
2021 cover design by Kirk Benshoff
2021 interior book design by Rob Steen
2021 color by Emmy Hernández
2011 interior book design by Colleen AF Venable
and Lawrence Lee Derks III

First edition, 2011
New edition, 2021

Printed in China by RR Donnelley Asia Printing Solutions Ltd.,
Dongguan City, Guangdong Province

Drawn with Staedtler graphite pencils on Strathmore 500 series Bristol
paper. Inked with Winsor & Newton Series 7 sable brushes and Speedball
India ink. Lettered with a combination of Speedball Hunt 107 crow quill nib
and Yaytime font. Colored with Clip Studio Paint.

Paperback: 10 9 8 7 6 5 4 3 2 1
Hardcover: 10 9 8 7 6 5 4 3 2 1